WHAT SHE *WANTS*

Samantha stood up in the waist-high water, completely furious. "Don't you dare pity me, Duncan Campbell. I knew exactly what I was doing and you did *not* take advantage of me."

His gaze swept over her body as the water from the ends of her hair ran down her naked flesh. He raised his burning blue eyes to hers.

"Good," he whispered. He cut though the water like a merman, cleanly and swiftly, his hands sliding around her waist, his arms flexing to bring her against him. "I'm glad to know that ye canna be coerced into anything ye dinna want to do."

Highland Magic

Tess Mallory

LOVE SPELL NEW YORK CITY

LOVE SPELL®

July 2005

Published by

Dorchester Publishing Co., Inc.
200 Madison Avenue
New York, NY 10016

ISBN 0-505-52624-7

The name "Love Spell" and its logo are trademarks of Dorchester Publishing Co., Inc.

Printed in the United States of America.

Visit us on the web at www.dorchesterpub.com.

To my husband, Bill—
If I were a mermaid, and you were a sailor,
I'd give up the ocean just to walk by your side,
every day of my life. Without you, this
book would not have happened.
I love you, forever.

ACKNOWLEDGMENTS

All my love and thanks to:
Special angels—Denise, Dawn, Steve & Melissa, Jan-Jan, Ellen & Greg, Jenny, Angus, and the writing team of Cathy Clamp and Cie Adams.

My amazing family—New Mommy Erin and little whosit, New Daddy Blake, Hedy, Thomas, Jordan, Cas, Jewell, & Daddo.

My life-affirming agent, Roberta Brown, and my understanding editor, Kate Seaver.

May the road rise up to meet all of you, always.

Highland Magic

Chapter One

"Dad, for the last time, I am not going to marry Duncan Campbell!"

Samantha Riley faced her father down in her usual fighting stance: hands on her hips, chin lifted, jaw locked. Retired Air Force Colonel Patrick Riley met her hands, chin, and jaw, and raised her one steely eyed glare.

"Why not?"

"Well, for one thing, I don't like him, and for another, I'm dating Luke right now," she said.

The retired colonel shook his head in disbelief. "Didn't you learn your lesson last time?" he demanded. "Why in the world you'd want to associate with the likes of Luke Carter the Third—hopefully the Last—is beyond me. He's just another spoiled, rich player, Sam, and is only going to bring you more heartache."

"It's my life, Dad," she said. "My love life to be specific. So would you please just butt out!"

His shoulders slumped and Sam was startled by the

sudden weariness in his eyes. The once chiseled features had begun to sag and soften and there was a noticeable tremor to his hands before he quickly stuffed them into the pockets of his khaki slacks. With an unfamiliar rush of panic, Sam realized that while she'd been in med school, her father had grown old.

He's just tired, she thought, brushing one long lock of blond hair back from her shoulders. *Or else he's trying a new kind of tactical ploy to undermine my frontal assault.*

It wouldn't be the first time her father had tried to guilt her into something she didn't want to do.

"I don't like that look in your eye," her father said, moving to his favorite leather chair and sitting down heavily. Samantha felt another jolt of panic. Her father never fought sitting down. He was really bringing out the big guilt guns this time, but she had to admit that he had never acted weak or sick to get her to do his bidding.

"And why has it been so long since you came to see me? You've been avoiding me."

Sam sighed, guilt rushing over her again. She used to spend at least one weekend a month with her father, even after starting med school. But over the last year and a half her visits to the small ranch outside of Wimberley, Texas had grown farther and farther apart. She'd avoided coming home and stayed in her apartment in Houston, giving excuses as to why she couldn't make the three-hour trip to see him.

She knew he'd never understand the real reason she'd stayed away, and since explaining would mean clueing her father in on her sex life, it wasn't even a consideration.

But by the end of January, she had known she had to face him. Jix MacGregor, her best friend of twenty years, and her husband, Jamie, had called and announced they were flying over from Scotland to stay for a couple of weeks, their visit to culminate in attending Austin's rendition of Mardi Gras. Sam, of course, had invited them to stay at the ranch, and would have to be there to welcome them.

Knowing there'd be things to do at the ranch and groceries to buy—her father was a strictly meat and potatoes man—Sam left her apartment in Houston and drove to the Crazy R Ranch. Her father had been happy to see her, and everything started out pleasantly enough, until she called Jix and Colonel Riley overheard the conversation.

Sam made the mistake of telling Jix she was going to Mardi Gras with a man Patrick Riley detested—playboy Luke Carter.

As a result, her father called her into his den for a "conference." Sam had rolled her eyes, having some idea of what was coming. They'd been having "conferences" ever since she turned fourteen and Jimmy Bradley asked her to the junior high homecoming dance. It had become her father's unspoken code for dealing with anything that had to do with Sam and the opposite sex.

The colonel opened the conversation by stating in a matter-of-fact voice that he wanted her to marry Duncan Campbell. It had gone downhill from there.

"I'm getting too old for this crap," she muttered.

"What was that?"

"Dad," she said, loudly and clearly, determined not to let him browbeat her, "I'm twenty-eight years old and a doctor—don't you think it's kind of ridiculous for you to keep trying to tell me who I should date?"

He gripped the cushioned arms of his chair and looked away, staring silently out the big picture window, which revealed the Texas Hill Country in all its winter glory. Sam followed his eyes.

The sprawling Riley ranch house sat on a craggy bluff overlooking the Blanco River. On the west side of the bluff the land sloped away, revealing a trail that curved down the sharp incline to a beautiful meadow-like stretch of land beside the sparkling water.

Her father had bought fifty acres of raw Hill Country land not long after her mother died, and even though it only had a small cabin on it, and they only visited it on weekends while her father was in the military, it had always been home. When Sam entered high school the colonel retired and invested in a new computer company. Two years later, he owned the company, and the Rileys were set for life.

He'd built a new house on their land and they'd moved to the fifty acres as he continued to pour his profits into building up what they now called the Crazy R Ranch. He bought up adjacent property, purchased the best horses in Texas, and hired the best trainers to go with them. By the time Sam entered the University of Texas at Austin, she was the daughter of an honest-to-goodness Texas rancher.

Right now the ranch was frozen after a recent dip into below-thirty-degree temperature, unusual for the Hill Country, and the view was one of rugged stoicism. Just like her father's face.

"Dad?"

He jerked his head back to her and she saw, with a sinking heart, that his hands were once again shaking.

"Are you feeling okay?" She moved to his side and slipped a practiced hand over his wrist, taking his pulse, counting the beats as she glanced down at her watch. But before she could make an assessment he shook off her hand and stood, resuming full battle mode.

"I'm just fine, except for the fact that my daughter continues to make a fool of herself over the wrong men!"

Sam's temper flared. "That's not fair. Even you have to admit that I've hardly dated since my fiasco with Mark!"

"If it hadn't been for Jixie, your trust fund would be history by now!"

Fury surged through her and Sam strode to the window, keeping her back to her father as she battled against turning and screaming at him. Would he never let her forget that she had almost married a scam artist? Would he never stop comparing her to Jix Ferguson, now MacGregor, who had "saved" her from marrying Mark the Rat? Much as she loved Jix, she longed to tell her father that her best friend's "rescue mission" had resulted in the two of them being sent back in time!

Jix Ferguson MacGregor had prophetic dreams, and four years ago had kidnapped Sam and taken her to Scotland to keep her from marrying the wrong man. There Sam and the wacky redhead, along with Jix's future husband, Jamie, did the impossible with the help of a magical green crystal in Jamie's sword—they had traveled back in time to 1605 and had an incredible adventure together. Sometimes Sam wondered if the whole thing had just been a crazy dream, but since Griffin Campbell—a time-traveling Scot they'd met in 1605 who ended up in the year 2003—was married to Jix and Sam's other best friend, Chelsea, she had to face reality, no matter how bizarre.

And then there was always Duncan Campbell, Griffin's cousin, a living, breathing source of irritation, and more proof that time travel was possible. Duncan had been saved from hanging in 1882 when Chelsea and

Griffin did their own jaunt through time and ended up in 1882, in San Marcos, Texas.

Duncan had been trying to get back to his own time, unsuccessfully, and his constant traveling through time had left him with a mysterious illness. Fortunately for him, when he came back to the year 2003 with Griffin and Chelsea, Sam was around to help.

Already confused about the direction her life was headed, Sam took a leave of absence from her last year of med school to ponder her future. As luck would have it Sam was in the perfect position to spend the next six months bringing the Scot back from the brink of collapse. It helped her, too, giving her an excuse for her father's questions on why she wasn't in med school.

Duncan's illness turned out to be an immune system deficiency that was treatable with antibiotics, vitamins, and a few herbal remedies she'd learned about during her foray into the past. After six months, Duncan recovered and she'd run like hell back to Houston where she'd finished med school and started a residency program in oncology. A little ironic, since the memory of Duncan had been eating at her insides ever since.

Sam took a deep breath and forced her thoughts away from the handsome, stubborn Duncan and back to her father's displeasure. Maybe she should tell the colonel exactly what his precious Jix had gotten her into four years ago!

Who am I kidding? He wouldn't believe me if I told him.

She could just imagine the look on his face, and the looks on the faces of the men in the little white coats after he called them to cart her off to the state hospital in Austin.

"My daughter?" he'd say to curious friends at parties. "Oh, yes, the stress of medical school was just too much for her. Went nuts. Thought she'd been traveling through time."

Well, it did sound nuts; nevertheless it was true. She tightened her jaw. Though he wouldn't be wrong about the stresses of med school getting to her.

"Come on, Dad," she said, her voice softening as she again noted the paleness of his face. "Let's make some lunch and watch Andy Griffith. You always like that."

"Don't you dare patronize me, young lady," he said gruffly. "I'm not an old man yet."

Sam rolled her eyes, her temper kicking back into gear. "Nobody said you were. Fine, you want to argue, let's argue!"

They glared at one another and Sam was suddenly seized with the need to poke the old bear with something that would really make him flinch.

"And while we're talking about my life," she said, "I need to tell you something." He looked up at her warily. "I'm turning down the residency program in Houston."

Sam finished the sentence almost triumphantly. There, that would show him that she was an adult, capable of making her own decisions.

Real disappointment darted through his faded blue eyes. In spite of her bravado, Sam felt a familiar surge of shame.

"Turned them down? But Samantha, that's one of the most prestigious oncology programs in the country. They only accept a handful every year." His shock was almost palpable.

Sam's throat tightened. Ever since she was a child it seemed she'd been disappointing her father. If she got a B on a test, why not an A? If she was the vice president of the student council, why not the president?

She hadn't shown any interest in the military other than battling the colonel throughout her teen years and went to UT instead of Baylor University, her father's alma mater. Her failures continued through college, and included partying too much and dating a long string of what he termed "inappropriate" men.

But when she'd decided to become a doctor he'd been so proud of her he'd popped nine or ten figurative buttons off his uniform. Of course, her decision had been followed soon after by her engagement to Mark the Rat, so his approval hadn't lasted too long, but it had given her a temporary heady rush of pleasure to know she'd finally done something right.

She took a step forward, uncertainty pressing her toward him. "Dad, I'm not saying I don't want to be a doctor. I just need some time to figure out where my life is going."

She expected him to fight back again, to launch into her and tell her how foolish she was being, how impetuous, how immature. In other words, one of their usual arguments. Instead, he sat back down in his chair and shook his head, looking as if he'd lost all hope.

"Like you say, it's your life," he said, his voice filled with a confusion that hurt her more than any amount of yelling could have. "Your decision. But I don't understand why you would turn down this opportunity."

"I have my reasons," she said. "Look, Dad, I've always worked hard to succeed and to make you proud."

His eyes came back to hers. "I am proud. I was proud. But if you're going to be as foolish in your career as you are in your love life—"

"I do not want to marry Duncan Campbell!" she exploded, clenching both fists in frustration. "I don't even want to date him! In fact, I can barely stand to be in the same room with him!"

"Why not?" Riley demanded, folding his arms over his chest. "He's a hard worker, an honest man, a smart man, and you could do a lot worse."

"Duncan Campbell and I are as far apart as—as—" she waved her hand toward the window. One of the ranch hands was walking across the wide vista, a dog following him, his tail wagging "—as me and Miguel!"

Colonel Riley's mouth dropped open. "I'm shocked."

Sam blinked rapidly and shook her head in confusion. "Pardon?"

"I know that I spoiled you after your mother died, and I know I shouldn't have given you everything you wanted, but I never realized that I had raised a snob!"

"A snob?" Sam stared at him in disbelief. "What in the world are you talking about?"

Her father gestured toward the window where the man was throwing a stick for the dog to fetch. "I can't believe I raised a daughter who would judge a man on his station in life, or his nationality! What counts in a man is not how much money he makes, but whether or not he has integrity and courage." He shook his head as he stared out the window again. "I'm disappointed in you, Samantha."

Sam had a hard time getting her breath, but she forced the air into her lungs. "So what else is new?" she muttered under her breath.

"What? Speak up if you have something to say."

"I'm worried about you, Dad."

He glanced back at her, startled. "Me? What are you talking about?"

She shook her head. "That man out there is Jesse Gonzales. He's been your head horse wrangler for the last five years. The *dog* is Miguel."

Confusion settled over his features again as Sam glared down at him.

9

"Miguel, Jesse," he blustered. "It wouldn't matter. If he's an honest, hardworking man, you wouldn't want him."

She turned away, flinging her arms up in the air. "Just because I don't want to marry Duncan Campbell doesn't mean I don't want to hook up with a decent guy! I took care of Duncan for six months, remember? Don't you think I'd know if we were at all compatible?"

Patrick Riley snorted in derision. "Compatible! You've been watching *Oprah* again, haven't you?"

"Dad, I am old enough to decide who I will date—and/or marry!" she said. "Duncan Campbell is conceited, arrogant, impatient, insufferable, and the most stubborn man I've ever met in my life!"

"I know it!" her father yelled back. "That's why I want you to marry him. The two of you are just alike!"

"Alike? We are not anything alike!" Sam stalked to the window and folded her arms across her chest.

"If you dislike the man so much, then I don't understand why you took a leave of absence from school to take care of him," her father said. "Samantha Jane, you don't make any sense at all."

Sam started to turn away from the window to continue the argument, but at that moment, out on the stretch of land between the house and the cliffside, Duncan Campbell strode across to talk to Jesse Gonzales.

As Sam watched his confident walk, she had that old twist-in-the-gut feeling she got every time she saw the man. After Duncan recovered from his illness Colonel Riley gave the man a job on the ranch. Duncan had apparently been thriving ever since, falling into his role as a cowboy and eventually becoming Jesse's assistant.

Now she watched the frustrating Scot as he walked

across the flat stretch of land, his hair—too long for a real cowboy, she noted smugly—dancing in the cold morning wind. Duncan's body was long and lean and he paused to bend over and pet Miguel, causing the snug jeans he wore to stretch across his taut rear end. Sam bit her lower lip as she watched, unable to turn away even though she wanted to, desperately.

It was just like Duncan to wear jeans so tight they were practically indecent, she thought. Just like him to wear an old faded flannel shirt that hugged his broad shoulders like a second skin. And just like him to straighten and turn toward the house, his blue eyes flashing with good humor under the brim of a black felt cowboy hat—until he caught sight of her in the window, staring down at him. And especially just like him to give her one of his sardonic, knowing smiles before turning back to talk to Jesse, as if she didn't even exist.

The sight of Duncan's lean, hard body brought to mind the days and nights she had cared for him in one of the small cabins on the ranch. They had constantly butted heads over her decisions concerning his care— no, they'd butted heads over *everything*.

She had wanted him. Desperately.

She'd survived taking care of him by always trying to act as a professional and keep a healthy distance between them, both physically and emotionally. But while she might have been able to somehow— miraculously—ignore his muscular body, she'd quickly found it was impossible to ignore Duncan Campbell the man. Intelligent, temperamental, impatient, rude, arrogant, frustrating, and callous, the jerk was completely irresistible.

The night before she left to go back to Houston, Sam had turned off her brain and climbed into bed with him for one glorious passionate fling and the best sex she'd ever had. The next morning she'd made a terrified beeline back to med school. She knew at the time that she was getting too attached to Duncan, that she cared too much. He was the main reason she'd limited her visits to her father in the last eighteen months. Although Duncan lived in the small cabin where she'd treated him, inevitably when she came to the ranch, the colonel would invite the man up to the house for supper. Spending her evening across from the Scot making polite conversation while electricity danced between them wasn't her idea of a fun time.

So she'd skipped Christmas at the ranch this year—she'd told her father she had the flu—and it had almost killed her. This was the first she'd seen her father in four or five months and she really didn't blame him for being hurt.

"We didn't get along," she said through gritted teeth, ignoring the voice in her head. *Liar,* it shouted. *There was one night you got along pretty damn good!*

"I don't wonder," her father said, new strength in his voice. "He's a real man, not one of these pretty boys or losers you usually run around with."

"Enough!" she said, fighting the urge to put her head through the plate glass window. She looked over her shoulder at her father, ignoring the ashen color of his skin, the sag of his shoulders, and the disappointment in his eyes. "Leave me alone, Dad," she said. "It's my life and I'm not going to live it for you."

"Why does that not surprise me?" he said, bitterness lacing the words as he shook his head in weary disgust.

Sam refused to let the pain cripple her. From long experience she hardened her heart, turned on her heel, and strode toward the door leading into the hall. She stopped at the doorway, suddenly unwilling to let him have the last word.

"And one more thing—" she began. She turned just in time to see her father push himself up from his chair, and crumple to the floor.

Chapter Two

Sam stood in the Crazy R Ranch stables, fighting the memories running through her mind. They played out like an old film, shimmering on a scratchy projector across her brain, except all in color, and all too real. Somehow the movie blocked out everything else around her—the distressed barnwood walls, the vaulted roof, the red doors opening to the stalls labeled with each horse's name. Even the smell of horse manure faded as the memory assaulted her.

In the surreal mental video, she stood in her father's den. They were shouting at each other. Had it been just a week ago? It seemed like a lifetime. The picture blurred, refocused, and suddenly she was standing in a hospital room, staring down at her father's pale, waxen face, wires and tubes running from his body to an assortment of monitors and machinery.

The stroke had been sudden and devastating, sending Patrick Riley into a coma. The doctors said there was some hope, as his brain waves were still active and the real damage was minimal. They didn't really know why he hadn't awakened, but Sam knew. She had broken his heart for the last time. He didn't want to come back to her.

She leaned against the smooth golden warmth of Seamus, the palomino horse she'd raised from a colt. She pressed against his side, disconnected somehow from her body.

Her dad was going to die.

Sam drew in a sharp breath and panic flooded through her. Now she was connected. Now she felt the electric power of fear and guilt and pain as it coursed through her body, down her veins, through her heart, into her fingertips.

For years she had prided herself on being practically emotionless, virtually free of soft feelings. Her mother had died when Sam was six. At the funeral she'd held on to her father's hand and cried inconsolably until he had gruffly told her to "be a little soldier." She'd gone numb as she suddenly realized that if her father stopped loving her, she would have no one. She had stopped crying. Since then she had perfected the art of a keeping a tight rein on her emotions.

Her stoic, almost hard facade had proved useful in pursuing a career in medicine. To be a doctor one had to be tough, calm, detached. And if her coping mechanism had more often than not taken the road of sarcasm and rudeness, well then, that was just the price she—and those around her—had to pay. In medical school she'd rationalized that saving lives was more important than being polite. And more than anything, Sam had wanted to save lives. Now she just wanted to save her father, and there was nothing she could do.

When Chelsea and Griffin had disappeared in 2003 after touching the green time-traveling crystals at Jacob's Well, Sam had been terrified her sweet, shy friend would never return. Jix had been distraught—the first time Sam had ever seen her really hysterical—and Sam had resolved that if Chelsea made it back, she was going to turn over a new leaf. She was going to appreciate her friends and family more and try to think before she spoke. She'd really done better; even Jix had commented on her efforts.

Of course, for the first six months after Chelsea's return, she'd had Duncan to rail at, so maybe she hadn't done as well as she thought.

Sam lifted her head and dragged in another ragged breath, shaking her blond hair back from her face. The horse shifted restlessly. She'd been with her father almost every minute since his collapse, but today Jix and Chelsea had insisted that she leave him and come out to the ranch for a shower and food and maybe a ride.

What she really wanted was a break from her thoughts and all the raw feelings she didn't want to face. Squaring her shoulders, she grasped the horse brush in her hand more firmly. She began working on Seamus's smooth golden coat again.

Stroke down, stroke down, stroke sideways, stroke sideways. Stroke down, stroke down . . . the repetitious movement soothed her, helping her stay numb. She swept one hand down Seamus's neck and the horse nickered softly, as if he understood.

"Sam?"

Samantha closed her eyes against the sound of Jix's voice. She wasn't up for another conversation filled with false cheerfulness and pious platitudes. She'd had more than enough of both ever since she'd called Jix and Chelsea from the Emergency Room. Duncan had been at her side as she watched the ER staff work over her father, poking him, prodding him, sticking tubes and needles into him. Sam was a doctor, but the sight of her father's body being invaded had sickened her. She had been thankful for Duncan's presence, but even more for his silence. Chelsea and Griffin showed up an hour later from Austin, and the MacGregors moved up their flight and arrived two days later to offer love and support.

"Sam?" Jix said again.

Sam looked up to find the familiar face of her best friend—wreathed in irrepressible red curls that framed concerned green eyes—peering over the top of Seamus's back.

She sighed and stepped away from grooming the friend whose company she preferred, to talk to the friend who was beginning to get on her nerves.

Ingrate, Sam silently rebuked herself. *Jix crossed an ocean to be here for you. Stop being such a witch.*

"Hi." Sam turned to carefully hang the horse brush on its accustomed nail on the wall of the stable, avoiding looking at Jix again. "I was just about to go for a ride."

Jix circled around the horse until she stood beside Samantha, her smile anxious, loving.

Please leave me alone.

Sam turned back to Seamus and wished she hadn't hung up the brush. Grooming the horse gave her a reason not to look at Jix. There was a saddle blanket draped across the side of the stall and she moved to hoist it down. Stay busy—those were her new watchwords.

"Can I come along? I haven't been riding in ages."

Jix's words were filled with bright, cheerful, terrible sympathy, and Sam closed her eyes again. Her survival instincts kicked into high gear. She opened her eyes and lifted the blanket onto Seamus's back, summoning courage, forcing a hard edge into her voice.

"That might be because you hate to ride."

Jix shook her head and her tentative smile widened. "Hey, I've gone on rides with you before. Don't you remember the time that you and I—"

"Jix, for the love of God, stop!" Sam lashed out with her last bit of angry control.

Jix stopped cold, a stricken look on her face. "Oh, Sam, I only—"

Sam held up one hand, palm outward, cutting off her friend's new attempt at comfort. "I am fine!" she said, biting off the words and flinging them savagely into the void between them. "Please just back off!"

She turned away, but Jix's silence spurred her to look back. Bad move. The depth of empathetic love mirrored in her best friend's eyes almost shattered the wall she had just rebuilt around her heart. Almost. Sam tightened her jaw and stared back. Jix blinked and the empathy faded to sadness.

"All right," she whispered. She lifted one hand toward Sam, and then let it fall back to her side. "If you need me . . ." her voice trailed away.

"Thanks." Sam bit out the word and turned back to the saddle blanket and smoothed it across Seamus's back, positioning it just so as she made sure the sides were even. When she looked back again, Jix was gone. Relief trembled through her.

Good, this was good. She could handle this. She could be a good little soldier. No problem.

Sam bent to pick up the saddle near her feet and then froze as another voice slammed into her from the door of the stable.

"I'd hoped that yer father's illness might have given ye a heart. 'Tis a pity to find that it has not."

Samantha gritted her teeth and turned to face him.

Duncan Campbell stood glaring at her, the reins of

18

the bridle on her father's favorite stallion stretched tautly between his hands. The man's golden brown hair, lightly streaked from the sun, danced in the wild wind that whipped through the wide-open stable doors, making him look as dangerous as the black stallion beside him. He wore a blue denim shirt tucked into faded jeans, and a sheepskin jacket hugged his broad shoulders, buttoned up tight.

The faded black cowboy hat he wore so rakishly looked strangely as though it belonged on the Highlander, as did the oval silver and gold-plated belt buckle engraved with a likeness of the Lone Star State. Though his clothing was different than when she first met him, his blue eyes were all too familiar—hot and dark and disapproving, gazing right into her soul.

Suddenly it was hard to breathe. "Get the hell out," she said. "Right now."

He walked past her, leading the horse to its stall as she glared at him.

"Midnight will be wantin' his oats," Duncan said, his tone casual, "so, ye won't mind if I ignore yer latest command, *yer highness.*"

The nickname, flung out like the insult that it was, sent a rush of color to her face. He hadn't called her that since their infamous bedpan argument back when he was still unable get out of bed and walk to the bathroom. At that time he'd accused her of being a control freak and an emasculator of men.

"Who said you could ride Midnight?" she demanded.

"Yer father," he said. He leaned against the railing, folding his arms over his chest. "I've been taking Midnight out almost every day for the last year, which ye'd know if ye had ever deigned to visit the man."

"None of this is your business," she told him.

He looked over at her and suddenly the blue ice of his gaze seemed to thaw, just a little. "Can ye not see that yer father—and yer friends—are just worried about ye?" he said.

Sam didn't want to talk to Duncan about Jix. In fact, she really didn't want to talk to him at all. "You obviously enjoy eavesdropping on private conversations," she said. "A gentleman would—"

"I'm nae gentleman," he interrupted, his voice soft, the sound sending another shiver across her skin. "I thought we settled that a long time ago."

Heat flooded through Samantha as she met his now fiery gaze.

He still wanted her. She'd always known he wanted her. That had never been the problem. The problem was, even though Duncan Campbell wanted her, lusted after her, she knew deep down that he didn't respect her. Maybe didn't even like her.

That was the real reason she'd run away to Houston—because if she stayed she knew she would let him seduce her again, or she would seduce him. And to make love to a man who wanted you only for your body would have to be the low point of any woman's life.

Right?

Yeah, dummy. Remember that, her protective inner voice said. Sam lifted her chin and her flushed skin cooled.

"Well?" he said. "Didn't we?"

"Yes, that is a question we have definitely settled," she said. "You are no gentleman."

"At least there's one thing we can agree on."

She followed him and stood outside the small enclosure, hands on her hips, her heart pounding painfully.

"Look," she said, "you may have coerced my father

into giving you his power of attorney, but that's only until I can get a judge to say otherwise. In the meantime, stay out of my way!"

After her father's collapse, Sam had eventually had to turn to the unhappy task of looking over Patrick Riley's finances, and had come across a paper designating what person, in the event of a debilitating illness, would hold his power of attorney.

She'd been shocked to find the name on the document was Duncan Campbell.

Duncan turned from pouring oats in a shallow trough and looked at her, his gaze unreadable.

"I dinna ask for the job."

"But you sure were willing to accept it after you found out that I would have to go through you any time I needed money until I receive my trust fund when I'm thirty-five!"

He smiled, but there was no humor in the blue eyes. "I dinna care about yer money," he said.

"No, you just get a great deal of joy out of having power over me."

"Power over ye?" Duncan shook his head and ran one hand through his hair, looking away from her in obvious disgust. "As if that would be possible. Though that's exactly what ye need—a man who willna put up with yer thick-headed stubbornness; a man who will put ye in yer place and keep ye there!"

"And I suppose you think you're the man to do it?" Sam narrowed her eyes and he narrowed his right back at her.

"Nay, I'm the last man who'd want to be tacklin' that job. But yer father tried to change my mind." He turned back to the horse. "He wanted me to marry ye."

Sam closed her eyes. If ever her father had gotten the last word it was now. No, she refused to believe there wouldn't be more words from Colonel Patrick Riley. He was going to wake up. In the meantime he'd left her to face his handiwork.

"He did not," she finally managed to say.

"Aye, he did. I told him again and again that it wasn't going to happen, but he was still determined to make it so." He glanced over at her. "Ye truly dinna know?"

Her face burned with humiliation as Duncan's gaze swept over her from her boot tips to the top of her tousled blond head.

She didn't answer and he finally sighed and turned away. "Yer old man was a smart one. That's why he hired me."

"Why?" Sam blurted, shocked out of her silence. "To marry me?"

"He'd hoped that even though ye insisted on dating such as Luke—what is his name?" But Sam had retreated to silence again and he shrugged. "Aye, Luke Whatsit and the rest of those weak-kneed sisters. He thought that if I were around, ye'd finally realize that ye had the real thing right under yer nose."

Sam shook her head in wonder. "Why, you insufferable, conceited ape." To her surprise he smiled at her insult as he turned to lean against the stallion. He crossed his arms over his chest as he examined her face leisurely.

"Thank ye."

She blinked. "For what?"

"Fer making my point."

"Which would be?"

He shrugged again. "I tried to tell him he was daft. So he found a way to bind us together." Duncan shook his head and then bent down beside Midnight to clean the mud from the stallion's hooves. "He knew if he put me in charge of the money, that it would give me power over ye, and he thought that would help to bend ye to my will."

Sam leaned back against the stall door behind her, the hard wood supporting her as she tried to swallow the lump in her throat. "My father apparently didn't— doesn't—know me very well."

"Aye, I agree with ye there. He was daft to think that I—or any man—could control Samantha Riley."

"He's not crazy," Sam said with irritation, "he's just stubborn."

Duncan put down Midnight's near front hoof and started on the near hind. "Well, then, at least ye came by it honestly."

She lifted her chin, stung by his condescension. "Honestly? Like you came by my father's estate? How long did it take you to talk my father into giving you authority over his money?"

One minute he was crouched beside Midnight, the next he was in front of her, his hands flat on either side of her head, his face inches away from hers. Sam felt a familiar thrill shudder through her body.

Duncan Campbell didn't have the pretty-boy good looks she told herself that she preferred in her men. Sam had spent many a long, sleepless night repeating that fact to her overly imaginative libido. As a way of fending off lurid midnight fantasies, however, the liturgy didn't have much power, because deep down, Sam knew she preferred Duncan's rough exterior over a more polished urban look.

Worse, Duncan was exactly the kind of guy she *could* care about. He wasn't handsome, but he was ruggedly beautiful, his face uniquely sculpted in strong, chiseled lines. He looked every bit the Scottish warrior, and if she hadn't known his history, hadn't known he had traveled in time from the year 1601, Sam could still have pictured him there, poised on a hill in Scotland, a wild Highlander. Why her father thought he was the man for her she couldn't imagine. He wasn't safe. He was the typical bad boy incarnate, and she wanted him.

A long, thin scar, pale against his tanned skin, ran from eyebrow to jaw along the left side of his face and only added to his mystique. He'd told her once that the jagged reminder of violence often repelled women he tried to seduce. Sometimes she feared there might be something desperately wrong with her, because every time she dared to look at the man, Sam wanted to press her lips to the flaw and touch her tongue to the smooth break in his uneven skin. She wanted to touch him now.

"I dinna talk yer father into anything, and don't ye ever say that again." His voice was soft, dangerous.

"Or what will you do?" she demanded, her chest rising and falling with the rush of her breath, the beat of her heart.

His jaw tightened as she continued to meet his angry eyes, and she almost groaned aloud as that telltale flame of desire ignited inside of her.

She'd always been a sucker for jaws that were due for a good clenching at any given moment, full lips that promised their kiss would take her one step closer to nirvana, and smile lines that carved their way out from the corners of hot, sexy, long-lashed eyes. Not that Duncan Campbell smiled often, but when he did, the man could light a rainy day. He wasn't smiling now.

"I will make ye wish that ye hadn't," he said, his eyes hard.

But what he promised wasn't violence, what he promised was seduction, pure and simple.

Sam took a deep breath. It was time to take back control, to show this man that in spite of her father's betrayal she was still the one calling the shots. She shoved past the barrier of his arm and walked back to Seamus, where she knelt to lift his heavy saddle from the ground. By the time she stood and heaved it onto the horse's back Duncan was already back in Midnight's stall, and Sam released a breath she didn't know she'd been holding. Silence filled the stable except for the soft sounds of horses moving around in their stalls.

She heard a thud and knew Duncan had unsaddled his horse and was probably grooming him now, his rough, square hands treating the horse with gentle competence.

Lucky Midnight.

Stop it, stupid. She fastened the cinch under the horse's belly and tugged on it as she tried to stop thinking about Duncan Campbell. She slipped the halter off Seamus's head and replaced it with the bridle, gently sliding the bit between his teeth. She'd ride out to the south forty and stay until the sun went down. That would take care of another day.

And then what? She pushed the question away. There was no tomorrow. She didn't dare look beyond today. If her father died without waking up, without giving her the chance to talk to him, to tell him—

"So where are ye running off to this time?"

She jumped at the sound of Duncan's voice so close behind her. Too close. She turned and forced herself to look up into his eyes.

"Imigh."

Sam spat out the Gaelic word for "get lost" and was shocked to see a real smile flash across the man's face for a split second.

"So ye remember the Gaelic I taught ye."

"You? Ha!" Sam turned back to her horse and raised her left foot to fit it snugly into the stirrup. She pulled up easily, slung her right leg over the saddle, and settled against the leather. Now she could look down on Mr. High-and-Mighty Duncan Campbell. Now she didn't have to crane her neck to look up at him and feel small and unimportant and helpless.

"Aye," he said, the fire returning to his blue eyes. "When ye cared for me, I taught ye the Gaelic, terrible as ye were at pronouncing the words."

"You only introduced me to the language," she said, gathering Seamus's reins in her left hand. "I took a community night course last summer—just for fun—and had a teacher from the Isle of Skye. So there, you, you—*rifi'neach.*"

Duncan's brows had darted up at the news that she had absorbed his few lessons and decided to learn the language on her own. Now he laughed at the word she flung at him, "ruffian."

"Did ye now? And why would ye want to learn the Gaelic?"

Sam shrugged. "It's a beautiful language."

Duncan nodded. "Aye. *Alainn.*" Sam felt her face grow warm at the way he said the word "beautiful," looking at her, as if he really meant something by it, when of course he didn't. Talk about a player. If only her father could see this side of the irritating Scotsman.

"Oh, and just for the record," she said, keeping her voice cool in spite of the heat in her face, "I never *cared* for you. I'm a doctor. I *treated* you."

The amusement vanished from his eyes. "And why

would ye think I meant anything different?" He backed away from her and frowned. "Ye have a problem, Dr. Riley, a serious one. Ye want so badly to be bedded that ye think any man who speaks to ye must want to do so." He shook his head. "I assure ye, 'tis not the case, in spite of yer father's entreaties on yer behalf. And in spite of one night when ye crawled into my bed."

Bright red spots danced in front of Samantha's eyes. She clenched the reins in her hands and glared down at Duncan, standing there looking so smug and so sexy and so absolutely infuriating.

"Po'g mo tho'n!" she shouted. "Kiss my arsc!" was way more satisfying when screamed in Gaelic. Digging her heels into Seamus's side, Sam sent the horse bolting past the Scot, out the stable doors, and into the great wide open.

Chapter Three

"I'm so worried about her. She hasn't even cried."

"Sam never cries."

"For pity sakes, Chelsea, her father is in a coma and will probably never wake up again—even Samantha should cry!"

"Do you think she really gave up her residency?"

At the sound of the voices, Duncan shifted on the couch in the den. For the last year and a half he'd been living and working on the Crazy R Ranch, spending most of his free time in the small hunting cabin Colonel Riley had offered as the room and board part of his salary.

Recently, however, the colonel had asked him to stay at the ranch house, citing several robberies on ranches in the area. Duncan had known that the tough-as-nails veteran wasn't worried about break-ins, and now the Scot realized belatedly that perhaps the man had known there was something wrong with his health all along. Maybe he'd wanted someone nearby in case he needed help.

Out of habit, Duncan had come up to the ranch house and taken his shower after his ride, then stretched out on the couch in the den for a little nap, completely forgetting the fact that Sam, along with the MacGregors, were staying there.

He opened his eyes and glanced around at Patrick Riley's favorite room, taking in the crackling fire in the huge rock fireplace, two leather couches, a large coffee table made from a slab of cedar, and two overstuffed dark brown chairs.

Duncan felt more at home on the Crazy R Ranch than anywhere else he'd ever lived, save Scotland. And yet, he continued to brood, his mood growing darker as the days passed. Colonel Riley's illness had only added to a depression that had begun after his return from 1882. No, if he were honest with himself, it had begun long before that.

In 1601, he had hated his life, his father, and the future that had been planned for him. The eldest son, he had been expected to marry well, act as his father's apprentice, and as the man grew older, take on the full responsibilities of his properties, one day becoming Chieftain. Fergus Campbell had expected those things from his eldest son, but after his mother died, Duncan rebelled against everything his father wanted from him.

Duncan had wanted adventure. He wanted to travel, to see what awaited him down each new road, on each new day. The last thing he wanted was to be tied down with obligations and duties. He and his father had butted heads for years, and then, one day, at the age of thirty-four, Duncan had simply had enough. Like a child, he had run away from home, fleeing to the hills where his cousins lived, and a special cave he had found there one summer.

It was in that grotto where he'd found the miraculous green crystals, and it was there he had begun his adventures through time, without a thought for anyone else but himself. Later, he would yearn for home and his own people, but first, there had been hard lessons to learn.

Duncan shifted on the cushions beneath him. He had a feeling that Samantha Riley had her own hard lessons ahead of her. Behind the couch on which he lay was a big gathering table, where he imagined Sam and Jix and Chelsea and their friends had perhaps played games in their youth, or enjoyed holiday dinners together.

At this particular moment in time, Jix and Chelsea sat there without Sam, talking to their husbands, trying to make sense out of Samantha Riley. It was a losing battle as far as he was concerned, but he was keeping his mouth shut. Still, he'd best make himself known. To do otherwise would make the situation even more awkward.

"She'll be all right," he said aloud, as he swung his legs off the couch and his feet to the floor.

Jix and Chelsea both jumped and then laughed at their reactions. Jix recovered first and smiled at him. What a lass. Too bad MacGregor had seen her first. She had spunk.

Samantha has spunk too, a devilish little voice in his head reminded him. *Aye, but Jix has a sweet and gentle spirit along with the spunk*, he replied. *Samantha Riley wouldna know gentle if it bit her on her—*

"Duncan! We didn't know you were there," Jix said. "Please, join us. You're part of the family now too."

Duncan felt a warmth encompass him at the sound

of her words and he fought the childish need to accept the invitation and truly become one of the group around the table.

"Nay, 'tis a thing for friends and family to discuss, not I," he said, trying to keep his voice pleasant, surprised at how harsh the words still came out.

"Och, come on, Duncan," Griffin said, frowning at him. "Ye were with Sam night and day for six months. Ye should be able to give Jix a little insight as to what's goin' on in her head."

Reluctantly, Duncan rose and walked over to the huge table, sliding in beside his cousin. Marriage obviously agreed with Griffin, he thought, as he watched the man beam down at his wife. Chelsea Brown had changed the girl-shy Scot into a confident husband. He was glad. Griffin deserved that kind of life.

The two men at the table looked as uncomfortable as he felt, but luckily Jix and Chelsea did most of the talking.

"So did she actually tell you that she was giving up her residency?" Chelsea said to Jix, her hand linked through Griffin's elbow, her gray eyes intense.

"Yes, and I couldn't believe it." Jix bit her lower lip and stared thoughtfully into space.

"Perhaps the lass has decided she doesna want to be a physician," Duncan said.

The four turned and looked at him as if he'd lost his mind.

"Colonel Riley's dream was—is—for Sam to be a doctor," Jix said gently.

"Perhaps Samantha has her own dreams," Duncan suggested, and then frowned. He'd been pretty hard on the lass earlier. Perhaps there was a reason she wasn't showing more emotion over her father's illness.

Jix shook her head. "I just don't understand. Sam always keeps her emotions, well, very controlled, but this is her father—" her voice broke and Jamie put his arm around his wife.

"Easy, darlin'," he said softly, "I know he was like a second father to ye too, and it's natural to be upset."

Jix looked up at him and burst into tears. "Then why isn't Sam upset?" she cried. "I don't understand. Colonel Riley was—is—a wonderful father."

"Aye, but everyone deals with these things in their own way," Jamie said. "Give her time."

Jix wiped away her tears and sat up straighter. "Time. Funny you should put it quite that way." She took a deep breath. "I had a dream last night."

The two men tensed, while Chelsea groaned out loud and leaned her head in both hands.

"Hey!" Jix admonished. "If it weren't for my dreams none of us would be together, just remember that!"

Duncan watched the interaction between the four, feeling again like an outsider. He knew that Jix Mac-Gregor had prophetic dreams. A dream she'd had about Samantha four years before was what had brought Jix and Jamie together, and ultimately, Chelsea and Griffin. It had also sent the four of them traveling through time.

"You're right, you're right," Chelsea said hastily, lifting her head and giving her friend a half smile. "Okay, what was it about?" She rushed on before Jix could speak. "And please tell me I wasn't in it!"

"No, it wasn't about any of us," Jix said, leaning toward her, warming to her subject. "It was about Samantha. She was in some wild, beautiful place that looked like the Highlands, and she was wearing a long, shimmering dress." Her eyes widened and flickered over to Duncan. "And there was a man with her, wearing a kilt—"

"Och, no, not another Scotsman," Jamie murmured.

"—but I couldn't see his face. He was some kind of servant to her, I think, at least he seemed to be very obedient."

"Now I know ye have to be wrong on this one," Griffin interjected. "An obedient Scotsman?" He chuckled and Chelsea poked him in the side with her elbow.

"Hush," she scolded lightly. "Go on, Jix."

Jix frowned in thought before continuing. "Well, there was another man who was tall and thin, with a long beard and hair. Oh, and he had a big staff."

Jamie grinned. "Sounds like Samantha's kind of guys—subservient and big-staffed. So what's the problem?"

Jix shook her head at him. "It's not funny, Jamie. I sensed Samantha was in some kind of danger. And then I saw a giant hourglass and the bottom had broken, and all the sand was running out and I could see them—I could see the crystals, glimmering in the grains of sand."

Duncan leaned toward her. "The crystals? Ye mean—"

"Yes, the green crystals that took us all through time and then back home again. But there were other crystals too that were lavender and blue and some like diamonds."

"Don't forget, not all of us got back home," Duncan reminded her.

Griffin shot a sympathetic glance his way. "Do ye still want to go back home so badly, laddie? I thought ye had made yer peace with the Lord's doing."

Duncan looked away before his cousin could see the guilt in his eyes. He'd made a grand fuss about not being able to get back to his own time period since leaving the year 1601. He'd told these friends how he had chased the crystals around the world and used them again and again, going from time to time, trying to get back home. They'd all been so sympathetic. If they knew the truth, he doubted they'd be so eager to invite him to their table.

"If He had anything to do with those crystals, then I'm not so sure the Lord knows what He's doing," he retorted.

"Ye dinna mean that," Griffin said. "Ye've always been a God-fearing man."

Duncan shrugged. "People change. 'Tis true that I've enjoyed experiencing this time, but I still want to go back again. To Scotland's past," he added. There, that much was true.

"I'm sorry I canna help ye at least return to Scotland in this time," Jamie said, shaking his dark head with obvious regret. "But with the Patriot Act, and the crackdown in security at airports and such, I canna dare risk getting a passport for ye as I did for Griffin."

Duncan nodded, admiring Jamie's willingness to bring up the sore subject between them. " 'Tis all right. Ye have a family to think about now. I dinna blame ye."

"Ooh, speaking of that, I'd better go and check on little James," Jix said, rising from the table. She patted Jamie on the shoulder and hurried out of the room to check on their son.

What would it be like, Duncan wondered, to have a child with someone you loved with your whole heart?

Duncan shifted in his chair. Their joy shouldn't make him uncomfortable, but it did.

"Well, James is sound asleep, sucking his thumb," Jix reported as she shut the door behind her and crossed to the table.

Jamie glanced back at Duncan. "I'm sorry my

sword didn't work for you. I don't understand why it didn't."

Duncan felt a familiar sinking of his spirit at the mention of Jamie's sword. The hilt of the MacGregor ancestral sword held a time-travel crystal that Jamie, Jix, and Samantha had accidentally used to travel to the year 1605. Jamie had brought the sword with him on this visit, and Duncan had eagerly taken the magical weapon in his hands, concentrating with all of his might on Scotland of the past. But the green stone had remained dim, and Duncan had remained in 2005.

"They have a mind of their own," Jix interjected, leaning against her husband, "showing up when they want, working when they please."

"Or maybe certain crystals work for certain people," Chelsea suggested. She frowned thoughtfully. "I've been doing some research on that possibility." She gave him a sympathetic smile. "But don't give up, Duncan, maybe the crystals will come back someday to Jacob's Well."

Duncan gave her a weary smile. The shy scientist, along with his cousin, Griffin, had experienced their own adventure through time, and thanks largely to Chelsea, had broken him out of a Texas jail back in 1882. If it hadn't been for them, he'd be dead, hung for stealing a horse.

"I look for them every day." Duncan ran one hand through his hair, feeling suddenly caged in. "Mayhap one day they will return."

"But even if they do," Griffin reminded him, "ye can only travel within this country. If ye return to 1601 in America, 'tis doubtful ye'd ever be able to make it from here to Scotland."

"Aye." Duncan looked away. Another secret. Another lie. "Still, I have to try."

"Oh, Duncan," Jix said, "I hate for you to start bouncing around time again. Remember what it did to you before."

He didn't respond. If he ever got the chance to travel through time again, he would take it.

Jamie shook his head slightly. "It's amazing how the crystals continue to appear and disappear. There has to be some explanation for it."

"There's no physical science that supports the existence of the crystals, let alone that explains how they work," Chelsea said.

"Now, come on, Chel," Jix said. "You can't apply the laws of science to magic!"

Jamie laughed and hugged her. His wife snuggled against him.

"Well, the crystal in my sword brought us together," Jamie said, "so I don't care what it is or how it works— I just know I don't want to ever use it again."

"I agree with the lad," Griffin said, squeezing Chelsea's hand. "I dinna care where I am, as long as I'm with my love." His wife nodded and gazed up at him adoringly.

Duncan looked away, the combined happiness of the two couples almost more than he could bear.

"So what about Sam?" Chelsea said. "Do we push her for an explanation on her lack of emotion about her dad?"

"Nay."

The four turned to look at Duncan again, all obviously surprised at his bold statement.

Mind yer own business, his insides prodded him. But he ignored the cautioning words. He knew better than anyone that Samantha just needed everyone to leave her alone. He couldn't sit there and allow her friends, good-hearted as they might be, to assault her with their questions and demands.

"Leave her alone for awhile," he said aloud. "She'll talk about it when she's ready." He shifted his glance to Jix. "If ye push the lass," he shrugged, " 'twill only make her more belligerent and more withdrawn as ye all well know."

Jix gave him a curious, thoughtful look and Duncan stood, suddenly anxious to get away from all of them.

"I think you're right," Jix said. "You know, when Sam was treating you for your illness, the two of you got pretty close."

He folded his arms over his chest, suddenly ill at ease. "I wouldna say that. We mostly argued."

Chelsea looked over at Jix and Duncan frowned at the gleam in her eyes. "But Samantha loves to argue, Duncan. Maybe that's what she needs now—someone to argue with."

"I think you're right, Chel." Jix rose and crossed to Duncan's side. She rested one hand on his arms and looked up at him earnestly. "Duncan, her father is in a coma—"

Her voice cracked a little over the word "father," and Jix's grief over Patrick Riley's illness touched him without warning.

"Aye," Duncan managed to say, "I know, and truly, I'm sorry for her. Patrick is one of the finest men I've ever known. He's been nothing but good to me." He shifted his feet and glanced toward the door.

"Don't take this the wrong way, but you irritate her six ways to Sunday. If you hang out with her, before long she'd give in to her real feelings and let them out."

"Thanks," Duncan said. "But I don't think—"

Chelsea hurried to his other side, tucking her hand into the crook of his elbow. "This way we can leave her alone, but if she needs us, you can let us know." She looked over at Jix. "Colonel Riley is like a father to us too," she whispered. "I can only imagine how Sam must really be feeling."

Griffin and Jamie exchanged glances, and together threw Duncan a combined look of sympathy.

"Ye might as well give in now, lad," Jamie said, and Griffin voiced his agreement.

"Aye, bucko, for the two of them will hound ye like a banshee's wail across the moors until ye do their bidding."

Duncan closed his eyes briefly, and all at once found himself nodding.

Anything to get out of this room.

"All right," he said, fighting to keep the desperation from his voice. "What do I have to do?"

Jix and Chelsea both gave a little sigh of relief, but instead of letting Duncan go, to his horror, they leaned more tightly against him.

"Eat lunch with her, go riding with her—"

"Take her to Mardi Gras!" Jix said.

Duncan blinked. "Take her to what?"

"It's a big party," she explained, leaning earnestly against him.

Duncan sent Jamie a fervent look of appeal, but the man just grinned back at him.

"In Austin," she went on. "Well, the original one is in New Orleans, but Austin throws its own version every year on Sixth Street."

"It's so much fun," Chelsea said, squeezing his arm, always a little more reserved than the irrepressible Jix, Duncan noted. "Everyone wears costumes and masks

38

and there's music and—" Chelsea sobered suddenly. "Maybe we shouldn't go," she said. "I mean, with the colonel in the hospital and all."

"But it will help cheer Sam up," Jix insisted. "The colonel would be the first to say give it a try!"

"Aye," Griffin said, "I have to agree."

Chelsea nodded and turned to her husband. "All right, let's do it! Griffin had a great time last year, didn't you, honey?"

"Jamie, too!" Jix said. "Remember, darling?"

Jamie and Griffin exchanged glances.

"Aye," Jamie said.

Griffin nodded. "Oh, aye," he said, obviously lying through his teeth.

"We'll have great costumes this year, won't we, Jix?"

Now Jix was beaming again. "My friend Jordan has agreed to let us borrow costumes from his special effects company. You aren't going to believe how incredible we're all going to look."

Duncan knew a scam when he heard one. "I dinna think I can attend yer Mardi Grass," he said, his hand on the doorknob. "There's too much work to be done here at the ranch."

"But Samantha needs us right now," Jix pleaded, her green eyes bright with what looked suspiciously like tears. Duncan almost groaned aloud. He was a sucker for a crying woman. Had never been able to resist them. It was his one weakness where the fairer sex was concerned. It was one of the reasons he had liked Samantha so much in the beginning. She never cried.

"Please, Duncan," Jix said, "you've got to help her. Sam's always liked you and really I think if you'd just give her a little encouragement that—"

"Jessica Isobel Xavier Ferguson MacGregor!" A loud, blunt voice from the opposite doorway stopped the woman in midsentence and Jix turned, her eyes wide with guilt.

Samantha stood in the doorway, hands on her hips, her furious gaze on all of them.

"Just what the hell do you all think you're doing?" she demanded.

Jix stepped forward. "Sam, it's not what you think. We were just trying—that is, we thought if Duncan—" her voice trailed away.

"You know, you've done a lot of rotten things to me over the years," Sam said to Jix, her voice soft with bitterness, "but I think this is the worst."

"Worse than kidnapping you and taking you to Scotland and getting you lost in time?" Chelsea asked incredulously.

Sam turned and narrowed her eyes. "Don't think I'm letting you off the hook!" Chelsea gulped. "What are you thinking, trying to pair me up with Duncan the Warrior King?"

"Dinna be so dramatic," Duncan moved to stand between Jix and Samantha. The girl was spoiled rotten. Couldn't she see that her best friend was worried about her? Tears hovered on Jix's eyelashes and he refused to stand back and let Sam berate the tenderhearted lass.

"You stay out of this!" Sam said.

"Ye're lucky to have friends that care so much about ye—Lord knows ye don't deserve them. Now why don't ye take a walk until ye calm down a bit."

Sam advanced on him, her fists clenched, her eyes narrow with fury. "Why don't you take a flying leap right up my—"

"Sam!" Chelsea cried.

Samantha stopped in her tracks. The fury ebbed from her face like water off a rock, and Duncan watched as her eyes turned to ice and her voice to steel. She glanced around at the five of them.

"Leave me alone," she said. "All of you."

Chapter Four

"Hey baby, I'll flash you if you'll flash me!"

"Whatcha got under that kilt, laddie?"

Duncan Campbell stood with his arms folded over his chest and leaned against the side of a building on Sixth Street in Austin, Texas. For the first time since coming to the twenty-first century, he felt inconspicuous, even though he wore Griffin's kilt, plaid, and full-sleeved shirt with the deeply cut front that Samantha had once told him looked "sissy."

Typical of the lass. Her choice in dates for the evening had reinforced his opinion that she didn't know a man from a jackanape, so he'd scarcely listen to her opinion about a man's clothing.

The thought of Samantha Riley made him frown and turn his gaze to search the crowd again. Where was she?

He'd been at this thing called Mardi Gras for two hours and was not particularly impressed. Granted, there had been an assortment of good-looking women raising their blouses to "flash" him from time to time, and while he was as appreciative of the female body as the next man, overall he found the whole thing a little silly.

He'd been approached at least ten times by different women, some asking him to have a drink, some asking him to lift his kilt, others asking for the gift of cheap plastic beads in return for "flashing," and finally a few who invited him to go home with them and "do the nasty."

He had finally found a pub—Mother Egan's was its unlikely name—and though different from any he'd ever been in, for a moment the feeling of being irrevocably lost in the wrong time faded slightly. He had downed a few whiskeys in defense of the cold night, then headed out again in search of his friends, only to be once more accosted by drunken women.

Duncan wasn't interested, not in leering at naked bodies of women without honor. Even though he was only thirty-four years old, his travels through time had given him an old soul. If he was going to have sex for the sake of sex, it had to be with someone he at least cared about.

Early on in the evening he'd gotten separated from Jix and Jamie MacGregor and their group, and so here he stood, waiting, watching for one of them to walk by.

Don't ye mean, waiting for Samantha to walk by? said a wicked little voice in his head.

The couples—and Duncan—had all met at the Riley ranch house to journey to this thing called Mardi Gras. He couldn't help but smile as he remembered the agonized look on his cousin Griffin's face, and that of Jamie MacGregor, as they stood fidgeting in their costumes. Served them right for being such henpecked—what was the word?—wusses. No woman would ever force Duncan Campbell to wear such creations.

Though he had to admit, Griffin's costume was amazing. Some kind of computer magic, Jix explained—though anything to do with computers was magic to him—had created an eerie likeness of a purple dragon's head that rose up from Griffin's shoulders and stretched five feet above him. It was dazzling, but Duncan would never have worn the garb.

Griffin had looked fairly miserable when they all gathered at the ranch house to set off for Austin, but every time Chelsea, clad in the simple dress of a Highland lass, smiled at him, his misery had changed to a duncelike bliss.

Jamie's getup was equally fantastic. He was apparently supposed to be the knight that went with the dragon. The knight's waist began at Jamie's shoulders and rose eight feet above him. From time to time the knight would slash his transparent sword through the crowd. MacGregor was actually delighted with his costume, though he kept complaining, but Duncan knew he was just trying to keep up a manly appearance.

Once again Duncan had felt lucky that he had no woman in his life trying to boss him around, trying to tell him what to do, trying to hold on to him the way Jix and Chelsea seemed to be constantly doing to their husbands, hugging and kissing and—

Duncan sighed, realized he had sighed, and scowled as he glanced up and down Sixth Street, hoping for a glimpse of the dragon or knight, or even the women.

Jix's costume had been simpler than anyone else's. No computer magic, just a damsel in distress—a mismatch if ever there was one—complete with medieval dress and chains around her wrists. Jamie had raised both brows when he saw them and whispered something in her ear that made her blush and smile.

Yes, Duncan was certainly glad he had no woman harassing him.

He had flatly refused to wear the costume Jix picked out for him. He would wear Jamie's kilt, he declared, or go in the usual clothing he wore while working on Colonel Riley's ranch, but he would not, under any condition, dress up like some movie character called "Shrek."

Jix had meekly agreed, which just proved that when a man stood up to a woman, she naturally backed down from her high horse. With the exception of Samantha Riley, of course.

Duncan's smile faded. The woman had a backbone like an iron rod and a will to match. His mouth quirked up again. However, if and when she ever capitulated, a man could be assured that he'd won a noble battle. He knew. She'd capitulated once, and it was a memory he often took out and replayed in his mind.

The thought of Samantha Riley naked and next to him in his bed entertained him for the next few moments until he brusquely pushed the memory away.

After returning from the year 1882 with Chelsea and Griffin, Duncan had been sure he was dying. His arm had begun to atrophy and a dragging fatigue had plagued him day and night. But an amazing thing, a woman physician, had taken care of him.

He'd been prepared to be grateful. Instead, he'd ended up wanting to throttle her—or kiss her until she was too sated to speak.

She was the most exasperating woman he'd ever met. They'd argued constantly, sniping and bickering at one another. But the truth was, his caustic wit had found an equal at last, and he'd secretly delighted in pushing her until her temper flared. She was blunt, sarcastic, and sexy as hell, and if she didn't know what was going on between them, he certainly did.

But it hadn't been until Sam's last night at the ranch that she'd given in to her feelings. He'd been surprised when his usual seductive innuendo had been met, not with her usual feigned indifference or snappy remark, but with hot, sensuous eyes and the burning touch of her hand on his chest. She'd melted into his arms and lost herself in passion, taking him along with her for the ride.

He smiled, remembering the way her long blond hair had fallen over her shoulder as she lifted herself over him, the waves tickling his jaw as she leaned down and captured his mouth. The way she had moved against him, uninhibited, fluid, totally unlike the stiff, unyielding woman who had taken care of him for six long months.

Of course, the next day she'd been the same cold, unemotional Samantha, bidding him a brief good-bye with a professional courtesy that had first angered and then amused him as she practically ran out the door, headed for Houston. He had shrugged and turned his attention to his new job on the ranch, thinking that was that.

But for some reason the memory of that night had haunted him. Why, he wasn't quite sure. It wasn't that he hadn't been in bed with beautiful women before.

He pictured Samantha for a moment—her perfectly symmetrical features, her changeable hazel eyes, her full lips made for a man to kiss, her ripe breasts made for a man to touch—

Duncan frowned and shifted against the building.

It wasn't like he hadn't had warmer women in his bed before—though for that one night she hadn't just been warm, she'd been a flame that danced against his skin and his lips. He saw her again in his mind's eye, rolling over on top of him, her mouth lowering to his, her eyes half-closed as she lifted herself—

He raked his hair back from his face and wiped away the slight moisture across his forehead. Must be warming up, he thought.

By the time morning came, before she'd risen and become Dr. Samantha Riley again, Sam'd been a goddess to him. If he were honest he'd admit that she had been like no other woman he'd ever bedded, but, as Sam was fond of saying, "So what?" That fact wouldn't keep him from leaping at the first chance he had to travel back in time again, not even if Sam came to him right now and lay naked and begging at his feet.

That image was a little harder to shake. The thought of Samantha putting herself in a position of submission—lying her perfect body down at his feet, gazing up at him with languid eyes inviting him to take her, to caress her, to do whatever he desired—

Duncan shook his head and released his pent-up breath, physically jarring himself back to reality. He'd been without a woman too long, he reasoned as he watched the crowd. That was all. He was only human, after all, and Samantha Riley, while a pain, would tempt the most stoic man.

After waiting another few minutes, he headed back to Mother Egan's for another whiskey or two, then returned to his vantage point. This time the drink softened his impatience and warmed him inside to the point that his mood became a more tranquil one, though he still wanted to go back to the ranch.

He could be in his cabin reading right about now, or maybe even catching a "show" on the "tellievision" up at the main house, or surfing the "Net." He still didn't quite understand the connection between standing on a curved board to ride the ocean's waves and using a computer, but that was just one small thing out of an infinite number of things he didn't understand about the twenty-first century.

Like the women here.

His gaze wandered over to a girl lifting her blouse in the street, letting every man look upon her bare breasts. In his day if a woman did that, she'd be disgraced. Her family would disown her. Here it seemed to be just part of the "fun." For a moment he wondered if Sam was somewhere in the crowd "flashing" her wares at strange men.

He straightened, alarmed, and then leaned back again. Of course she wasn't. Even in this devilish place, Samantha and Jix and Chelsea were true ladies.

But what if Sam's date—his lip curled back at the thought of the man she'd brought with her this night—didn't protect her in this wild crowd? What if—

He forced out the pent-up breath he was holding. Samantha Riley, more than any woman he'd ever known, could take care of herself.

Duncan stomped his feet to get his circulation going again and moved to the other end of the building to peruse the crowd from another direction. Why Samantha had chosen to go to the Mardi Gras with Luke Carter he would never understand. The man was arrogant and egotistical—what could she possibly see in him?

Yes, he was better off without a woman in his life, especially a woman like Samantha Riley. Hot with desire one minute, an ice goddess the next. He was definitely glad that she'd dragged along her insipid escort to this ridiculous—

Duncan stopped thinking, uncrossed his arms, and straightened away from the wall.

Across the street, Samantha Riley stood in all of her

costumed glory. She tossed her pale blond hair back from her creamy white shoulders, and her eyes, as slanted as a cat's, danced with impatience as she gazed out at the crowd around her. Her gown hugged the upper part of her body and the sight of her soft curves sent a surge of heat through him that chased away the cold.

She then scowled, shifting her attention to something on the street. The crowd parted and Duncan could see her handsome date on his knees in front of her.

Duncan grinned and wondered if the man was simply worshipping at her feet, or, as he suspected, begging for mercy.

Samantha Riley watched her date empty his stomach against the Sixth Street curb as the girl beside him giggled and wavered drunkenly. Sam groaned aloud and wondered why she had ever agreed to attend Austin's version of Mardi Gras as she glanced up and down the street, looking for Jix or Chelsea.

And on the heels of that question was another—Why did her father always have to be right? Even in a coma in the hospital, he was right. Luke Carter had been nothing but a complete bore, and had turned out to be, with the exception of Duncan Campbell, the most conceited—and fickle—man she'd ever met.

First, Luke had made fun of her costume. Not that she cared what he thought, but Jix's face had fallen at his critical remarks and Sam had wanted to punch him.

She glanced down at the costume that had been created by one of the hottest up-and-coming special effects companies in the world. One of Jix's kooky friends owned the company, and the loan had apparently been a big favor on his part. Only Jix MacGregor would think that this filmy, iridescent fairy queen costume would be Sam's choice. She should never have given Jix carte blanche on the costumes while she was still in Houston.

She glanced up. Okay, she had to admit that her costume was pretty incredible. She never would have ordered it for herself, but it was amazing.

Rising up above her head and also reaching downward almost to the ground, two translucent blue-green wings fluttered slowly open and shut. Sam swept one hand backward, into the wings, and it was like passing her fingers through a movie projection.

There were two buttons on the back of the silver rhinestone-studded belt she wore, one that turned on the wings and one that started the color flow. Bored, she reached back and pressed the second button. As she watched, colors pumped through the wings, starting at the base of each and pulsating through to the fragile wing tips—first deep green, then kelly green, blue-green, peacock blue, sky blue fading into deep blue, violet blue, lavender, and on and on through the color spectrum.

The dress was made from an iridescent fabric that changed color too, with every movement of her body, in shades of blue and violet and green. The neckline was cut low and the sleeves long, and she'd been the hit of Sixth Street in the first few minutes. Even now, people all around her were oohing and ahing and stopping to stare. Jix and Chelsea had been nothing less than thrilled at her success.

So why wasn't I thrilled? Sam thought as Luke threw up again at her feet. The blue-haired girl beside him took a deep drag from her cigarette and knelt down beside him. After Samantha and Luke had gotten separated from Jix and Chelsea in the crowd, Luke had picked up the girl, who looked like she was about nineteen years old, and had been practically making out with her in the street ever since. Sam ignored them both as she looked around, hoping to catch sight of a knight or a dragon.

I'm such a grump. I didn't even thank Jix for the costume. She was just trying to do something nice for me and as usual, I have to whine and moan. Maybe that's why I'm here with Luke Carter instead of some-one I give a damn about.

A sudden gust of wind sent her long, blond hair into her face and she pried it away from her eyes, praying her contacts wouldn't pop out. The disposable con-tacts that Jix had insisted on were actually her favorite part of the costume. They had changed her grayish hazel eyes to a beautiful, clear lavender. For once, Sam was glad she had listened to her friend. According to the eye doctor, she could wear them for a month or more before she even had to take them out.

She couldn't wait to see her father's face when he saw her in this—Sam closed her eyes. Her father was in a coma. Her father wasn't going to see anything. She'd spent every night with him since his stroke, but Jix had begged her to take this one night off from her vigil at his side. She never should have agreed.

Luke retched again and she pulled the skirt of her dress out of the way.

"Poor Lukey, baby," the girl crooned. She glanced up at Sam. "Maybe he needs some coffee."

"You think?" Sam asked dryly. "Excellent idea, Tiffany, why don't you—"

"My name is Buffy," the girl interrupted, frowning.

"Of course it is. Here," Sam dug in her purse and handed her ten dollars. "Go and buy him some coffee."

"Gee, thanks. You want me to bring you some?" She reached down and pulled Luke up to a semi-standing position. The no-longer-so-handsome man smiled at her through half-closed eyes.

"Is zat you, Shamantha?" he asked.

"No, it's Queen Maeve," Sam said. "Go, leave, I order you."

Buffy frowned at her again and then shrugged, tugging Luke after her. He stumbled along, oblivious, but in fairly good hands.

Great. Now, all she had to do was find Jix and tell her that as far as she was concerned the party was over. But the street had suddenly grown more crowded and Sam felt her frustration mount as she found she couldn't move forward. At this point she'd even be happy to see Duncan if he walked by. She shot another glance around, standing on her tiptoes, trying to see over the heads of the press of humanity surrounding her.

Duncan had asked her to go with him to Mardi Gras and she'd delighted in turning him down. Not that her rejection had made a dent in his day. Still, she'd been determined to show him that while he might be her father's choice, he certainly wasn't hers.

Shoving her elbow into a man with a big beer belly standing behind her, Sam reached around the back of the rhinestone-studded belt she wore and found the switch that turned off the wings. They disappeared and she sighed, feeling oddly relieved.

At last the crowd began to surge away from her, and Sam lifted the hem of her gossamer skirt and stepped over Luke's vomit, and headed back down the street.

She hurried on, but still couldn't make much progress. All at once she realized she didn't want to find Jix. If her friend saw her, she'd be relentless in trying to talk her into staying. Sam kept her head down.

Pushing through the crowd, she jabbed a big guy wearing a Hell's Angels black leather jacket in the side, and made it to the sidewalk. More than anything she wanted to get out of her costume and head for the hospital. She glanced up at a big clock outside one of the bars. One A.M. Too late. By the time she went home and changed, it would be morning. She should never have left her father's side in the first place.

On the sidewalk the throng wasn't quite so heavy, but as she took a step forward, a familiar voice stopped her in her tracks.

"Going my way?"

A man in a giant beer bottle costume almost plowed her down, and Sam stepped out of the way. A shadowy figure stood leaning against the side of a building, his arms folded across his chest, his dark blue eyes raking over her with an infuriating boldness. She met his stare and raked him right back.

The sign overhead, advertising a bar called Friends, blocked the glow from the city streetlight, and cast a shadow over the man, cloaking his right side in darkness and illuminating his left. The symbolism wasn't lost on Samantha. If ever there was a man of darkness and light, it was this one. He was tall, over six foot, with a well-chiseled face, firm lips, and a five o'clock shadow darkening the well defined jaw and chin. A long curved scar ran from jaw to eyebrow and it gleamed in the light. A tiny shiver of anticipation ran up Sam's spine.

Duncan.

His broad shoulders stretched the limits of the cream-colored, full-sleeved shirt he wore. The front of it was cut in a vee, and exposed a muscled, rippling chest dusted with golden hair. His shirt was tucked into the waist of a green and cream plaid kilt, and below, well-muscled calves were laced into rough, knee-high leather boots.

She wanted him.

One booted foot braced in front of the other as he leaned against the brick building, but he straightened, a knowing smile on his face. That look—as if he knew that she wanted him, desired him, craved his touch, and that he deserved nothing less than her adoration— wiped away whatever lovesick puppy look she'd inadvertently let cross her face. She stared at him coolly, one hand on her hip.

Duncan moved toward her, his body as taut and sinuous as a leopard's as he moved to her side. She opened her mouth to demand what he wanted, but before she could speak she was swept into his arms. Sam lost her breath as he bent his head to hers.

He smelled like whiskey and spice and cold nights in front of a blazing fire—no, strike that—he was the fire, his heat all she needed to keep her warm. She looked up into his hooded gaze and suddenly her self-preservation kicked in. Before his lips touched hers, she pushed her way out of his arms and headed down the street again.

Duncan fell into step beside her, assuming an air of casual camaraderie. She slid him a sideways look as she tried to get her heartbeat under control. What was he up to?

"So yer pretty laddie couldna hold his whiskey, eh?" he asked, his arm slipping around her waist in a comfortable, nonsexual way.

Sam enjoyed the sensation for a minute, then registered his touch and slapped his hand away. Why did she ever let her guard down around Griffin Campbell's time-traveling jerk of a cousin? Hadn't she learned the hard way that she couldn't trust him?

"My pretty laddie was a boring, condescending jerk."

"Aye, I could have told ye that." Sam could see Duncan was a little better for drink himself. "Och, yes," he said, nodding to himself, "I did tell ye that—when ye turned me down for this—this—" he looked around and shook his head "—whatever the hell this is."

"Mardi Gras," she said tersely, lifting her skirt to step over spilled beer. "And what's wrong with it? Not fun enough for you? Not exciting enough? Oh, that's right, I forgot, you're the king of excitement, the prince of thrill, the—"

She was jerked to a stop as Duncan pulled her into his arms again. He gazed down at her lazily, his full lips curving up in a smile, his blue eyes languid with whiskey and desire.

"Aye, but the thrill was yours, lass, as well ye know." He bent his head and this time Sam didn't react fast enough. His mouth seared down into hers, the whiskey on his tongue like a smooth liquor. Sam started to resist, but instead her hands slipped up to his chest and she clutched his shirt as she dragged him closer and kissed him back with a year and a half of pent-up, self-imposed, celibate frustration.

Don't do it, her smarter side warned, even as she pressed against the hard length of him. *You'll regret it. Don't forget, you've been down this road before.* A sudden picture of how she'd looked the morning after their night together as she'd stood in front of the bathroom mirror, repeating one simple mantra—stupid, stupid, stupid—over and over, made Sam break the passionate kiss. But it was too late. He had won.

Duncan gazed down at her, laughing softly. "Och, I knew ye couldna resist me, lass. One night wasna nearly enough for either of us."

Sam sucked in a cold breath of air and her brain kicked back into gear.

In retrospect it probably wasn't the kindest, nor the wisest thing she could have done, but she was tired, it was late, and Duncan Campbell was just too conceited and too damn sexy for his own—or anyone else's—good.

Her knee came up and Duncan went down as too late her conscience shouted no, no, no.

Chapter Five

Duncan groaned from the bucket seat of Samantha's Nissan Sentra as he pressed an ice-filled plastic sandwich bag to his crotch. Sam actually felt bad about her literal knee-jerk reaction to the Scot's conceited assumption that she wanted him, even if she did, but her remorse faded as he continued to glare at her.

"It was your own fault," she said, feeling cranky and tired. "You shouldn't have grabbed me like that." She glanced over. He sat leaning against the door, his blue eyes filled with pain and malice.

"So now what, you aren't going to talk to me?"

He continued to stare at her silently, one muscle in his jaw throbbing.

"Well, fine!" Sam snapped, and slammed her hands down on the steering wheel. "I couldn't care less!"

After kneeing Duncan, she'd decided her work there was done and had walked away, but he had somehow managed to catch up with her, threatening swift and complete retribution if she didn't take him back to the ranch.

Seeing the very real pain on his face, and remembering that she was, after all, still bound by the Hippocratic oath, Sam had bought him a bag of ice from a street vendor and then helped him out to the parking lot and her car. And now she was getting the silent treatment.

That's gratitude for you, she thought.

The quiet stretched awkwardly between them during the long ride back to the Crazy R Ranch, but Sam was determined not to be the first one to break the tension. She drummed her fingers on the steering wheel, and then as she turned off of 290 West onto Ranch Road 12, she stole a glance his way. He stared stubbornly out the window.

Sam dared a look at the ice bag in his lap and saw that the ziplock top had come unzipped, the ice was melting and Duncan was about to get a rude awakening.

"Duncan—"

"Dinna bother to speak to me, woman!" Duncan said. "There is nothing ye have to say that I would want to hear."

"But Duncan—"

"I mean it!" He leaned toward her, stabbing one finger in her direction. "Dinna bother apologizing now when ye've probably damaged my jewels and rendered me impotent for the rest of my life!"

Sam glared back at him. "You stupid, asinine ape. I just wanted to tell you that your stupid, vastly overrated jewels are about to be quick-frozen."

Duncan drew in a sharp breath as the ice water gushed over the top of the bag and into his lap. Sam had to give him credit. He didn't yell, didn't cuss, and scarcely moved. He simply continued to sit there glaring at her, while his kilt soaked up the water and the stain spread across the green plaid.

"Sorry," she muttered.

The anger in Duncan's gaze flickered into something less lethal and one corner of his mouth quirked up. "Now, I bet that hurt ye more than yer attack on my nether regions hurt me, didn't it?"

Sam relaxed her shoulders. "I overreacted. I admit it. I was tired, you were drunk, so let's just chalk it up to Mardi Gras and forget it."

"I wasna drunk," he said, glowering again.

"Okay, whatever." She waved one hand, no longer amused, just exhausted and tired of dealing with Duncan Campbell. They were close to the turnoff to the ranch and she couldn't wait to get out of the car and away from him.

Of course, they'd be sleeping under the same roof. Her father had informed her on her first night back that Duncan now spent his nights at the ranch house. He'd been a little vague as to why, saying something about burglaries in the area. Now she knew that it had all been a ruse, to keep him near her. Chelsea and Griffin had brought their own car to Austin, and would be taking Jix and Jamie to stay in Duncan's usual refuge, the hunting cabin, before going home to their own little place near the Devil's Backbone that they'd purchased last year.

So that meant she and Duncan would be alone in the house tonight. She wondered suddenly if he still slept in the nude. That had been another fight they'd had regularly when she took care of him. He'd refused to wear pajamas. The thought of Duncan lying under his sheet, naked and beautiful just down the hall from her in the empty house, made her tighten her grip on the steering wheel.

"We're almost home," she said and feigned a yawn. "I'm going right to bed." She swallowed hard. "To sleep. I'm going right to sleep."

"I need ye to do something for me," Duncan said, leaning toward her. He was close, too close. Her heartbeat quickened.

"Do you have your seat belt on?" she demanded, refusing to look at him. "Get it back on, Duncan, before I get a ticket."

"Samantha, this is important."

Sam took a deep breath and released it, then turned to look at him, forcing a casual tone. "What do you want?"

"I need to stop by Jacob's Well before goin' to the ranch."

She frowned. "Jacob's Well?" That was one request she hadn't expected. "What for?"

"I check it every evening, but I dinna have a chance today, what with all the plannin' and makin' ready for the festivities." He tried to say the words lightly, but Sam could hear the veiled anxiety in his voice.

"Well, I guess I owe you that much," she said.

Duncan nodded. "Aye, that ye do." He scowled at her. "If I canna have children 'twill be yer fault."

She flushed. "I already said I went too far. I admit it. I'm sorry. It won't happen again. Now just shut up so I can find the turn."

Duncan's mouth curved up in satisfaction and Sam immediately regretted admitting anything to the frustrating man.

"Thank ye, lass. I accept yer apology."

He turned to look out the window at the passing countryside again. Lightning flashed in the distance. He turned back to her, his blue eyes unreadable. "There's a storm coming."

They drove a few minutes in silence, and then Sam couldn't help it. She had to ask.

"Duncan, what if you can never go back?" She glanced over. He was staring out the window.

"I dinna ever entertain that thought."

The sign for Jacob's Well Road loomed suddenly out of the darkness and she maneuvered the turn easily. There were no streetlights out here and the night seemed to close in around them, broken only by the sight of the lightning in the distance.

"But what if you can't?" Sam insisted. "Have you ever thought about what you'll do? With your life?"

He stared out the window. "Yer father used to ask me that verra question. I'll tell ye what I would like to have been able to tell him—I have no life in this century. No permanent life."

Depression settled over Sam and she shook away the sudden sensation, berating herself harshly.

What, you thought he was going to say that if he could have you in his life that he'd be happy to stay forever? Don't be such a twit!

Ridiculous. She didn't want a relationship with Duncan Campbell. Obviously she'd been around Jix and Chelsea for too long. Just because they'd hooked up with time-traveling Scots and found their happily-ever-after didn't mean it would or could happen to her.

She glanced out the window to keep from looking at him. Even though it was pitch dark out in the country, she could see the gray storm clouds rolling across the sky, lit from behind by more lightning.

Since it was too late to knock at the door of the owner of Jacob's Well, Sam circled around to the other side of Cypress Creek. They could walk down the creek bank to the spring. There was better light from that side of the well anyway, though it wasn't as scenic.

She came to a stop and killed the motor, then climbed out and slammed the door of the car behind her. She shivered as the night wind shimmied over her skin. Jix had refused to let her bring a coat to Mardi Gras, saying it would ruin the effect of the costume. Without speaking, Duncan took the plaid he had draped across his right shoulder and placed it around her, like a shawl. Sam took it gratefully, but didn't speak. He seemed even less anxious than she to break their silence and so they walked side by side, each lost in thought.

Lightning split the sky and Sam jumped and reached out instinctively. Duncan's hand closed around hers and she looked up, startled, into his eyes. The clouds above them lit up again, sending Duncan's face into stark relief, light and shadow carving his lips and nose and lifted brows as the rain began to fall.

Suddenly, one side of his mouth quirked up and Sam smiled back. Duncan started to run, pulling her along behind him, grinning back at her. Sam laughed as they ran, the two of them stumbling over the rough ground, like children turned loose on a playground. They reached the creek bank and stopped, both breathing hard. Sam bent over to catch her breath, still laughing. Duncan straightened, his chest heaving.

"I'm gettin' too old fer this sort of thing," he said.

"Well, you *are* four hundred years old," she reminded him. She straightened, sobering. "You're feeling all right, aren't you? I mean, you haven't had any signs of a relapse?"

Duncan shook his head and took her hand again. "Nay, lass, yer cure was a lasting one. At least, so far. Come on."

They walked in companionable silence down the side of the creek until they reached what was known as

Jacob's Well. Sam felt a little twinge of civic pride as they approached the well-known Wimberley landmark.

It was actually a spring, the birthplace of Cypress Creek. The deep pool called the "well" made a mossy green circle in the middle of the still water where the creek began. The green became darker, mixed with blue as the hole stretched downward into the heart of the earth. Sam knew from newspaper articles on the subject that four different chambers had been mapped by divers, and it was thought that there were more besides those, but the deeper underground caverns had never been completely explored.

Sam turned to tell Duncan they'd have to cross the creek, only to find him staring at her.

His eyes were dark and hot, and she felt a little thrill rush through her.

"Ye look like the queen of the fairies," he said. "Shimmering and delicate."

Sam laughed. "Don't let the costume fool you. The only thing delicate about me is my underwear."

Now why did I say that?

Duncan took a step closer to her and she turned away, her heart beating wildly. She could feel him standing behind her, and she knew, knew he was about to put his arms around her, about to turn her in his arms, about to kiss her. She couldn't bear it again. Not tonight. Not when she knew she meant nothing to him. She whirled around, taking a step back at the same time.

"Did you grow up believing in fairies?"

The spell broken, he looked away, toward the water, laughing a little. "Aye. The fairy folk. My mother told me tales of the Tuatha De Danaan when I was a boy. They were the ancient gods of Ireland and Scotland and were said to be the first inhabitants. But when invaders came, they turned themselves invisible and went below the earth to live."

"Was there a fairy queen? I mean," Sam stumbled over the words, "I know there wasn't really a fairy queen, but did people believe there was?"

"In my time? Some did, some didn't." He stared into the distance, his blue eyes soft with memory. "In more ancient times, aye, they did. Queen Brigid was the daughter of Dagda, the good god, and was a beautiful, magical being who had the power to seduce any man." He shot her a smile and Sam felt herself blushing again.

"You're making that up," she said.

Duncan shook his head. "Nay."

"Well, thanks, but I don't think I'm quite fairy queen material," Sam said, a touch of her usual sarcasm creeping into her voice.

Duncan turned back to her and lifted one hand to smooth a fine lock of her blond hair, drifting in the night breeze, back from her face.

"Ye are beautiful, Samantha." His hand dropped away. "Come on, then, we'll have to go across and climb the limestone," Duncan said. "Else I canna see into the pool."

Sam started to follow him as he stepped into the shallow water at the edge. He held one hand up to stop her.

"Nay, lass, ye'll ruin yer dress, and then Jix will have my head for certain. Ye'd best stay here."

Sam frowned in irritation. "You aren't the boss of me," she said. "I can lift the skirt or you can carry me across."

Duncan rolled his eyes and put his hands on his hips. "Just stay here. Damnation but if ye aren't the most stubborn woman I ever met." He turned and headed across the creek.

She started to tell him off, but as Duncan continued into the water, something leapt up inside of her—fear, dark and piercing—and she knew she had to stop him. What was going on? She didn't have intuitive moments—that was Jix's realm. She was all about the here and the now.

But as she watched Duncan crossing the creek, the fear swept over her again and she had to speak. Something was going to happen and she had to be with him when it did.

"Duncan!"

"Aye?" Duncan paused and looked back at her.

"Take me with you. Please?"

Sam's heart felt as if it had stopped beating. He stared at her, his gaze confused. The softly spoken plea had tumbled out before she could stop it, and yet she didn't regret it. Slowly he crossed back to her and gazed down into her eyes for a long moment, before suddenly bending down to pick her up in his arms.

Sam gasped involuntarily as his hands closed around her legs and her waist and his face came very close to hers. He tossed the long train of her dress over his shoulder and started across the water.

"Thanks," she said, and fought the desire to kiss the curve of his neck as he carried her across.

"No problem." He lowered her to the bank on the other side.

She started to climb up the stark limestone rocks jutting out slightly over the pool and Duncan took her elbow. She jerked her arm away from him. "I can do it myself."

He frowned, then shrugged and pushed past her. "I've no doubt in the world that ye can."

They climbed in silence until Duncan stopped near the top, feet apart, gazing down into the water like a gypsy seeking the future in a crystal ball.

Sam hung back, her position a few feet lower than his. She watched him, her pulse quickening as lightning continued to strike in the distance, lighting the darkness every few minutes. His face was strained, anxious, and for the first time she realized exactly how much Duncan truly wanted to return to his own time. He would never be happy here.

"The crystals aren't there," he finally announced. "They're always near the surface."

"I'm sorry, Duncan," she said.

He turned and stared at her, his face lit by the lightning, then encased by the darkness, back and forth, back and forth, as the storm raged in the distance. It was mesmerizing. He was mesmerizing.

"Ye mean that, don't ye, lass?" He smiled then, and for the first time ever, Sam saw uncertainty in his eyes. "Are ye so anxious to have me leave?"

Sam started to deny his words, but caught herself just in time. She shrugged. "I just know how badly you want to go."

Duncan looked away. "Aye." When he turned back again, his vulnerability was gone, as if it had never been there. "Come, lass, let's get out of here before the rain starts in earnest."

They made their way down the limestone and when they reached the shallow crossing again, Duncan picked her up with ease. His arms were so strong, and Sam felt so incredibly weary. She laid her head on his shoulder and sighed. Duncan stopped moving and Sam lifted her head to find they were only halfway across the creek. She looked up at Duncan to ask why he had stopped, but the words stilled in her throat.

He gazed down at her, his blue eyes dark and filled with pain, and her heart contracted as she slid one hand up his chest, over the crystal necklace to his neck, to his lips. She moved her hand to the scar that began at his lower jaw and traced the pale mark upward with her fingertips. Duncan closed his eyes at her touch. She could feel his jaw tense beneath her fingers and, emboldened by the fact that he wasn't looking at her, Sam kissed him.

With a groan, Duncan let her slide to her feet, her back to Jacob's Well as he gathered her to him, his mouth seeking hers. The cold water danced around her ankles but she didn't care; the heat between them was enough to stave off the chill. His lips burned across her skin, her face, her mouth, her neck, and his hands tightened around her waist.

As they stood there, intertwined, Sam had a brief, startling burst of honesty within. Suddenly she admitted, if only to herself, that she wasn't immune to Duncan Campbell, that there was a reason his words often cut her to the quick. He was the only man she'd ever met who had the same fire as she, the only man who'd ever seemed strong enough to accept her for who she was.

"Duncan . . ." Sam whispered against his lips.

Lightning struck the ground not ten yards away, and Sam shuddered. Duncan's face was illuminated in the darkness, and he jerked his head up as the storm began a cacophony of brilliance against the backdrop of the night. His hands slipped away from her and he took a step forward, toward Jacob's Well.

His eyes were fixed, dazed. The stark limestone wall rose up in front of him like the bones of some neolithic beast, and his shadow played across them in an eerie, flickering dance. Samantha began to tremble as he took another step forward, the water rising to his knees.

"Duncan, don't—" she began, but he held up one hand.

"I saw them," he said, tension rippling through his voice. "When that big flash hit the ground, I saw them. The crystals are there."

Sam's throat tightened. He took another step and Sam felt that sense of impending doom once again and cried out for him to stop, but the thunder pounded down just then and swallowed her voice.

Duncan reached deeper water and began to swim, then paused when he reached the middle of the pool, and dove beneath the surface.

For a second Sam thought her heart might stop. Was he gone? Would he really leave without even saying good-bye?

Relief swept through her as he burst out of the water again. In two strong strokes he reached the limestone bank and pulled himself up on the ledge, then stood, his kilt dripping around his knees. The first real smile Sam had ever seen him smile stretched across his face, dazzling her with its intensity.

"The crystals are back!" he shouted.

Sam was suddenly grateful for the storm, grateful for the lightning that allowed her to see Duncan for a few moments more. His dark hair fell around his face as he ducked his head. Sam watched his lips moving silently and wondered if he might be praying. There was so much she didn't know about Duncan Campbell, and now she never would. She swallowed hard. It was better this way. Better for him. Better for her.

Duncan lifted his head, his gaze seeking hers.

"Lass," he said, "I dare not wait. They might disappear before I could return."

Sam attempted a smile. "I know." Her words sounded weak even to her own ears. She tried again. "I know!" she called. "It's all right, Duncan. I'll tell Jix and everyone what happened."

He nodded. "I want to thank ye," he said, and she thought she heard regret in his tone. Or was that just what she wanted to believe?

She shook her head. "I didn't do anything."

"Aye, ye saved my life," he said. "I never properly thanked ye, but I do now. Thank Jix and Jamie, and Chelsea and Griffin as well," he said. "Tell them that I will bless them every day of my life for their kindness to me."

Sam nodded silently. She couldn't respond. Her throat was too tight. She lowered her gaze and stared at the water rushing around her feet.

"Samantha."

Sam felt the warmth of his voice envelope her. She looked up to meet Duncan's blue eyes.

"Ye are a strong and valiant woman," he said, "and if it were possible I would stay here"—his lips curved up—"if only to give ye someone to argue with each and every day." His smile faded. "Dinna spend too much time blaming yerself about yer father, lass," he said, "for life is too short to agonize over what ye wish ye had done differently. Start from here and go forward."

Sam lifted her chin and blinked back tears. "I've told you before, but you just don't listen." A tremulous smile played across her lips. "You aren't the boss of me."

Duncan chuckled, then laughed out loud, throwing his arms wide, raising them to the lightning in the sky.

"Aye, I know it lass!" he cried. "And woe to the man

that ever tries to tell ye otherwise!" He grinned and lowered his arms, then sat down on the ledge and slid easily into the water. He bobbed up and down beside the limestone and glanced over at her again. "By the by, I left a signed paper on yer desk this day, turning the management of yer father's estate back to ye. 'Tis all legal accordin' to Jamie's lawyer."

Sam stared at him. She wanted to tell him she didn't care about money or legalities or anything except him. She wanted to beg him to stay, to tell him that there was more to her than a pretty face and a caustic wit. She wanted to, but she couldn't take the risk. He was leaving. There was no reason to bare her soul now.

Duncan tossed her another smile and swam to the middle. Sam took a step forward. She'd been wrong about so much where Duncan was concerned. She'd wasted so much time.

"Duncan!"

Take me with you.

The words leapt, unbidden, back into her mind, and this time she pushed them away.

Leaving would solve nothing. Traveling with Duncan back in time would only add to her guilt, and rob her of the chance of begging her father's forgiveness if he ever woke up.

And yet, the words danced through her mind again.

Take me with you.

"Aye?" He looked at her, impatience beginning to show on his face.

Coward.

Samantha closed her eyes against the pain darting through her. She couldn't leave. She had to stay and face the choices she had made.

"I'll miss you," she said, risking that much honesty.

"Aye," he said, his blue eyes gentle and suddenly brand new to her. "And I will miss ye, too."

"Take care," Sam whispered.

"Good-bye, lass. And one last thing—"

"Yes?" she said, breathless.

"Yer father loves ye very much. Never doubt that."

A sob welled up in her throat and she fought it down, swallowed it down as Duncan winked, and dove beneath the water.

Thunder rocked the atmosphere and Sam's heart raced, as if keeping time with the streaks of lightning that traveled now, one after the other, from the sky to the earth. Closer and closer they came, and she shifted uneasily in the water. Nothing had happened within the pool, at least nothing she would have expected. No explosions, no whirlwinds, no flashes of light. Was Duncan gone? Had the crystals worked?

Slogging back to the limestone bank, not caring if she ruined her dress, she climbed up the rocks, this time continuing to the place Duncan had stood only moments before. She hurried out to the rough edge and looked down. The sky lit up again and she could see Duncan beneath the water, and near him, a green, twinkling light.

Lightning flashed again. It wasn't safe to stay, but she refused to leave until he was gone. What if he changed his mind? What if the crystals didn't work?

Lightning struck the ground on the other side of the creek, leaving the smell of brimstone in the air, and then struck again at the base of the limestone, the impact sending her to her knees.

"Duncan!" she shouted.

Her heart thudded in her chest as she looked up. The thunder had stopped, and all at once a dreadful calm fell, breathless, around her. Suddenly she knew Duncan had to get out of the water.

"Duncan!" Sam tried to call to him again, but the words were a faint, hoarse cry. The air around her seemed to thicken with each passing second as she tried desperately to scream his name, without success.

Too late. The bolt of lightning pierced the sky and plunged downward into the heart of Jacob's Well. Sam screamed as the energy hit the water and sent it flooding upward in an iridescent geyser eight feet tall. She quit breathing as the tower of water collapsed back into the pool and something floated to the top— Duncan, a cluster of emerald-green crystals clutched tightly in his hand.

Sam didn't hesitate. She stood, poised on the rock, ready to dive, when thunder cracked above her and another bolt of lightning streaked down.

It was as though time had stopped. Sam saw the lightning in front of her, thin and bright and solid, reaching for the crystals clutched in Duncan's hand.

Then time started again, and she watched the piercing radiance of the lightning find the crystals in Duncan's hand in a terrible finale of light and sound, then a brilliant green energy pulsed upward from them, through the air, through the night, headed directly for her.

Sam's last memory before the explosion of light shattered the night and swept her away was the sight of Duncan's face, like white chalk against the dark water of Jacob's Well.

Chapter Six

Duncan opened his eyes to silence and the horror-filled gazes of six men staring down at him as if they had seen a ghost.

He lay flat on his back in a soft green clearing—a glen, he realized—feeling as though he'd been pelted with rocks. There were trees behind the men, with bright green leaves, swaying in the breeze. He tried to move and a searing pain laced up his spine.

Duncan moaned and the six men took a step back. He opened his mouth to explain, and found he couldn't speak, either. He could blink his eyes, but that was all. Damnation.

What had happened?

Time travel for him usually involved a brief bit of amnesia afterward, and this time was no exception. His memory returned in pieces. He had been in the water at Jacob's Well. The crystals had returned. Samantha had told him good-bye. It had been dark and there'd been a storm.

Wherever he was now it was daytime. The sun shone high in a hazy blue sky and beyond the men and the trees were emerald green hills that faded to purple.

He had made it to Scotland. He had never told anyone that it was possible to travel not only from time to time, but from place to place.

At the moment his latest foray into the past seemed to have left him paralyzed. If so, he might be regretting his decision to leave Texas. That is, if the hulking men standing motionless from shock let him live long enough to regret it. Apparently he had appeared out of thin air right in front of them. Not good.

The men were all huge, clad in dirty leather tunics and leggings, with ill-made bags slung around their necks to rest against their waists. Three held bows and arrows, while two had staffs and the sixth man a sword in a roughly made scabbard at his side. Out hunting, no doubt. In Scotland it was hard to differentiate between time periods, as men in the Highlands didn't dress according to style, but to tradition. Changes were slow in coming to the more obscure areas. But as he appraised the six, Duncan felt certain that he had made it to some part of Scotland's past.

The man with the sword, apparently the leader, recovered from his shock and began to speak in a kind of Gaelic Duncan recognized.

"A demon," the man whispered, drawing his sword from the scabbard at his side. The weapon was strange, short, almost leaf-shaped, and rough-looking. Unrefined. It looked almost . . . Roman.

Duncan blinked again. The language. The sword. Was it possible? Could he actually have made it back to the right time period? Truth be known, he had almost given up on the possibility, though he had kept trying. Lord knew he'd been trying for a very long time.

Once again he attempted to move his arms, his legs—any part of his body—with no success. He tried to speak. If he had by some miracle ended up in the right time, these were a superstitious people who worshipped goddesses and gods, fairies and tree spirits, and feared demons. If he could speak, he might be able to convince them that he wasn't anything to be feared, but a good spirit, perhaps even a god, with the ability to appear in front of them his proof.

But as long as he lay frozen in place, the men would think what they liked, and take action accordingly.

Duncan managed to swallow. He wiggled one finger. If he just had a few minutes . . .

The leader moved toward him. One of the other men, a bowman, followed him, his eyes wide with fear.

"Ye must kill it, Flynn," the bowman said in the same language as the first, "afore it regains its power. Kill it now!"

The other men murmured their agreement as Duncan fought to speak. His tongue regained its movement and he ran it over his lips. That was a mistake.

"Aye," the one called Flynn said in a hushed voice, "see how it licks its lips in anticipation of our blood."

"Kill it, quick!" someone cried.

"But dinna get too close!" another warned.

Duncan felt the panic tighten its hold on his throat. To come this far, to try so hard to make things right, only to be thwarted at the end by six frightened barbarians. It wasn't right.

Dear God Almighty, he prayed, *ye brought me here for a reason. To change what I damaged. To set right what I made wrong. Dinna let it end this way. Dinna let me die without saving Talamar.*

75

Flynn moved within sword length of the prostrate man, his bearded face furrowed with anxiety. Duncan tried to convey to him through his eyes that he meant no harm, that he wasn't a demon, only a man, but the big hunter slowly raised his sword above his head with both hands. Duncan drew in a quick, shallow breath. The man lowered his sword.

"He looks to be a man, Murdagh," he said, as indecision darted across his face.

"Aye, aye, 'tis a trick," the one called Murdagh insisted. "It means to fool ye, Flynn. Kill it now, while ye still can!"

Flynn raised the blade again.

Murdagh joined Flynn, and stood on Duncan's other side. He held a long spear.

So it ends like this, Duncan thought. *All of my striving, all of my efforts, all for nothing. If I'd stayed in Texas, I could have lived and perhaps found some kind of happiness.*

The image of Samantha Riley came to him then, blocking the very real one of Flynn's fiercely scowling face.

Samantha, with her shining blond hair, her soft pink lips, her biting wit, her inner strength. If he had stayed, could she have loved him? He had seen something in her eyes there at the creek as he held her, as he kissed her. He should have stayed.

'Tis too late now for regrets.

Duncan looked up into Flynn's suddenly determined eyes, glad he was able to at least face his end with courage.

He prepared to die.

She was surrounded by green. Green water, green crystals, green air, green trees, green grass. Green.

Samantha opened her eyes.

She lay on her stomach, her face pressed into the ground. Layers of decomposed leaves, pungent beneath her nose, made her sneeze, bringing her back to cognizant thought. She sat up and groggily realized the green surrounding her was the dense foliage of trees and bushes and thick underbrush.

For a minute she sat still, trying to regain her equilibrium, trying to remember just how she had ended up in the woods clad in her Mardi Gras costume. Jix would be furious if her friend's inventive costume had been damaged. Quickly Sam checked the outfit and groaned as she saw several tears in the diaphanous skirt.

Sam staggered to her feet and brushed the twigs and leaves from the iridescent material, then groaned again. A water stain darkened the beautiful dress, beginning at the hemline and reaching upward by about a foot all the way around.

"Jix is going to kill me!" she muttered.

Jix? Where was Jix? More important—where was *she?*

She frowned and put out a hand to steady herself against a smooth-barked tree. Had she and her date drank too much and passed out? No, she hadn't had a thing to drink all night. And she was no longer on Sixth Street but—but where? In a forest? A forest in downtown Austin?

Alarmed, she glanced around and breathed a sigh of relief. Good. Luke Carter was nowhere in sight. What a loser. Even Duncan Campbell would've been a better date than—

Sam gasped and clapped one hand over her mouth. Memory, dark and sweet, surged through her—Duncan holding her as they stood together in the swirling waters of Cypress Creek; Duncan kissing her, his mouth hot and urgent. Duncan. The creek. Jacob's Well. The crystals. The storm with the terrible lightning that had plummeted down into the water and . . . and . . . what had happened?

Her heart began to pound as she relived that moment after Duncan dove beneath the water to touch the time crystals. Lightning had struck, and suddenly Duncan had been floating on the top of the water, the crystals in his hand. Had the lightning struck Duncan? Was he lying in the creek even now while she stood here daydreaming and dull-eyed?

Sam's medical training rushed to the forefront and she started walking, then stopped and looked around, disoriented and dizzy.

Where was she? There weren't any thick woods like these around Jacob's Well, were there? These trees—she'd never seen anything like them in Texas.

Feeling a little panicky, Sam pushed aside the long, flexible branch of a bush blocking her way and started moving again. She fought her way through the underbrush until she reached the edge of the woods.

No, not the edge of the woods, she realized, but the edge of a clearing. And in the clearing lay Duncan Campbell. And standing over him was a very large, very un-Texan-looking man holding a very large sword.

Raised.

Over Duncan.

Understanding flooded through Samantha in seconds. They weren't in Texas. They weren't in the twenty-first century. The lightning. Somehow it had hit the crystals in Duncan's hand and ricocheted into her, sending her tumbling through time with him.

She had to think fast. What would stop these barbarians? A distraction—she needed to create a distraction. Without a second's hesitation, Samantha stepped out of the shelter of the trees.

"Stop!" she shouted.

The look on the faces of the men told her she had succeeded in distracting them from killing Duncan. She must look a sight in her shimmering gown and long blond hair. Surely she could convince them not to hurt Duncan. On second thought, maybe she needed to be more concerned about herself, she realized, as the startled looks on the men's faces shifted into open lust, their gazes locked on the sight of her cleavage. The man holding the sword started toward her.

"Stop!" she shouted again, a tremor of fear dancing down her spine. "Stay where you are!"

The man stopped and turned back to his comrades. They all began to talk in gibberish to one another in low voices. No, not gibberish. Gaelic, or what sounded like some kind of Gaelic, though not what she'd learned from Duncan and her summer course.

Samantha inwardly groaned. Great. Why didn't Duncan get up? They had seconds in which to run like hell. The men seemed to come to some kind of consensus, and the one with the sword started toward Duncan again.

"Wait!" she cried, switching to what she could remember of Gaelic. It wasn't exactly the same as theirs, but maybe a few of the words were similar enough to register. "Do not harm him!"

Sam took a step toward the six men, putting on her "I'm-a-doctor-so-don't-mess-with-me" look. Duncan's life once again depended on her. She stopped at his stretched-out feet, and her confidence faltered. He lay flat on his back, unmoving. What was wrong with him? He should be on his feet by now, taking advantage of the distraction she was providing.

"This man is innocent!" she proclaimed, or at least hoped that was what she was saying. "You must leave at once!"

The men continued to stare at her in confusion, unmoving. Duncan continued to lie motionless as well. Sam's temper flared and she nudged him with her foot, hissing, then adding, "Duncan Campbell, you dullwitted excuse for a man, get up and let's get the hell out of here!"

His voice came back to her, hoarse and faint, but still hard as iron. "What do ye think, that I'm takin' a beauty sleep? I canna move!"

Sam knelt quickly at his side. Of course, something was wrong with him, and instead of helping him, she was griping at him. No wonder he'd chosen time travel instead of a nice little cottage on the Blanco with her in the kitchen. Scratch that. No wonder he'd chosen time travel instead of her.

"Are you hurt?" she said. Should she help him sit up? No, if he'd been injured she needed to assess his situation before moving him. She lifted his arm and found it to be heavy and unwieldy. She began checking out his limbs for breaks. "Are you in pain?"

"I canna move," he said, "but a minute ago I couldn't speak, so I think I'll be all right."

"I think you need to let your doctor be the judge of that," she retorted, then lowered her voice. "Duncan," she said, "where are we?"

"We're in Scotland," he said under his breath. "In the past. Just give me a few minutes to get my muscles working again and we'll get out of here."

Sam's eyes widened as the huge man towering near them took a step forward. His sword was raised again.

"That may be more time than we have, laddie," she said.

Duncan's blue eyes widened and he whispered back urgently, "Listen, Samantha Riley, if ever there was a time when ye should do what I say and ask questions later, this is it."

"Tell me," she said.

"Where are yer damned wings?"

"My wings?" His question threw her.

"Be ready to turn them on when I say, but right now, repeat what I tell ye."

Duncan began speaking in low tones, but his Gaelic was unlike any she'd ever heard. Still, she reiterated what he told her, addressing the circle of men in her most confident voice. In a matter of seconds, the man threatening them had lowered his sword once again and the rest had backed away, looking half-afraid, half-skeptical.

"Now, stand up and turn on yer wings," Duncan said.

Sam stood and reached around to the back of the belt. She pushed the switch. The holographic wings flooded into place, instantly pulsating with life and color as they swept up above her. Almost in unison the six hunters fell to their knees, flung out their arms, and bowed their faces to the ground.

Samantha drew in a sharp breath. "What in the world did you say to them?"

"Och, nothing much. Only that ye are the queen of the Tuatha De Danaan, the fairy folk, and I am yer human consort, and that if they give us shelter and food, ye will come and listen to their bequests, but if they do not, ye will destroy them all."

Sam stared at him aghast. "Are you *trying* to get us killed? What in the world possessed you to tell them such a thing?"

"Do ye have a better idea?"

She swallowed hard. "Yes, I could tell them that you're the devil and they should kill you immediately."

"How do ye think I ended up with a sword dangling over my head? They already think I'm the devil's spawn because I appeared out of thin air in front of them! I'm trying to convince them that we're the good guys. Just try to act like a fairy queen until they leave."

"Leave? What makes you think they're going to leave?" Sam asked as she surveyed the bowing and fawning men. "They look like they're ready to build a shrine."

The man with the sword stood up, took a step forward and fell to his knees again, then hesitantly spoke.

"What's he saying?" Sam asked.

Duncan frowned. "He is begging yer forgiveness, but asks if ye would please show them some magic."

"Right. Of course," Sam said with a sigh. "And another adventure begins. Where's Jix Ferguson when I need her?"

Brogan, the high priest of the village of Nirdagh, sat on a crude bench beside a rough wooden table and stared into the water-filled, carved wooden bowl atop it. Dancing across the liquid surface were glints of sunlight that had made their way through the cracks in the parchment-covered windows of his home.

Any villager who dared to enter the quarters of the high priest would see only their leader beginning his daily habit of *scrying* in order to predict any malady or blessing that might befall his people. In truth, he was simply thinking, and admiring his own reflection.

It was a handsome image, he decided. A strong jawline, aquiline nose, a well-formed mouth. His chin was a trifle weak, but he had compensated for that by growing a beard. It wasn't thick, but it did help cover the flaw. The lines of his forty years of living were carved deeply into his leatherlike skin, and he knew they helped him to project an image of wisdom and power.

His mouth lifted in a rueful smile. Power over thirty or forty dirty, ignorant villagers. He leaned his head in his hands. How had he come to this? Once he'd been the leader of a lucrative band of thieves and charlatans, until one of them had turned on him. Damn Padrais to the lowest circle of hell for his treason.

Brogan sighed. If it hadn't been for his ability to twist disaster to his own advantage, by now his dust would have been scattered to the wind. Three years. Three years since he had been really clean or seen any sign of civilization. But he was alive. He felt a little cheered. And not in shackles. After all, he'd learned at a young age that it was every man—or in his case, boy—for himself.

Considering the fact that he'd been born to a prostitute who beat him more than she fed him, he hadn't done too badly for himself. He was warm and dry and well-fed, though the food was plain, and when Talamar married Laird Gwain he would have enough gold to strike out on his own again and make an even better life for himself. Yes, life was good.

He straightened, casting a glance at the entrance to his shelter. It wouldn't do to let any of the villagers catch him unawares. He didn't possess a real door; he had only the hides of the furry Scottish cattle to keep out the stares of the curious. It was a mild day, and he had the brown hide pulled back to let in some sunlight and heat. It was never warm enough for him here.

After being stabbed and left for dead on the wayside by Padrais and his cronies, Brogan had pressed his hand against his wound and crawled for hours until he reached a cave. He'd collapsed inside, unconscious. When he awoke some time later, it was to the sight of a rounded ceiling covered in beautiful, sparkling crystals, blue and lavender and some clear like diamonds. As he stood, he realized that he was no longer in pain. He looked down and saw that his stab wound was gone, as if it had never been there in the first place. He held a blue crystal in his hand and at his feet lay a wooden staff, embedded at one end with several long green crystals, different from any of those in the cavern.

He was still a little weak, so he picked it up and leaned upon it, and found he was suddenly overcome by thirst. He left the cave and searched for water, finding a spring not too far away where he drank to his heart's content.

When he tried to find the cave again, it was gone, though he searched for hours. Much, much later, he had stumbled into the small village of Nirdagh, where the townspeople had gathered around him, talking in loud, excited voices about the return of the missing staff of the Tuatha De Danaan. A beautiful young woman had stepped forward and welcomed him, telling him that the one who found the staff of the ancient gods would be named their high priest.

Gradually, over the days that followed, as he was treated like royalty, he learned from the young woman, Talamar, that the crystals were the jewels of the Tuatha De Danaan, the fairy folk, who once lived in Scotland as gods and goddesses. Brogan remembered the fairy tales, told to him by his grandmother on cold Scottish nights, and he eagerly assured the villagers that he was, indeed, destined to be high priest. That in fact, he had been injured and Queen Brigid herself had come to him and healed him with a beautiful crystal.

It was this story that seemed to seal the deal with the villagers and especially with the young woman who appeared to be their leader. Later he learned that her father had once been laird over a large amount of land, including their village. Upon his untimely death, Talamar had inherited all of the property. The villagers treated her as their princess, and she had performed the offices of their high priestess until he arrived with the staff, though she didn't seem upset by his arrival.

"It is Brigid's doing," she told him. "She has given her staff to ye, Brogan, and I would never think of opposing her will."

Familiar with the practice of paying homage to the fairies through tributes of meat and bread and milk, which the high priest would naturally oversee, Brogan saw the ancient beliefs of the villagers as a way to survive—and thrive—without having to do a thing in return except pretend that he believed in their fairies, and occasionally make up tasks and rituals for the villagers to perform, supposedly relayed to him by Queen Brigid. Although Talamar sometimes frowned at these reports, she had never opposed him and so far his luck had held.

His smile wavered back at him in the watery bowl. Over the last few months the tributes of food and precious metal broaches and weapons had increased. Bad weather and poor crops had pushed the inhabitants of the village to give more to their high priest, as through him they beseeched Brigid for help and comfort.

Brogan stuck one long finger in the water and stirred it, sending ripples across his angular reflection that spread out to the edges of the bowl, disrupting the image of lazy brown eyes and lank, dark hair. The lazy eyes were filled with a sudden panic as a new thought struck the high priest.

If the village's bad luck continued, they might think their high priest didn't know what he was doing, since Queen Brigid didn't seem to be listening to their heartfelt pleas. He needed to come up with a plan, a way to assure the people of Nirdagh that she was still watching over them and approved of their sacrifices of goat and grain, given to the high priest every full moon.

Already he'd planned the distraction of a wedding between Princess Talamar and Laird Gwain of Innisbar, a village some miles to the north. That little alliance had been a real coup for him, with Gwain promising him a pot of gold for convincing the village elders to give the favored girl in marriage.

A noise at the doorway stirred Brogan from his brooding and focused his attention on the bowl of water once again. He let his eyes roll back in his head at the unmistakable sound of shuffling footsteps hesitantly mounting the steps to his home.

"Oh, great Brigid," he muttered, loud enough to be heard, "tell us, oh Brigid, why it is you withhold your blessings from us. Give us vision, sweet Brigid, of what sacrifice you desire."

Slowly he released his breath and allowed his eyes to return to normal before shifting his gaze to the doorway. One of the chief elders of the village, Aleric, stood outside the door, head bowed, glancing up from time to time as he patiently waited.

Brogan gestured for him to enter. Aleric's dark eyes were anxious, and the high priest stood, recognizing immediately that something had happened, something that needed his attention.

"What is it, Aleric?" Brogan asked somberly, giving his voice the deep, thoughtful timbre that denoted his importance and connection to the Otherworld of the deities.

"She's come," the man said, his voice faint and filled with awe.

Brogan frowned. "She? Who has come?"

The man swallowed and with great difficulty managed to form the name.

"Queen Brigid is in the clearing," he finally got out.

Brogan frowned. What kind of new nonsense was this? Ah well, timing was everything. Perhaps he could turn this event—whatever it was—to his advantage. He pretended to ponder the man's words, then slowly stood and crossed to the corner of the room where his staff leaned. He picked it up and faced Aleric solemnly.

"Show me," he said.

Samantha stared down at the prostrate man. She couldn't even do card tricks, let alone any displays of believable magic besides her wings. She glanced up at the holographic beauties still towering over her. How long would the batteries last?

"And me without my rabbit," she muttered. "Can you move yet?"

Duncan lifted one hand, then his foot. "A few minutes more perhaps."

"We don't have a few minutes more!" she hissed. "We've got to get out of here."

The men began raising their heads at the whispered conversation between the queen and her companion. They began whispering themselves, their voices confused and edged with suspicion.

"I'll tell them that I displeased you and you rendered me unable to move to teach me a lesson," Duncan said. "That should give them a few second thoughts should they decide to attack again."

Duncan spoke quickly in the strange language and

the men nodded, then began murmuring excitedly to one another, darting looks of fear in her direction.

"Now this I could get used to," Sam said. "Men looking scared to death when I speak."

Duncan lifted one brow. "I should think that was just business as usual with ye, lass."

"Uh-oh."

Duncan looked up, alert. "Uh-oh, what?"

Sam nodded toward the men still on their knees. Behind them a procession was approaching. At the head of the group was a man carrying a carved wooden staff crowned at the top with three large green crystals.

"Damn," Duncan whispered. "Brogan."

"What does 'brogan' mean?" she said, then blinked as she got a good look at the crystals in the staff. "Duncan, do you see—"

"Aye, lass, I do."

The man's black hair hung in a braid down his back and he wore a long brown robe tied in the middle with a knotted sash. He had the dark, burning eyes of a zealot. Sam swallowed hard.

Duncan moved to his knees with another groan. "Let's get out of here."

"Too late." Sam's heart began to pound as the man with the staff continued to walk toward them.

The six men rushed anxiously to the tall man holding the staff. Duncan leaned forward, looking almost as if he were trying to make eye contact with the tall man. The man finally turned and looked directly at the Scot, then away from him to Sam, and Duncan seemed to visibly relax.

"'Twill be all right," Duncan said. "But I have the feeling ye're about to have to defend yer claims to the throne of Tir Na Nog."

"Tir na what?" Sam said, a sudden panic sweeping over her as the tall man walked toward her.

"Maybe ye'd best act like ye canna neither understand nor speak their language," Duncan said thoughtfully.

"There's no acting to it!" She shot him a disparaging look. "This doesn't sound like Gaelic to me," she said. "Are you sure we're in Scotland?"

"Aye, just a very ancient Scotland. The language wasna quite the same then. I can be yer interpreter. Since ye are descended from the gods, it would make sense that ye couldna be bothered to learn a mere human's language." He nodded. "Aye, I can make them believe that."

The tall man paused and turned back to mutter to the man behind him. The crowd was beginning to swell with people that had apparently followed him from their village.

"Damn it, Duncan," she hissed, "I can't be here. My father needs me!" Her throat tightened at the thought of him awakening without her and dying before she could make things right.

Duncan pulled himself to a more upright position. "And I'll get ye back to him, soon, I promise."

He rattled off a few sentences in the strange, guttural tongue, and the tall man turned around, his dark eyes narrowing

Sam drew in a sharp breath. "Why did I ever go with you to Jacob's Well?"

"Whist, lass, it isn't every day that a girl finds herself on a braw, bonny adventure through time."

"That's what you think," she said. "Once was enough."

"That's where ye're wrong, my queen." One corner

of his mouth edged up and his blue eyes mocked her. "Once is never enough."

"Shut up and get up," she snapped. "I'm not facing these Neanderthals on my own."

"Aye, then give me a hand."

Sam sniffed and stepped over his legs to stand a few feet away, her hands folded demurely across her gown. "Help yourself. I'm a queen. How would it look for me to be bending down and dragging a mere mortal to his feet? Besides, you once told me that you didn't need anyone's help, especially mine."

Duncan's gaze glittered up at her, but he replied respectfully, apparently taking his role to heart.

"Ye're right, my queen," he said. "I don't." He took a deep breath and using the ground for leverage, pushed himself up. He staggered upright, then leaned over, balancing his hands on his knees for support as he caught his breath again.

"Here he comes." Sam lifted her chin with haughty precision and faced the tall man.

"Dinna show fear or confusion. Ye are the queen of the fairies, remember!"

He stopped a good five feet away from her. Upon closer inspection, the man, obviously a leader of some kind, wasn't as old as Sam had initially thought, though his face was creased with several deep lines and his dark hair had a touch of silver. Fiftyish? Maybe a little younger.

His dark brown eyes looked younger than his features, and there was intelligence mirrored there. Maybe he could be reasoned with. Maybe she could talk him into letting them go. Maybe he was deciding whether to use wood or charcoal around the stake on which he would be burning her.

The man gazed into her eyes for a long moment and

Sam tried to look cold and haughty, as would befit a fairy queen.

She guessed.

Who knew what a fairy queen should act like? Maybe she should be nice. Or maybe she should try and show him she was someone to be reckoned with. Sam took a step back and lifted her arms to the sky, speaking in a thundering voice.

"Oh Lord," she said, "grant me the serenity to accept the things I can't change, the courage to change the things I can, and the wisdom to know the difference!"

She reached around to the back of the belt and switched the mechanism to "color flow." The wings at her back began to change, every color of the rainbow surging through the shimmering, transparent creations. The crowd, including the tall man, gasped.

"What the bloody hell do ye think ye're doin'?" Duncan hissed. Sam dropped her arms to her side.

"Letting them know I mean business. Do you think it worked?"

"Aye, I think it did," Duncan said.

The tall man's face was filled with awe and fear. He took another step closer to her, and all at once, the crystals in his staff began to glow.

The tall man stood staring at the crystals in stunned amazement. He lifted the staff and whirled toward the crowd shaking it above his head. His hand trembled, along with his voice.

"Unseelie!" he shouted. "Unseelie!"

Chapter Seven

Sam looked uncertainly at Duncan. "Is that good or bad?" she asked.

"Now ye've done it," he said. "We're damned for sure."

"I've done it? I didn't make the damned crystals glow!" She looked wildly from Duncan to the crowd. "Well, don't just stand there, do something!"

"What did you have in mind?" Duncan took a step back as the crowd advanced on them.

"What does 'Unseelie' mean?"

"It means that we are part of the demonic, evil fairy court, instead of the good one."

Sam grabbed Duncan's arm and jerked him back beside her. "So tell them that we aren't. Tell them we're the good ones!"

"I'm not sure they're in a mood to listen," he said grimly. "Do ye see any pitchforks among them?"

"You're a lot of help. Should we run for it?"

"Wait a minute." Duncan slipped his hand around her waist and pulled her against him.

"Damn it, Duncan, this is hardly the time—"

"Shut up, lass."

Sam felt his hands at her back and then all at once the beautiful, shimmering, ever-changing wings disappeared. He spun her back to face the crowd. The people stood in stunned amazement. He said something to them and they all nodded and murmured to one another.

"What did you say?"

"That although ye are a fairy queen, that for now, ye want to walk among them as a human female, and ye removed yer wings to prove this to them."

"Oh-kay," she said.

"Now, touch my face very gently."

"Why?"

Duncan cursed under his breath. "Just do it!"

"All right!" She turned and lifted her hand to his face.

"Smile at me."

"Duncan—"

"Just smile, woman!"

Sam narrowed her eyes and plastered a beatific smile on her face. "Is this good enough?" she asked as she caressed his jaw with her fingertips. He needed a shave. Her fingers slid over the rough surface until she touched the smoothness of where his scar began. She hesitated and Duncan moved away from her touch.

"Just what is it you're trying to prove?"

"That ye are a kind and benevolent queen. Now watch."

To her astonishment, Duncan sagged to his knees, his rugged face suddenly wreathed in ecstasy. He began to babble in the Gaelic-sounding language, but the only words Sam could make out were "Seelie" and "queen" as he swayed from side to side, his hands clasped in front of him.

"I thought the Seelie thing was bad," she hissed at him, while keeping a smile on her face. The crowd still stood in apparent amazement, and not knowing what else to do, she raised her hand and waved to them à la Queen Elizabeth.

"No, the Seelies are the good fairies, the Unseelie are the bad. I told them that you aren't a bad fairy, but a very good fairy who will bless them with joy and prosperity if they will but welcome you with open arms. I used your kindness to me as an example of how good you really are. I've also told them that you and I have to converse in the language of the Tuatha De Danaan."

"You should've gone into politics."

"Now—kiss me," Duncan ordered.

"What? Why should I—"

"I'm yer consort, damn it. Kiss me."

Duncan's whispered voice was sharp with impatience. "Before ye get us both killed."

She narrowed her eyes. "Fine, I'll do it, but I won't like it."

Leaning over, she pecked him on the mouth, but Duncan reached up and cupped her face in his hands, possessing her lips with a heat that sent a shudder through her body. As they separated, his eyes told her what was evident, that he knew she had enjoyed the kiss as much as he had. Sam straightened, quickly resuming her smile and her queenly posture.

The villagers looked unconvinced and the tall man was still frowning, when all at once Sam saw someone pushing through the crowd to the front. It was a young woman with long, red-gold hair and green, green eyes. She reminded Sam of a much younger Jix. The girl/woman spoke rapidly to the tall man, and whatever she said caused his frown to deepen, then she turned toward Sam and sank to her knees.

"What's going on?' She turned to Duncan, only to find he had a stunned look on his face. His eyes were fixed on the young woman bowed to the earth.

"Talamar," he whispered, slowly rising to his feet.

"Who? What's happening?"

"Turn yer wings back on," he said, his voice sounding dazed. "But wave the other hand, as if ye are using magic to do so."

She frowned at him, but did as he said, waving one hand in the air à la David Copperfield, and at the same time reaching behind her waist with the other to flip the switch on her belt. The dazzling, diaphanous wings appeared once again and the crowd gasped and stepped back, but this time they had tentative smiles on their faces. The young woman glanced up to see what had happened, and the smile on her face made her even more beautiful than she already was.

Sam stole a look at Duncan. No wonder he was staring. A man would have to be dead not to notice this young woman. But why had he said "Talamar"?

The excited chatter of the crowd brought her back to the business at hand. Apparently she'd done the right thing and the villagers were no longer on the verge of frying them. The tall man with the staff, however, didn't look in the least happy.

"What's his problem?" she said, keeping the royal smile plastered on her face.

Duncan came out of his trance and took her hand. "Dinna worry about him. All right, that's enough, dinna overdo it." He sank back down to his knees and kissed her hand. "Ye are a success as a fairy queen. I'd best be watching my back, else one of these villagers might see themselves taking my place with the fair Brigid."

"Brigid? Oh—the queen of the Tuatha De Danaan. I get it." She lifted his chin and smiled down at him, trying to radiate aristocratic goodwill. "Regardless of whether or not anyone stabs you in the back," she told him, "I promise you, your consorting days are definitely numbered."

"So where are we? And more important—when?" Sam asked.

Duncan turned from staring out the one small window the stone hut boasted. There were no panes of glass, only paper coated with grease, but the window opened outward, hinged with a crude apparatus.

They'd been led to the stone shelter by the tall man, Brogan, the high priest. He had remained silent as they walked from the forest to the village, less than a half-mile away.

Duncan took his silence to mean that the priest didn't recognize him. Good news. Brogan had already killed him once, or at least thought he had. The man's lack of recognition meant Duncan had finally done it—he'd finally made it back to the right time. God had answered his prayers and given him a chance to undo his terrible mistake.

They'd been given a supper of porridge and ale, their servers muttering deep apologies that the food was so plain and unfit for the Queen and her consort. Sam had played her part of benevolent deity to the hilt, with just the right combination of kindness and haughty indifference.

Not too different from her actual personality, Duncan thought. He rubbed his forehead to ease the headache that was always a result of traveling through time. He glanced over at Sam, where she stood looking around at their crude quarters with disgust on her face. She had a bruise on her cheek and suddenly he wondered if their journey through time had caused it.

"Are ye feeling all right?" he asked. She shot him a sharp look.

"Why? Are you feeling bad?"

Sam crossed the room and seized his left arm, shoving back the sleeve, her cool fingers sliding over his skin with professional ease. Back during his time in 1882, before Chelsea and Griffin came to his rescue, his left arm had begun to atrophy. Sam's treatment after his arrival in the year 2003 had restored his muscle tone fully. She stroked his skin again and Duncan watched her face carefully. She might act detached, but he knew she had to feel the electricity that was always there between them.

"It looks all right." She glanced up at him. "What about the rest of you?"

"I'm fine. I merely asked if ye were all right." He reached over and wiped a trace of dirt from her face. "Och, I thought it was a bruise."

Sam flinched at his touch and for some reason her reaction bothered him.

"Sorry," he said, "I should know better than to touch the queen." He said the words lightly, but the undercurrent of truth was there between them.

She opened her mouth to speak, snapped it shut, then started again. "That's right," she said, her voice hard. "So hands off. And don't try to distract me—where are we and when are we and by the way, who's the girl?"

Duncan leaned against the bare wall of the hut.

There was a mattress on the floor and a stool in the corner. A rough wooden table made from planks stood opposite it with a bench beside it. A stone fireplace took up most of one wall, and he was grateful for the small fire burning there. Even in the summer, Scotland was chilly at night.

Sam started pacing the small confines of the room like a trapped animal. Duncan liked watching her as she moved across the room. The diaphanous fairy-queen gown was a little worse for its tumble through time, dirty around the hemline, torn up the side to just above her knee and at the neckline, exposing soft, creamy skin in both places.

There was so much energy connected with Samantha. Too bad he couldn't find a way to disengage her mouth from her motor.

"I dinna know exactly where or when we are," he said, folding his arms over his chest. "I know we are somewhere in Scotland, and a verra long time ago."

Sam stopped pacing. "I'm from the year 2005, remember? The *1800s* are a very long time ago to me! Have you ever been to this time period before?" She asked, her nervousness radiating out from her in waves.

Duncan looked away. "I've been to some ancient times, aye."

"And the girl?"

He raised one brow, trying to appear nonchalant. "I dinna know what girl ye are blathering about." It was a flimsy evasion, and one he knew she wouldn't let stand.

"You are such a liar."

He narrowed his eyes at her, hoping to intimidate her into dropping the subject. "Ye are lucky that I respect yer father so much, else those might be the last words ye ever said."

"You know it's the truth."

He had nothing to say to that, since, it was, indeed the truth.

Sam brushed her hair back from her face and gave him an exasperated look. "Duncan, it's obvious that you know that girl. The one who seemed to be defending us. And if you know her, then that means you've been here before. So don't bother lying to me, just tell me what's going on?"

He couldn't deny her words. His own shock when he first saw Talamar had betrayed him. But he didn't have to tell her everything.

"Aye, I've been here before—satisfied?"

"Not even a little. You've been here before, to this very place? This very time?"

"Aye."

"What year is it? And who is the girl?"

"I dinna know the exact year, but I surmise that it is sometime around 880 AD"

"880 AD?" Samantha went pale at his words. "Are you kidding?"

"Dinna be afraid," he said, "I'll get ye back home."

Sam shook her head at him. "Oh, no, don't you dare start patronizing me. I'm not scared. Do I look scared?" she demanded, as she tossed her hair back from her shoulder.

In that moment Duncan wished he could tell her exactly how she looked—fiery and beautiful, her lavender eyes snapping with temper as she sought desperately to keep her fear at bay.

She began talking and pacing again. "So we're in Scotland, in the ninth century—where in Scotland?"

"The Highlands."

"Where in the Highlands?"

"Near the northwest coast."

She came to a stop again and put her hands on her hips as she faced him. "So who's the girl?"

Duncan sighed. "Her name is Talamar. She's the daughter of a local laird and is said to be the only one who has ever seen the fairy folk face to face. No doubt yer performance today convinced her that ye were one of them, and she did us a favor by helping convince the crowd and the high priest."

"So what is—was—she to you when you were here before?"

Duncan kept his face carefully impassive. "Nothing."

Sam rolled her eyes. "We'll come back to that one. Who was that man with the staff?"

"Brogan, the high priest."

"High priest of what?"

Duncan arched one brow. "What do ye think? The high priest of the Tuatha De Danaan."

Sam nodded thoughtfully and shot him a knowing look. "So that's why you wanted me to pretend to be the fairy queen."

He shrugged. "Ye were dressed for the part."

"There were green crystals at the top of his staff. Why do you think they started glowing when he walked up?"

"I dinna know," he admitted, straightening away from the wall and rubbing the back of his neck. He moved away from her.

"Are they the same as our time travel crystals? Do you think that means we might be able to use the crystal in his staff to get back home again? What happened to the crystals you were holding in Jacob's Well?"

"I dinna know," he said again.

"Well, what *do* you know?" Sam grabbed him by the arm and forced him to turn back to her. He could see the fear in her eyes, saw her trying to keep her brave front in place, as usual, with the power of her anger. He placed his hands carefully on her shoulders, trying to calm her with his touch.

"Look," he said softly, "I know ye are afraid, no matter what ye say, but I'll do the best I can to get ye home again."

He watched as she swallowed hard and the fury seemed to drain out of her. "I'm sorry," she said, and looked up at him, surprising him not only with her apology, but with the glimmer of tears in her eyes. "Of course it isn't your fault that I'm here. I just need to be home, with my father. I'm not afraid of being here, Duncan. I'm afraid of never getting home again. What if this time I can't get back? Now, when my father needs me most?"

"Aye, lass," he said. "I know how ye're feeling, believe me. The crystals are unreliable, 'tis true, but they also seem to have their own sense of timing, if ye ken my meaning." She shook her head. "For instance," he went on, "why were you sent back with me?"

Sam frowned and shook her head. "All I remember is seeing the lightning hit the crystals in your hand and then a green light ricocheted up and hit me."

"Why dinna the lightning kill me? Why dinna the lightning destroy the crystals and keep me from going through time?" Duncan tucked a stray hair behind her ear and moved his other hand to the back of her neck. "I dinna know. But what I've learned in my travels is that there is usually a purpose in what the crystals do."

"You mean, like bringing Jix and Jamie together, and Griffin and Chelsea?"

"Aye, like that."

"And you and Talamar?"

Duncan took a step back and let his hands fall back to his side. "Aye, perhaps."

Sam nodded, and then closed her eyes and swayed toward him. Duncan caught her before she fell and swept her up into his arms.

"Put me down," she said, with no strength at all in her voice.

Brogan moved away from his vantage point below the window. As he made his way back to his hut he thought about what he'd heard. It had been an unlikely sounding conversation between one of the Blessed Ones and her consort.

While the more educated, well-traveled side of his mind dismissed the claims of the beautiful blond-haired woman, the teachings of his childhood, as well as his own eyes, prodded him to believe. Her consort had appeared out of thin air, according to the men of the village, and how else could her glorious wings be explained?

Eavesdropping on the couple seemed an advantageous way to find out more without letting the two strangers know his doubts. By doing so he'd discovered that Queen Brigid had a temper, though that was nothing new in goddesses. But there was something strange, not only about the language in which they spoke, but in how they acted toward one another.

In the privacy of their room there had been no obeisance on the part of Duncan, the consort, toward the queen. In fact, he acted as if he were in charge, rather than she.

Strange. Exceedingly strange.

Brogan entered his hut and took a seat at the table, deciding he would have to keep a close eye on the two of them, though a respectful eye. It was presently to his advantage that the strange woman was here, claiming to be the fairy queen. He could take credit for her appearance and tell the villagers that he had beseeched her in his prayers to come to them. He would have to be careful, though. If she truly was the fairy queen, she might know if he claimed credit. It would not do to anger her.

He had many questions for the woman regardless of whether she was the fairy queen or not. When he approached her in the clearing, the crystals in the staff had begun to glow. Indeed, he had felt them trembling right down into the wooden staff itself.

When Talamar had told him that the green crystals in the staff belonged to the Tuatha De Danaan, he'd thought her beliefs childish and simply used them to his own advantage.

But if it was true . . . all of his learning and his travels had not prepared him for this possibility. Could there truly be such a thing as magic?

He stroked his beard as a new thought hit him. In the meantime, how did he keep his position as the high priest in the village? Would his office be considered unnecessary now? Before, he had been the only one who could supposedly communicate with the fairy queen. Now, she was here in the flesh.

The sun dipped low in the sky as Brogan pondered the situation, and by the time the moon had risen above the village, his apprehension had risen as well. He looked around the hut he had usurped from Aleric, plotting how he could protect himself from either the fairy queen's magic, or the ruse of two people who might be better at trickery than he himself.

Duncan lay beside Samantha, listening to her even, steady breathing. The cool night air slipped over his bare chest as the wind whistled through cracks in the shutters pulled tightly over the one window.

The mattress that had been provided for them was only slightly dirty and stuffed with goose down. In addition, they'd been given a light coverlet to protect them against the breezy Scottish nights. These comforts were no doubt considered luxuries to the villagers. Duncan felt a moment's discomfort over their deception, but quickly dismissed it. Survival came first.

He pushed the coverlet back and laced his fingers behind his head as he stared at the ceiling. No matter how many times he traveled through time he would never get used to the fact that it could be dead winter in one time period, only to arrive at a place where the summer sun was shining. He sighed. It was wonderful, in any case, to be back in his native country, even hundreds of years before his own time.

He glanced over at Sam and spared a fleeting moment to wonder if she was really all right. After her near fainting spell she'd managed to take off her gown, leaving the thin underdress on as a nightgown. She'd stretched out on the mattress and had been asleep within seconds. He was glad because he could only imagine her objections to him sharing the same bed. He had no intention of sleeping on the floor though, and with Samantha asleep, he hadn't had to fight her for his side of the bed. A good night's rest would help both of them more than anything, he reasoned.

A sudden gust of wind shook the hut and Samantha stirred in her sleep, turned toward him, then snuggled down under the crude coverlet again.

Duncan raised up on one elbow and gazed down at her. How could a woman be so beautiful on the outside and so filled with anger on the inside? Asleep she looked like such an innocent with her creamy skin, her slightly parted rose-colored lips, the long lashes across her flushed cheeks, the childlike way she curled her fingers under her chin. He lifted his own hand and grazed the side of her face lightly, feeling the burn that always danced down his nerves when he touched her.

They were so much alike, he and Sam. She hid her pain inside, twisting it into barbed words and sarcastic insults. To hear Jamie and Griffin tell it, she had always been a no-nonsense kind of person who believed in "telling it like it is," but this bitterness, this anger, inside of her stemmed from her father's collapse. Aye, he knew what had caused her pain. Guilt. And he understood why she had chosen to hide her most vulnerable emotions behind the cold and cynical mask she wore. He brushed a wave of blond hair back from her face.

If she had cared to hear he could have told her that her pretense solved nothing. Walls only begat walls, and the pain of letting down a loved one never went away. Worst of all, even the highest walls could not keep out the sheer force of love.

Thoughts of Talamar smiling up at him in their past time together, lifting her lips to his, darted into his mind. He pushed them away. These were the kind of thoughts he could not allow himself to have. He must keep Talamar at a distance in order to avoid making the same mistake twice.

He turned his attention back to the woman beside him. What had Samantha been like as a child? he wondered. When her mother was alive? He pictured a five-year-old Samantha, tiny and precious, laughing at something her mother had said, throwing herself into her father's arms when he came home from work.

Duncan pulled his hand back from her hair, frowning at his own weakness. Foolish. Lying here making up fairy tales about Samantha's childhood. He smiled grimly. For all he knew she had been as big a brat as a child as she was now.

Resolutely he lay back down and turned away from her to stare at the rough stone wall in front of him. All at once, softness pressed against his back and one long leg edged between his. He groaned as Sam curled behind him. She was asleep, unconsciously molding her body against his.

Duncan sucked in a deep breath and tried not to feel the cushion of her breasts pressing against his back, nor the pressure of her legs, fitted perfectly against his, one arm wrapped across his waist. He should have been able to ignore the sensations coursing through him, or else push her away, but instead he lay there, feeling her touch, wanting to turn and take her in his arms.

Will ye never learn? He clenched his jaw against the need that burned inside of him. *Think with your brain this time, laddie! Ye have a chance to make things right—dinna hurt another lass in the meantime!*

Duncan closed his eyes and thought of Talamar. Talamar with her sunshine hair and her eyes like the green hills of Scotland. Talamar with her trusting heart and her willing soul. He had been overjoyed to see her alive and well. It wasn't too late. He could correct his mistakes.

Suddenly weary, Duncan cradled his aching head in both hands. Talamar had come to him an innocent and he had led her down the path of mindless desire with no thought for the consequences. How many times had he longed to take back what he had done? How many times had he berated himself for his selfish pursuit of what he had deemed love? His lustful actions had placed her in danger and ultimately been responsible for her death.

He had carried his guilt with him for so long. Finally, he had the chance to right his wrongs. Nothing must stand in his way.

Samantha shifted against him, making him draw in a sharp breath, bringing his thoughts back to her.

Samantha. He had already crossed the line with her, succumbed to his physical longings. And yet, he did not regret the one night they had spent together. Even though she'd acted afterward as if they had never made love, had never held one another, never caressed one another. He understood why. She was afraid to let him get too close, and rightly so. She had instinctively recognized him for what he was—a man who would lead her to ruin.

Smart girl. He would get her back home again, safely, somehow, and he would keep Talamar from dying. After that, he cared not what happened to him.

Duncan eased to his back. Samantha shifted with his movement and threw her arm across his chest, then, still asleep, kissed his shoulder. Morning seemed very far away. He closed his eyes and prayed for strength.

Chapter Eight

Samantha woke up feeling warm and secure, and with a start, realized why. She had molded herself against Duncan during the night, wrapping her arm around his waist and throwing her leg across his! He was snoring and she carefully, slowly, untwined her limbs from his, hoping he had fallen asleep before she'd made a fool of herself yet again. When she was sure he was still asleep, she rose from the bed and grabbed his plaid from the floor.

To escape the stuffiness of the hut, she pulled back the heavy hide that covered the doorway and slipped outside.

First things first. After checking to make sure no one was around, she found a clump of bushes and relieved herself with a sigh. Fairy queens probably didn't have bodily functions, so that might be a problem while they were in the village. She'd have to make sure no one saw her doing normal human things. She grimaced in the darkness. Of course, she'd want privacy for this sort of thing anyway, but she'd have to make sure that no one even suspected what she was doing. She finished her business and then tramped back to the thatched stone hut, where she paused outside the doorway and shivered at the realization of where she was and what had happened.

Lost in time. She'd done this before, with Jix and Jamie, and remembered how terrified she'd been at first. Eventually they'd all found one another again and spent the rest of their adventure in 1605 together. But this time, even with Duncan beside her, she felt alone. There was something he wasn't telling her. She sensed it, knew it from the way he had watched Brogan. The way he looked at Talamar.

She yawned. She couldn't even remember falling asleep after Duncan picked her up in his arms. She'd been exhausted, unusually so, probably a by-product of their travel through time, like Duncan had said. She ran one hand up and down her arm, remembering Duncan's health problems from his time travel. But he'd traveled many, many times before he'd started having symptoms. This was only her second time around. Surely she'd be all right in a day or so. She'd better be, because she doubted there was a friendly neighborhood pharmacy where she could fill a prescription.

Sam glanced up at the night sky and was seized by a sudden awe at the sight of the constellations above. Glittering diamonds on velvet. They looked the same as they did from Texas, although in slightly different places. No matter what the time period, she supposed there was always the constant of the stars to give comfort. But there was scant comfort there for her tonight.

This was no adventure, no exciting jaunt. Jix might have seen it that way, but she couldn't. She didn't want to be here. She couldn't stay here. She had to get back to Texas and make things right with her father before he died. She couldn't stay in Scotland's past.

How had they ended up in Scotland anyway? That was something she would ask Duncan in the morning. Wasn't there some rule about it being impossible to travel through time to another place? If you started out in Texas and journeyed to the past, you'd still be in the same place in Texas, albeit a different time. So what had happened to get them to Scotland?

She shivered and pulled Duncan's plaid more tightly around her shoulders. If only she knew what would happen next. The crowd of villagers in the clearing had totally unnerved her, not that she would ever admit it to Duncan. She'd admitted enough to him tonight out of exhaustion and fear. There was no way she was going to keep playing damsel in distress to his knight in shining armor. She was quite capable of taking care of herself, and even capable of getting back to her own time by herself if it came down to it. Besides, Duncan definitely didn't fancy himself as her savior.

For some reason Duncan acting as her savior wasn't the turn-off it should have been and Sam lifted her face to the night air, forcing Duncan from her mind. The wind swept down as she stood there and her hair danced in the air.

How could this be happening? How could she be standing in ancient Scotland for the second time in her life? She didn't want to think about it anymore tonight. Casting another look around, she hurried back into the hut.

Duncan lay asleep on his back, one arm thrown across his forehead as she slipped back in beside him. Careful not to wake him, she cuddled up against him again, for warmth, she told herself. Of course, only for warmth. After all, survival was the first order of business. Growing up as an air force brat had taught her that if nothing else.

In the morning she'd talk to Duncan about the the high priest's staff. If Duncan had been here before, knew these people, then he had to know whether or not the crystals in the staff would take them home again.

She gazed at his face as he lay sleeping beside her. His scar was pale in the moonlight, and not for the first time she longed to touch the sensitive skin. Why it intrigued her so, she didn't understand. She'd asked him once, during his convalescence at the ranch, how he'd gotten the scar. He'd told her he received it in a battle, that it was a badge of honor. Then he'd smiled. It was that smile that had given him away. She'd known he was lying.

But why? What was the big deal that he couldn't tell her? It had miffed her and she'd only spoken to him in monosyllables for about a week. She'd finally given up on ever knowing. A sudden thought sent an unfamiliar sensation through her. What if it had something to do with Talamar? What if he'd been defending her in the past because he was madly in love with her and—

She suddenly blinked and turned away from the Scot's broad shoulders.

I will not do this to myself, she vowed.

Duncan wasn't for her. Not even if he agreed to go back to her time. They'd kill each other in a week. Soon she'd find a way to return home, and Duncan Campbell would be just an irritating memory.

"What do you mean, beauty is only skin deep?" Samantha demanded. "What's that supposed to mean?"

Duncan glared at the fuming woman standing on the other side of their small hut. She had her di-

111

aphanous gown on once again with the "magical" belt in place, her hands on her hips, and a scowl on her lovely face.

She'd awakened him at dawn, demanding to know more about his first visit to this place, demanding to know if the staff of the high priest could take them back home, demanding to know how they had ended up in Scotland instead of Texas of the past, demanding to know more about his relationship with Talamar.

All in all she was a very demanding woman. He folded his arms over his chest.

"That means that ye might be beautiful, but if ye ever hope to find a mate, ye might want to work on yer communication skills."

She opened her mouth to speak, but Duncan cut her off.

"Samantha. Do ye really want to spend this time arguing, or do ye want to prepare for all the villagers who are going to be at your door any minute?"

He could see her weighing his suggestion and realizing he was right, but she was just stubborn enough to refuse. She raised one eyebrow in his direction, folded her arms across her shimmering, generous bosom, and to his amazement, nodded.

"All right. What do I need to know?"

He started to speak, but this time she cut him off.

"But you *are* going to answer my questions later," she said flatly. "And we *are* going to talk about how I can get back home again as soon as possible. So count on it."

"Grand," he said, "I canna wait. Now, the first thing ye need to know is that these people are very superstitious. If anything bad happens in the village they take it to mean that the fairies are angry because of something they've done, or didn't do. It might mean that one person is at fault and in a matter of moments ye can go from being a well-loved part of the community to being burned at the stake." His voice was grim.

Sam moved to the small ramshackle stool in the corner of the room and sat down, carefully spreading her dress around her. "All right," she acknowledged.

"Their beliefs go back hundreds, even thousands of years. Christianity hasn't made it this far into the Highlands, or if it did, it didn't take."

"So am I supposed to be a fairy or a goddess?" Sam asked.

"A little of both. The story goes that the first inhabitants of the British Isles were the Tuatha De Danaan—the People of Dana—and when the Sons of Mil invaded—"

"Who?" she interrupted.

Duncan sliced the air with his hand. "Doesna matter. Humans coming to the isle. Anyway, the Tuatha De Danaan had to flee the land, so they became invisible and went underground to live, but still had the power to reappear in different forms whenever they pleased. These became the fairy folk, called the Sidhe—"

"The Shee?" Sam interrupted again. "I like the sound of that. Must have been a woman who came up with it, because if a man had created the myth, they would've been called the Hee."

Duncan rolled his eyes. "Spoken like a true women's lover; now as I was saying—"

"Women's what?" Sam was staring at him, a slight smile playing around her lips.

He frowned. "Women's lover, ye know, these lasses who hate men and would rather have sex with each other."

Sam starting laughing and Duncan frowned.

"Do ye want to know about the villagers or no?" he said.

She kept laughing and Duncan glared at her as she leaned forward, holding her sides and gasping. Finally she brought her laughter under control and managed to answer him.

"Women's *libbers*," she said, trying to catch her breath and wiping tears from her eyes. "Oh, that's the best laugh I've had in a long time."

"Glad to be of service," he said shortly. "But—"

"And for your information, Mr. Male Chauvinist Pig, women's libbers are women who advocate equal rights for women, nothing more. Women who have sex with each other are called lesbians."

He blinked at her. Had she just called him a pig? "Did ye call me a pig?" he said.

"Yes, but not just any kind of pig," she said. "A male chauvinist pig."

Duncan could feel the heat rising in his face. *Control, laddie, control. She loves to bait ye.*

"And what does that mean?"

"It means that you think women are helpless and men are smarter and better and we're just here to fulfill your every desire."

One corner of his mouth lifted. "And are ye no here to do exactly that? I remember one night—"

She was on her feet, the laughter gone from her face. "You'd do well to forget that night, Duncan. It's never going to happen again."

He smiled, crossed the room, and stopped in front of her. "Aye," he said softly, "I can guarantee that it will not."

The color rushed away from Sam's face, then just as quickly flooded back into her pale cheeks. "Good, just as long as we're clear on that."

"Aye. We're crystal on that, and as I was—"

"Speaking of crystals—"

"At the moment," he interrupted, taking back control of the conversation, "we'll finish our history lesson, so that ye will understand how serious our situation really is."

"You mean more serious than being trapped in time?" she said.

"I mean being trapped in time and at the mercy of people who, if they find out ye were tricking them, might just burn ye at the stake," he said.

She sighed. "I knew the burning at the stake thing was going to come up sooner or later."

"Do ye want to know the rest of this story or not?"

Sam moved to the bed and flounced down on it, sliding across the coverlet to lie on her stomach. "Fine, piggy boy," she said, "tell me."

"Dinna call me that," he ordered. The woman was enough to drive a man crazy. To keep from strangling her with his bare hands he continued his history lesson, refusing to let his gaze linger on the way she was so enticingly draped on the bed where they'd slept together the night before, not touching, not kissing, not holding one another.

"The Tuatha De Danaan were not happy about being pushed off of their islands. They began destroying the wheat and milk of the Sons of Mil, and so the Sons of Mil made a treaty with the King of the Sidhe—"

"Wait, the Sidhe and the Tuatha De Danaan are the same people?"

"Basically, yes. And the King of the Sidhe, Dagda, or the good god, decreed that the fairy folk would stop destroying their goods. After that, the humans kept them happy with sacrifices of wheat and milk throughout the ages." Duncan finished the tale and Sam

115

looked up at him with a frown on her face, her chin in her hand.

"So if the Tuatha De Danaan were so powerful, why didn't they just destroy the Sons of Mil?"

Duncan shrugged. "Maybe they didn't believe in killing human beings."

"Right. Just wheat and milk." She slid off the bed and stretched, pulling the shimmering fabric of her dress tight across her long, lithe body. Every curve moved beneath the material and Duncan stared in fascination, only to be caught in the act when Sam turned toward him. A knowing, smug smile eased over her perfect face.

"So is that it?" she asked.

"Aye."

"Any advice on how I should act?"

His brows knit together thoughtfully. So he was a piggy boy, was he? "Well, a queen is usually arrogant, haughty, and selfish. So, in other words, just be yerself, ye'll do fine."

"Very funny—piggy boy." She straightened her shoulders and turned toward the doorway. "Well, c'-mon, consort, my followers await."

Duncan moved to pull the heavy hide back from the doorway. "Let me do the talking," he said.

Sam jerked the covering back down and glared up at him. "I'm not going to just stand there like some kind of mute dummy. Forget it. I'll tell you what I want to say and you can translate."

Duncan frowned. "Ye can tell me what ye'd like to say and then if I think it's all right, I'll translate it. Ye'll put yer foot in it for sure if ye're no careful."

Sam narrowed her eyes. "You are the most frustrating man I've ever met."

"And ye are the most stubborn woman I've ever

known, so we're even." He jerked back the hide from the doorway again.

She lifted her skirts and slid past him with a twitch of her hips. "No, Duncan, until I get back to my father, we are not close to even."

"Oh, consort, consort darling, do bring me another walnut, and this time, crack it with your teeth."

Sam lounged back against the "couch" the villagers had provided and smiled gleefully as Duncan approached with a handful of the precious sweetmeats, as yet unshelled.

She had been torturing him all day, ordering him here and ordering him there. While the villagers couldn't understand what she said to him, Sam had quickly let the Scot know if he didn't obey her every command that she would throw a fit, telling them in very clear body language that the Queen of the Fairies was very, very unhappy with her beloved consort.

The villagers had gathered that morning, slack-jawed in her presence, along with Brogan, and she knew Duncan was working hard to assuage any suspicions the high priest might have about the pair.

The villagers had apparently risen before dawn and prepared a beautiful bower for their queen. At the edge of the forest, a pallet, made from another coverlet filled with down, had been placed on an ornately carved wooden piece that resembled a kind of lounging couch.

Duncan found out and told her that a woodworker had been carving it for months, preparing it for the Feast Day celebration a few weeks away. The villagers had deemed it more important for this special occasion.

Sam had taken care to school her features when she looked at the beautiful artwork. Spirals and whorls adorned the edges of the curved back of the piece. There was a smooth surface for the pallet, raised slightly in the middle that dipped down again, giving a perfect resting place for her legs. The pallet had been covered with a cloth of a deep green hue and embellished with embroidered leaves and flowers. It must have taken months to create.

But instead of fawning over the beautiful work, as she wanted, Sam was careful to only give the anxious villagers a queenly smile of approval, as befit her station. Duncan, in turn, gave her an approving, covert nod. As if he'd thought she'd do something stupid and she had pleasantly surprised him.

Jerk. Piggy boy jerk. Male chauvinist piggy boy jerk.

Still, she had to smile at the thought of having him at her beck-and-call indefinitely. It gave her ideas. Bad ideas. Ideas she shouldn't be entertaining. She took a deep breath and raised her chin as Duncan dropped to one knee beside her. She was glad to see that he was keeping up the act, feigning an adoring look at his queen.

"I will crack the nut for ye," he said in English, "but ye can forget me risking my dental work."

Sam grinned. When she took over Duncan's medical care in 2003, she'd insisted on him going to the dentist in spite of his protests. He'd admitted later he was glad she'd forced him to go.

"Oh, all right," she said, feigning a sigh, "I only wanted to see if you were willing to do anything I asked. Obviously you have a lot to learn as a consort." She leaned down and planted a kiss on his mouth. Duncan smiled back at her, but his eyes promised retribution.

By late afternoon the game had lost its appeal and

Sam was exhausted from holding court. Brogan, the high priest, stepped forward during this latest lull, and knelt before her. The man's dark braid fell over the shoulder of the dark brown robe he wore, and she could see a bald spot at the very back of his head. A fly landed in the middle of the spot, like a helicopter on a helipad. Sam yawned, then realized the man wasn't getting up.

"What's wrong with him?"

"He's waiting for ye to give permission for him to rise," Duncan said from his rigid position beside her couch. He'd been standing like a frozen sentinel for the last hour or so and she wondered if he was tired. Maybe she should ask him to sit down with her.

He glanced over at her. "Ye've been doing this most of the day—do ye not know yet what ye are supposed to do?"

The words were said pleasantly, but the look in his eyes was anything but. He hadn't forgiven her yet for that piggy boy remark. Things were looking up.

"Bite me," Sam said in an equally cordial voice. "Tell him to rise."

Duncan obeyed. The priest stood awkwardly and lifted enigmatic brown eyes to hers. He was a mystery, Sam thought, and perhaps a dangerous one, though she didn't really sense that from him. Still, she wasn't sure he bought the whole fairy queen gambit. He spoke then and Sam was delighted to realize she recognized a lot of the words. Maybe after hearing the language all day she was beginning to catch on, to replace her knowledge of Gaelic with this slightly different version.

"Brogan wants to know if everything is all right— my queen." Duncan said, adding the last two words as if an afterthought.

Sam draped one arm over the top of the couch and

gazed up at him from beneath lowered lashes. "Why wouldn't it be?"

"He's not accustomed to yer sour looks like I am," he said, his voice still smooth and even.

She smiled over at Brogan. "Tell him that I appreciate his concern, and that it isn't often I find such kindness in humans." She glanced back at Duncan. "Lord knows that's the truth."

While Duncan spoke to the priest, she looked up and once again admired the trellis the villagers had made from intertwined vines. They arched over the couch and were covered with delightful tiny white and purple flowers. She yawned again.

At first it had been a novelty to lie here and be worshipped—every woman's dream—but as the day wore on she had grown weary of keeping her plastic smile glued in place as Duncan related the requests of her followers. All day long they had come to her, humbly bowing down before her, asking for good weather, for bountiful crops, for healthy animals, healthy children, an easy childbirth—and harder requests, such as bringing a deceased relative back to life.

With Duncan's help—and she had to admit, she had needed his counsel—she was able to give vague but sympathetic answers to the people of Nirdagh.

She felt horrible. She had tricked these good, innocent people into believing that she could help them, when in truth she and Duncan were just using them. Duncan didn't seem worried about it. In fact, he had seemed a little preoccupied all day, his gaze searching the crowds of people coming to her—they had come from other villages too, apparently—almost as though he were looking for someone. Someone young and redheaded perhaps?

She looked up at him again as he nodded to Brogan and moved back to her side.

"He asks if there is anything he can do for you," Duncan said.

"What did he have in mind?" She tucked her hands under her chin and gazed up at Duncan with languid eyes.

"Probably not what ye have in mind," Duncan said easily. He glanced over at the esthetic-looking man. "Funny, I dinna think he was yer type."

Sam batted her eyes at him. "You weren't either but that didn't stop me."

Duncan inclined his head, apparently unmoved by her words. "Shall I ask him to grace yer bed this night?" he asked. "Ye said that my days as yer consort were numbered. I'm sure Brogan would be happy to take my place." He folded his arms over his chest and gave the priest an assessing look, then nodded and turned back to her. "Aye, I think it would be possible to rid him of the fleas, and I wouldna worry about the rash he complained of this morning. I wager it isn't catching."

"Ask him where his staff is today."

Duncan's taunting eyes gleamed. "Probably where most men keep them."

Sam felt a surge of familiar irritation at the innuendo, but as his gaze locked with hers, her annoyance quickly shifted into another emotion that was much more dangerous. She looked away.

"Duncan," she said, "Ask him. I want to go home."

To her surprise, Duncan spoke to the high priest and he nodded and hurried away. "I asked him to bring the staff to ye. Satisfied?"

Sam leaned her head on her palm, suddenly ravenous. "No. I won't be satisfied until I'm home again. Hand me that bowl of apples, slave."

But Duncan wasn't listening. He was staring past her, his deep blue eyes glimmering with something she'd rarely seen. Kindness. Concern.

She followed the direction of his gaze. Talamar stood a few feet away, her long-lashed green eyes filled with devotion and awe as she looked upon the fairy queen. Now Sam got a good, close look at the woman who had championed them in the glen.

Her hair was a wondrous mixture of reds and golds and blonds that reached past her knees. When she'd first appeared in the glen Sam had thought her to be in her mid-twenties, but now that she had a closer look, she saw that the girl looked barely twenty, if that. Sam turned to glare at Duncan who was still gazing at the young woman like one mesmerized.

Talamar wore a deep green garment of worsted wool that accentuated the color of her eyes. A thin leather cord hung around her neck and disappeared under the garment. She was diminutive and fragile, and her pointed chin and high cheekbones made her look almost like an elf or a fairy herself.

As the new supplicant fell to her knees, Sam glanced at Duncan and saw a faint, gentle smile curve across his lips. She swallowed hard and lifted her chin.

"Why have you come so late?" Sam demanded, her voice harsh. Duncan shot her a look and frowned, but translated the words. Sam caught only a couple of words this time.

The girl looked up, startled no doubt by the displeasure in the queen's voice. Her lower lip trembled and she ducked her head again, a flow of words rushing out in tones of supplication.

"She says that she wanted to let the villagers have their chance to present their needs to you and leave her own for last." Duncan said the words politely to Samantha, but his eyes were shooting daggers. "Now quit being such a witch to the lass. She's done nothing to ye."

Sam glared back at him. *No, but I bet she's done a lot to you—and you enjoyed every second of it.*

"Should I ask her name even though I already know it?" she inquired, careful to keep her tone without even a hint of jealousy. Why should she be jealous? If Duncan had fooled around in the past with this young thing what was it to her? Nothing at all.

"Aye, I would use her name. 'Twill help convince her that ye are who ye say ye are."

"Right. Lie to the customer, they'll never know the difference." Duncan frowned at her, and she plastered the plastic smile back on her face. "Talamar," she said loudly and beckoned for her to come forward.

Talamar's eyes widened at the use of her name by the fairy queen and she quickly obeyed, hurrying to kneel at Sam's feet.

"Be nice," Duncan said in a low voice.

"Tell her that I have chosen her to be my hand-maiden while I am here."

Duncan folded his arms over his chest. "Why?" he demanded.

Sam smiled up at him, trying to look innocent. "Why not? I regret speaking harshly to her. And it doesn't do any harm to curry favor with someone in power while we're here."

"She has no power," Duncan said.

"How do you know? If her father is the laird—"

"Was. He's dead now. The village looks up to her

123

though, and respects her. Only the high priest ranks as high as she."

"Tell her I wish for her to be my handmaiden or there will be a scene."

Duncan bowed to her, and then knelt beside Talamar, speaking softly. Just the tone of his voice sent a rush of jealousy coursing through Sam's body. Talamar looked up at her as he finished speaking, a genuinely happy smile on her face. She nodded energetically, babbling to Duncan, then seized his hand and shook it.

Sam felt her face grow hot as she sat there and watched Duncan staring down at the girl so tenderly. She gritted her teeth, then stood and thrust her hand toward her consort, palm up. Duncan looked up. Striking a queenly pose, Sam reached over and gently grasped Duncan's face, her thumb at his chin, her fingers curved around his jawline.

"I get it," she said, her voice loving. "You never wanted to go back to 1601, you wanted to come here—to her." Her nails bit into his skin. "So what am I, Duncan? Collateral damage? I don't think so. You're going to make sure I get back home and then you can stay here with your girlfriend, but you *are* going to help me get back home first."

She drew him upward until he stood erect, then slipped her arms around his neck and pulled him down to meet her lips. He could scarcely resist, not in front of Talamar and the others of the village still watching. To do so would be to blow their cover entirely. Her other hand moved to cup his face and she deepened the kiss, forcing his mouth to open to hers, forcing him to at least act as if he cared for her, as if he really was her consort.

He had no choice but to respond. When Sam stepped back from him, he had a dazed look on his face, and so did Talamar. The girl looked from Sam to Duncan and then back again, as if confused.

Sam lifted her chin and gave the girl a languid smile as she slid one hand up Duncan's chest. "Payback's rough," she said sweetly.

Talamar blinked and bowed her head, backing away from the queen. She stopped a few feet away and began speaking again, to Duncan, but this time she didn't look at him. Duncan nodded and translated, keeping his eyes carefully averted from the queen.

"She says she is honored to be your handmaiden and wants to know how she may serve you."

"Tell her I want clean clothes for both of us—I want to see how talented the village seamstresses and weavers are—and decent food instead of the slop we had last night."

Duncan stared straight ahead, his features composed, but his eyes glittered. "Aye, I will tell her." He spoke to the girl and she nodded, and then bowed to Sam again before rushing away. As soon as she was gone, Duncan turned to Sam.

"What the hell was that kiss about?" he muttered under his breath.

"Didn't you enjoy it, my consort?" Sam crooned, sliding her hands over his shoulders and pulling his head down to hers. "Or isn't that the way your lovely Talamar treated you when you were here last time?"

He started to speak, but her tongue flicked out to touch his lips once, twice, and then she kissed him again, her fingers laced in his dark hair. Duncan stood motionless for a moment, simply enduring her kiss, when all at once he gathered her to him, crushing her against his chest. His mouth opened to hers, but this time he took charge of the kiss, ravaging her lips, burning his tongue into her mouth, forcing her to feel the long, hard length of him through the thin material of her dress.

For a moment Sam forgot where they were, forgot Duncan didn't care anything about her and thought her only an annoying brat. Her pulse quickened and her heart pounded as he devoured her lips, her throat, the line of her jaw, the curve of her neck, sending hot tremors of desire under her skin and into her veins.

It was when his hand covered her breast that she remembered where they were. She pushed him away and he grinned down at her, challenge in his eyes. The villagers had gathered around them and were openly gaping at the two.

"Is that how ye like it, my queen?" he asked, his voice a caress. "Would ye like me to lay ye down right here and show yer people how the fairy folk mate?"

Sam's face flushed with heat. "What I would like is for you to go straight to hell," she said, keeping a smile on her face.

"Ah, good, ye havena forgotten how we must act in front of these fine people, if I am to play yer loving consort."

"All they know is my tone of voice," she said, "like dogs." His face darkened and her smile broadened. "But the truth is, I'm the queen. So from now on you'd better remember—I'm on top. I call the shots. If I want to kiss you, I'll kiss you. If I say jump, you say how high. Get it? Got it? Good."

Duncan bowed toward her from the waist, his hand over his heart, but as he straightened, his eyes met hers, blue and intense. He took a step forward and grasped her chin in his hand as he bent his head to hers, almost, but not quite, touching her lips.

"Be careful how ye play with fire, my queen," he whispered, his breath warm against her mouth. "Or ye may get burned."

Chapter Nine

The high priest leaned back against a large oak tree on a slight rise overlooking the village and watched as Queen Brigid went into her hut and her consort headed in the opposite direction. He balanced the long staff he held across his knees. Queen Brigid had seen all the villagers that day and listened to their requests, and the high priest's standing had increased substantially in the eyes of the village. The thank-you offerings should be piling up around his borrowed quarters by nightfall.

He didn't know who or what this woman and her companion really were, but at present he had decided to simply wait and keep a watchful eye on the two of them. He'd seen too much in his life to believe in things like fairies or elves or even God. The two of them had to be up to something, and he planned to find out what. Until then, the presence of the queen was helping him, so he would just watch and wait.

Maybe he would discover the secret behind the woman's wings.

Brogan glanced down at the staff lying across his legs. Her consort had told him that the queen requested his staff. Why? Did she plan to use it to proclaim the man, Duncan, the new high priest? Perhaps he should refuse to bring it to them. Or perhaps he should bring it to them at a time when no one else was around and somehow coerce the truth out of the two of them. But then, what if she really was the queen of the Tuatha De Danaan? He'd best hedge his bets.

"Ye wished to see me, Brogan?"

He glanced up to find Talamar gazing down at him, her green eyes hesitant, as always.

"Aye," he said, rising and assuming his persona of high priest. "I wished to inform ye that I have sent a message to Laird Gwain and received an answer." He smiled as if about to bestow a rare gift upon her, for truly, it was. "Laird Gwain desires a handfasting with you on Feast Day and will be here within the week."

She drew in a ragged breath and Brogan could see her visibly gathering courage. "My father was the only one who could command me to wed," she said.

Brogan pretended to be sympathetic, nodding and stroking his ragged beard in feigned contemplation. "Of course, of course, however, yer father is dead, and it falls to the elders of the village to guide ye in these decisions."

"But ye are not an elder," Talamar said, her voice faint, her eyes confused.

The soft breeze lifted one long strand of red-gold hair into the air and Brogan admired her beauty for a moment.

Her father, Noric, had been a powerful laird with more land than any other man in Caledonia. The well-respected leader of Nirdagh had fallen from his horse three years ago, lethally bashing his head against a stone, and leaving the decision of her marriage up to the village elders, and eventually to Brogan.

Marriages were made to strengthen alliances. Brogan had offered Talamar his devoted friendship, while he looked for a way to profit from marrying her—and her dowry of land—to someone who would reward the efforts of the high priest. He had found the perfect man for Talamar in Laird Gwain.

At the time the grand idea came to him, the girl had thought herself in love with a young man from Innisbar, but Brogan had quickly put an end to that. He smiled to himself at the thought of how cleverly he had handled that little problem. And really, Talamar would be better off for his subterfuge. What woman wouldn't want to be the wife of a powerful man like Gwain?

As the high priest it had been fairly easy—especially after making his deal with Gwain—to convince the elders that marrying Talamar to Laird Gwain was the best way to protect the village and the province against attacks from the Danes. They didn't need to know about the gold Gwain had promised Brogan if the marriage actually took place.

"Nay, I am not an elder," Brogan said, addressing Talamar's statement, "but as the village's high priest, I am above the elders, as ye well know." He cupped her chin in his hand and lifted her face to his. Talamar kept her eyes downcast. "I only want yer happiness, my dear."

Talamar's lashes swept up and her green eyes met his in an unusually frank appraisal. "Did Laird Gwain promise ye something if ye would convince the elders I should marry him?"

Brogan dropped his hand away from her face and stepped back, shaking his head in open astonishment. "I have no idea what ye are talking about, child. Surely if ye married Gwain it wouldna benefit me."

Talamar lowered her gaze. "Not unless ye had an agreement with Gwain that if ye arranged the hand-fasting and the elders gave their permission, he in turn would grant ye a boon, either land or gold." She looked up, her lower lip trembling.

The high priest allowed his face to go slack as he pressed one hand to his chest, as if truly insulted. The girl was smarter than he'd thought.

"I am wounded, fair lady, that ye would think such a thing of me. The union between ye and Gwain would be a benefit not only to yerself, but to the village of Nirdagh. Gwain's protection from Danish invaders would be invaluable." He frowned at her like a loving father. "'Tis only a matter of time before they reach us, ye know." He sighed. "But I dinna expect one as young as ye are to understand the necessity of such things."

"I understand perfectly," she said. "But I do not know Lord Gwain. My father loved my mother and he always told me that he wouldna have me marry except for love."

"Yer father wanted ye to marry a man of equal station," Brogan reminded her, careful to keep a look of sympathy on his face. "And he wouldna want ye to be alone. And what of yer duty to the people of Nirdagh? Would ye leave our village open to plunder and murder?"

She looked away from him. "If I must, I will deed land to Gwain in return for his protection," she said. "But I dinna want to marry a man I dinna love."

"Ye would insult Prince Gwain with such an offer. And why should he accept such an arrangement? If he marries ye, he will have both yerself and yer lands." Brogan shook his head. "Ah, the impetuosity of youth. The idealism." He placed his hands on her shoulders with all the gentleness of a loving uncle. "My child, I understand yer feelings, but unfortunately in life, sometimes we must do what is expedient, not what our heart desires. Yer father knew that."

"What do ye mean," she asked. "My father followed his heart, always. He adored my mother."

"Aye, he did, but 'twas not always the case."

She stepped back from his touch, her gaze startled. "That is not true."

"I dinna want to tell ye this, but I see that I must. Yer father was in love with another woman before his marriage to yer mother was arranged," Brogan told her, shaking his head.

"What woman?" she whispered, lifting her hand to her heart.

"A woman not of his station. A common woman who was beautiful and vivacious. Her name is unimportant now. He wanted to marry her, but his father and mother wouldna hear of it, and because he was an obedient son, he married the girl they chose for him." The tale practically created itself as he spoke, and Brogan felt pleased that he'd not lost his talent at making up stories.

"I dinna believe it," she said, her gaze shifting away from him, her eyes filling with tears.

He moved to cup her shoulders again. "Perhaps that is why he told ye he wanted ye to marry for love—because he was unable to do so, but he himself did the right thing, and love came out of his sacrifice."

"And now he is dead." The tears spilled over her

cheeks as she turned back to him. "Now I will never know what he would have bid me do."

"There, there, now." Brogan smoothed the moisture from her cheek with his thumb. "Dinna cry. Ye havena even met the laird. How do ye know ye willna love him? Will ye at least meet with him?"

Talamar nodded, blinking back her tears. "Aye, I will meet the man." She turned to leave, but stopped and turned, her eyes bright with hope. "The queen."

Brogan frowned. "What about the queen?"

"She can tell me if I should marry Gwain," she said, almost breathless with excitement. "She will know."

The high priest opened his mouth, then closed it. This was something he hadn't expected. Still, why would Queen Brigid—or whoever she really was— object to the marriage of the princess to the rich, well-mannered laird? But if she did, it would ruin his plans.

"The queen may not wish to become involved in our foolish little problems," he said. "I am not sure we should disturb her with such a question."

"I am her handmaiden now. She will allow it, I know she will. She is very kind," Talamar said, and alarm rang through Brogan's body. "But first I will do as you ask," she went on, "I will meet the laird. As ye said, perhaps 'twill be love at first sight." She wiped away her lingering tears with the back of her hand like a child.

Brogan released his breath and patted her on the back. He really was fond of the girl, but this was business. "Verra well, my child. Wash yer face, then, and when the laird arrives, we will speak of it again."

She nodded and walked quickly away toward the forest.

Brogan turned away, stroking his beard thoughtfully. What if the fairy queen gave Talamar permission to refuse Laird Gwain's offer? As he hurried off to Aleric's hut he began to devise an alternate plan.

Duncan was extremely confused.

After Samantha jerked away from him and stalked off to their hut, he had headed for the glen. Now he paced back and forth in the clearing, trying to come to terms with himself.

How many times had he imagined once again meeting Talamar? How many times had he dreamed of sweeping her into his arms and kissing her senseless?

Now he had finally returned, was finally back, had finally met her again face to face.

How could it be that he no longer loved her?

Ever since he'd been forced to leave Talamar, years and years ago, he'd been trying to return to ninth-century Scotland. He had yearned for Talamar for so long and agonized over the death of the young woman. He had dreamed of touching her again, kissing her again, and now, when he had finally obtained his goal and reached the right time period, he found, upon looking into her eyes, that he felt nothing for her but affection.

He had been stunned when he first saw her, but by the time she presented herself to Samantha that morning he had been prepared to feel that same burning desire he'd always felt, and had been prepared to fight it.

But when he looked down into her green eyes as she paid her homage to the queen, he found he was gazing at a girl, albeit a beautiful one. And there was no burning desire, no raging attraction. No love, save for that of perhaps an older brother for his younger sister.

What had happened? Had his treks through time somehow changed his love for Talamar? Or was it something else?

He ran one hand through his hair as suspicion darted through his mind. No. It couldn't be because of Samantha. He and the lass just liked sparring with one another to keep their hand in at the game of love. It was a game they both enjoyed. It didn't mean anything, just as their one night together hadn't meant anything.

Had it?

Sometimes he thought he saw something in Samantha's eyes, something that hinted she might have deeper feelings for him, like that night at Jacob's Well. When she thought he was leaving forever, there had been a moment that she looked as though it would really matter to her.

Did it?

He headed out of the clearing, back to the village. When he reached the hut he shared with Samantha he hesitated, then sat down on the stone step outside the hide door. Duncan folded his arms over his chest and observed the comings and goings of the villagers. From his vantage point he had a good view of the village marketplace, a small area in the center of town where people bartered supplies or just stopped to chat with neighbors.

Today there were a few farmers set up in the square, their wares displayed on crude tables, but he remembered other times when the village had been packed with vendors. One particularly sunny spring morning he and Talamar had walked amidst the almost fair-like event, watching street performers and laughing at the antics of a man with a pet squirrel. He had bought her a green ribbon that matched her eyes and had tied it in her hair and kissed her.

The memory didn't have the poignancy that it once had.

All right. Duncan took a deep breath and released it slowly as he tried to organize his thoughts.

He didn't love Talamar anymore for whatever reason. But that didn't change what he had to do. That didn't change the fact that this time he had to make sure she married Laird Gwain and as a result, stayed alive.

In his first journey to this time, his love for Talamar had caused her to refuse marriage to the laird. Right after that a series of calamities had befallen the village—bad water, tainted milk, a fire, poor crops—and as a result, Brogan had decreed it was Talamar's fault. Duncan had been saved for a sacrifice of blood to the gods—an event that had actually sent him tumbling back through time again as the high priest Brogan passed his staff of crystals over the body of the "sacrifice." But before he disappeared, he'd seen Talamar die by fire.

He shook his head to try and clear the memory from his mind. It hadn't happened yet. He still had time to make sure things went the way they were supposed to. Talamar must marry Lord Gwain. She must not die burned at the stake.

But he also had to make sure Samantha got back home.

Unfortunately, Duncan wasn't sure how exactly to help Samanatha return to her father. As much as he had traveled through time he still understood little of the mechanics. He and Sam were at the mercy of the unpredictable crystals.

Duncan glanced up at the sky. The sun was going down and already a chilly breeze was sweeping through the marketplace and people were hurrying home to prepare their suppers and feed their children. He and Sam's own supper would no doubt soon appear in the hands of Talamar or some other willing servant of the queen.

He frowned. Maybe he could make Samantha understand that there was no need to panic. The time travel crystals had a mind of their own and if they didn't want you to end up in the right place at the right time, you wouldn't. If they did, you would. It was as simple as that. You often had to play the waiting game.

Are ye sure there isn't some other reason, lad, that ye are in no hurry to help Samantha return home? Do ye have some ulterior motive, like perhaps wanting her to remain in the past with ye?

The thought danced through his head and he stood up abruptly, refusing to entertain any such notion.

Ridiculous. He and Samantha were about as suited for one another as a hawk and a wolf. It was time to tell her the truth about Talamar; she must understand why he had to protect the girl.

Twilight touched the village. Duncan turned and went inside the hut, pushing aside the taunting little voice in his head that reminded him he and Samanatha weren't hawk and wolf, but man and woman.

Samantha took the news rather well, considering.

Duncan had settled her on the mattress, facing him, then decided that was a mistake. Staring deeply into Samantha's lavender cycs—he loved those lavender contacts—and watching the subtle interplay of emotion there might be more than he could handle at the moment. If she turned vulnerable, he knew he would take her in his arms, and that would be a terrible mistake.

Who was he kidding? Samantha, vulnerable?

Still, she'd been through a lot. Maybe they should sit at the table. Aye, having a table between them could only help matters. He had started to suggest it when she spoke, a frown marring her smooth forehead.

"Before you get started on the fair Talamar—how is

it that we were able to travel to Scotland from Texas?" she asked. "I thought the crystals only allowed a person to travel to the same place, just in a different time?"

"Aye, but it's possible," he said, "as ye are well aware of now, to use the crystals to transverse time and space to any country of yer choosing. However, it's risky and inaccurate and I suspect it's how I ended up almost dying."

"You mean the stress of traveling to a different place as well as a different time might have caused your illness?"

He nodded. "Aye, at least that's my theory."

"Why didn't you tell me about this when I was treating you?" she demanded.

He shrugged. "I dinna think it mattered. What was done was done."

She rolled her eyes. "All right, never mind, but then that means we could travel back to twenty-first century Texas from here, right?" Her voice was filled with hope.

"Aye, I suppose," he said more slowly as a new thought dawned upon him. He realized that there was no way he could let Samantha travel back to her home in Texas without his help. What if she got lost in time the way he had been for so long?

He'd heard the whole story of her adventure with Jamie and Jix and was convinced that the only way the three had made it back was due to the strength of the mental union formed by all three of them concentrating on getting back to the year 2001. Maybe the addition of Samantha's mental concentration this time was what had allowed him to make it back to this time period.

The crystals were operated by thought, but sometimes they seemed to have a mind of their own.

"But it might not be worth risking our health," she was saying, half to herself. "We could always fly over from Scotland, or I could, and then you'd be back in Scotland at least and I wouldn't have to listen to you complain about missing your own country any more and—"

"Do ye want to hear my story or no?" he said crossly, in truth trying to turn her from this line of thinking. He needed more time to consider how best to see Samantha home safely.

"Lead on, MacDuff," she said with a wave of one hand.

"Dinna call me by that name," he said. "Verra well. I was in Madagascar, still trying to return to my own time of 1601, but it occurred to me that perhaps I should first simply try and return to Scotland of any time and work from there. So when the crystals appeared to me, in a water grotto, I concentrated on Scotland. It worked. I appeared in the forest and wandered into the village of Nirdagh, posing as a bard, and 'twas there that I met Talamar and . . ." he hesitated.

"And?" Sam said, arching one brow.

"And I fell in love with her."

There, he'd said it. She was frowning, but at least she wasn't screaming and there were no blunt objects handy.

"You can sing?" she asked.

" 'Tis not the point. I fell in love with Talamar," he said again, a little louder.

"In love. With Talamar." Sam shook her head, her gaze skeptical. "Duncan, she's a baby."

"Aye, she is very young." He hurried on with his tale. "I know, I know, in yer time I would be considered a rogue, but in this time 'tis nothing wrong with an older man marrying a much younger woman."

Her eyes widened. "Did you marry her? Is that what this is all about?"

He shook his head. "Nay. I wanted to marry her, but before I could, the village elders, led by Brogan, declared her a witch and I a demon. Seems that someone did see me appear in the forest after all. But the truth of the matter was that I had prevented Brogan from sealing a deal with Laird Gwain. He had arranged for the fatherless girl to marry the laird, and in return, Gwain agreed to give him part of the girl's dowry in gold. It was a sweet deal, but one that wasn't going to happen because Talamar was in love with me and refused to marry the laird. If I had not interfered, she would not have died."

"You couldn't have known that," Sam said. "It was Brogan's fault. Funny, I wouldn't take him for a violent person."

"Aye, to be fair, I dinna think that Brogan intended for her to actually burn, only to scare her into marrying Gwain. But the fire got out of hand and it was too late." Duncan rose from the bed. He paced across the room with his hands behind his back and stopped at the doorway. He pulled back the rough hide covering the opening and stared out at the village.

"I'm sorry, Duncan," she said softly.

"It's strange. Here I am and Talamar is alive, but I've mourned her loss and grieved over her for a very long time, and the pain is still there, as if she is still dead."

He felt a touch and looked down, surprised to find Samantha beside him, her hand on his arm. "That must have been awful," she said. "How did you get away?"

Duncan looked away from her again. "I was stretched out in the center of the standing stones to have my blood shed. I don't know if Brogan would have gone through with it or not. He looked verra nervous, but he passed his staff over me in some kind of ritual and the crystals began to glow." Duncan glanced down at her. "I was transported to another time."

"So, that's why you came back here—to save her."

He hesitated and then nodded. "Aye."

"Then why does she act like she doesn't know you?"

He let the hide drop back over the doorway and turned, leaning against the wall beside it. "She doesna remember me. You and I arrived a few months earlier than the last time I was here." He frowned, trying to sort it out, then shrugged. "At least as far as she is concerned, she doesna know me and that's a good thing."

Samantha gave him a pointed look. "But you know her and still love her. That must make it hard on the old ego." She poked him in the stomach with her finger.

"I'm not concerned right now with romance," Duncan said, irritated. "I'm trying to save the girl's life. Ye can see that, can't ye?"

She nodded. "Oh, sure, I see it—'girl' being the definitive word in that sentence. And I can see why you were so happy about finding the crystals in Jacob's Well. It must have been terrible to be separated from your soulmate all this time."

Duncan cleared his throat. "Aye. So ye understand why my attention must be on making sure Talamar marries the right man this time?"

"Oh, I understand." She moved away from him, her shoulders looking tense beneath her tattered dress. When she spoke, her words were clipped, emotionless. "What about helping me get back to my own time?"

His mind raced. He had planned to get Brogan's staff for her or else search for a grotto—the crystals always appeared, sooner or later—but he couldn't send

141

her traveling through time alone. He'd have to take her back and he couldn't do that until he helped Talamar.

"Ye canna travel back alone," he said. She whirled around and looked up at him, her eyes filled with challenge.

"Why not?"

"I believe that it was only the sheer power of your mind, linked with the minds of Jamie and Jix that allowed the three of ye to return to yer own time. Do ye not remember that I've been bouncing around by myself for a verra long time, trying to return to my own home?"

"Or so you said, but now the truth comes out. You were trying to come back to her." She lifted her chin and Duncan knew that look. "Well," she said, "then you'll just have to come back with me."

Duncan took a deep breath and expelled it, dragging one hand through his hair. "Aye, after I help Talamar, I will help ye return."

Samantha narrowed her eyes. "And how long will that take?"

He shrugged. "As long as it takes."

She turned on her heel and walked to the small window in the room, lifting her arms to rest on the wooden sill as she balanced her chin on top of them.

She seemed calm. Too calm. Duncan had sailed enough to know that when a storm was coming the water got very still. He had fought enough with Samantha to know the same was true for her.

"There's something you don't understand," she said.

"What dinna I understand?"

She looked over her shoulder, her eyes like lavender diamonds as she spoke softly. "That I don't give a damn about your little quest to save Talamar. That I don't care if you think it's up to the crystals where and when they deposit me. I've got to get back to my father." She turned back to the window and shook her head. "I can't stay here."

Duncan crossed the room to her side and laid his hand on her shoulder. She jerked away from his touch and turned to glare up at him.

"I can't wait on you and I can't communicate with Brogan, so you've got to help me," she said sharply. "He never came back with the staff today. I need you to make him bring me the staff, so I can return to the twenty-first century. I will take the risk of traveling on my own. If you don't help me get the staff I'll find a way do it on my own."

"That would be a mistake," he said. "Besides, there's no hurry about yer return."

Her eyes widened in fury. "Of course there is! My father is dying!"

"This is *time travel* we're dealing with, remember? It doesna matter how long ye remain in the past, if the crystals are willing to take ye back to the right place and the right time, then ye can stay a week in the ninth century or a year—and still end up at yer father's side in time to make things right with him."

Samantha shook her head. "How do I know that's true? You'd tell me anything to save your precious Talamar."

Duncan took her hands between his and spoke softly. "I promise ye, lass. I'll help ye, but it must be in my own time and my own way. Trust me."

She pulled her hands away. "I'm tired," she said, her voice flat. "I want to get ready for bed."

Duncan hesitated as he gazed down at her. Should he tell her that he was no longer in love with Talamar? Would that make her trust him more?

He started to speak, then realized what he had just

promised her. If he traveled back to her time then he would have to begin once again to find his way home.

Well, it was done. He wouldn't go back on his word and he wouldn't let Samantha wander through time on her own.

At the same time, he wouldn't allow himself to become more involved with her than he was already. There was no way Samantha Riley would stay in the past with him, and so there was no reason to reveal what possible feelings he might have for her.

"I'll wait outside," he said, and turned away.

Chapter Ten

Samantha felt as though she'd been hit by a sledge hammer. Duncan was in love with Talamar. Of course he was. It figured. You travel back in time with a man, thinking he might secretly have the hots for you, only to discover that he was trying to get back to an old girlfriend. Riley's luck.

But it didn't work this time, the old flippancy. Duncan's words had pierced her heart and brought her true feelings to light. When he told her about his "mission," she'd suddenly had to acknowledge all the feelings she'd been trying to keep buried inside of her for a year and a half. She loved Duncan Campbell.

"Oh, hell," she said aloud, and pulled the dress over her head. She was down to the thin slip that came with her costume when the hide over the doorway lifted and Duncan came back in.

His eyes were downcast, his face thoughtful, and then he glanced up and saw her.

Sam had an idea of the picture she made, the sheer

silk plainly outlining her body, her breasts, her long legs. Feeling a need to make him suffer just a little, she raised her arms over her head and yawned, arching her back slightly, stretching like a cat.

Heat flickered in Duncan's eyes and she suddenly remembered his warning a few days before about playing with fire. Suddenly she didn't want to play.

"I'm so tired," she said quickly, pulling back the feather-filled coverlet and slipping underneath it with another yawn. " 'Night."

She turned away from him and closed her eyes, silently berating herself for her cowardice. But her very real fatigue overshadowed her thoughts and she slipped easily into a state between waking and sleeping, her mind playing with dreams and rearranging reality.

When the coverlet lifted and Duncan slid in beside her, she accepted the direction her dreams were headed. After all, she was still a woman and if she couldn't have physical comfort in real life, at least she could in her dreams. She felt his hand smooth down her arm, over her hip and along her thigh, and shivered at his touch. His hand moved to her waist and slid over her stomach, pulling her back against the hard length of his naked body.

It seemed only natural in the dream to turn in his arms. Only natural to open her mouth to his kiss, to the heat of his tongue. Somewhere between his first touch and his mouth on her breast, Sam woke up and realized it wasn't a dream at all, but by then she didn't care. Duncan in real life was better than any dream.

She kissed the side of his jaw and licked the smooth curve of his scar even as his hands and mouth moved over her skin, sending shivers of delight coursing through her.

Duncan. How was it that in his arms everything felt

all right again? How was it that his touch made her forget everything but his blue eyes gazing down into her soul? She tried to pull herself to full consciousness, but his mouth was doing amazing things, making that extremely difficult.

Don't forget. He loves another woman. Doesn't he?

But as he slipped his warm hand between her legs, her nipple taut between his lips, all coherent thought left her. He moved to kiss her and she clung to him, letting him take her mouth as he stoked heat down below with his touch, letting him burn himself into her with his mouth as he moved from her lips to her neck, back to her breast again.

He was in perfect control, and even in the midst of the fire he was stoking with his body, she couldn't allow it, couldn't let him conquer her without a fight. She rolled on top of him, loving the sound of his gasp as she took him into her, the steel of him, the flame of him, and as she reached for the fire, just when she was about to find that elusive peak, he stilled beneath her and she groaned aloud.

"Patience," he whispered against her ear. Then he began to move and Duncan was not just inside of her but filling her, impaling her, empowering her, completing her with every stroke, every surge of his taut, powerful body. She found the heat and felt every ember burning brighter inside her skin, building as he took her higher and higher, deeper and deeper, harder and hotter, until the brilliance burst inside of her and she lost herself in the raging inferno of Duncan, shattered against him even as he shuddered under her, burned equally by her fire and her heat.

Sam wrapped her arms around him and rested her head on his chest, unwilling to let him leave her, unwilling to let him slip away, knowing that this was just sex for him, but so much more for her, and hating herself for her weakness.

Duncan lay beside Samantha hating himself for his weakness. Not only was he letting Samantha believe he still loved Talamar, but he was taking what she offered him with no thought of how their lovemaking would affect her future. He glanced over where she lay sleeping, as limp as a rag doll. On the other hand, perhaps she was using him for her own reasons, for comfort, for reassurance. For sex.

He frowned at the thought for some reason. Wouldn't it be better for them both if that were the case? But there had been something about the look in her eyes as she lay beneath him, the soft catch in her throat as he moved within her, that said there was more to it for her.

And for ye?

Duncan ignored the question and gazed at Sam's face for a long moment, then reached over and stroked one finger down the smooth line of her jaw. She had kissed his scar during their lovemaking. Come to think of it, she had done that the first time they made love. No other woman had ever done that before.

The raw vulnerability in her face as she slept should have made Duncan turn away, but instead, it drew her to him. He kissed her forehead gently and she smiled in her sleep.

When she looked like this, sweet and soft and unprotected, he wanted to take her in his arms again. He wanted to protect her and make her world all right again. He wanted to make sure she got home again. He wanted to love her.

Duncan felt the shock roll through him and he eased

away from the sleeping woman, sliding out of bed without a sound.

Love her?

No, he didn't love Samantha Riley. She was brash and rude and hard-nosed and argumentative and utterly unfeminine.

Except when she laughed or when she teased him or when she genuinely smiled at someone or when she lay boneless and content in his bed. Then she was utterly and completely woman.

Duncan picked up his clothes and slowly dressed, his eyes never leaving the sight of the gentle movement of Samantha's chest as it rose and fell with each breath she took.

He refused to let his need for her confuse him or lead him astray. He was here to correct the mistakes he had made in the past. If he could make sure Talamar married Gwain, then she wouldn't die and he would be free of the chokehold of his guilt. If he failed, then it would all happen again and Talamar would die. Even if he didn't love her as he once had, he still had to protect her and make sure things came out right.

He closed his eyes against the memory of Talamar's death and when he opened them again, Samantha was lying on her side, leaning on her elbow as she gazed up at him, a warm smile curving her lips.

"Hello, my consort. You have served your queen well. Now come back to bed and do it again."

Duncan swallowed hard and took a step back. "Sorry," he said, hearing the brusqueness of his voice but unable to prevent it. "There's something I need to take care of."

Sam blinked and the tender look faded from her gaze as she sat up. The coverlet fell away from her body, revealing her in all of her naked glory. "Right now?" she demanded.

The hard tone in her voice made his decision suddenly a lot easier. "Aye. Go to sleep, lass. Ye've got another big day tomorrow."

He headed out the door even as Samantha called after him.

"Duncan?" The first time her cry was almost a plea. He stumbled down the stone steps on the other side of the doorway before his conscience got the better of him.

"Duncan!" The second time it was a demand. Duncan strode across the village marketplace, not daring to look back.

"DUNCAN CAMPBELL GET BACK HERE!" The third time it was Samantha the queen and he could just about picture the fury on her face and the murder in her eyes.

Duncan kept walking. It was starting to rain and he welcomed the cold, wet punishment against his skin.

Someone was talking, disturbing her nap. Sam opened one eye and peered at the young woman kneeling in front of her. She was beautiful with her long, dark hair and dark blue eyes. What was in the water around here that the natives produced such perfectly featured children?

She was little more than a child, maybe sixteen. It was hard to readjust her thinking to this time period, when girls were given in marriage when they were twelve.

"Duncan, what does she want?" she asked crossly. She hadn't forgiven him for disappearing the night before. Brogan had coerced her into seeing petitioners again all morning and Duncan had reappeared right on schedule, just as the first one walked up.

After the last of the villagers had slipped away, happy as clams to have seen the queen, Duncan had spread a coarse blanket on the ground beside her bower and together they had enjoyed a good lunch of bread and cheese and apples, with some kind of boiled meat that was really tasty. She didn't ask what it was. She didn't want to know if she was eating squirrels or some other unappetizing fare.

After lunch, she'd slipped onto her couch and fallen asleep. Now, as she peeked out at the girl waiting in front of her, she saw that Duncan had stretched out on the blanket and fallen asleep too.

We should have gone back to the hut, she mused, *but we might not have slept much.*

She was still trying to sort out her feelings after their passionate lovemaking the night before. Duncan hadn't come back to bed at all and she had finally fallen asleep again. When she awakened, it was as if it had truly been a dream. But her body ached deliciously and she knew it had been all too real, just as the realization that she loved Duncan could no longer be denied.

Sam felt nervous and uneasy. She wasn't used to feeling this way, out of control, vulnerable. If Duncan found out, he would feel sorry for her, pity her, but he wouldn't love her. He already loved Talamar. So now she had to find a way to push the Scot out of her heart before it shattered. That meant no more late nights in his arms.

Yeah, so remember that next time, stupid.

Duncan spoke to the young girl kneeling in front of Sam, and the girl answered him in that strange, lilting language. Sam was still drowsy and only half listening to their conversation. Finally Duncan turned to her.

"She has a request for the queen," he said.

"Tell her I already closed the request line," she said with her eyes shut. "The wizard is gone for the day. Tell her to come back tomorrow."

"She's very upset. Can ye not listen to her?"

Sam opened her eyes and saw that once again, Duncan had a sympathetic gleam in his gaze. Why couldn't he ever look like that when she asked something of him?

"Fine," she said, pushing herself up to a sitting position. "What does she want? Freckle removal? A fertility potion? For me to put a hex on her mother?"

She scratched the back of her neck and got a sudden whiff of her own body odor. Ugh. How had Duncan tolerated her enough to make love to her? In spite of a sponge bath that morning with a bowl of water and a rag, she still smelled extremely ripe in her disheveled fairy gown.

Talamar was having some of the village women sew special clothing for the queen. Sam hadn't wanted to wait and told Duncan she'd take anything that was clean, but he'd cautioned her not to forget she was the queen of the fairies. To accept common clothing would be to cause suspicion.

"Funny," Duncan drawled, pulling her back to the matter at hand. "She wants ye to find her a husband."

"Maybe she could take you after I'm finished with you," she said, leaning back against the couch again.

Duncan's eyes sparkled as he turned back to the girl and spoke. Her blue eyes lit up, her rose-colored lips curving up as she boldly raked him over with her glance.

"Did you actually tell her that?" Sam asked in disgust.

He shrugged. "How was I to know, my queen? I might as well have a—what do you call it in your time—a backup."

"Very funny. Now tell her that I won't be finished with you for a long time—at least until you help me get out of here—don't say that part—so she shouldn't hold her breath."

Duncan related the message and the girl's face drooped in disappointment.

"Now she's heartbroken," Sam said with a sigh. "Tell her I'll try to find someone else for her. Someone a little younger and not such a grouch."

"Yes, my queen," Duncan said, amused. He spoke to the girl again, who nodded as she rose to her feet, then bowed and hurried away.

"What did you tell her?"

"That I'd meet her in the woods at midnight."

Sam narrowed her eyes at him. "If you get caught with some elder's daughter, don't expect me to come and bail you out." She stretched again. "Gosh, are you as bored as I am? What do people do around here for fun, besides watch the rain?"

"Most people are too busy just trying to survive to worry about fun, my queen," he said, lying down on the blanket again, leaning on one elbow as he faced her.

"And I'm so filthy," she complained, dragging one hand through her hair. "What I wouldn't give for a shower!"

Duncan lifted both brows. "Why don't you go to the spring?"

Sam's hand stilled in her hair. She lowered it as she slowly straightened on the wooden chaise. "Spring? There's a spring near here?"

"Of course. Dinna ye think they would have to have a source of water for the village?"

"But you didn't tell me."

One corner of his mouth quirked up. "Didn't I? My apologies, my queen."

Sam jumped up from the couch. "You—you—jerk!" she said, glaring down at him. "Talamar! Talamar, come here!"

The girl came running from one of the huts, her skirt lifted to clear the ground, her face anxious.

"Talamar," Sam said imperiously, "take me to the spring and bring me a towel and, oh, some soap, please."

The girl stared at her blankly and Sam shook her head, frustrated by her inability to communicate with her apart from Duncan.

"I'll take ye to the spring," Duncan said.

"No thanks! Just tell Talamar what I said," she ordered.

"Yer wish is my command, yer highness."

"And quit calling me that!"

"Yes, yer highness." He chuckled as he stood and talked to Talamar briefly.

The girl nodded and pointed to the woods, then bowed her head, obviously awaiting the queen's pleasure.

To her surprise, Duncan turned to her with apology in his eyes. "I'm sorry, lass," he said. "I truly dinna think to tell ye."

"Well, you should have," Sam grumbled.

"Aye. Still, I think I'd better go with ye, else how will ye communicate with yer handmaiden?"

"I'll manage." Sam took Talamar by the arm and turned her toward the forest. "In the meantime, why don't you go and do something constructive?"

"Aye, I could do that." He stroked his chin thoughtfully. "Or I could find young Diersa and help combat her loneliness."

"Diersa? Is that her name?" Sam asked. "It figures. Probably the equivalent of this century's 'Buffy' or 'Tiffany.'"

"Diersa?" Talamar asked, then spoke rapidly to Duncan. He threw his head back and laughed.

"What did she say?"

"She said to be careful of her cousin, Diersa, that she is a—" he paused.

"A ho?" Sam suggested.

He frowned at her. "I dinna ken what that means. But in my time we called such women a 'light skirt,' meaning one that would bed any man who looked at her twice."

"Then you'd better hurry," Sam said sweetly, "before someone else gets your place in line. C'mon, Talamar," she dragged the girl forward, "and for your sake, I hope there's a Jacuzzi in this damn spring."

Talamar led her deep into the forest, directing her to step over thick vines that crossed the hard-packed path evidently used often by the village. Sam enjoyed the walk, enjoyed burning off some energy. Duncan made her so angry. How dare he drop his veiled innuendoes? How dare he toy with her emotions? How dare he make love to her when he was in love with a teenybopper?

She walked right into Talamar and muttered an apology as she looked up. Talamar had stopped in the pathway and was gesturing for Sam to proceed her past a huge tree that looked as if it had been there since the dawn of time. Sam made her way around it and stopped, dumbstruck.

In front of her was one of the most beautiful sights she'd ever seen. In the midst of silver birch and black alder, juniper trees and rowan, a brook carved a curving path through the rock, sending sparkling water gushing down the slight incline and over round stones that formed a two-foot-high waterfall, splashing down into a pool big enough for two or three people.

"Talamar," she said with a sigh. "I forgive you everything."

Sam stripped off her clothes with a vengeance and stepped down into the clear pool of water. To her surprise and delight the water was warm. Apparently even Scotland had a few hot springs. The water came up to her waist and she sank down into the comforting warmth. What she wouldn't give for some scented candles and three or four Hershey bars. But she wasn't going to complain. No way.

The rocks lining the pool were stacked too neatly to be natural, and Sam realized someone had actually built this pool within the stream. Smart people. She hadn't given them enough credit. But she was willing to bet big money a woman had been behind it. With another heartfelt sigh, she leaned her head back against a stone.

Talamar leaned over the edge of the pool and pantomimed drying off, then disappeared into the forest, presumably to fetch a towel, or what passed for a towel in this century.

Sam closed her eyes and for the first time in months, felt every muscle in her body actually relax.

"Feeling better?" a deep voice asked.

Sam jerked her head backward in surprise, slamming it into the stone. Then she opened her eyes. Duncan knelt beside the brook, smiling down at her. Her first instinct was to cover her nakedness in the water, but then she reasoned it wasn't anything he hadn't seen before.

"Go away," she said.

"Sorry. Didn't mean to startle ye."

She closed her eyes. "Go away, Duncan."

There was silence and after a moment Sam felt a sharp stab of disappointment as she realized he must have left. She opened her eyes to find him exactly where he'd been before. But this time he wasn't looking at her face.

Suddenly she felt oddly exposed to him. As though she was baring more than her body, as if he could see all the feelings and emotions she tried so hard to hide. She sat up in the water, wrapping her arms across her breasts.

"Can't I have a moment's peace?" she demanded.

"I wanted to make sure ye were all right."

She looked at him warily. "Why? Never mind. I can't talk to you like this," she said, indicating her lack of clothing with a wave of her hand. "When Talamar brings my towel, then we'll talk."

He held up a large piece of thick cloth. "I brought it. After all, I am yer consort." He gestured to another pile of cloth beside him on the ground. "And I insisted on bringing ye some clean clothing. 'Tis the finest they have available until the women finish sewing yer queenly garments."

"Great," she said wearily. "All right, I'll get out, but first turn around."

"No need to disturb yourself." He pulled over his head the brown tunic he wore, and dropped it to the ground.

Sam's mouth went suddenly dry. It had been a long time since she'd seen Duncan without his shirt. Their fierce lovemaking the night before had been in near darkness. His broad chest was muscled, golden with a tan from the Texas sun, as well as a light dusting of hair curling there. His arms were thick and strong.

"What do you think you're doing?" she asked, willing strength into her suddenly choked voice.

"Takin' a bath," he said as he loosened the drawstring around his waist that held up the slim trousers all the men of the period wore. The pants fell to the ground and Sam instinctively closed her eyes. To look upon Duncan Campbell naked was to court disaster.

"Get in the water, Duncan," she said tersely.

She heard a splash and dared to open one eye halfway. Most of the Scot was safely underwater and she breathed a sigh of relief.

Duncan leaned back against the stone wall of the pool. His biceps gleamed in the sunlight that streamed through the treetops overhead and a fine stream of water ran down his furred chest. Water droplets glistened on his face and Sam once again had the urge to kiss his scar. She shook her head and forced her gaze away.

"You never answered my question yesterday."

"What question?"

"About getting the staff from Brogan so that I can get back to my father."

The tension around his mouth softened unexpectedly. "I've explained the difficulties there, lass. I'll do the best I can, but you may need to be a little patient."

"So why are you here invading my space instead of making sure Talamar marries whatsisname so I *can* go home. Patience is not one of my many virtues."

"Last night ye liked my invasion," he said softly.

Sam's gaze collided with his as his eyes caressed her face, then slipped down over her breasts. She could almost feel his touch. She refused to look below his chin, refused to notice how close to the water's surface certain parts of him were, refused to let his naked nearness distract her from her question, which, of course, was why he was naked at all. To distract her.

It was working.

"So let me ask you this—how does your deep and abiding love for Talamar work in with what happened last night?" she said, closing her eyes against the sight of him. "What am I, Duncan?" She opened her eyes, hoping he could see her anger and not her pain. "Just a good time?"

He looked away. "Lass, I'm sorry. I shouldna have taken ye last night. It wasna right."

Sam frowned. "What are you talking about? You didn't 'take' me. I gave myself to you."

"But ye were asleep, ye were exhausted. I took advantage and I'm ashamed."

She stood up in the waist-high water, completely furious. "Don't you dare pity me, Duncan Campbell. I knew exactly what I was doing and you did not take advantage of me."

His gaze swept over her body as the water from the ends of her hair ran down her breasts and pooled over her nipples before dripping in teardrops to the water below. He raised his burning blue eyes to hers.

"Good," he whispered. He cut through the water like a merman, clean and swift, his hands sliding around her waist, his arms flexing to bring her against him. "I'm glad to know that ye canna be coerced into anything ye dinna want to do."

Chapter Eleven

"That's right," she managed to answer, frozen in place against Duncan's wet, hard, dripping body.

Sam gasped as her cold, naked skin collided with his and he bent his head to hers, possessing her mouth for one searing moment before he slid down her body and took one breast between his lips.

Sam let her head drop back as her arms curved across his shoulders, helpless to do anything but feel his power and his need. The pleasure seemed to go on for hours as his mouth burned over her body and his fingers painted a path of fire across her back, across her shoulders, across her stomach and down, down, down to the part of her that cried out for his touch.

She sagged in the water and only Duncan's strength kept her aloft as he stroked her mouth above and her body below. Then, when she thought she could stand no more, that she would die if he didn't fill her with his heat, he stepped between the silk of her legs.

The sound of a man clearing his throat made Sam gasp and slide down into the water as Duncan turned with a scowl, his broad body blocking hers. He spoke sharply in the garbled almost-Gaelic and Sam made out his words—"What do you want?"

She peeked around Duncan's waist and saw it was Brogan standing above them beside the stream, the staff in his hand. Great. How would a fairy queen/goddess handle being caught in flagrante delecto by one of her priests?

The priest's voice was laced with apology, but Sam thought she detected something else in his tone. As Duncan lectured him, probably on the necessity of making his presence known a little sooner—who knew how long the man had been standing there—she peered around Duncan again in time to see a glint of suspicion dart through Brogan's dark brown eyes. She caught Duncan's last words.

"Leave us now!"

Brogan bowed and placed the staff on the ground, then walked quickly away. When she was sure he was gone, Sam moved toward the side of the pool again. Duncan moved to intercept her, blocking her way. He slid one hand up the side of her neck, cradling her face with his thumb along her cheek and his fingers tangled in the soft hair at the nape of her neck. He lowered his mouth almost to hers, stopping bare centimeters from her lips.

"Now, where were we?"

Samantha ran her tongue across her lips, hardened her heart, and pulled away from his gentle hands. "We were getting out of the water and using that staff to go back home. You did ask him to bring it. Thank you, Duncan."

Duncan looked away from her. "I asked him to bring it so that when the time is right, ye may return to yer own time," he said.

"Come back with me now, Duncan," she whispered. She moved against him, slipping her hands up around his neck again.

Duncan stared down into her eyes for a moment and then shook his head.

"I'm sorry, lass, I canna. And I canna let ye go either."

Sam bit back the sudden angry reply that rushed to her lips and backed away from him. "That's what you think," she whispered. She climbed out, dried off, and got dressed in record time.

The fresh clothing Duncan had brought for her felt warm and clean, but Sam barely noticed as she pulled the long, coarse, violet-colored dress over her head. She felt stunned and empty as she picked up the staff.

Duncan got out of the pool and stood dripping beside her. She met his challenging gaze coolly. He bent and grabbed his plaid from the ground and used it to dry off, then pulled on his clothes, never taking his eyes from her.

The crystals in the staff gleamed in the fading sunlight, but they gave off no inner glow of their own.

Duncan's dark brows knit together over stormy blue eyes.

"Don't look at me like that," she said.

"Give me the staff, lass," he said.

Samantha took a step back from him and tightened her grip on the wooden staff, her ticket home. "No."

Sam thought she saw a flash of pain in his eyes, but it was gone so fast she was left to wonder if it had been there at all.

"I am saddened for ye, Samantha," he said, taking another step forward.

"Why?" She put the staff behind her.

"Because ye dinna trust anyone. Ye dinna trust that I will get ye back to yer own time. Ye put on a grand show of needin' no one. Ye canna never risk opening yerself to anyone, not even yer best friends." He shook his head. "Not even yer father."

Once again Sam felt as if she had been struck. "Don't you dare talk about my father," she whispered. "You don't know anything about my relationship with him."

He cocked one brow. "Don't I?"

The wind picked up just then, lifting Duncan's waving hair, sending the dark brown strands back from the rugged lines of his face. She gazed at him for a long moment. In his olive green tunic and trews, with the stubble of beard across his face, he looked for all the world like a rugged Robin Hood. Too bad he had his own Maid Marian in this century.

"Yer father took a great liking to me," he went on, moving to sit on a large stone near the stream. "We used to sit in front of the fireplace in his den and talk."

Sam's throat tightened. "About me?"

"He loved ye dearly. He was verra proud of ye."

She whirled. "He's not dead. Don't talk as if he is."

"Ye treated him like he was, most of his life," he said.

"I didn't."

"Ye did. Disregarding anything he ever told ye, going yer own way no matter what he advised. Dating any man that ye knew would break his heart."

"He tried to control my entire life!" Sam shouted, pushed beyond her control. "And nothing I ever did was good enough! Nothing! He said terrible things to me!" But how could Duncan understand the hurt that her father's criticism had left in her soul? How could he understand that the last thing he'd ever said to her was an expression of his disappointment in her?

"Och, did he now?"

"Yes!" She spat the word out.

"Well, then that's different. When I was a lad, my father told me that he wished I'd never been born. I suppose yer father must have said something similar to ye." He stood, his hands at his side, his voice even.

Sam frowned. His father had said that? What an awful thing to say to a child. "No, of course my father never said that."

Duncan walked a few steps to the side and casually glanced down at the spring beside them. "My father once beat me until I couldna walk and he couldna lift his arm again." He glanced over at her. "I suppose yer father was a harsh taskmaster as well."

Sam ran her tongue over her lips, trying to ignore the sharp stab of sympathy his words sent into her heart. She could imagine a young Duncan taking his punishment stoically, locking his jaw against the pain as he fought to keep from crying out.

"No," she finally said. "Of course he wasn't, at least not like that. He never raised his hand against me."

"Och, I see." Duncan nodded. "Of course, there are other kinds of abuse. He must have called ye names."

"No."

"Made fun of ye?"

"Of course not."

He nodded again. "So what ye are saying is that yer father never abused ye, never shamed ye, and in fact, was more proud of ye than any man could ever be."

"No," she whispered. Her hands loosened around the staff and it sagged sideways toward Duncan. "He wasn't proud of me."

"Of course he was."

Duncan stepped forward and jerked the staff out of her hand. Startled, Sam lunged for it, but he grabbed her around the waist and held her, even as he moved the staff out of reach.

"Give it to me, Duncan."

"Sorry, lass. I told ye, when I finish what I came here to do, I'll help ye return. Until then, ye'll have to be patient."

For a moment as Duncan gazed down at her, Sam saw the familiar fire ignite in his blue eyes. He still wanted her. He loved another woman, but he wanted her.

"Let me go," she said between clenched teeth.

His fingers flexed against her back, and then he slowly released her. Sam turned and started back through the forest.

"Where are ye goin'?" he asked.

She stopped in her tracks. "I don't know," she said, determined not to cry in front of him. "But don't try to stop me."

Duncan started to say something, but instead, turned on his heel and headed the other way.

By the end of the second week of their stay in the past, Sam had just about had it. Trying to come up with the appropriate responses and remain kind and benevolent all day, every day, as a steady stream of petitioners came to her, was draining her completely.

Not to mention the fact that she was dealing with a growing depression over Duncan's fears about her traveling through time alone. Not to mention the fact that he had hidden the staff with the crystals. Brogan was not amused. Not to mention the fact that she was in love with a time-traveling jerk who was in love with someone else.

After she'd gotten over her initial anger, Sam'd realized that his refusal to let her try it alone must mean he cared something about her. But not enough, apparently, to leave history to its own devices and help her return to her father.

Weary from day after day of hearing the villager's requests, she'd finally asked Duncan to tell Brogan that she would only see petitioners in the mornings, every other day. To hell with this benevolent matriarch crap. What use was there in being a queen if you couldn't make the rules?

Too bad she couldn't make up some rules that Duncan would have to obey, like making love to her at least every other night. Since their argument at the spring they'd maintained a cool civility in their dealings as queen and consort. In public, he was courteous and did a lot of hand-kissing. In private, he barely spoke to her.

Now that the morning's line of supplicants had finally all been seen, Sam lay on the chaise lounge beneath her flowery bower enjoying listening to Talamar as she strummed a four-stringed instrument and sang. She had a lovely voice. Of course she did. Everything about Talamar was lovely.

Sam sighed and then stretched, enjoying the feel of her new clothing. She'd made a very queen-like decision a few days before and had informed Talamar— through Duncan of course—that she wanted the village seamstresses to make not dresses for her clothing, but tunics and trews like the men in the village.

Talamar had been openly shocked, but had bobbed her head in acknowledgement.

At least now if Sam had to stay in this time period a little longer, she would be warmer and more comfortable. The dresses Talamar had been suppling up to this point were beautiful, but a tad chilly. Today, though, she wore a long-sleeved tunic made from a soft wool and dyed to a beautiful golden color, with trews of a soft brown. Her blond hair took on a new sheen against the cloth.

Talamar had provided four brand new sets of clothing, tunics and trews, and one dress that Talamar had insisted on. The village cobbler had made her a pair of soft brown boots to go with them and for the first time in days, Sam felt like her old self. Sort of. But it was okay. It was all okay. This was all temporary. Just temporary. She'd find a way to get home.

Sam glanced around. Not a sign of Duncan, as usual. For the last few days he had appeared briefly every morning to translate the requests of the villagers, and then disappeared again until the evening meal. He would eat, pretend to adore her, and then disappear until well after she'd gone to sleep. Fine, that was fine. The less she had to see him, the better.

Every time she looked at him all she could think of was the night he'd made love to her and then that moment in the spring when she'd thought, oh so briefly, that he might truly care for her.

Sam shook her head, as though she could banish all thoughts of Duncan. She was restless. If she had to stay in this time for a while, she had to do more than lie around all day.

She glanced over at her handmaiden, clad today in a dark green long-sleeved gown with a sleeveless overgown of brown. Talamar looked like a wood nymph. With sudden inspiration, Sam interrupted Talamar's singing.

"Talamar."

The girl stopped plucking the strings and looked up. Sam hesitated. Duncan was nowhere in sight to translate her idea.

Sam straightened. This was ridiculous. She could communicate with Talamar, surely, if only through sign language and the little bit of their Gaelic tongue she'd managed to pick up. She didn't need Duncan. She didn't need him at all. With a queenly smile, she "walked" two fingers across the wood of the chaise lounge, and then pointed to the forest behind them.

Talamar nodded eagerly in answer to the question, and set aside her instrument. Samantha rose and gathered up a few loose flowers that some of the villagers had brought her that day.

I could get used to being worshipped, she thought. She turned and walked toward the forest, with Talamar close behind.

At first she had hated the girl, especially after learning she was Duncan's "lost love," and in the beginning Sam had worked her handmaiden hard—go here, fetch that, brush this, and on and on, relentlessly.

But the girl had been so willing, so sweet-natured in doing everything she asked, that by the end of their first week together, Sam had realized she couldn't keep up her arrogant demands, not even to make Duncan mad—and it did make him oh, so mad. And she couldn't hate someone as sweet and guileless as Talamar. Not even if Duncan Campbell was in love with her.

Duncan had made a fervent, steely-jawed vow to make sure she got back home as quickly as possible. His promise was not so much reassuring as it was insulting. He'd made it clear that he would be happy to be rid of her.

The girl dipped in a curtsy and said something too quickly for Sam to understand. She shook her head and Talamar repeated the sentence. Sam still didn't get it and shook her head again. Talamar moved ahead on the path leading into the forest and gestured for the queen to follow her. Picking up her skirt, Sam hurried after her, wishing fervently for an old pair of jeans and a warm sweater.

Each and every morning of her stay in Nirdagh, she woke up to find clean clothing at the end of her bed. Today she had donned the plain, deep violet gown left there, along with an undershift.

As Sam walked behind Talamar she adjusted the rhinestone-studded belt housing the holographic equipment. She continued to wear it every day just in case she needed to prove her magical abilities on the spur of the moment.

In addition, she also wore a small red velvet drawstring purse around her waist. Talamar had left it for her one morning and Sam quite liked the look of it. She'd drawn its dangling handle under her belt to hold it at her side; it added a splash of color against the brown.

Before long Sam caught up with a smiling Talamar. She stood in a small clearing that gave way to five new trails leading in five different directions.

Sam wished she could ask where all the trails led, but what would be the point? Even if she knew how to ask, she wouldn't be able to understand more than a word or two of what the girl said. She blew out her breath in exasperation. It was so awful not being able to communicate on her own, and even worse, to have to depend on Duncan.

Talamar was ahead of her again, moving uphill, and Sam followed, until at last she looked up to find her guide had stopped. They had walked all the way through the forest and had arrived at the top of a hill. Sam blinked in amazement. Huge neolithic stones with beautiful carvings of swirls and figures on their sides created a circle around the edge of the craggy mound.

A fairy ring.

Sam stared at the ancient artifacts and began walking toward them. A brisk breeze swept down through the clearing and she stumbled to a stop as she recognized the smell of salt. The sea. It would be wonderful to see the ocean. Duncan had told her, during a rare conversation, that it was nearby. She suspected he was spending most of his time there when he wasn't trailing Talamar around the village.

He followed the girl constantly. Not overtly. To the casual eye he was gazing out at the forest, or talking to an old lady peeling apples over near the common kitchen, but Sam knew what he was really doing. He was watching over Talamar. And yet she never saw him approach the girl.

One night, when Duncan hadn't come to bed, she'd gone outside, determined to catch him in the act of making mad, passionate love to the young princess. Instead, she'd found him sitting on a rock in the marketplace, staring up at the night sky, looking more forlorn than anyone she'd ever seen. She ducked behind a tree before he saw her and hurried back to their cabin, knowing that nothing in the world could make Duncan Campbell look so sad but unrequited love.

And yet she didn't resent Talamar. It wasn't her fault that Duncan was in love with her. She didn't act as if she knew the man existed most of the time, though she was polite whenever he spoke to her. It was obvious Talamar gave Duncan the respect due the fairy queen's consort, and nothing more.

I didn't come out here to think about Duncan, Sam admonished herself. I came out here to have some fun.

With that in mind, Sam practically skipped into the ring of stones, intent on catching a glimpse of the sea. Almost at once, Talamar started shouting. Sam stopped and turned back toward the girl with a frown. She couldn't understand what the girl was saying, but from the way she was standing outside the circle, waving her arms and motioning for Sam to come back to her, it was obvious that Talamar didn't want Sam to go inside the circle. Sam hesitated. The girl's face was wreathed in fear.

"How do I say, 'It's okay'?" Sam muttered. She settled on smiling broadly at the girl and waving. Talamar shook her head at her and motioned to her again.

"I'm just going to look at the ocean," Sam called, trying not to sound impatient. "I am, after all, the freaking queen of the fairies, so I guess I can walk through their fairy ring." She turned to continue her way through the ring, when suddenly Talamar was at her side, dragging her backward.

"What do you think you're doing?" she said, trying to keep her footing as the girl pulled her by the arm to a place a few feet outside of the stone ring. She frowned at Talamar and turned to go back into the ring.

Talamar shouted a word Sam had come to understand, since the girl used it so often.

"Please!" Talamar cried and grabbed her again.

Sam looked down at the hand gripping her arm. She

171

frowned and Talamar quickly let go. "I want to see the ocean, do you understand o-cean?"

Talamar began to babble again, pointing in the opposite direction, almost grabbing Samantha's arm, and then jerking her hand back. There was such a frantic look on her face that Sam finally gave in.

"All right, all right! I'll come back later—by myself!" she added, and followed the girl down the path leading away from the stones.

They returned to the clearing and this time Talamar chose a different, narrower avenue. She paused, making sure Sam was behind her, then led Sam deeper into the forest, where the trees grew closer together and most of the sunlight was blocked by the intertwined branches and leaves above.

Sam slowed her pace as the calm of the quiet forest spoke to her soul. There was a lot to be said for peace, she decided; if only she could find a little for her mind as well.

The girl stopped ahead beside a huge boulder—it was amazing that Scotland hadn't sunk into the ocean from the sheer weight of all the rocks on top of the country—and Sam halted beside her.

"All right," she said, then switched to her broken Gaelic. "I am here. What?"

Talamar frowned and Sam knew she had once again butchered a sentence, so she just lifted both hands and shrugged, hoping it translated to "Well? What do you want?"

Talamar smiled and pointed to another rock dwarfed by the huge one.

"Okay, another rock, what's so special about—" Sam quit talking and stared. It wasn't another rock, it was a giant *egg*.

172

Chapter Twelve

Three feet tall and about two feet wide, the shell of the egg was a pale blue with splotches of pale green here and there and one deep ochre spot in the middle.

"What is it?" Sam whispered.

Talamar said something she couldn't understand.

"What? I don't know those words. Can I touch it?" Sam stroked the air around the egg and looked to Talamar for permission.

The girl nodded eagerly. Sam sank down to her knees in front of the amazing discovery, wondering why she felt so drawn to the huge egg. It was like a fascinating sculpture. She ran her hands lightly over the smooth surface.

"It's so beautiful," she said. "Is it a dinosaur egg? No, dummy, they didn't have dinosaurs in this time period." She glanced up. "I wish I could really talk to you." Talamar watched her, uncomprehending. "Talk?" Sam opened and closed her mouth and then pointed back at the girl. "Understand?"

Talamar frowned, then her face lit up and she nodded, beckoning Sam to follow her once again. Curious, Sam stood and hurried after her. The girl led her around the huge boulder to the other side where to her surprise, Sam saw that it wasn't a boulder at all, but a cave. She stared at the twenty-foot-high entrance, wondering what the dark interior held. As Talamar waved toward the opening, Sam realized she needn't have wondered. They were going inside.

Talamar walked into the cave, and when Sam didn't immediately follow her, she came back, an anxious expression on her face.

"Are you sure this is safe?" Sam said, as she followed the girl into the cave. She glanced up as Talamar gestured again for her to follow. "I just hope there aren't any bats in here."

While the entrance was broad and high, as Sam moved farther into the cave she discovered that the ground sloped suddenly downward and she had to duck to keep from hitting her head on the rocks above. The broad walls of the cave narrowed to a passageway about four feet wide, and Sam had a moment of claustrophobia before the walls widened again. The pathway ended in a huge cavern and Sam looked up, stumbling to a stop, absolutely stunned.

The high ceiling of the cavern, as well as the walls, were covered in crystals, beautiful multicolored crystals. They lit the room, filled with their own luminescence, reminding Sam of the way the green crystals in Jacob's Well had glowed. The predominant color of the crystals seemed to be lavender, but there were spots of blue crystals as well, and a few clear diamondlike formations. With a surge of excitement, Sam searched the vast expanse of crystalline for green crystals but, to her disappointment, couldn't see a one.

Talamar started chattering, waving first toward a blue crystal and then a lavender, apparently trying to tell Sam something about the beautiful creations. Sam let her talk as she moved to one curved wall where a nest of clear crystals jutted out in a quartzlike formation.

"They are so beautiful," she whispered, and, unable to resist, reached out and touched one diamondlike gem. The crystal had six nonsymmetrical sides and was about an inch in diameter and four or five inches long. It was the most dazzling thing she'd ever seen.

"I hope, my queen, that ye are pleased with my care of yer precious gems," Talamar was saying, "I havena allowed any to be touched or removed, except for the ones ye gave me. I have awaited ycr return."

"That's fine," Sam said, turning to smile at the girl, "because I think that—"

Her mouth fell open. Talamar had spoken to her and she had understood every word she said! Sam rushed over to the girl.

"Say that again," she said. "Talk to me!"

Talamar smiled and shook her head. She said something in her odd language and Sam couldn't understand but a word or two.

"Am I going nuts? I understood you a second ago as plain as day!" She stared at the girl, who didn't seem perplexed at all. Sam pantomimed talking with her hand, and then looked questioningly at Talamar, who nodded eagerly and crossed over to the clear crystal formation.

Sam followed more slowly. Talamar pointed to the crystal and as Sam drew near, the girl hesitantly extended her hand. Sam hesitated too, but finally surrendered her own hand. Talamar began talking again as she placed her queen's fingers on the clear crystal.

"Do ye not remember, my queen, how this fairy stone allows us to speak to one another?" she said, her words spoken in the clearest English Sam had ever heard.

"Of—of course," Sam said. "I—I had forgotten."

"I am sorry, my queen, that I did not bring ye here before," Talamar said anxiously. "I supposed that for some reason ye dinna want to use the stones this time."

"No, I just misplaced mine and—" Sam stopped. "This time?"

"Aye, my queen. And now that we can understand each other, may I tell ye that this incarnation of yerself is the most beautiful one of all!"

"Yes, er, thank you, Talamar." *This incarnation?* Sam's brain was on overload. Was the girl trying to say that she had actually spoken to the fairy queen before? Sam dragged in a deep breath and tried to keep her equilibrium. The crystals, she had to focus on the crystals and find out if they were like the green ones that had sent her and Duncan through time.

"I would like to test your knowledge of the stones," she said, thinking fast.

"Yes, my queen?"

"Tell me what magic the blue and lavender stones hold."

Talamar dipped her head. "Yes, my queen. The lavender stones hold the power of contentment. All who wear this sacred stone are blessed with a feeling of peace and good temperament." She touched the neckline of her *leine*. A leather cord was looped around her neck and disappeared under her garment. "I am never without mine."

Sam nodded and gazed back up at the sparkling

sight above her. "Do all the villagers have one of these crystals?"

Talamar looked confused. "No, my queen. Ye have given only myself permission to wear yer stones. Not even Brogan knows of them, except for those in his staff."

"Of course," Sam said hastily, "I knew that. I was just—er—testing you."

Talamar smiled and inclined her head again. "Thank ye, my queen."

"And what of the blue crystals?" Sam said, trying to assume a more haughty air. She'd really let that queenly attitude slide and it took a little effort to get it back. "Do you know of their powers?"

"Aye, my queen," Talamar said with another brief curtsy. "The blue stones hold the magic of healing."

"Healing?" Samantha echoed the word. "You mean you can use it, to heal someone from sickness? I mean, tell me how it is used."

"The healing stone is verra unpredictable," the girl said. "At times it will heal completely, and at other times only causes the sick one to improve somewhat."

A healing crystal! If she could get back to her father, she could use the magical stone to heal him! She had to return home before it was too late. As if she could read Sam's mind, Talamar spoke again.

"It canna bring one back from the dead, of course."

Sam's eyes widened. "No, no, of course it can't," she agreed.

"For death and life are in the hands of the good God," she said, then added, "Oh, and the blue crystals can only be used once." Talamar looked at Sam, an expectant expression on her face, and Sam suddenly remembered she was supposed to be quizzing the girl.

"Excellent," Sam said, "I'm very proud of you."

Talamar bit her lower lip and ducked her head with pleasure. She was an odd combination of beauty and shyness, and suddenly the girl reminded Sam of both Chelsea and Jix. The thought of her friends sent a pang through her heart. She had to get back to them and to her father. She knew what her next question would be.

"Very good, indeed. Excellent. But, Talamar, where are my green crystals? I confess, it has been so long since I was here that I do not remember if they were in this cavern or not."

Talamar gave her a strange look, but answered. "No, my queen. Because the green crystals are forbidden to all humans, ye hid them and dinna tell anyone where they are. The only green crystals are those in the staff of the high priest, which ye rendered impotent."

"Brogan is impotent? Oh, you mean the crystals, of course." Of course. Riley's luck.

"Only yer magic can cause the crystals in the staff to work again. That is one reason I knew it was ye in the glen. The crystals were glowing!"

"Very good, Talamar." Her thoughts were racing. Surely there must be something she could learn from the girl about the time travel crystals. Perhaps something about the way they worked.

"Tell me, why do the green crystals work at some times and not at others?"

"The magic of the green crystals is connected with the magic of nature itself."

"What do you mean?" Sam ran her fingers across the clear crystal again.

"With nature—the creations of the good God," Talamar clarified.

"You mean like plants? Things that grow?"

"Earth, wind, fire, air—all of creation interconnects with the green crystals, for only then, as ye taught me yerself, may the energy of life be fashioned into the portal opening to other worlds." She smiled. "But ye also taught me that the crystals seem to do as they will, at times."

Sam tried to keep her surprise from showing. Talamar knew that the green crystals allowed people to travel through time. She supposed Talamar viewed it as just another magical power of the fairies. "Very good again, Talamar. Er, why then are the green crystals usually found in water?"

"Are they, my queen? This I did not know. Thank ye for granting me such knowledge."

Oops.

"Should we be returning to the village, my queen?" Talamar asked. "It will be dark soon."

"Yes, we'd better go, but tell me, is there a way we can take a piece of this clear crystal with us so that you and I may always be able to converse?" Sam smiled at Talamar.

"There are some smaller crystals, which have fallen to the ground, my queen," Talamar said, crossing the cave and pointing to a small collection of the precious stones. "Choose whichever pleases ye, and I will fashion a necklace for ye."

"Wonderful." Sam moved to kneel beside the sparkling brilliantly colored gems. She selected a clear crystal about a half of an inch in diameter and about two inches long, then picked up a bigger blue one, and after a moment's hesitation, a smaller lavender one. "Never know when you might need one of these," she said.

"Yes, my queen."

Sam drank in the awe-inspiring sight of the crystal

cavern once more, and then turned to go. She couldn't wait to tell Duncan about this—or wait a minute— why should she tell him? Maybe she'd just pretend that she had learned the language Talamar spoke all by herself! A smile curved her lips. It would serve the arrogant jerk right.

After giving Talamar careful instructions not to reveal the cave to anyone else, even Duncan, Sam followed her back into the sunlight. She breathed a sigh of relief. While the cave had been fascinating, there was something about it that left a feeling of uneasiness in her bones. As they passed the big egg she gave it a pat, resolving to visit it again to see if it would hatch. It would help pass the time and she was curious about what might be inside.

They headed back the way they had come, through the forest, until they returned to the clearing. Sam stopped and looked in the direction of the standing stones. Talamar stood uncertainly beside her.

"All right," Sam said, "now that I can understand you, why don't you want me to go and look at the ocean from the cliff? I promise you I won't fall in." She smiled at the girl whose face had turned ashen.

"Please, my queen, do not leave me yet. There is so much I wish to speak to ye about."

"Leave you?" Sam gestured toward the path leading to the cliff and the stones. "You mean if I go inside the ring it will take me away?"

Talamar shook her head. "Please, my queen, do not jest with me. Danger is coming to Nirdagh, and we need your help."

Sam let the girl pull her back along the path toward the village, but she kept glancing back.

Maybe there was another way back home besides the green crystals.

* * *

Duncan watched Talamar and Samantha come back to the village. He fully trusted Talamar to take care of the queen, and had been glad to learn an hour before from one of the villagers that the two had gone for a walk in the forest. He hoped that perhaps the two women might begin building a friendship. There was no real way to know how long he and Samantha would have to stay in the past. It wouldn't hurt Samantha to have a friend.

Samantha and Talamar paused in the middle of the mostly deserted square and spoke fervently to one another. Duncan sat up straighter. Spoke to one another?

He stood and waited until Talamar moved off, no doubt running yet another errand for her queen, before crossing casually to Samantha.

"Have a nice walk?" he asked.

Sam glanced up at him. He knew her well enough by now to know when she was hiding something. Whatever it was, it was something big. She was practically vibrating with excitement.

"Yes, we had a lovely walk," Samantha said, moving past him. Duncan caught up and fell into step beside her.

"Where did ye go?"

"Oh, just around, you know, she took me into the forest, showed me the neighborhood 7-Eleven, that kind of thing."

"Verra funny. Where did ye really go?"

Sam stopped walking, her stubborn chin thrust toward him. "I don't have to tell you where I went, Duncan. You certainly don't keep me apprised of your whereabouts."

"Did Talamar show you something special?" he insisted.

An enigmatic smile curved across Sam's lips. "Yes, as a matter of fact, she did."

"What?"

Her lashes dipped down and then back up as her unnaturally lavender eyes gleamed in triumph. "Probably not the same special thing she showed you," she said, "but pretty amazing all the same."

She walked away, a swing to her hips, and Duncan ran one hand through his hair and followed.

"Samantha," he called. She stopped and waited for him. "I need to talk to ye."

"Really? Well, that's too bad, because I'm busy. Talamar and I have things to do."

"The two of ye seem to be getting along well."

Sam looked thoughtful, and surprisingly complacent. "Yes," she said, "she's a nice girl. She reminds me of Jix and Chelsea combined. She has Jix's exuberance for life tempered by Chelsea's shyness."

Duncan couldn't help but smile at the mental image those words invoked. "Aye, I have seen some of both in her myself. So," he went on, "ye aren't finding the language barrier such a deterrent anymore?"

She shook her head, the soft blond hair sliding across her shoulders, bringing back the memory of an all-too-recent night when the sweet-smelling locks had spilled over her shoulder and onto his chest as she devoured his lips like a woman starved for love. He blinked and pushed the images away.

"Oh, no," she said, "I'm starting to catch on to the language rather quickly. Talamar's helping me." She turned and headed toward their hut.

Duncan didn't follow. He was afraid to be alone with Sam when she was awake. Every night he swore to himself he wasn't going to go back to the hut, that he would sleep under the stars, and every night he eventually returned to the hut to lie beside her.

In the last two weeks he had tried to feel again his old love for Talamar, if only to convince himself that he had truly ever loved her.

But no matter how many times he approached Talamar and spoke to her, once even taking her hand, he felt no more for her than the affection of a friend. He would protect her, yes. He would make sure that she married the right man, yes. But he did not love her and never would. He was lost to the passion of a blond-haired goddess; Samantha had thoroughly enchanted him and he had eyes for no other.

For the first time in a long time, he was afraid; afraid he truly did love Samantha; afraid if he told her, she would expect him not only to go with her to her time, but to stay there.

Could he stay with her in the future? Could he resign himself to never returning to his own time of 1601 again? Now that he could make right what he'd done to Talamar, afterward there would be nothing stopping him from returning to his own time, his own home. Nothing except taking Samantha home again. But if Jix Ferguson's theories were true, the crystals allowed travelers to return to their homes when the time was right.

Perhaps once he'd made sure Talamar would be safe, and Samantha was reunited with her father, the time would be right for him to return home.

Return to what?

The question spun around his mind, but he cared not for the answer. He would return to duty, to his father, to marrying a woman of his father's choice. He would return to the responsibilities he had deserted so long ago.

But he would leave Samantha behind in 2005. He would never ask her to stay with him in the barbaric past.

Duncan dragged his fingers through his hair and started toward the hut, then stopped. Finally he turned and went the other way.

Sam entered their cottage and was happy to see that someone—probably on Talamar's orders—had a blazing fire going. The days were growing rapidly colder. Or maybe Duncan had done it. He wasn't a lazy man, she'd give him that.

She sat down on the bed and opened her hand to stare down at the blue, lavender, and clear crystals in her hand.

The more she thought about it, the more sure she was that Duncan must have known about these crystals. He had traveled through time over and over again, but she'd never even thought to ask him how he managed to communicate with all the people he'd met throughout the past.

And while Duncan knew Gaelic fluently of course, the language spoken in the ninth century had to be vastly different from that of 1601. If it turned out that he had let her struggle through two weeks of listening to him translate what all those villagers were asking, she might just drive one of these crystals through his heart.

She stroked the clear crystal and unbidden, a different image came to her mind, an image of Duncan driving himself into her, hot and hard in the night. He hadn't made love to her since her "dream" and she missed him with an ache hidden deep inside of her.

Sam put the crystals back in her velvet bag and lay back on the bed, staring at the ceiling, wishing Duncan were there beside her, wishing he would come to her in her dreams again, her dreams that were reality. She fell asleep, dreaming of Duncan, but in the morning when she awoke, she was alone.

Chapter Thirteen

"What's wrong, Talamar?" Sam asked.

It was so wonderful to actually be able to speak to the young woman. Since their day at the cave the two had quickly become good friends, and on this unusually sunny afternoon they sat picnicking beside the spring, after enjoying a leisurely soak.

Talamar's red-gold hair had a natural wave that was beautiful, and as she watched it dry, long and lustrous, Sam felt a twinge of jealousy, but pushed it away. It was like being jealous of a teenager. And today Talamar looked like a very unhappy teen. She seemed sad or worried.

She looked up at Sam's question, her eyes somber. "I was just thinking how much I will miss the spring, and Nirdagh."

Sam frowned. "Miss it? Why? Where are you going?"

The girl began packing their uneaten food back into the beautiful woven basket. "After my marriage to Laird Gwain, I will return with him to his home in Innisbar."

"Who is Laird Gwain?" Sam asked.

"He is laird over much of this part of Caledonia. He is the best choice for a husband for me."

"The best choice?" Sam stopped with a roast leg of some kind of fowl halfway to her mouth. She lowered it. "Do you love him?"

Talamar shrugged. "I dinna know the man."

Sam shook her head. "Then I don't understand. Why are you going to marry him?"

Talamar folded a cloth napkin and laid it carefully into the basket, her eyes downcast. She obviously was trying to hide her real feelings. "It isna my decision," she said.

"Oh?" A prickle of suspicion ran up Sam's spine. "Then whose is it?"

"The elders and the high priest."

"Why? Why do they want you to marry this man?" Sam had an idea what was coming. She'd read enough romance novels to know that in the past women were given in marriage to forge alliances or gain property. The girl's next words confirmed her thoughts.

"Villages up and down the coast have been attacked and invaded by the Danes. We fear we will be next, and Laird Gwain offers protection."

"In return for you, right?" Sam sat back, shaking her head. "And you've agreed to this?"

"I canna allow the people of the village, who depend upon me, to suffer just because I dinna want to marry the man. 'Twould not be so bad if it wasn't that—" she stopped.

"If it wasn't what?" Sam leaned toward her.

Talamar looked up, her eyes bright with unshed

tears. "If it wasn't that I love another man." A sob broke free from her as she bent her head, her shoulders shaking with silent emotion.

Sam brushed one long lock of hair back from the girl's face, her chest tightening with apprehension. "And who is it that you love?"

Talamar shook her head, her fingers pressed to her lips. "Oh, my queen, I beg ye, do not ask me to say."

Sam sighed. Of course Talamar didn't want to tell her. Duncan was the queen's consort. The poor girl probably thought if she admitted her love for him, the queen would turn her into a frog or something. She drew in a deep breath.

"And what if I, queen of the Tuatha De Danaan, told you not to marry Laird Gwain?"

Talamar's head came up and a tentative light shone in her gaze. "But, my queen, then what of my village? My people?"

Sam snorted in disgust. "From the looks of those huntsmen who brought us into the village that first day, I'd say there was no shortage of able-bodied men for defense!"

"Aye," she agreed, "but the invaders have better weapons, and more men. Laird Gwain would provide both for our protection."

Samantha's mind raced. There had to be a way to solve both problems. "A tribute could be paid to Laird Gwain," she said, then leaned forward, suddenly inspired with the answer. "I will offer Laird Gwain some of the magical blue healing crystals in return for his protection of the village."

Talamar's mouth dropped open. "Ye would do that for me? To keep me from a loveless marriage?"

Sam swallowed hard as she suddenly realized that

by saving the girl from this man, Gwain, she was leaving her available for Duncan.

"Yes," she said resolutely. "Love is part of the life energy that keeps our world in balance. When that energy is abused by human beings, it disrupts the flow of nature." She smiled, impressed with her spur of the moment explanation.

Talamar stared at her, her lower lip quivering, then she threw herself prostrate on the ground and wept, her body shaking with convulsive sobs.

Sam didn't know what to do. Extreme emotion in the form of tears was something she wasn't accustomed to dealing with. Jix always covered her pain with jokes and laughter. Chelsea used logic. She hid her own pain with anger or sarcasm. Tears didn't usually enter into the mix.

She patted the girl gingerly on the back. "Don't cry, Talamar," she said uncertainly. "Everything is going to be all right. You'll see."

Talamar looked up, her face streaked with tears, her smile lit from within. "May the good God bless ye, my queen," she whispered. "I am yer obedient servant, today and forever."

Sam shook her head and to her own surprise, reached out and smoothed Talamar's tears from her cheek. "No, sweetie," she said, "you are my friend, and from this day forth you will not walk behind me, but at my side."

The girl was openly shocked. "Oh, no, my queen, I could not. 'Twould not be seemly."

Sam rose to her feet, assuming her queenly air. "But I decree it," she said. "It is my wish. Are you saying you oppose your queen's wishes?"

Talamar gulped and flattened herself back against the ground. "Oh, no, my queen, never, never!"

189

Sam grinned, but felt an unfamiliar pang of compassion. She'd never wanted a little sister, but maybe it wouldn't have been so bad. She knelt down and took Talamar's hand, pulling her up with her until she was standing at her side.

"I'll talk to the elders and Brogan," she said. "It's time these big strong men stopped hiding behind little girls." She patted her hand and drew her along beside her. "And then later, you and I are going to have a long talk about women's rights."

"What are ye trying to do?" Duncan demanded.

Samantha looked up, startled, and plunged the carved bone needle she held into her middle finger.

"Ow!" She glared at the man. "What are you trying to do? Give me blood poisoning? There's no telling where this needle has been."

She stuck the needle into the leather she had spent the last hour trying to fashion into a large shoulder bag. During her walks in the forest recently, she'd seen herbs that might come in handy around the village and she wanted something besides a basket to gather them in.

It had been a week since Talamar had taken her to the crystal cave and the days had been long and boring, outside of her daily walk to visit the egg. The villagers wouldn't allow her to do a thing. No cooking, no cleaning, nothing. After their picnic that day, she'd asked Talamar for ideas on something to occupy the rest of the afternoon.

Embroidery, Talamar had explained hesitantly, was the only work for ladies and queens.

So of course, Sam had promptly asked for leather, leather cording, and a large needle. Now she tossed the leather beside her on the chaise lounge. The late afternoon breeze lifted her hair and sent it drifting against her face. She raked it back with one hand while she examined her finger. It was just a small puncture wound. She spared a thought for tetanus but dismissed it as wasted energy. There was nothing she could do about it anyway.

Duncan continued to glare down at her and Sam fought the urge to stick out her tongue. Instead, she stuck her finger in her mouth and glared back.

He looked wonderful in spite of the daggers he was shooting her with his eyes. The long-sleeved gray leine he wore was a little too small and showed off his broad shoulders to their best advantage. The ninth century version of a shirt reached past his hips and a broad leather belt was buckled over it at the waist. Leather leggings clung to Duncan's muscled thighs, disappearing into knee-high, roughed-out leather boots.

Sam found she wasn't breathing. She drew in a deep, ragged breath and reminded herself that he was an insufferable jerk, but then realized that as a deterrent the thought was losing strength. She loved him anyway, damn it.

"For your information," she told Duncan, her words garbled around her hurt finger. "I'm trying to stay busy so I don't go out of my mind."

"I'm not talking about yer sewing." he said. Sam lowered her finger, her pain forgotten. Duncan was upset, really upset about something.

"Then what are you talking about?"

"Why are ye interfering in Talamar's life?"

"Oh, she told you?" Sam picked up the leather and needle again and frowned down at the small bloodstain on her new clothing. Great.

"Nay," he said, "I overheard her telling a friend. Ye

canna go sticking yer nose in the business of this village."

"Why not? I'm their queen, aren't I?"

"Ye dinna know anything about this time period or how things work. Dinna be filling Talamar's head with yer women's lovers nonsense here."

"Stop frowning at me," she said with a yawn. "How many times do I have to remind you that you aren't the boss of me?" She stood and brushed off the leggings she wore.

"Stop it," he ordered.

"Stop what?"

"Stop interfering in Talamar's marriage."

Sam lowered her arm and sat up. "Don't tell me you want her to marry someone she doesn't love?" She couldn't hide the slight surge of hope in her voice.

"Of course not," he said. A few of the village elders walked by and Duncan bowed to them, then turned back to the queen. "But we canna interfere in events of the past."

Sam pulled her legs up to her chest and laced her fingers around her knees. "Why not? Jix and Jamie and I did, and nothing bad happened."

"Ye were lucky, then, or maybe ye just dinna know what results yer actions led to. After all, ye weren't there to see, were ye?" He clasped his hands behind his back and walked back and forth in front of the couch beneath the bower.

She narrowed her eyes. He was certainly acting nervous. "What's going on, Duncan? Why are you acting so strangely?"

"Strangely?" He stopped pacing and stood still. "I'm not."

"You know," she said, watching his eyes, "Talamar

told me she didn't want to marry Gwain because she was in love with someone else."

Surprise flashed into his gaze, but he quickly turned away from her, nodding to another villager as the man walked by.

"Did she now?" he said, his voice casual.

"Yes. Do you know who she's in love with?"

He looked back at her, lifting one shoulder in an eloquent shrug. "Perhaps she's beginning to remember how she once felt about me."

Sam resisted the urge to stab him with her needle. "Come here and I'll let some of the air out of that big head of yours," she said. "She doesn't remember you."

The area near them was now deserted. Duncan shoved Sam's legs over and sat down beside her. He placed his palms on either side of her head and brought his face close to hers as she pressed backward against the softness of the cushion beneath her.

"Stay out of this, Samantha," he said slowly and defiantly as the muscles in his arms trembled. "Yer interference could result in terrible consequences—for all of us, as ye well know."

Sam resisted the urge to lick the throbbing vein in his neck. "What could be so terrible about saving Talamar from marrying a man she doesn't know, let alone love?"

"This is another time, another place, Samantha. Surely ye remember what I told ye happened before."

Sam shook her head. "All right, granted we have to be careful, but I don't understand. I would think that if you love Talamar you wouldn't want her to marry someone else." She frowned. For a moment she thought she saw hesitation in his eyes, but then it was gone and his usual steely reserve was back in place. "Do you really love her?" she asked. "Or is that just

193

your way of keeping me at arm's length? I assure you, a simple 'I'm just not that into you' would suffice."

"Just dinna meddle in Talamar's life," he said, his mouth so close she thought for a moment he was going to kiss her. She wanted desperately to kiss him. But that would be stupid. Really stupid.

"She needs someone to help her." Sam ran her tongue over her lips, fighting her weaker self. His gaze followed her tongue, but he didn't touch her.

"I will help her," he said, his voice slightly distracted. " 'Tis my right, not yers."

She arched one brow at him. He was beautiful and frustrating and all too near.

"Of course, because you love her, and you think she loves you too." Jealousy began to burn inside of her, deep and dark. "Is that where you spend your nights, Duncan? In her arms? I didn't think so, because I thought you realized the danger this time, but maybe I was wrong."

"Talamar must wed Gwain," Duncan said, the muscles in his arms like iron cords. "Now, do what I say and stay out of it!"

Sam felt fury surge up inside of her and it was all she could do not to slug him. But there were better ways to get revenge. She leaned forward and deliberately, slowly, licked her way up Duncan's scar.

He closed his eyes. When she leaned back again, his eyes flew open, and two intense blue shards of glass shimmered back at her. With an oath he rose and stalked away.

Samantha waited until he was out of sight, then picked up the piece of leather again and stabbed the needle into it over and over again in frustration before finally throwing it to the ground.

Enough was enough. She had to find that damned staff. Duncan or no Duncan, she had to get home.

The next day, early in the morning, Laird Gwain arrived in Nirdagh with a small army. Duncan stood back as the clustered groups of horsemen and archers rode in and began pitching camp just outside the village. So as not to be noticed, Duncan stood a good way off and wore a hooded cloak pulled low over his eyes. A short, bearded man dismounting from a beautiful gray horse caught his attention immediately.

The man's finely made leine was covered with a fur-trimmed robe, clasped at one shoulder with a large silver brooch. His trews and short boots were of the finest leather. His hair and beard were gray and he walked with a slight limp that lessened the longer he moved forward.

This was Gwain? Duncan stared in disbelief. This hard-eyed, craggy-faced, stiff-kneed old man? The first time Duncan had come to this time period, everything had gone wrong long before Gwain ever came upon the scene.

Whenever he made plans to return and correct his mistake, he had never thought further than saving Talamar's life. But now, one glance at the cold and cynical face of Gwain told him there might be worse things than death.

Brogan came sweeping onto the scene just then, his own furry cloak over his usual long brown leine. The days were beginning to grow chillier, but Duncan felt sure the robe was a symbol of power and wealth to both men.

The high priest greeted Gwain and bowed to the man several times. They engaged in a long conversation that ended with Gwain nodding and following the priest into the village. Two of the laird's men followed, one carrying a large ornate chair, the other Gwain's sword.

Duncan waited a moment, and then fell into step behind them. When Brogan gestured for the man to enter one of the larger huts in the village, Duncan walked on past. When he was sure it was safe, he doubled back. The two men now stood outside the doorway, their arms folded over their chest.

Guards. Duncan walked past the building and then slipped between a stand of slender trees to the left of the hut, where, as he had hoped, a tiny open window gave him a portal for eavesdropping.

"Ye have one of the Blessed Ones here, in yer village?" The Laird of Innisbar, Gwain, asked the high priest, his dark eyes mirroring his disbelief.

Brogan shifted uneasily on the stool opposite Gwain's ornately carved chair. Said aloud, it sounded foolish.

The laird had brought with him a wagonful of luxury items, including his bed, his bedding, a sumptuous rug from the Far East, and the chair on which he sat. All of the high rents the laird demanded from his tenants must be paying off. Surrounded by such luxury, Brogan felt a stab of envy. But Gwain was a new ally, a new opportunity, and one he didn't intend to lose.

"Aye," Brogan said, leaning toward the skeptical man. "I would not have believed it myself, had I not seen it with my own eyes."

"What exactly did ye see?" Gwain's iron-gray hair fell waving to his shoulders, while his beard and mustache were trimmed closely around his well-worn face. It gave Gwain a kingly air, and Brogan decided to cut his own straggling beard and long, braided hair after

Gwain had left the village with Talamar. Soon, with the power of the gold Gwain would give him, he would become a man of respect and wealth too.

"The woman has hair the color of wheat and eyes more purple than the heather."

Gwain shrugged. "I have bedded women from the northlands with wheat-colored hair and strangely hued eyes."

"Aye," the high priest said, "but did any of them have *wings?*"

The laird rose from his chair and walked to the single window in the house, then turned back, his gaze thunderous. "Do ye think me a fool, Brogan? What game are ye playing with this preposterous story?"

" 'Tis the truth, I swear it! Believe me, I could hardly believe my eyes, but she has beautiful wings!"

"Made from linen or silk, perhaps."

Brogan shook his head. "Nay, my laird, these are wings that tower above her head and stretch below. They shimmer and ye can see completely through them, but most remarkable of all, the colors in the wings are constantly changing—blue, purple, green, yellow—and she can make them disappear! I, too, have had my doubts, but I can find no other explanation for it but magic!"

Gwain stroked his short beard and then walked slowly back to his chair. "And have ye seen her fly?"

Brogan blinked. "Well, no. . . ."

"Or have ye seen her change size or turn a man into a beast or has she summoned any magical beings to her side?"

Brogan fiddled with his long sash. "Well, no, she only has her consort at her side."

Gwain's gaze sharpened. "And he is an elf? A gnome? A centaur?"

"No," Brogan said. "He's a human."

Gwain nodded and sat down again. "Then there could be another explanation." He held up one hand as Brogan started to protest. "I dinna know what the explanation might be, I'm only saying, since ye've seen no evidence of magic besides the wondrous wings, it's possible that 'tis a trick. Why, in Rome I once saw a man make a pig disappear. We will discuss this later," he added with a wave of his hand, "right now we have more important issues to review."

Brogan fell silent. Gwain was not a stupid man, but educated and well-traveled. He could understand the man's doubts, but Brogan did not wish for Gwain to cause the villagers to doubt their beliefs. Even though they had spent the morning giving tribute to the fairy queen that should rightly go to Brogan, surely she would leave soon.

Once Gwain saw the fairy's queen's wings, he was sure the man would concur with his evaluation. In the meantime, he would not oppose him.

"Ye mean yer proposed marriage to Talamar," he said.

Gwain sat up a little straighter and leaned slightly toward Brogan. Brogan hid a smile. The man was eager.

"Aye. Ye did say she was young, did ye not?"

"Eighteen years." Brogan was glad Talamar looked even younger. Lord Gwain would be pleased when he met the girl.

Gwain frowned. "Adequate. What of her figure and countenance?"

"Small-figured, but with ample bosom, and a beautiful face."

"Hair?"

"Red with glints of gold."

Gwain frowned again. "A redhead. They are usually feisty of spirit. I like an obedient woman."

"Talamar is not feisty," Brogan assured him hastily. "She is demure and obedient to the core."

"Ye say she is small. Can she bear a babe?"

"Oh, aye, sir, her hips are made for childbirth."

Gwain leaned back and smiled. "Well, then, bring the lass to me. I want to meet her."

"Of course, my laird." Brogan stood and bowed, and headed for the doorway. He stopped at the draped hide opening and turned back. "My laird," he said deferentially, "there is still the matter of our agreement."

Gwain was staring with lustful eyes at the window. He shifted his gaze to Brogan and nodded. "If I like the girl, ye will have yer agreement, and yer payment."

Brogan bowed halfway. "I will fetch her to ye, straightaway."

As he pushed through the hide door, he smiled, confident that everything was going according to plan.

Duncan sank to his heels and waited tensely for Talamar to be brought to Gwain. Within minutes, he looked up to see the girl being walked quickly toward the building by Brogan, his arm under her elbow. Duncan stood and listened.

"Welcome, Laird Gwain." Talamar's lyrical voice drifted down to Duncan.

"My greetings to ye, fair bride," Gwain said. Duncan could hear the proprietary tone in his voice and it made him nervous. In this day and age, women were little less than chattel. Men ruled the world for the most part, and what Talamar wanted wasn't going to mean a thing. He smiled though, as he waited for the girl to speak up. She had a gentle heart, but a strong spirit. If she didn't want to marry Gwain, there was no way she would agree to wed the steely-eyed laird.

"With no disrespect intended," she said, "I have not yet agreed to the marriage."

Duncan could hear a shuffling sound as if the man had pushed his chair back and stood.

"And why not?" Gwain's voice was sharp, angry.

"I dinna know ye, my laird."

Quick, thudding steps echoed across the wooden floor of the building, and then he heard something that sounded like a slap as Talamar cried out.

"Now do ye know me?" Laird Gwain's voice was smug. "Here is how it is, my dear Talamar. Ye will marry me, because if ye do not, I will lay waste to this village with my army. Ye need not fear the Danes. Ye need fear me."

Duncan clenched his fists and it was all he could do not to rush inside. His hand fell on the sword newly placed at his side—a gift from Samantha via the villagers' tribute. He could take the two guards at the door. It was the rest of the army he wasn't sure about. But if he heard any more violence, he would do so and devil take the hindmost.

Brogan spoke then, his words so low and fearful that Duncan couldn't make them out.

"Do ye agree to the marriage or no?" Gwain demanded.

Duncan could barely hear Talamar's reply, but it drifted down to him like a bird on the wing.

"Aye," she intoned.

He leaned against the building as the full portent of what he had overhead sunk in. By saving Talamar for Gwain, he was sentencing her to a life of misery.

More steps inside, quick and light, and Duncan

moved to peer around the corner as he heard the rough slide of the cowhide being pulled back from the door. Talamar rushed out, her hand to her face, headed toward the queen's bower. Samantha had been seeing petitioners again today. He felt a sudden rush of fear.

What if Samantha made good on her promise to tell Gwain that he couldn't marry Talamar? The man would cut Sam down without a second thought, even if he believed her to be the fairy queen. He was just arrogant enough to think he could get away with it. Besides, Gwain didn't seem the religious type.

Duncan started forward, and then pulled back as the hide on the doorway lifted again. Brogan walked out, head down, a very unhappy look on his face. He passed by and Duncan waited a moment before heading in the other direction.

First he would find Talamar and make sure she was all right, then he would talk to Samantha, then he would beat the hell out of Gwain and Brogan.

Chapter Fourteen

She couldn't find the damned staff.

Sam stretched out on the wooden chaise lounge. As soon as Duncan had left her the day before, she'd started searching for the staff, to no avail. She'd looked in the forest, in the village, in the clearing. Today she would look in the cave Talamar had taken her to near the standing stones.

Brogan had wakened her at the crack of dawn, telling her that this was the Day of Offering and would she be so kind as to please dress and come outside. Apparently, word had spread about the queen being willing to now speak to the villagers herself and everyone was very excited about it. Brogan had been positively gloating as he led her out to the bower.

Sam glared down at the ground beside the chaise lounge. She wanted to sit up, but there was no space left to put her feet.

Once a month the villagers paid homage to their

goddess by offering tribute. All day long the villagers had been bringing food and goods to her—fruit, nuts, vegetables, jewelry, knives, even a sword and scabbard, which Duncan had been thrilled to attach to his belt before he left her side hours ago.

She'd told the people they didn't have to give her anything, but they'd insisted and to refuse them seemed to be a horrible insult, so she'd accepted more and more gifts throughout the day until she was surrounded by all the offerings. It had something to do with the arrival of Laird Gwain; maybe they were trying to curry her favor so she'd bless this sham of a marriage they had planned. She'd yet to meet the man, but she couldn't wait to tell him to his face that Talamar was not going to be his bride.

She looked around. Where was Duncan? As usual, nowhere to be seen.

She'd ignored him the previous night when he actually came to the cottage before she fell asleep. She'd wondered at his change in behavior, but hadn't trusted herself to exchange civil words with him. He'd ignored her right back and she'd finally gone to bed, alone. He'd sat in the darkness and stared at the walls. In the morning, his side of the bed wasn't mussed, but he was gone, and this time he didn't reappear when she started seeing the villagers. She'd felt a sharp pang of apprehension. Now that she could speak to them herself, was he going to abandon her? No, of course he wouldn't.

Don't be so melodramatic, she scolded.

As the morning passed, Brogan had seemed less and less happy about the villagers giving her gifts. She needed to talk to Duncan about what to do with all of the stuff given her that day, and about Talamar's marriage. If he thought that conversation was over, he had another think coming.

That is if he ever deigned to show up again. She frowned. Earlier, she'd sent Talamar to fetch her new cloak and the girl had been gone for a very long time. When she returned she'd been strangely subdued, her cheeks unnaturally flushed. Now she seemed to be avoiding looking at her "queen," keeping her face averted as much as possible.

Had Duncan and Talamar been together? Had Duncan listened to Sam's arguments against Talamar and Gwain's marriage and decided, after all, that love was more important than history? If so, Sam had only herself to blame.

Sam shifted on the couch again. After two weeks it seemed to be getting more and more uncomfortable, and the soft rain that came almost every afternoon had turned the cushion to a mushy, moldy mess. She'd thought about asking for a new one, but now that she'd been around the villagers for a while, hearing their deepest needs and dreams almost daily as she watched how hard they worked, she hated to put any more on their weary shoulders. So she endured the lumpy cushion and took naps on her own mold-free bed. Too bad all she'd done lately was sleep there.

Sam leaned her chin on her hand. How much longer could she bear this? Maybe she would tell Duncan he couldn't sleep beside her anymore. Maybe she'd tell him she wanted a new consort. Somebody young and handsome and—she straightened, suddenly wide awake. Somebody like the hunk standing in front of her.

"My queen, may I approach?"

This was no villager. This was a soldier. One of Gwain's army?

Talamar had strung the clear crystal on a beautiful silk cord and Sam wore it all the time now beneath her leine. She glanced around. Duncan was still nowhere in sight, so she would speak to this petitioner by herself.

"Approach," she told the soldier, happy to see he actually understood her and moved forward to fall to one knee. She turned to ask Talamar for some fresh fruit, only to find the girl staring dumbstruck at the man, looking as if she'd seen a ghost.

Sam turned back to the young man, taking time for a longer appraisal. He had hair as blond as her own and was very tall. Viking blood? Danish? Likely, with all the raids of the Norsemen upon northern Scotland. Since the discovery of the clear crystal, Talamar had told her queen a lot of Caledonia's history.

He filled out his simple blue tunic well, as did all of Gwain's soldiers, and he wore a rough leather jerkin over it, laced up the front. His leggings were leather, too, and he carried a sword at his side.

Sam looked over at Talamar again. Now she looked like a ghost herself. The girl's hands trembled, even clasped in front of her.

"Talamar? Are you ill?"

She didn't answer, but continued to stare at the kneeling young man.

"Talamar?" Sam sharpened her voice and the girl blinked as if coming out of a trance, and turned toward her. Sam frowned. She had a mark on the left side of her face.

"Did you hurt yourself?" she asked. "Your face is bruised."

"Aye, my queen, I—I fell down."

"Go and lie down," she ordered. "I'll come and check you out in a few minutes, all right?"

"If ye please, my queen, I would rather stay."

"All right, but after I hear this man's plea, I want you to do as I say. No arguments."

"Yes, my queen."

Sam turned back. "All right, soldier, tell me your name and your request."

He started to speak, his head still down, but Sam stopped him. "Stand up, man," she interrupted, suddenly irritable. "I don't care to look at the top of your head while you're talking."

The man stood, dutifully, and met her eyes with hesitation. His eyes were a light blue, nowhere near as beautiful as Duncan's, but nice. "My name is Finn," he said. "My request is not a simple one."

Sam leaned back against the curve of the couch and lifted one brow. Every single person who had come to her since her arrival had said his or her request was simple, easy for the fairy queen's magic.

"Indeed? You intrigue me, soldier. What is your desire?" It was interesting how he hadn't looked at Talamar once, even though she seemed to know the man. Curiouser and curiouser.

"A year ago I was in love with a girl in this village, but she rejected my suit."

Talamar's swift intake of breath made Sam turn. The girl seemed extremely agitated and her face was growing red. Maybe she had a fever. Sam'd have to check her out after Fabio was finished with his request.

The man was waiting on her and she turned her attention back to him with a wave of her hand.

"Yes, yes, go on."

"In a fit of anger I left and joined my—joined Laird

Gwain's army. Now I wish to make known to this girl my regrets."

Sam yawned, delicately covering her mouth with one hand. Brother. These people didn't know how to do anything for themselves.

"I would think that was hardly a request needing my magic."

"Aye," he agreed as his gaze darted over to Talamar and Sam congratulated herself for her intuition. They *did* know each other. "But I fear 'twill take powerful magic for her to ever forgive me. You see, since that time I have learned that her rejection, which came by a messenger to my village, had not been sent by her."

Sam smiled. Now, this was more like it. A real live soap opera. Who needed reality TV? "And who had sent it?"

He shook his head again, pain darting into his handsome face. "I dinna know, my queen. I should have come here and begged her to change her mind, but instead, I ran, and more is my shame because of it."

"How do you know she didn't send the message?" she asked. "Perhaps you only want to believe the message didn't come from your love."

He shook his head, solemn as a village elder. "No, my queen. The messenger was forced to serve in Laird Gwain's army after delivering the message, and during a battle against the Danes, he was mortally wounded. I carried him back to our camp, where he admitted to me that he had been paid to tell me the lie. He died before I could find out who had sent him."

Talamar moved suddenly behind Sam's couch and bent to whisper in her ear. "My queen, I think I will take yer leave. My head, it aches terribly."

"Of course, Talamar," Sam said in concern. "I'll be right there."

The girl hurried away without a backward glance and Sam hoped she was all right. A real illness in this backward time—just the thought of it made her shudder.

"What was your name again?"

"Finn, my queen."

"Well, Finn, let me think about your problem for a day or two. Perhaps I will be able to help you. In the meantime . . ." she paused and gave him a lazy smile.

"Yes, my queen?"

She rose and reached up to caress the tall man's face. "Perhaps you will grant a request for me."

Duncan saw Talamar leave Samantha's side and run into the forest. She was crying. She had returned to the queen's side after her abuse at the hand of Gwain that morning, and Duncan had hesitated to approach her. But now he followed her, his jaw clenched.

If Sam had hurt the girl's feelings after all that had happened to her this day—

He pushed through some low bushes into a clearing, but stopped as he realized Talamar stood a few feet away. Her head was bowed and she covered her face with her hands as she sobbed uncontrollably.

Duncan moved to her side, turning her and taking her in his arms. The girl rested her head against his chest and continued to weep. He lifted her face and smoothed her tears away with his thumb. Her cheek was bruised from Lord Gwain's abuse. *How can a man hit a woman like that?* he wondered, feeling thunderous. Talamar was a tiny little thing. Gwain was a coward and much, much worse. How could Duncan let her marry such a man?

"I willna let Gwain hurt ye again," he said.

At his touch, Talamar looked up at him, startled. "How did ye know?"

"A little bird told me."

She began crying again and Duncan led her over to a huge stone at the center of the clearing.

"Dinna cry," he said, making her sit, trying to think of words of comfort. The Talamar he had known in the past was not given to tears. Or at least he'd never seen her cry. He put his arm around her and she pressed her cheek against his chest and clung to him tightly. He wanted to tell her that she didn't have to marry Gwain, but he couldn't. If he interfered, it could mean her life. Again.

"'Twas bad enough," she said, "to know I must marry Gwain, but now—now—!" she sobbed against him.

"What, lass?" he said, patting her awkwardly, realizing how much he had grown used to Samantha's stoic control. "Now what?"

Quickly, one word tumbling over the other, she told him that she'd just learned the man she had loved for years, named Finn, had not rejected her as she supposed.

"A year ago I received a message," she said, leaning against him, her fingers knotted in his shirt. "A messenger came and told me that Finn dinna love me anymore and that I must forget him as he was leaving to join Laird Gwain's army."

"And this wasn't true?" Duncan asked.

She shook her head. "Today he came to the queen and told her that someone had sent a messenger to him as well, telling him that I was rejecting his offer of marriage. He was so upset that he ran away and joined

Gwain's army." She shook against him. "Why did he not come to me in person? Why did he believe I would do such a thing? I loved him!"

Duncan patted her back, trying to sort out the paradoxes created by time travel. Before when he had visited this time period, Talamar had never mentioned anyone named Finn, much less that she had been in love with him.

"But he's here now?"

She gulped back her sobs to answer him. "Aye, Finn is here. But now I am betrothed to Laird Gwain." She started crying again and pressed her face against his chest.

How was it he'd never realized how truly young Talamar was? Beautiful, aye. Sweet of spirit, of course. But she was scarcely a woman. She was still a girl. Samantha would have told Gwain off and kicked dirt in his face. She would not sit crying, waiting to be rescued. Talamar had the promise of strength as she got older, but Samantha was strong. It was an amazing revelation.

"I have but one hope," she went on, wiping her tears away with one hand, hanging on to Duncan with the other. "The queen has said she will tell the elders and Brogan that I do not have to marry Laird Gwain."

Duncan sighed. He'd overheard Talamar telling one of her friends the same thing. That was how he'd known of Samantha's interference.

"She says that she will promise Laird Gwain magical crystals in return for releasing me from our marriage plans."

Duncan drew in a sharp breath. He hadn't known that. What was Samantha up to?

"She told ye this?"

Talamar pulled away from him, her eyes suddenly filled with fear. "Perhaps I should not have told ye, but since ye are her consort—"

He pulled her back to him. In this world he had never even kissed her, let alone seduced her. In this world he could be her friend, her confidant, and rest in the knowledge that he was no longer in love with her. She looked up at him.

"Are ye all right, Duncan?"

"Aye," he said, kissing her lightly on the forehead. "And yer troubles, they will all work out. Ye have my word on it."

The bushes scratched Sam's face, but she refused to move. She'd sent Finn out to look for Duncan and he'd come back, his jaw tense, to report that her consort was in the forest with her handmaiden, Talamar. She thanked him and then dragged him along with her to investigate.

She watched in chagrin as Talamar and Duncan spoke together fervently. The girl had been crying, that much was certain, as was the fact that Duncan's eyes were filled with compassion. He'd put his arms around her and held her tightly. In return Talamar had thrown her arms around his waist and he'd kissed her. On the forehead, but still, it was a kiss.

Impulsively, Sam grabbed Finn's hand and backed into the clearing, pulling him with her.

"Why you wicked boy," she said, and then laughed loudly. She flung herself against him and put her arms around his neck. "Kiss me," she whispered.

"What, my queen?" he asked softly and anxiously, his hands rigid at his side.

"Hold me, you dolt, and kiss me, quick!"

He automatically put his hands on her waist, then, wild-eyed, leaned down and pecked her on the cheek. She rolled her eyes. Where was a good Casanova when you needed one?

She laughed again and tugged on Finn's hand, leading him into the clearing. She made a big show of stopping in shock as she saw Duncan and Talamar.

"Oh, dear," she said, pressing her fingers against her lips with an impish giggle. "We didn't know anyone was here."

Talamar sank into a curtsy and Duncan rose, folding his arms across his chest.

"And just who are 'we'?" her consort asked, his blue eyes curious, but not jealous.

Suddenly Sam felt more foolish than she ever had before. What was she doing? Acting like a kid in junior high trying to make the boy she liked jealous? To what depths had she sunk in this ancient land?

Gathering her wits quickly, she smiled at Duncan. "I was just joking," she said, keeping in mind the clear crystal she now wore around her neck was translating everything she said to Finn and Talamar. "This is Finn and he has a problem. I thought you might like to give him the man's point of view."

Duncan frowned, slowly lowering his arms to his side. "Did ye say Finn?"

Talamar looked up, her face pale.

"Yes," Sam said, returning his frown, "why do the two of you act as if I'd said—"

Before she could continue, Talamar whirled and ran out of the clearing. Sam turned on Duncan with a vengeance.

"Now what have you done? I could see she'd been crying. What did you do to her?"

212

Finn took a step forward, his face like a thunder-cloud. "Aye, I'd care to know the answer to that question as well," he said, his fists clenched.

"Down, boy, I'll take care of this." Sam put her hands on her hips. "Well? What have you got to say for yourself?"

Duncan's gaze traveled over her, then shifted to Finn, and back to her. He narrowed his eyes.

"How does he know what ye are saying?" Duncan asked.

Sam smiled up at him, knowing she had to take her shots where she found them. "Wouldn't you like to know?"

"Aye, I would. I know ye couldna possibly have learned this language in this amount of time." He narrowed his eyes. "Tell me what's going on, Samantha."

Finn's mouth dropped open. "My queen, how can ye let him speak to ye in such a manner?" His hand fell to his sword. "Allow me to run him through for ye."

Sam shook her head. "Not yet, my friend. He still hasn't answered my question. What did you do to Talamar?"

Duncan threw up his hands in disgust. "I dinna do anything to the girl," he said. "She ran into the forest crying and I asked her what was wrong. She seemed to need someone to talk to. So we talked. Satisfied?"

"Hardly. Finn?"

Finn fell to one knee beside her. "Yes, my queen? Yer will is my command."

"Och, laddie, ye dinna know what ye're saying."

Sam glared at Duncan and knelt down beside the man, stroking his long blond hair back from his face. "Look at me, Finn."

He glanced up, his lower lip trembling.

"Could you follow the young lady that was just here

and make sure she's all right?" She glanced up at the treetops. "In fact, it's lunchtime. Why don't you see if she'd like something to eat?"

He visibly swallowed and then nodded. "If it is yer will, my queen."

"It is." She looked up at Duncan and arched one brow. "See if she needs someone to talk to."

"Aye, my queen." He rose, ducked his head in an awkward attempt at a bow, and hurried away in the direction Talamar had gone.

Duncan watched him leave, shaking his head, a strange smile on his lips. "For a fake fairy queen, sometimes ye really do create some magic."

"Thanks for noticing," she said. He turned to walk away and she grabbed him by the arm and pulled him to a stop. "Oh, no you don't. I'm not finished with you."

One corner of his mouth quirked up. "Aren't ye, lass?"

She flushed. "It's obvious that Finn and Talamar know each other."

"Aye, 'tis a bit more than that. They're in love."

Sam's brows went up. "How do you know?"

Duncan shrugged. "She told me."

Sam swallowed hard and took a step toward him, reaching her hand out to touch his arm, then letting it fall back to her side. "I'm sorry, Duncan. But maybe it's all for the best."

"The best?" He grinned suddenly, the gesture so unexpected that her heart leapt up at the sight. " 'Tis the best news I've had in a hundred years."

Sam shook her head. "What are you talking about? You love Talamar. How can this be good news for you? It's bad enough you think you have to let her marry another man, but now to find out she loves someone else—" Sam broke off, suddenly overwhelmed at the thought of how Duncan must feel. The smile on his face had to be bravado, nothing more. She was well acquainted with the façade of keeping up a good front.

"I'm fine, lass."

"Look, Duncan," she said softly, lifting her hand again and this time letting it rest on his arm, "you don't have to pretend with me. I know your heart is breaking."

The humor left his face and his eyes darkened to azure as he covered her hand with his own.

"Aye," he said, his voice gruff, "ye can see through me, can't ye lass? And I need someone to talk to, in private. Are ye up for it?"

Samantha hesitated, but how could she say no? Duncan was her friend. Her friend? Yes, in spite of everything, he was. And she loved him. And wasn't love all about sacrifice and putting the other person first? A new concept for her, but she suddenly understood it.

"All right," she said.

"Thank ye, lass." He started walking, pulling her along with him, one step for every two of hers, making her run to keep up.

"Where are we going?" she asked.

"To a place of true magic," he told her.

Samantha's face when she saw the ocean was worth the thirty–minute walk it had taken them to get to the isolated beach. Duncan had spent a good deal of the last week exploring their surroundings, trying not to be around Samantha any more than necessary, and he'd found the path leading to this beautiful, peaceful place.

"It's incredible," she said in a hushed voice. Her eyes glimmered with unshed tears, and surprised, Duncan turned and tried to see the view through her eyes, as if for the first time.

The ocean off the west coast of Scotland had a wildness about it in any age, but this one in particular. The dark water stretched to the horizon, seeming to go on forever, not a ship in sight, no people, no docks, nothing but the endless sea. Above, birds flew in lazy circles as the waves rushed away from the tundra-colored sand and then surged back again, breaking against rocks jutting from the water. Farther down the beach the waves crashed against a stark, craggy cliff that no man had ever climbed.

It was a blessedly clear day, and above the ocean pink, wispy clouds stood out in faint relief against the deep blue heavenly bowl above them.

"I feel like I'm at the top of the world," Sam said.

"Aye, ye almost are." Duncan took her hand and she looked at him, startled, as if she'd forgotten he was even there. Then the familiar wariness came back to her eyes as she allowed him to pull her across the beach to a smooth stone. "Sit down," he said. "Let's talk."

Her long blond hair hung over her shoulder and he reached out and curled a lock around his fingers. He wound the strand again and pulled her gently closer, leaning his head down toward her.

What was it about the lass that made him want to kiss her every time he got near her? Chemistry, she had told him once before. But it was more than that. It had to be.

"No," she said, her hand closing over his. "I will not be your rebound love affair. I will, however, listen to you vent or rage or anything you need to do."

He released her hair, his hands dropping to his thighs as he stared out at the vast panorama in front of him.

"First, tell me how it is that ye can now converse with Talamar." He watched her from the corner of his eyes and saw her smile.

Sam shrugged. "Oh, well, you know I'm pretty good with languages and Talamar and I have just learned to understand one another through gestures and—"

"Do ye think me a fool?"

Samantha lifted her chin and slid him a smile.

"Don't push your luck. I'm trying to do you a favor here."

"Samantha," Duncan's eyes were weary. "Can ye not tell me?"

A flush of shame surged into her face. Here she was again, causing pain when she could be offering comfort. What was wrong with her? Were her games more important than Duncan's feelings?

Sam reached under the edge of her dress and pulled out the leather cord with the clear crystal strung on it. Duncan cradled the crystal in his hand. His head was very near hers as he examined the stone, and she had to steel herself not to kiss his scar, so close, so very close.

"What is it? Not our crystal, 'tis clear."

Her heart fluttered a little at the "our," but she took a deep breath and managed to sound nonchalant. "Turns out there are more kinds of magical crystals than just the green ones. Talamar took me to a cave that was full of them—these and also blue and lavender ones."

He glanced up at her. "But no—"

"No," she said quickly. "No green ones. Apparently

the 'fairy queen,' that is the real one—" she shook her head "—what am I saying?"

"Go on," Duncan urged.

"Talamar told me she's had dealings in the past with the fairy queen, who showed her where this cave of crystals is so that she could help guard it from anyone who would use the crystals for their own purposes. The blue crystals are for healing, the clear for communication— they translate the language of the wearer into the language of whomever she's speaking to. Oh, and the lavender ones give the wearer a sense of peace. Sort of a martini in a rock."

"Does Talamar know where the green crystals are kept?"

Sam shook her head. "Talamar says the queen wouldn't show her where the green crystals are kept because they're forbidden to humans."

"There's no such thing as fairies," Duncan said, frowning in perplexity. "I wonder who the woman really was?"

Sam's gaze grew thoughtful. "I wouldn't be so sure. I mean, the green crystals did send us through time, didn't they? What else can they be but magic?"

"Dinna put yer faith in such things," he said abruptly, letting the crystal fall back to her chest.

"But Duncan," Sam looked out at the ocean and he saw pain dart across her face, "If I can get back home again, I could use a blue crystal to help my father." Her eyes came back to him. "Do you think if we asked the real Tuatha De Danaan to help us that—"

Duncan cut her off, his voice hard. "Listen to yerself. Practical, hard-nosed Samantha Riley tripping off into a fairy tale of magical cures. Ye'd do better to get on yer knees and ask the Almighty for a way back to yer father."

"I have," she said flatly. "Sorry I shared."

Duncan closed his eyes and the sharp tang of the sea breeze struck him in the face as if he deserved a slap. He did.

He opened his eyes and looked into her closed face. "I'm sorry, lass. I just dinna want ye to get yer hopes up."

Samantha stared at him for a long moment, and then dropped her gaze. "I won't." Her eyes flashed back up at him. "I'm not stupid, Duncan."

"Nay, lass, I never thought ye were." The silence stretched between them. "Why did ye quit yer residency?" he asked. "Ye never did say."

She pulled her feet up on the rock and wrapped her arms around her legs. "No, I didn't."

"Come on, lass. I'm about to share some of my deepest feelings with ye. Can ye not give me one of yers?"

She looked out to sea for a long moment, and then swiveled around to face him. "All right. I quit because I just wasn't sure I wanted to do it anymore."

"Why not?"

She shrugged, her head bent, her hair falling across her face. "Maybe I was afraid I couldn't do it."

Duncan folded his arms across his chest. "Now who's the liar?"

She jerked her head up and glared at him, then the corner of her mouth eased up. "Okay, I knew I could do it."

"Then what?"

Sam rolled her eyes and released her breath in exasperation. "I didn't want the responsibility, okay? There, now you know. I'm a coward."

Duncan shook his head. "Nay, lass, never that."

"Yes, I am." She released her legs and let her feet slap down on the sand. "My first week in my oncology residency, I had a patient with leukemia and there wasn't much hope for him. I did everything I could for him, but it looked like he was going to die."

"I'm sorry, lass, but surely ye knew when ye went into the medical profession that ye couldna save everyone?"

Sam's voice grew passionate. "But I want to save everyone!" She pulled her legs back up and wrapped her arms around them. "He was five years old."

"Och," Duncan said, "it must be hardest when it's a child."

"But he didn't die." She glanced up at him and he could see the shadow in her eyes. "I just didn't know enough. There was a new treatment and one of the on-cologists on staff told me about it. If it had been left to me, that boy would be dead. That's why I turned down my place in the program."

Duncan frowned. "Isna the residency supposed to be a time of learning? Are ye not supervised by an older doctor with more experience?" She nodded as the wind tossed her hair around her face. "Then he wouldna have died, lass." He laid one hand on her shoulder and squeezed. "Ye are too hard on yerself."

Sam turned her gaze to the sea. "After that, I didn't know anymore if I wanted to hold life and death in my hands."

He cupped her chin in his hand and turned her back to face him. Her lavender eyes glistened and for a moment he didn't know what to do, what to say. Here was Samantha as he had dreamed of her, vulnerable, open, honest. Here was his chance to give her comfort.

"Ah, lass, there is yer mistake," he said softly.

"Mistake?"

"Aye, 'tis never entirely in yer hands," he said. "The

Almighty is the master of life and death. To say otherwise is to take on such a burden that it will eventually crush ye. Ye do yer best, and that is all ye can do."

Sam blinked at him. "That makes sense," she said.

"Aye." He leaned down closer, drawn to her like never before, but just before his lips touched hers, she jerked back and frowned.

"You're just trying to distract me so you don't have to tell me how you feel about losing Talamar, aren't you?"

Sam slid to the edge of the rock again and plopped her feet back to the sand as she folded her arms over her chest.

Duncan dragged in a deep breath. He'd made the decision to tell Samantha that he no longer loved Talamar. Now all he had to do was actually say the words out loud. But before he could, she spoke again.

"You know, I'm not surprised that you love her."

Duncan blinked. "Ye aren't?"

"Although in the beginning I couldn't imagine you falling in love with anyone."

The breeze drifted over the water and lifted soft tendrils of her hair, sending them to dance in the air. Duncan was enjoying watching the picture she made, when her words sunk in.

"Why not?" he demanded.

"I couldn't even imagine you falling in *like*." She tucked a strand of hair behind her ear and looked back at him. "But now I can see that if it had to happen, then it makes sense it would be with someone like Talamar."

"What do ye mean—someone like Talamar?"

Sam shrugged. "Well, she's sweet and gentle and cute as a bug and completely helpless. The helpless part is the clincher."

Duncan had been nodding as she spoke, but frowned when she got to the last sentence. "And why should her helplessness make me desire her?"

She leaned into the wind, her hair streaming back from her face and Duncan's pulse quickened. She looked like a sea nymph or a selkie, newly changed upon the land. Her laughter rang out across the waves and echoed back to him.

"I never said you desired Talamar," she said. "You desire me. I said I could see why you could fall in love with her."

"I dinna follow," he said, refusing to rise to her baited remark about wanting her.

"It's obvious, isn't it?" Sam turned toward him, her lavender eyes steady. "Let's face it, Duncan, you're a card-carrying male chauvinist, as I've said all along. You want to call the shots. You're a rescuer and you like women who act like they need you. If a women is strong and can take care of herself, you might sleep with her, but you'd never want to marry her."

Duncan frowned again. The woman thought she had an answer for everything. "And why not?"

"Because a women like that is too complicated for you. You want a little wifey who will do what you say when you say, fetch and carry, iron your little socks and have dinner on the table at five P.M." She looked thoughtful for a moment. "I bet you'd even like her to wear pearls and heels."

"What in the hell are ye talking about?" Duncan said.

"You've felt the fire between us," she said, "during every argument, every confrontation, every difference of opinion. You've felt it when there was nothing to argue about."

"And when did that ever happen?" Duncan stood

and walked to her side. She smiled up at him. What was she playing at now?

"Not often," she admitted, "but the point is, the fire is always there, but it's bothersome, it's trouble, it doesn't stroke your ego, and you don't want to deal with a woman who has a little spirit, a little flame to her personality." She tossed a rock into the ocean.

"I think I've dealt with it several times now," he said. He reached out and captured her hand in his.

She shook her head. "I'm not just talking about sex, Duncan."

"I know what ye're talking about," he whispered. He lifted his hand to her face and slid his fingers into her hair, pulling her toward him. "Ye're talking about what happens anytime we stop fighting long enough for this—"

He leaned down to take her mouth with his. Her lips were cool and sweet and he kissed her gently, barely touching, letting his tongue graze hers. He moved his hand to her waist and she lifted hers to his chest as she opened her mouth to him, urging him closer. Duncan deepened the kiss, almost groaning aloud as he knelt and lowered her to the sand. He broke their embrace and she smoothed his hair back from his face as he gazed down at her.

"You don't need a woman who will obey your every command," she said. She arched her body to meet his lips as he kissed her collarbone. "You need a woman who will give you trouble every day of your life."

"Trouble is not what I'm wanting from ye today, lass," he murmured against her skin.

The pale violet leine she wore was laced up the front. Slowly Duncan lifted the end of the leather cord

223

holding it together and pulled. The cloth parted to reveal the beauty of her creamy breasts beneath.

"Oh," she said softly, "but trouble is what I'm going to give you, laddie."

Chapter Fifteen

Sam sat up and let the sleeves of the garment fall to her wrists, then tossed it aside. She laid back down, arms above her head, her eyes half-closed, her lips inviting, her hair spread out like a mermaid's across the sand. Duncan stretched out beside her and skimmed his fingers lightly across the sensitive tips of her breasts. She held his gaze like a wanton and he grew hard as he watched the fire ignite in her eyes from his touch.

She slid her hands up to the vee of his shirt and knotting her fists there, jerked the material, rending it all the way to his waist. Then she pushed him backward to the sand, but before she could straddle him, he stopped her.

"Not this time, lass. This time, I'm on top."

Sam frowned and opened her mouth to protest, but he stopped her words with a kiss, and then pushed her backward. She eased back down to the sand, silently watching him, her face flushed with anticipation.

She'd already kicked off her shoes, but she'd worn those damn leggings again. Duncan untied them and impatiently tugged the leather down. Sam raised her hips to help him remove the last of her clothing, but the trews clung to her skin and he couldn't get them over her feet.

"Leave them," she whispered. "Just touch me."

The sight of her, lying there, half-naked, bound by her own clothing, sent a ripple of heat through him and he ripped the leather tie from his own leggings as he covered her body with his own. She rolled naked and hot beneath him and her arms came around around his neck to draw him closer. He held himself above her as the tip of her pink tongue flickered out to touch his scar. He groaned aloud as she traced his skin upward, her breasts pressed against his chest, her hips tilted to his.

"Take me, Duncan," she said, her mouth moving against his face. "Now."

Duncan entered her and she moaned, arching under him. The binding of her leggings kept her from completely opening to him, but that made it all the better, tighter, hotter, and he lost himself inside of her. She was like warm honey and Duncan closed his eyes as he stroked into all of her heat; then he had to look at her, and looking at her meant he had to kiss her, had to possess her mouth again before sliding his lips down her neck to her breast, where his touch made her cry out in wonder.

Her head was back, her eyes closed, her arms outstretched against the sand as he kept a dark rhythm below that matched every thud of his heart. Each sweet thrust only served to ignite his need for her. Higher and higher he took her, as he gazed down into her liquid eyes that glazed with need until at last she arched against him one last time, her arms pressing back, fingers clutching at the sand beneath her as her body shuddered with release and she lay limp and sated. But he wasn't finished.

"Open yer eyes," he said harshly, and her lavender eyes swept up at him, startled, as he locked his gaze with hers, letting her see the desire inside of him, letting her know how much he wanted her, needed her, wanting her to show him the same. He saw himself in the glazed reflection of her eyes and just for a moment, a second, he saw what he'd been looking for—the spark beyond desire, the surrender.

"This is part of ye too, Samantha Riley," he whispered against her hair as he moved inside of her, "the woman who is not afraid to be soft."

"But what about the part that dares to be strong?" she asked, breathless.

"Aye," he murmured, "I admire her. I even desire her. But ye dinna need to be strong because ye fear the softness."

"I don't want to be hurt," she said against his mouth and slid her hands down his back as she tilted her hips upward. "There. There—" She arched against him, her words soft, scattered. "It's easier—not to let myself feel. To—stay strong."

He moved away from her and she cried out her protest, but Duncan reached for her feet and with a hard yank, pulled off the leggings binding her, then returned and buried himself inside of her, loving the soft cry she made.

"Do ye feel that?" he whispered.

"Duncan . . ." His name was a plea and he gathered her close, taking her high and hard, making her close her eyes and gasp and reach up to clutch his shoulders as he told her exactly who she was and who he was, and what truly lay between them. He tasted her breasts again, this time roughly, possessively, and she urged him on, meeting his thrusts below as he held her hips tightly and surged inside of her, trying not to fall off the earth.

Then she cried out again and opened her eyes and Duncan saw the real Samantha, staring back at him, startled and frightened by the sheer, overwhelming passion and honesty of their lovemaking. He wanted to reassure her, but she closed her eyes and shuddered, giving herself over to the moment, surrendering control and reaching her peak. To see her tremble and feel her yield and give and accept, in spite of her fear, sent emotion welling up inside him, and then it was his turn to shatter. He welcomed the oblivion of her sweetness and fire as he rocked into shooting stars and then into tranquil darkness.

But as he lay beside her in their dazed aftermath, one arm flung across her waist, one leg intertwined with hers, rationale returned and Duncan knew he was lost.

Irrevocably. Irretrievably.

God help him, it was true. He loved Samantha Riley.

Samantha opened her eyes to the sound of the ocean and for a minute she didn't know where she was. She tried to sit up but something heavy was draped across her leg.

Duncan.

She fell back against the sand and closed her eyes against the flickering moonlight. Flickering? She peeked out again from under one eyelid and saw a fire burning. Sometime during the night Duncan had risen and built a fire, then sprawled beside her and covered her legs with one of his. Sam groaned.

How was it possible that once again she had been so stupid? The man was a walking aphrodisiac.

She had sand all over her and no telling what kind of little microscopic organisms were crawling up her legs right now while Duncan snored beside her and weighed her down, keeping her from moving, keeping her from sitting up, keeping her from running away—

His leg slid against her skin and Sam drew in a sharp breath. She turned her head to bark at him, to tell him to get the hell off of her, but her words died before they were formed.

Duncan's face was mere inches away and her throat tightened as she let her gaze skim over his dark brows, over his long lashes lying in crescents against his golden skin. He'd been scraping his beard off with a sharp knife since their arrival—she knew because she'd caught him at it one day and asked if he needed any help. He replied that he wasn't quite ready to have his throat slit yet.

She smiled at the memory. Her smile faded and she lifted her hand to his face, gliding her fingers over the rough beard along his jawline, letting them slide up the ragged scar. Her heart pounded beneath her ribs as she leaned closer to his lips, the beat almost drowning out her thoughts as she brushed her mouth against his, then jerked away.

She couldn't love Duncan Campbell. She couldn't. He wasn't going back with her to stay, only to make sure she got home. She already felt guilty about that— what if he couldn't make it back again to Scotland's past? What if he died trying? And to love him and lose him would be more than she could bear.

Wriggling a bit, she managed to twist her way out from under his leg and rose from the sand. She wrapped her arms around herself and walked toward the ocean, feeling freer, and at the same time more trapped, than she'd ever felt in her life.

Whoever imagined I would someday stand naked by the sea in ancient Scotland? she mused in dazed wonder as she looked out at the dark ocean. The half moon lit the black, choppy waves and she shivered. *Whoever imagined I would someday let Duncan Campbell into my heart?*

Sam turned away from the water, fighting the sudden rush of tears as she stumbled over to pick up her clothing. She dressed quickly, feeling frantic and possessed by the need to get away from Duncan—but there was nowhere to go. Except home.

What if Duncan wanted her to stay in the past with him? Would she do it? No, she couldn't stay here. She couldn't remain in the past with a man who needed a woman who was soft and tender and vulnerable—all the things she refused to be. And her father was waiting for her—for her and the blue crystal that might save his life. While Duncan was playing hero to Talamar, her dad was dying.

Sam started to head down the beach, but quickly realized she didn't know which way to go. She hadn't paid much attention when Duncan had led her there. Her mind had been spinning with too many other things. She glanced down the long stretch of sand, watching the waves crash against a rugged outcropping of rocks near a cliff. Idly she wondered if that was the same cliff on which the standing stones rested.

Just then the moon came out from behind a cloud and lit the side of the cliff, painting it. The wind whipped up and she shivered and turned to go back to the fire, then screamed as a dark shadow suddenly blocked her way.

"It's me, lass, it's me!" Duncan's arms went around her and she almost passed out from relief.

Sam clung to him, trying to stay upright. "You scared me to death! Don't ever do that again!"

"Sorry, lass. I woke up and saw ye walking away from me. Where were ye going?"

"Nowhere," she said.

"Good." Dropping a quick kiss on her shoulder, he let the plaid around his waist fall to the ground as he walked naked into the ocean.

"What are you doing?" she hissed. She picked up the plaid and followed him down to the water's edge.

He looked back at her and Samantha felt the strangest sense of deja vu. Of course. Jacob's Well. The night he'd said goodbye and then dove beneath the water to find the crystals. A shiver of premonition danced down her spine.

"I'm swimming to the cliff."

"Why?"

"Because it's there?"

Sam looked out across the water. The cliff was a good fifty yards from the edge of the beach and even in the moonlight she could make out jagged rocks with powerful waves crashing against them. The tide was coming back in. If Duncan tried to swim out there now he could get caught in an undertow—or worse.

She laid her hand on his arm. "No, Duncan, don't. Please don't."

He blinked. "I think that is the first time ye've ever asked me to do anything."

"What are you talking about?" She shook her head at him, perplexed by his words. "I've asked you every day to help me go home."

Duncan grinned and put his arm around here. "Nay, every day ye *tell* me to help ye go home."

She wrapped the plaid around his waist and felt a shiver of fear at the thought of losing him.

"This is serious. Please? See, I even said it a second time."

"And who said there's no such thing as miracles?" he said lightly. His face grew somber and he leaned down to kiss her. Duncan's mouth lingered on her lips for a moment and Samantha felt a sweet, swift pang in her heart.

"Not me," she said. "Miracles are all I have left."

Brogan was not pleased. His plan had not included hitting women. Talamar was sweet and kind and—he shook his head and paced the small confines of his borrowed room.

This was all getting too complicated. Back in his days as a thief, he didn't get involved with those he was robbing. It was a quick grab in the street, or he'd sneak into a home at night when all were asleep. Even the trickery he'd pulled, making an aristocrat believe that he was another aristocrat who needed a loan over a poker table, then disappearing the next day to parts unknown with the money—none of it involved truly knowing the people.

"I've grown soft," he muttered to himself. No, if the truth be known, he'd always been soft. His mother's beatings had made him strong, but she'd had a friend, Ceara, who had been kind to him. She told him stories and tucked him into bed at night when he was a boy.

She had wanted her own child, but the frequent diseases she'd acquired through her trade, prostitution, had left her barren. So she had mothered Brogan. And while she hadn't exactly taught him right from wrong—she obviously didn't know herself—she had at least instilled in him a compassion that unfortunately for him reared its ugly head from time to time.

This was one of those times.

Well, he would have to get past it. He kicked the wooden bowl that Aleric used to feed his pet mongrel. It spun across the room as he continued to pace, his hands behind his back.

This was too important to ruin. If Talamar married Gwain, the payment for Brogan's assistance would set him free from this miserable, dirty little village and the responsibilities of being the high priest. He could set himself up somewhere as a nobleman. He could buy land or maybe purchase a pub.

He stopped and stroked his beard. Yes, a pub. He would call it Talamar's Tavern, in honor of the woman who had helped him obtain his freedom. Surely that would count for something, wouldn't it?

Though he wasn't exactly sure who his grand gesture might please.

The fairy queen had not yet spoken with Laird Gwain. The laird had avoided meeting with the woman; why, Brogan wasn't sure. Perhaps if Queen Brizid told him to his face not to marry Talamar, Gwain knew he would be forced to comply or else face her wrath.

Though she didn't seem very wrathful. He'd seen some displays of temper, nothing new for fairies or goddesses, as far as he knew, but overall she'd been extremely kind. She'd even offered to give him all the tribute the villagers had recently brought to her.

That was extremely ungoddesslike. The Tuatha De Danaan were well known for their possessive natures where tribute was concerned. In all the ancient stories, even such crude offerings as milk and wheat were fought over among the fairy lords and ladies.

He frowned. Perhaps he should go and speak with Queen Brigid directly, ask her if she approved of the marriage between Laird Gwain and Talamar. If she did not, he'd have to be prepared to turn the situation to his advantage.

"Talamar, I need to talk to you."

It was the day after the fantastic night of lovemaking Sam had spent with Duncan on the beach. Sam had given Talamar the day off, but apparently the girl didn't know the meaning of the words and was hard at work. Sam stood beside her, trying to decide exactly what to say. She'd spent most of the morning thinking everything through.

The girl looked up from the loom where she was weaving a length of beautiful green cloth, her eyes questioning. "Is everything all right, my queen?" she asked.

"Yes, everything's fine, I just need to ask you something. Come with me into my hut."

"Yes, my queen." Talamar rose from her work and followed Sam out of the big community building that housed the kitchen and another large room where sewing and weaving went on year round. Sam couldn't help but be impressed daily by the way the villagers all helped one another and lived in comparative peace together, pooling their efforts and talents to survive.

It was rainy and chilly this day, and she led Talamar quickly through the drizzle to the hut she shared with

Duncan. This was a day for warm drinks beside a fire, not the forest, although she'd wanted to check on her little egg friend. She would do that tomorrow, for sure. She looked up at the trees near the edge of the marketplace. The green leaves were no longer so bright. Summer was waning. Time was passing, and she was still trapped in the past. With Duncan. Sam clasped the warm cloak that Talamar had given her that morning more tightly around her shoulders.

After the last tumultuous round of lovemaking with Duncan on the beach just before dawn, she had dressed and asked him to take her back to the village. He had led her there, as silent as she was, but once in the comfort of their bed he had taken her in his arms again and made her almost weep as he simply held her tenderly.

She'd risen late and left him there asleep to hurry to the spring alone. There she had scrubbed the sand from her skin in the warm waters as the rain came down and mingled with the tears on her cheeks.

She had to get home. She had to get away from Duncan before he broke her heart. It was only a matter of time. She knew it. She'd known it all along. It was why she had battled him from the first day, taunting him, shooting barbed, sarcastic words his way in a futile attempt to keep him at a distance.

"How may I assist you, my queen?" Talamar asked as Sam sat down on the stool near the stone fireplace where a fire was blazing. The girl stood next to her, patiently waiting.

"I need to ask you a question." Sam lifted her chin, striving to look just a little more imperious. She wanted—no, she *needed*—for Talamar to be truthful with her.

Duncan said he had fallen in love with Talamar in

the past. He hadn't said a word about not loving her anymore. Had he been meeting Talamar secretly? Had Duncan slept with Talamar? But the girl loved Finn—or so Duncan had said. Samantha took a deep breath. She had to know.

"What are your feelings toward my consort?"

"Yer—yer consort?" The girl's eyes widened. "Sir Duncan? I dinna ken yer meaning, my queen."

"Sir Duncan—I saw you with him in the forest yesterday. The two of you seemed—friendly."

Talamar's mouth dropped open and then she fell to her knees, her hands clasped in front of her. "Oh, my queen, no! 'Tis not what ye are thinking, I assure ye. I am in love with Finn and—" she stopped abruptly and hung her head.

Sam stared down at her. "Duncan said you and Finn were in love, but I was so distracted I didn't put it all together. You're the girl that sent him the message saying you didn't love him!"

She shook her head. "I dinna send that message, my queen. But I received a message too—I thought from Finn—saying he dinna love me anymore! Only yesterday—when ye kindly sent him after me—did we discover the terrible travesty that has been done to us both." Her face twisted and she clutched at Sam's skirt.

"Oh, please dinna take him from me!" Tears ran down Talamar's face and there was fear in her eyes.

Sam raised both brows. "Don't take who away from you?"

"Oh, forgive me, my queen," Talamar begged, "but please dinna take Finn for yer own. I love him and we have only now been reunited after so long! I beg of ye to do this one thing for me!" Her green eyes sparkled with the duality of fear and courage and for the first time Samantha realized that Talamar deserved her respect.

"Oh, for gosh's sake—get up, Talamar," Sam said. The girl looked up cautiously. "Come on, get up."

Talamar got to her feet, but stood with her head bowed as she continued to sniffle.

"Now, look at me," Sam ordered. Talamar raised her head and blinked back tears. "I do not want Finn," she said slowly and succinctly. "And may I take this to mean that you do not want Duncan?"

"Nay, my queen, nay. Sir Duncan is too old for me by far!" She clapped one hand over her mouth. "Not that he is old, my queen."

"You'd be surprised." Sam grinned. "So you and Duncan haven't—you know?"

Talamar looked appalled. "Nay, my queen. I am a virgin. 'Tis part of the reason Gwain wants me so badly."

"Bastard," Sam muttered.

"My queen?"

"Never mind." She stared into the fire, thoughtful. "So it's Finn you want. Well, what do you know!"

"Yes, my queen, and this is why I dinna wish to marry Laird Gwain."

"Well, gee, can you guess what was at the top of my to-do list today?"

Talamar frowned. "My queen? I dinna ken what a to-do list might be."

"Well, it's a list of things I need 'to do' today, get it?"

The girl's face cleared. "Aye, I understand now. What is at the top of that list, my queen?"

"Talamar," Sam said, suddenly tired of the whole bowing and scraping situation, "could you please stop with the 'my queen' address and call me Samantha?"

"Oh, my queen, I could not!" she said aghast. "And

why would ye have me call ye such a strange name, my queen, when yer name is Brigid?"

Oh, darn. "Of course it is," Sam said quickly. "Samantha is a—er—an elven name given to me by an old friend from the Elf Kingdom."

"Oh, I see, my queen," Talamar nodded, thoughtfully.

"And it would please me if you would use this name when speaking to me."

The girl bit her lower lip. "Of course, I will do whatsoever ye command, my queen, but are ye certain this is yer wish?"

"Yes, I'm sure. Now, that's taken care of—back to my question. Guess what's at the top of my to-do list?"

Talamar shook her head. "I dinna know, my—I mean, Samantha."

Sam smiled broadly. "Right at the top of the page it says, 'Get Talamar out of her betrothal to Laird Whatsisname'."

"His name is Laird Gwain, my—Samantha."

"Well, whatever his name is, soon he will be the ex-Mr. Laird Gwain—" she could see Talamar's confusion deepening with every word she spoke, and she gave up and sighed. "Never mind. All you have to know is that I'm going to make sure that you don't marry Laird Gwain and that you do marry Finn, your one true love."

Talamar eyes were filled with sudden, fervent worshipful adoration, and she fell back to her knees on the hard wooden floor.

"Oh, my queen!" she cried, and burst into tears.

Sam sighed and patted her head. "So we'll work on the whole name business later. Right now, we'd better find Laird Gwain and Brogan and get this betrothal broken."

The hide over the door was suddenly pulled back and Duncan stepped into the room, his eyes hard, his jaw set.

"Like hell you will," he said.

Chapter Sixteen

Duncan stood glaring at Samantha. After their wonderful night together, he'd had a hard time turning his thoughts back to Talamar's situation, but eventually he'd been able to put Samantha at least partially out of his mind.

By late afternoon he'd sought refuge in the woods, reexamining the options left to him. The rain poured down softly on the treetops above him, their leaves so thick that only a bare bit of the wetness fell to him. He hadn't minded. It kept him awake and alert as he thought things through.

If Talamar refused to marry Gwain because of her love for Finn, everything pointed to the same disastrous end as before. Duncan had no army, no power that could stop Gwain and Brogan from exacting their revenge. History would repeat itself, only this time, Finn would be sentenced to death instead of Duncan. The third man in the triangle had changed, but nothing else.

Duncan had frowned at the thought. He would not allow Talamar to reject Gwain and send herself and her people into chaos, while he walked away unscathed. He had to make her understand that in life there were often hard and painful decisions that must be made. Sometimes a person had to do what was best for everyone else, and their own needs be damned. He had promised Talamar it would work out all right, though, and he couldn't in good conscience let her marry Gwain. No, he had to think of some other way to keep Talamar from ending up on the top of a bonfire.

It had taken hours for him to sort it all out and decide on how he could best approach Talamar about the situation. By the time he had reached the village again, the rain had stopped, the sun was beginning to set, and he was starving. He'd been wondering where Sam might be as he arrived at the doorway to the hut just in time to hear her promising Talamar she wouldn't have to marry Gwain.

Grand. Another mess he would have to unravel. That was all he needed—Samantha confronting Gwain.

"Like hell you will," Duncan repeated as he moved farther into the room.

Sam's chin came up and she shot him a warning look. "I beg your pardon?"

"My queen—Samantha—" Talamar said, and Duncan looked at her in surprise. "—Why are ye begging yer consort's pardon?"

"It's a figure of speech back in Fairyland," she said shortly. "Duncan, keep quiet. Talamar, please leave us. You and I will speak later."

"Yes my quee—Samantha." The girl sank into a deep, lovely curtsy, and then rose and hurried out of the room. As soon as she was gone, Sam jumped up and turned on Duncan in a fury.

"Are you trying to screw this up?" she asked. "All we need is for one person to suspect that I'm not really the fairy queen and this whole gambit is going to come down around our ears."

"So is that why Talamar is calling ye Samantha?" he said sharply. "To help keep our secret?" She started to explain but he held up one hand. "It doesna matter. All we need to blow this whole thing is for ye to stick yer nose in once again where it doesna belong!" Duncan turned and paced across the room, swearing under his breath.

"What is your problem?" Sam's brows pressed together above furious lavender eyes as her fingers stroked the clear crystal strung around her neck. "Talamar is in love with Finn and I'm trying to save her from a loveless marriage to Laird Whatsisname! What's the use of pretending to be a queen if I can't use my influence to help her? I think—"

"No, the problem is, ye dinna think!" Duncan interrupted her. "Ye just do whatever the hell ye want and devil take the hindmost!"

Sam frowned. "What does that even mean?"

"Never mind!" he shouted. "Ye will not speak to Laird Gwain about ending Talamar's betrothal to him so that Finn can marry her!"

Sam's hand flew to her throat in an oddly vulnerable gesture, then she let it fall back to her side, clenched tightly. "Why?" she demanded. "Because you plan to do the same thing, but marry her yourself?"

"Marry her my—" he stared at her in disbelief.

What was wrong with the woman? After all they had been through together—after the passion and closeness they had shared only the night before—was it possible that Samantha still didn't understand the depth of his feelings for her? And more importantly, was she capable of loving him back the way he loved her?

Duncan felt his anger drain away as he realized all at once what he had done. He'd placed himself in a dangerous position, worse than any he'd ever encountered in all of his travels. He'd given his heart to a woman without knowing first how she felt about him; without knowing if that woman was even able to give herself and her love to him.

What had he been thinking?

He felt naked as he stood there in front of Samantha Riley, her cold gaze meeting his. Aye, she loved to feel his skin touching hers, but was that all there was to it for her? And if he admitted his love to her, would her eyes soften, her lips part, her heart melt with equal love for him, or would she smile cynically and laugh in his face?

All at once Duncan wasn't quite sure he could bear it if she scorned him. Suddenly, Duncan knew that the tough shield he'd kept around his heart for so long was gone—shattered by his love for a woman who quite possibly didn't love him.

He had to do something to protect himself from the fall that he knew was coming.

"Well?" she said. "Do you want to marry Talamar? Do you still love her?" She folded her arms over her chest, narrowed her eyes, and jutted out her chin in that stubborn attitude he knew so well, and all at once it was easy to lie.

"Yes," he said. "I do."

Brogan stood in stunned silence just outside the door of the fairy queen's hut, then jumped back and pretended he was merely passing by as the queen's consort came barreling out of the doorway. He had understood every word of their conversation. He wasn't sure why the queen and her consort had not spoken in their own language as they had done when they first arrived. The queen had used the villagers language more recently, though, so perhaps out of habit the two used that language just now. It mattered not. What mattered was that their conversation almost wholly proved that the woman was a fraud. She had said she was pretending to be the queen.

He smiled and kept walking in the direction of Laird Gwain's quarters. Everything was going to be fine now. She couldn't stop the wedding and he wasn't worried in the least that Duncan wanted to marry the girl. Everything was going to go according to his plan. The high priest smiled. He had an army on his side.

Samantha waited until Duncan walked away without a backward glance before she moved. Then she grabbed her cloak and hurried out of the hut, heading for the forest. She put one foot in front of the other, her eyes unseeing, her heart pounding, until she reached the shelter of the tall trees. Then she ran, blindly, tears streaming down her cheeks, her hair flying behind her as she dodged the saplings and alders and rowan trees and jumped over rocks and small bushes until she was too winded to go any further.

She dropped to the ground and wept. She cried until there was nothing left inside of her to cry, until she lay gasping for breath on the forest floor.

I have to get out of here.

Sam pushed herself up from the ground and wiped the moisture from her face with both hands.

I have to go home. I have to take the blue crystal back to my father.

Yes. That would save her. Concentrate on getting home again, not on Duncan's betrayal. She never should have taken her attention from the goal in the first place. If the cave in the forest held blue and lavender and clear crystals that contained magical powers, then the green ones had to be somewhere nearby—or she had to find someone who knew where they were.

She clenched her fingers in the deteriorated leaves beneath her and fought for control as tears threatened her again. Sam dragged her sleeve across her face again and staggered to her feet, accidentally kicking a stone and sending it to collide with another larger rock. She blinked as sudden intuition rushed over her.

The standing stones.

She'd read a book once—fictional—of how a nurse had once traveled back in time through the magic of a circle of standing stones. Maybe there was another way to get home besides the green crystals.

Sam gathered her skirts up and headed through the woods, searching for the path that would lead her to the fairy ring. Whatever it took, she was going to go home.

"So she isna the Queen of the Tuatha De Danaan at all," Brogan said. He finished his story and watched Laird Gwain's eyes for his reaction.

Gwain sat sprawled in his thronelike chair beside a table laden with food. He was dressed in burgundy velvet this chilly day and the fire behind him in the fireplace sent a pleasing light over his repast. He plucked an apple from the dish in front of him and gazed at its likewise rosy hue.

"I told ye from the beginning that it was foolish to think she was," Gwain reminded him. He polished the apple on his sleeve and took a bite, chewing noisily.

"Aye, my laird," Brogan agreed. "It was the wings that made me believe. I still dinna understand how they are possible if she isna who she says she is, but I must be certain before I take any action."

"Action?" The man took another bite and Brogan shifted impatiently in his own ramshackle chair. Ever since Gwain had arrived the man had done nothing but sleep and eat. The village would have to work hard for the next month to replace the amount of food and bread and drink that the laird and his men had consumed.

Brogan straightened, a little surprised that concern for the villagers would enter his head. He wasn't going to be here next month. He planned to be far away—a pile of gold would allow him to seek his fortune elsewhere.

The so-called fairy queen and her consort would not stop him from accomplishing his goal.

"Yes," he said, "I need yer help, my laird, to prove that she isna one of the Sidhe at all. Will ye help me?"

Gwain shrugged. "Why do I care whether she is or no?"

Brogan leaned toward him, his hands clasped tightly together. "Because, my laird, if she is who she says she is, then ye will not be marrying Talamar."

Gwain dropped the apple core he held and it fell to the floor. "What?!" he shouted.

"She doesna want ye to marry Talamar, and should Queen Brigid forbid it, the elders would never allow the union. But dinna fash yerself," Brogan added hastily. He shrank back as the man began sputtering and rose from his chair to tower over him. "If we prove that she isna the fairy queen, then nothing she says will matter, do ye ken?" he finished, his voice strained.

Gwain sat back down, his pudgy hands clenching

the arms of his chair. "I had hoped to leave yer village intact, but if the elders oppose me—"

"But why risk any of yer men, my laird?" Brogan said, his heart pounding painfully. He had everything all figured out. He couldn't allow Gwain to ruin things. "When we can easily solve this problem through other means, ye ken?"

"Aye, I ken," Gwain said, his eyes hard. "Tell me yer plan and then I will tell ye if I will help ye, or if I will burn yer village to the ground and take what I want."

Duncan tossed back a shot of the ancient equivalent of whiskey. He'd get over Sam. He'd find a way to send her back to her own time and then he would make a life here in the past, and gradually he would forget Samantha Riley.

He poured another drink from the earthenware bottle on the table and downed it, relishing the burn down his throat. It was almost sensual, almost like the way his skin felt when Samantha touched her tongue to his scar or slid her fingers across his chest, though nothing could quite compare.

He leaned back against the rough wooden interior of what passed for a pub in Nirdagh. He'd only visited the place a few times since arriving, as he found it depressing. Besides, he had to keep his wits about him. But today . . .

A huge fireplace dwarfed the small, dark building filled with a few tables and benches. There were two small windows near the top of one wall, but otherwise there was no light save for a couple of precious candles on the bar near the entryway.

Darkness was good. He wanted the darkness. He

wanted to slip into the shadows and never come out again. The lie to Samantha about loving Talamar had been a spur of the moment decision, brought on by his own sudden panic and fear. He'd been a coward. If his father could just see him now he would laugh himself sick. A Campbell brought low by his love for a woman. God knew his mother had never felt that kind of love from her husband. Perhaps that was one reason Duncan had always doubted it existed.

He poured another drink and then closed his eyes to make the darkness deeper, more all-consuming. But the darkness brought other memories—the darkness of his cabin in Texas where he and Samantha had first made love, the darkness in the hut they shared, broken only by the faint glow of the embers in the fireplace, the darkness of the ocean as she stared out at it, mesmerized by its endless beauty, as he was mesmerized by hers.

Samantha's beauty and fiery spirit had intoxicated him, as had the heat of her body against his, and her need for his touch. She'd made him feel more alive than any woman ever had.

Was that why he'd lost his great and abiding love for Talamar? Or had he ever truly loved her? He'd felt such guilt over her death—had he convinced himself his love had been real to prove that she had not died simply because he had flirted and won her like some kind of prize?

And was his love for Samantha any more real? Didn't he feel guilty for bringing her here, keeping her from her father? He'd started out in lust with her—was it possible that the feeling hadn't changed?

It would be easier to think so. Anything would be easier than this. Duncan opened his eyes to the darkness and pushed the drink away. Just as it was easier to blame Samantha for not trusting him, when it was as much his fault as hers. He had accused her of being unwilling to take a chance, to open herself to him, but he was guilty of the very same thing. Instead of being open and honest with her, he had lied in order to protect his own fearful heart.

Aye, his hands were not clean where Samantha Riley was concerned. He was a coward.

He deserved whatever came next, but Samantha Riley did not. He was going to save her if it was the last thing he ever did.

And well it might be.

Sam checked to make sure she had everything. She had the blue crystal in the red velvet bag dangling from the rhinestone-encrusted belt that housed her holographic wings. She had on leggings and a warm leine and her leather shoes. She was as prepared as she could possibly be. The clear crystal was around her neck. The leather bag she had sewn together herself was filled with bread and fruit and nuts, just in case she ended up lost in time. A lump formed in her throat and she swallowed hard. Sam threw her cloak around her shoulders and headed out of the hut.

There weren't many people around this late in the afternoon. Talamar was nowhere in sight, thank goodness. She didn't want the girl's company. With any luck, the girl was wrapping herself in Finn's arms in some secluded place. A pang of guilt laced through Sam. She hoped they enjoyed their tryst while they could. Without the clout of the fairy queen, their love was doomed.

She hurried down the pathway through the forest and arrived at the clearing where the trail divided in a matter of minutes, then stood and tried to get her bearings. She was turned around, but finally remembered which path led to the stones. Her thin leather soles were little protection from the hard dirt beneath her feet, but she didn't care. She hurried up the trail until at last she came to the flat area where patches of grass and dirt were surrounded by the huge neolithic stones.

Sam crossed the circle to the sheer drop of the cliff and stood staring out at the gray-green waves crashing against the wall below. To the right was the beach where she and Duncan had loved—no, she wouldn't use that word—where they'd had had sex all night. If he loved Talamar, that was all it could have been. At least the girl didn't love him back. At least she would be spared from a life of misery with a man who loved one woman and slept with another.

Sadness filled Sam's heart as she watched the waves wash up against the tundra-colored sand, until she thought she would die from the pain. She closed her eyes against it, shoved it away, and then opened her eyes again, back in control.

"All right," she said aloud, "it's time to stop dreaming and return home."

Sam started back across the circle and stopped in the middle, gazing around at the stones.

Now what? She should have asked Talamar, but somehow she hadn't been able to bear seeing the girl right now. Not that it was Talamar's fault, any of it. Talamar couldn't help it if Duncan loved her.

She hadn't told Talamar good-bye. The girl would understand, though. Talamar thought Sam was Queen Brigid, so the next time the real fairy queen showed up, the girl would just think it was Samantha. Sam shook her head. Crazy things were starting to make sense— she'd been in the past too long.

If you leave, Talamar will have to marry Gwain.

Resolutely, Sam moved to the center of the circle and looked up, wishing a storm would blow up and carry her out of Oz. She didn't want Talamar to have to marry Gwain, but maybe Duncan was right, as much as she hated to admit it. Maybe Talamar had to marry Gwain in order to keep the universe on the right track. Duncan had more experience in these things. He had seen firsthand what interfering in the past could do, so who was she to think she knew better?

Oh, hell. Who did she think she was fooling? She was a woman, that's who she was. And she was Talamar's friend. She couldn't leave Talamar in the clutches of Gwain.

She had to save the girl. "All right," she said aloud. "I'll save Talamar and then try this. It's time travel, right? I have plenty of time."

She released her pent-up breath in a long sigh and then tried to take a step forward. Tried. She couldn't move. It was as if the air had been turned to gelatin and her legs to bags of sand.

"What's going on?" she muttered.

Suddenly she felt sleepy. Terribly, terribly sleepy. Her body was heavy, so very heavy. She felt as if she were being dragged downward. Down, down, down, into the hill. Into the hill?

Sam's eyes flew open and she looked down. Her feet were disappearing into the earth. When she sank to her ankles, she found her voice.

"Duncan! Talamar! Somebody help me!"

As if by magic, Talamar appeared. The girl hurried up the path from the forest and stood, looking frantic, outside the stones. Then she raced across the clearing and took Samantha's hand and suddenly Sam's legs worked again, as if they'd been unbound by some invisible force. She stumbled forward with Talamar's arm around her waist and together they made it out of the circle before both collapsing to the ground.

"What was that?" Sam asked, trying to get control over her breathing, as well as the tremor coursing through her body. "What happened?"

Talamar gave Sam a very strange look. "Were ye trying to return home, my—Samantha?"

"Yes—No—" Sam held one hand up to her head and thought fast. She'd forgotten that Talamar believed this was how the real fairy queen traveled between Fairyland and earth. "I feel faint," she said, swooning back to the ground.

"I will get Sir Duncan," Talamar said, and ran into the forest, back toward the village.

"No!" Sam shouted, but the girl was too quick for her. She tried to get up but her legs were still shaking too badly. Had it been quicksand? No, of course not. How could the stones still be standing if the ground were that soft? There was more to it than any simple explanation.

She shivered at the memory of how it had felt—as if something were sucking at her, holding her in place, trying to pull her down into the ground. She wrapped her arm around her knees and pulled them to her chest. Her feet were covered with dirt and she brushed the dark earth from her feet, sending the particles flying. She felt almost as if the dirt itself were somehow alive.

Sam froze as a strange feeling crept over her. She was being watched. She looked over her shoulder, back at the stone circle. No one was there, but she shivered again.

Don't think about it, she commanded. *You just have a case of the heebie-jeebies. Duncan will be here soon.*

To rescue you? Another voice in her brain scoffed. Sam clenched her jaw. What was she, some poor, defenseless damsel in distress? She didn't need Duncan, or any man, to rescue her. She tried to stand, but her legs were still like rubber and she sat back down heavily. Taking a deep breath, she willed her body to relax.

In the distance, across the ocean, the brilliant scarlet sun was setting against distant purple hills. Sam watched as stone shadows danced across the circle over the smooth, even surface of the clearing. Her shoulders stiffened. There were no disturbances in the ground, no evidence that anything at all had happened.

"Samantha!"

Sam jerked her head toward the sound of Duncan's voice and saw the tall Scot crashing through the forest, coming toward her, followed by Talamar. She schooled her features not to show any of the turmoil she still felt inside, and with monumental effort, forced strength into her legs to stand.

"Are ye all right, lass?" Duncan said, grabbing her by both arms and steadying her as she stood swaying in front of him. "Talamar said ye collapsed."

Sam wanted nothing more than to lay her head on his broad chest and feel his arms around her, but she knew to do so would be to show weakness to him. That was something she would never do again.

"I'm fine," she said faintly, still feeling dazed. "I just, I started feeling a little faint. It must be a result of our"—she glanced over at Talamar—"our travels."

He gazed down at her, his blue eyes grazing over her features as if searching for the truth.

"It's more than that," he said. "Ye look almost as if ye've seen a ghost."

She hesitated, then shook her head and laughed, pulling away from him. "Don't be ridiculous. I don't believe in ghosts. I barely believe in"—she looked at Talamar again—"gnomes." She raked her fingers through her hair, feeling suddenly, inexplicably weary. "I'm fine, really I'm fine." She turned to go but Duncan stopped her, one hand on her arm.

"Where did this feeling of faintness happen?" he asked. She glanced back up at him. The dark stubble of his beard shadowed his jawline, except for his scar.

She took a deep, ragged breath. "In the circle," she said, pointing. "Out there."

Duncan started walking toward the ring of stones, but Talamar stepped in front of him, twisting her hands together.

"Sir Duncan, please dinna go into the fairy ring. No human is allowed!"

"Why not?"

The girl licked her lips and spoke. "This is the sacred Circle of Brigid, and only the fairy folk are allowed within. There is much magic here for those who know how to summon it." She glanced over at Sam. "My queen, why did ye step into the circle if ye dinna wish to return to yer own world? Why were ye so frightened?"

Sam shifted her feet and almost fell. Duncan was instantly at her side again, but she pulled away from him.

"Since when do I answer to you, Talamar?" she said sharply. "Just because we're friends, don't overstep your bounds."

Talamar hung her head and Sam turned blindly, choosing a path and walking quickly away from the two.

Behind her she could hear Duncan and Talamar talking. She quickened her pace in case he tried to follow her. Unlikely, but with Duncan and his cursed sense of obligatory honor, you never knew. He might still think he owed her something for their few fleeting nights of passion. Well, she didn't want any payment that would help assuage his guilt. She hoped his conscience pricked him for the rest of his life.

Sam turned a corner and saw the rocky surface of the crystal cavern up ahead, and as she got nearer she saw the large egg. She stopped in her tracks. She sank down to her knees beside it and ran one hand across the warm surface.

What was it about this egg that made her feel so comforted every time she saw it? It was silly how protective she felt of it.

Must be my biological clock, she thought grimly. *Like any kid would want me for a mother.*

Just then something moved inside of the egg and she smiled and smoothed the shell with her fingers. "You really are in there," she mused aloud. "I was afraid maybe you were just a leftover that had never hatched." She rapped on the top of the shell. "When are you coming out? I won't be here much longer."

"Leaving us, are ye?"

She looked up into Duncan's thoughtful gaze. "Yes," she said, unable to meet his eyes for long. She turned back to the egg. "I'm going to find a way home. Soon."

"So that's what all of that was about at the circle? Ye thought there was some magic there that would take ye home again?"

"I thought it was worth a try." She wasn't about to tell him she hadn't actually tried. He might jump to the right conclusion that she planned to return to the circle later on.

"And ye were not even going to say good-bye?"

She shrugged, keeping her gaze on the egg. "I didn't think it mattered if I did or not." She could feel Duncan's eyes on her, but she refused to look up at him.

Finally he sighed and knelt beside her, running his hand over the egg. "And who is this little friend?"

He was too close to her. His dark hair fell over his face and she had to stop herself to keep from smoothing it back for him. She snatched her hand away from the egg and stood, suddenly afraid Duncan would touch her. If he touched her, it didn't matter what she knew was true, she would still melt into his arms.

"I don't know," she said, backing up, trying to move away from him as she shook dirt from her leine. "And I won't be here to find out," she added, turning to walk away.

"Oh, ye might be," Duncan said, and she looked back, planning on telling him what he could do with his pessimism. But he stood staring down at the egg. She followed his gaze.

The top of the egg had cracked.

"Oh, no!" she said, her hand covering her heart. "Did I crack the egg? Will the little—whatever it is—die?" If she were responsible for hurting some small creature—well, that would be the perfect end to a perfect day.

He knelt back beside it. "Nay, 'tis the thing inside busting out."

"Don't call it a 'thing'," she said. "It's a baby of some kind."

Duncan rolled his eyes. "Women can make even an egg cracking a sentimental moment."

"That's right," she said. "That's why we're called women. Oh, look!"

The top of the egg cracked more, and one big section lifted up and back. One little clawlike hand poked out.

"What is it?" Sam whispered as she bent down to get a closer look. The little claw was a greenish-blue color.

"I have no idea," Duncan said. He carefully removed the large piece of shell. The claw disappeared back inside. "It might be—"

A scaly head with a little horn on top popped out of the hole and Samantha squealed and jumped back, colliding with Duncan and sending him sprawling. Two big amber eyes blinked at them and a large, bird-like mouth opened and closed, exposing a long, serpentine tongue.

"It's a dinosaur," Sam said, awestruck. The shell shuddered and cracked again, and then shattered. The little beast lifted two iridescent green wings and moved them open, then closed, open, then closed, as it continued to stare at the two of them.

"It's a dragon," Duncan whispered.

Chapter Seventeen

"A dragon? It can't be," Sam said, stunned by Duncan's words.

"Why not? This is Scotland, land of magic and hidden mysteries. Anything is possible here."

The little dragon tumbled the rest of the way out of the shell. The creature was a dark green-blue with gleaming scales of the same color running down his backbone and up to the top of its head. As it moved, Sam saw variations of iridescent blues and greens that colored the tough scales across its back, with faint speckles of silver. It had skin like a lizard and its small, iridescent green wings reminded Sam of bat wings, only larger. Its head was too big for its body and its large amber eyes blinked in babylike confusion as it looked around. Duncan moved cautiously backward as it began to toddle across the forest floor.

"I'm going to call it Blinky," Sam said. It was silly how happy the birth of the little dragon had suddenly made her feel. She stood and took a tentative step toward him. "Hi, Blinky," she said softly, holding out her hand.

"Blinky? 'Tis hardly a name for an ancient beastie that will someday terrorize the countryside. Look out, it may take yer fingers off if ye offer them to it." Duncan frowned and put his hand to the sword at his side. "I should kill it now and give it a quick, painless death."

"You will not!" Sam cried, moving between the man and the dragon.

"Look out!" Duncan shouted as the animal opened its large mouth and . . . licked her hand.

Sam laughed and bent down to pick it up. "Let's take him back to the village," she said. "Ugh, it weighs a ton!" Giving up, she sat down beside the dragon and patted it on the head. "It thinks I'm its mother," she said as the creature rubbed its head against her arm.

"Of course it does." Duncan sat back down beside her and linked his hands over one leg and smiled. "After all, ye are the original Dragon Lady."

Sam felt her happiness slip away as she stroked Blinky's warm, lizardlike skin. "I'm sure you don't think I could be a mother to anything," she retorted.

Duncan had a thoughtful look on his face as he gazed at the little dragon. "I confess, the vision of ye dandling a babe on each knee isna one that seems likely to me, but not because ye wouldna make a good mother."

"Then why?"

He shook his head. "Because I canna imagine ye ever wanting to be a mother. That would mean giving a part of yerself to someone that ye could never walk away from. Ye would have to take a step in faith, one ye could never take back."

Sam stared at him, his meaning washing over her

like a flood. "You don't think I'm capable of loving anyone—not even my own child."

"Nay, I dinna say that," he said. "I think if ye had the choice, ye wouldna want to have a child because then ye would have to love it, and that would lay ye open to the pain ye've been running from yer whole life."

She closed her eyes against the sudden tears. That was twice in one day she'd been reduced to this weakness, a weakness she was damned if she'd let Duncan see. She hid her face against the little dragon's neck until she regained her composure, then lifted her head to glare at him.

"And what about you, Duncan? Can you see yourself taking on the grown-up responsibilities of raising a child? That might cut down on your time-traveling romps, don't you think? Or are you one of those men who sires your bastards and then leaves without a second thought?"

Red flooded Duncan's face and she saw, with satisfaction, that she'd hit a nerve. "If I ever sire a child," he said, "ye can bet that I'll stay around to make sure he is raised correctly."

"Oh, and only you would know how to do that. His mother wouldn't be smart enough to raise him on her own."

Duncan looked stung. "I dinna say that."

"You didn't have to," Sam leaned her head against the little dragon. "Well, thank you for the psychoanalysis, Dr. Freud, but while I'm here, I think I'll see if the green crystals might be in Talamar's cave."

She got up. *Should I tie something around the little dragon's neck so it won't wander away?* she thought, and then remembered she wasn't going to be here anyway. She was trying to figure out if Talamar would be willing to take on the responsibility of the little creature when she felt Duncan's hand on her arm. She looked down at his fingers as if they were some vile creature and he dropped them away.

"There canna be green crystals in that cave, for there is no water."

"That's just your theory."

" 'Tis been my experience." Duncan rubbed the back of his neck and released his breath explosively. "Why do ye not understand that even if ye find the crystals, ye may not arrive back in the right time anyway, especially if ye only have the power of one person's energy?"

"Jix and Jamie and I didn't have a problem with it," she said.

The little dragon snuffled among the small plants near the cave. It began munching some tender stalks, making its way around the edge of the huge rock face.

"I've told ye that I suspect it was the strength of all three of yer minds and energy," he said. "So do ye realize if ye try to go alone, ye may end up somewhere else, alone?"

The thought of being alone, trapped in another time, sent an icy rush of fear dancing down her spine. "I have to try," she said.

"No, ye don't," Duncan said, determination in his voice. "Ye will wait until I can go with ye."

"I'm going as soon as I find the crystals!" She glared at him. "And since you hid the staff—an act I don't think Brogan is very happy about, by the way—I'll have to find more."

"No, ye won't."

"*Yes*, I will, and in the meantime, you are going to help me keep Talamar from marrying Gwain and keep her from being chicken fried by a bunch of pitchfork-toting villagers!"

Duncan started to speak again, but the anger faded from his eyes and he smiled and shook his head. "Don't ye know by now, lass? Ye aren't the boss of me?"

Sam couldn't help but return his smile, faintly. "Maybe I'm starting to believe my own press as the fairy queen."

"Or maybe ye are not the fairy queen at all!" a loud voice from behind them cried.

Samantha and Duncan scrambled to their feet. A group of armed men approached them. In the fore-front were Brogan and a sour-looking man who had to be Laird Gwain. Of course, the men belonged to the laird. She swallowed hard and lifted her chin.

"How dare you say such a thing, High Priest? I hereby remove you from the priesthood of my follow-ing," she said, blustering her way through. "Begone!" She waved one hand in his direction. "And never re-turn!"

There, if that worked, then she'd be saved having to fight Brogan along with Gwain when it came time to talk to them about Talamar. She looked at him haught-ily, and suddenly realized he was holding the crystal staff.

"Where did you get that?" she demanded.

"Aye," Duncan said, "the queen has need of the staff."

"Yer pardon, my queen, but as the high priest I also have need of the staff of the Tuatha De Danaan." Brogan glanced over at Duncan. "Since yer consort would not return it to me, I had him followed until he led me to it."

"I am very displeased with you, Brogan," Sam said.

He inclined his head. "Again, yer pardon, my queen. However, we are here for a specific purpose."

"What is it?" she said. Brogan's mouth might be making the right words, but his eyes were a different matter. He knew. He knew she wasn't the fairy queen.

"We would see yer wings, my queen," Brogan said.

"What is happening here?" Talamar pushed her way through the crowd and turned to face the men, putting herself between Sam and Brogan. "How dare ye accost the queen of the Tuatha De Danaan in this manner?"

"How do we know she is who she claims to be?" Brogan said. Gwain continued to stand silently beside him, his arms crossed over his broad chest.

"It's all right, Talamar," Samantha said. "When I rain down destruction upon these men, I will not harm you or the village."

Brogan stepped forward, the crystal staff in his hand, but kept his distance from the queen. "If I am wrong, then I will take the punishment," he said. "We would see yer wings, my queen."

Sam hesitated. She hadn't turned on the holographic wings in several weeks. What if they no longer worked? What if the battery had run down? She glanced over at Duncan and he moved to stand behind her. Luckily they had their backs against a stand of trees.

"All right," she said, "though I do this only because it pleases me to do so."

"Lame," Duncan said under his breath, "extremely lame."

"Shut up," she mumbled under her breath. Then Sam held out both arms as Duncan flipped the switch on the back of the glittering belt she always wore.

It didn't work.

Sam took a deep breath as Duncan flicked the switch again.

Nothing.

"Well, my queen," Brogan said. "We are waiting."

"Do something," Sam whispered. She lifted her arms over her head à la first grade ballet class and then lowered them slowly once again as the Scot jiggled the switch one last time.

Suddenly, to her vast relief, the wings shimmered into being and the crowd of men stepped back, low murmurs of awe accompanying their movement.

"There!" she said triumphantly as the colors surged above her in dazzling beauty. "Now, to show that I am a benevolent queen, I'm willing to forgive you for this indiscretion, however—"

"My queen, yer pardon," Brogan said with a half-bow. "But there is more that we must ask of ye."

Gwain hadn't moved and he continued to stare at her, his beady little eyes narrowed. It made her nervous.

"What is it, Brogan?" she asked, trying to maintain her queenly attitude.

"Would ye please follow us, my queen?"

Sam looked at Duncan and he shrugged. "Very well, but make it quick."

"No, my queen!" Talamar cried. " 'Tis a trick! Do not go with them!"

"Take the girl," Gwain said, "and bring her along."

Two of his men grabbed Talamar as she twisted against them. Duncan started toward them, but Sam held him back as she realized that one of the soldiers holding the girl was Finn. Duncan saw him too, but continued to glower as he stood next to Sam. Talamar looked up at Finn and stopped struggling. She flashed Sam a look begging her to be cautious.

Torn between trusting Finn to take care of Talamar and wondering if he was part of the whole setup, Sam caught Finn's eye and he inclined his head ever so slightly. Whether that meant he would take care of Talamar or that it was okay for Sam to go with Gwain, she wasn't sure, but there was no time to figure it out. Gwain's men pressed forward and pushed Talamar, Duncan, and Sam toward Brogan.

Brogan bowed again and started up the path leading away from the cave. Sam glanced back, suddenly remembering the little dragon. It was nowhere in sight. That was good, because these guys would probably have shot at it with their bows and arrows for sport, or carved it up with their swords for dinner. She shivered at the thought and hurried up the path, with Duncan close behind.

Before long she saw where they were going—to the fairy ring. Great. No doubt they wanted her to stand in the center and see if she would be transported back to her fairy kingdom. Her recent experience in the ring made her throat tight as they neared the standing stones and she stopped with the rest of the crowd outside the circle.

"Why are we here?" she asked Brogan.

"There is something I wish ye to see," the man said smoothly. He walked around the perimeter of the stones, toward the cliff, and curious, Samantha followed him. Duncan walked beside her, his brow furrowed.

"I'll watch yer back," he said softly, and then moved to walk behind her.

When they reached the edge of the cliff, Sam turned to Brogan and lifted one brow. "Well, why are we here?"

"We would like to see ye fly, my queen," he said, his dark eyes gleaming with triumph.

Sam ran her tongue over her lips. "Fly?"

"Aye, my queen." Brogan gestured to Gwain, beside him. "Laird Gwain wishes to see ye fly, as do we all." The men nodded and muttered their assent.

"Where are the elders?" Sam asked, suddenly realizing none of the villagers were present.

Talamar spoke up. "Aye, where? We dinna have the right to ask aught of the Blessed Ones," she declared loudly.

"Thank you, my dear," Sam said. "You will be assured a place in Valhalla."

"That's Viking mythology," Duncan muttered from behind her.

"But right now," she went on as if he hadn't spoken, and pretended to yawn, "I'm tired." She turned to go. "Perhaps tomorrow."

Gwain inclined his head and two men seized Duncan and hauled him toward the cliff. One of them ripped the sword from his side and threw it aside.

"What are you doing?" Sam yelled, her heart pounding as the soldiers wrapped a long rope around Duncan's chest, binding his arms to his side. They tied the other end around one of the large standing stones. "I demand that you release my consort right this minute! If you don't I'll—I'll—"

"What will ye do, my queen?" Gwain asked.

She spun back to him, fury pumping through her veins, along with fear.

"I'll bring a plague to this land! I'll destroy your army!"

"What about something simple?" Gwain said, a set of discolored teeth showing as he smiled. "Turn one of us into a frog or a bird, and then we'll believe, oh Queen."

Sam's pulse quickened with fear. This was a dangerous man. He was not blinded by folklore and magical beliefs. He was a soldier and believed only what he could see.

266

"I do not follow the commands of *humans,*" she said. "Now release my consort, or I promise, you will regret it."

Gwain lifted one hand and Sam turned in time to see the soldiers throw Duncan over the cliff.

"NO!"

Sam screamed and lunged toward the men, barely catching herself at the edge. She looked down. Duncan dangled from the long rope they had anchored around his waist. The Scot looked up, fury in his eyes. For once, she knew it wasn't directed toward her.

"Do ye see, Brogan?" Gwain said, walking casually over to stand beside her. "If she could fly, she would be hovering in the air beside her lover, or else we would lie dead at her feet, or be hopping down to the spring." One corner of his mouth curved up in malevolent delight. "This is no deity, no queen of the Sidhe. This is a mere woman who has somehow fooled all of ye."

"But the wings," Brogan said, his voice uncertain.

"Aye, I canna explain the wings, but—"

"You bastard!" Sam cut him off and headed toward him, fists clenched. "You bring Duncan back up here right now or I'll show you what a mere woman can do!"

Two archers filled their bows and pointed them straight at her heart. Before she could even react, Finn stepped forward and brought his sword crashing down on top of the drawn arrows.

"Seize him!" Gwain shouted. "Take him and Talamar back to the village!"

Four swords were turned on Finn and he lowered his own. "I am sorry, my queen," Finn said.

"Please, my queen," Talamar pleaded, as the men dragged her away after him, "spare the village from yer plague!"

Sam watched the soldiers march them away, wishing she could reassure Talamar, knowing to do so would be to show weakness.

"So you will penalize a man for showing his allegiance to me, will you?" she said, trying to bluff her way back to some kind of equality. "Just wait until—"

Suddenly a sound like the roar of a lion, only a hundred times worse, swept over the circle quelling her words. The men furthest away from the laird threw down their weapons and screamed like little girls as they ran into the forest.

"What's going on?" Gwain demanded. "Hold yer ground, men, or risk my wrath!"

But the men continued to flee, parting to make way for whatever was running full tilt toward the standing stones.

Sam caught her breath as she saw her baby dragon running straight toward her, sporadic bursts of fire from its mouth cutting a wide swath through the crowd of men.

"What the hell!" Gwain shouted. "Kill it! What's wrong with ye, men? Kill the blasted beast!"

Sam's heart almost stopped as the archers nearest her fitted an arrow to their bows, but Blinky sent a burst of flame with pinpoint precision and set not only their weapons on fire, but their clothing as well. The men ran screaming down the path toward the spring. The rest of Gwain's men backed away, leaving a wide circle around Samantha, Gwain, and Brogan. Brogan's eyes widened and he took a step back as the little dragon advanced.

Sam glanced back over one shoulder. The men who had thrown Duncan over the cliff were gone. If Duncan could just hang on a little longer—she turned back to Gwain.

"Some band of brave soldiers you've got there," Sam said, and smiled lovingly down at the little dragon who faced her a few yards away. "Blinky, darling," she said, and jerked her thumb at her enemies. "Sic 'em."

Fire, red-hot and red-yellow, leaped from the small dragon's mouth and Gwain and Brogan dove to either side to escape the flames. Wild-eyed they both stumbled to their feet and took off running toward the village.

Sam patted the dragon's head. "Very good job, Blinky, my sweet," she said hastily, and turned to hurry toward the cliff with the little dragon bouncing along behind her. Together they peered over the edge. Duncan still dangled there like a pendulum.

"Can you climb up?" she yelled.

"Nay," he called back. "They tied my hands together."

Sam grabbed the rope and tugged, but his dead weight was too heavy for her to lift. "I can do this," she said, "I just have to be smart."

Her hands trembling, she grabbed the rope again and strained backward, putting the full force of her weight behind the effort. Her feet slipped out from under her and she fell flat on her tailbone.

"Ouch!" Her hands were blistered and burned from the rope. Okay, so that wouldn't work. Wasn't there something about using a lever to pull someone up with a rope? Or was that the way to move a rock? Oh, why hadn't she paid more attention in physics? If only Chelsea were here, she'd know what to do.

Despair swept over her, but the sound of Duncan's voice propelled her back to her feet. "I'm coming, Duncan. Hang on!"

"The knot in the rope," he called, " 'tis slipping!"

Wildly she looked around, trying to find a way to save him. Something wet touched her hand and she looked down to find Blinky licking her fingers, gazing up at her in concern. She patted the dragon's head. "Not now, Blinky, I've got to find a way to save Duncan." She gave the dragon a desperate look. "Understand save Duncan?" Blinky blinked at her. "That's what I thought. Hey—!"

She ran over to the rope. "Maybe there's some way that you could help me pull him up." Sam tested the rope. It was taut. If she could just somehow manage to loop it around Blinky's neck—no, that would hurt the little dragon, maybe strangle it. That wouldn't work.

"Think, think, think!" she said aloud.

"Dinna strain yerself, lass."

Sam whirled toward the cliff. Blinky hovered in midair, his batlike wings flapping up and down, front claws firmly locked in the back of Duncan's leine.

In stunned amazement, she watched as the little dragon carefully flew Duncan up over the side of the cliff and gently touched him down in front of Samantha, before settling beside him on the ground and folding his wings back into place. Duncan pushed the loosened ropes upward and freed himself.

"Oh, Duncan!" she cried, running toward him. He smiled wearily at her and opened his arms. Sam fell to her knees and threw her arms around Blinky's neck. "Isn't Blinky wonderful, Duncan? You saved him!"

"Aye," Duncan grumbled. " 'Tis a bloody miracle."

Sam smiled up at him. "Well, we were due one." She stood and started brushing dirt from his clothing, trying to keep him from seeing how badly her hands trembled. "Are you all right?"

"Aye," he nodded. "Just a little winded." He reached down and patted Blinky on the head. "Thanks, friend."

"We've got to get out of here," Sam said, hooking

one arm through his. "Who knows how long they'll stay scared of one little dragon."

His hands fell away from her arms and he nodded. "We'll have to hide until night." He ran one hand through his disheveled hair. "There's nothing near here that will shield us."

"I know where we can hide," Sam said, grabbing his arm. "Just follow me."

"A sure recipe for disaster if ever there was one," he muttered. "Lead on, MacRiley."

She grinned. In spite of the danger they were in, in spite of the fact that Duncan loved Talamar, for some reason she felt lighter. Duncan was still alive. He hadn't crashed to the rocks below. Life was still full of infinite possibilities.

"Now you're starting to catch on," she said, and led the way.

"Please, Laird Gwain, dinna blame Finn. He only sought to protect me."

Brogan didn't like the look of panic and anguish in Talamar's green eyes. She'd never done anything to harm him. If there were just some way to gain his fortune without forcing her into this—but things had gone too far now. He glanced over to where Gwain paced back and forth in front of the large fireplace of the common building, his hands clasped behind his back. The laird was determined now not only to marry Talamar, but to destroy Queen Brigid, her consort, and their small friend.

Gwain still didn't believe the woman was one of the Blessed Ones. Brogan, on the other hand, had become a believer when the bewinged creature obeyed the queen and sent its first blast of fire his way.

The laird had argued that if the "queen" were truly of the Tuatha De Danaan, she would have used magic to save her consort. And, he'd added, he'd seen many a strange creature in this wild part of Caledonia.

The incredible wings continued to convince Brogan, though Gwain kept dismissing them. Perhaps the laird didn't want to believe, because then the man would have to admit there was something larger and more powerful than he.

He couldn't understand why she'd said she was pretending to be the queen, but maybe it had been a trap. Yes! A test, and one he had failed miserably.

"Take this man out and put him in stocks!" Gwain shouted just then, startling Brogan from his reverie. The laird was pointing at Finn, and Talamar wept openly at the man's feet as she begged for his life.

"Please," Talamar begged, "do not harm him!"

"Perhaps the laird would consider yer request," Brogan said, stepping forward into the firelight that flickered on the floor beside Gwain, "if ye honored yer betrothal to him."

Talamar looked up, her eyes filled with fear. She ducked her head and wiped away her tears with the hem of her skirt, then slowly rose to her feet, strangely calm.

"Nay, my love," Finn said, straining against the hands of the two men holding him between them. "Dinna do it! I'd rather die!"

"That can be arranged. Take him away," Gwain ordered.

"Dinna kill him," the girl said softly.

"Dinna do it, Talamar!" Finn shouted as they dragged him to the door. "Please, I beg of ye, dinna agree to marry him!"

Talamar lifted her eyes to Gwain. "Dinna kill him," she said again.

Finally he nodded. "Dinna kill him," he told his soldiers, a smile edging across his florid face. "Put him in stocks for now."

The door closed with finality behind Finn and his captors, and Gwain smiled at Talamar.

"Now, my dear, ye have something to say to me?"

"Aye," she whispered. "Let Finn live and give him his freedom, and I will marry ye."

Gwain nodded again. "Verra well. Once we are truly married, I will release him."

Her chin lifted. "No tricks," she said.

Gwain shook his head, his gaze roaming over her as if he already had the right. "No tricks," he agreed. "However . . ." he reached out and grabbed her arm and yanked her against him. "Ye must seal this bargain with a kiss."

Brogan watched with new uneasiness as the girl stiffened in the older man's embrace, obviously steeling herself against the touch of his lips. When she stayed unmoved and unyielding, the man forced her mouth to open and thrust his tongue into her with the finesse of a peasant taking his first virgin. Brogan swallowed hard.

Gwain broke the kiss finally and squeezed the girl tightly against him. "The wedding will be held tomorrow," he declared. "Now, go and prepare yerself, girl." He shoved her toward the doorway.

Talamar's face was pale as she took two steps forward, lifted her hand to her forehead, and with a moan, collapsed to the floor.

Brogan reached her first and knelt at her side. He slid one cool hand over her forehead. "She is feverish," he said. He glanced up at Gwain, fear dancing down his spine. "The fairy queen said she would send a plague upon us! This may be the beginning of it!"

Gwain looked uneasy. "Ye said she was not the queen of the Tuatha De Danaan."

"Perhaps I was mistaken," Brogan said. "Perhaps I misunderstood." He ran his tongue across his dry lips. "After all, she does have wings and a dragon."

Talamar moaned. Her face was flushed. Brogan put his arm around her shoulders and lifted her against his chest to keep her from the cold floor. "We can discuss this more, but first, let us take care of yer betrothed."

"Put her on my bed," Gwain said, and turned back to stare into the fire.

"Ye could get the fever yerself if—"

"I willna lie with the girl!" Gwain snapped. "Do ye think me a fool?" He ran his hand over his sharp, pointed beard, his beady eyes darting to the girl and then back to the high priest as Brogan had two men lift her and take her to Gwain's quarters.

Brogan moved to stand beside Gwain. Perhaps there was a way out of this mess he'd helped create. "I have thought of another way to know for certain if she is one of the Blessed Ones. I don't know why I didn't think of it sooner."

"Well, tell me quickly! What is it?" the laird demanded.

"We must bring her an offering of gold, my laird," Brogan said.

"Gold?" Gwain turned and stared at him.

"Aye." Brogan could hardly keep from licking his lips at the thought of Gwain giving him a nice pile of gold to offer Queen Brigid. Then he would take part of the gold for himself and offer the rest to the fairy queen, appeasing her. Then he would run. Talamar wouldn't have to marry Gwain and everyone would be happy. Well, everyone except Gwain, but that wasn't his problem.

"Ye must bring the gold to me and I will place it in the center of the standing stones on the next full moon," Brogan said. "If this woman is the queen of the Tuatha De Danaan, then she will turn away from such an offering. The fairyfolk have no need of gold."

That lie would give him time to steal part of the gold and find a way to get the rest to the queen. Brogan smiled. He was fortunate that Gwain seemed to know next to nothing of the legends of the Sidhe. Fairies loved gold.

"I have a better way to find out if they are who they claim to be," Gwain said as he stared into the fire. His dark eyes reflected the flames and his face was carved into rough plains by the shadows leaping upon his skin.

Brogan frowned. "What way, my laird?"

Gwain turned back to the high priest. "Set them on fire."

Chapter Eighteen

Sam and Duncan had walked for a couple of hours to put time and distance between themselves and the village, finally making camp in a crag with steep stone walls that hid them from casual view. They'd slept a good part of the day and awakened hungry and thirsty, and as far as Sam was concerned, ready to do battle against Gwain and his minions. But Duncan was infuriatingly practical, as always.

"We've got to find some way to help Finn and Talamar," Sam said, pacing back and forth across the flat stones beneath her feet.

"Aye, lass," Duncan agreed, "and we will. But first we must finish eating, else we'll have no strength to do anything for them. Be patient."

She'd been patient when they'd gone scouting for a spring and found it. The little dragon had been the happiest of the three at the sight of the flowing water and jumped right in, flapping its wings in the sparkling pool formed by the smooth rocks at the bottom.

She'd been patient when Duncan insisted that she eat, and he had gone hunting, bringing her back some nuts and berries and, to her disgust, a squirrel that he proceeded to skin and roast over the fire he built.

Now, however, the sun was going down and she'd lost her patience.

"How can you sit there and do nothing," she said, pausing in the middle of the cave to stare at him, "when Finn and Talamar may be in danger?"

Duncan looked up from his position by the fire, his jaw locked in mid-chew, his brows raised in surprise.

"I'm no doing nothing," he said. "I'm eating."

"I mean—doing nothing to help them! We've got to return to the village!"

"I'm eating," he said again, reasonably, as he held up another piece of squirrel meat and brushed off a small speck of dirt, "and I'm thinking."

Sam rolled her eyes and sat down beside him. Already the leine she wore was growing the worse for wear. She was used to Talamar bringing her a clean garment every morning, and realized, belatedly, that she had grown very spoiled during her time in the past. Talamar had literally waited on her hand and foot.

"Well, stop thinking and start doing!" She stomped her foot on the ground like an impatient child.

Duncan glared in her direction and tore another strip of meat from the carcass on top of the plaid, which he'd spread across his lap.

"We canna go off half-cocked. Gwain willna have killed them yet. He wants to marry Talamar, remember?"

"But he doesn't want to marry Finn," Sam reminded him. "So what's to stop Gwain from killing him?"

Duncan shrugged and took another bite. "Nothing."

Sam jumped to her feet, furious. "That's exactly what I'm talking about—this attitude of total disregard for human life! What is wrong with you?"

A slow smile eased across Duncan's face as he looked up at her. "Ye surprise me, lass."

His soft tone took some of the fire from her anger, but she continued to frown down at him.

"Why? Or dare I ask?" she added, caustically.

"I dinna think ye would care so much about someone ye barely know."

"I'm a doctor. That's what we do," she informed him.

He shrugged and took another bite of meat. "I'm wondering why ye often seem to treat strangers better than ye treat yer own family and friends?"

His words struck Sam like a physical blow. "What do you mean?"

Duncan glanced up and stopped in mid-chew, as if he just realized what he'd said. "I dinna mean a thing, lass."

Sam folded her arms over her chest, a slow, hot flush staining her cheeks as she glared at Duncan.

"Oh, come on, Duncan, don't hold back. I can take it."

Duncan wiped the back of one hand across his mouth. "Aye, lass, I've no doubt that ye can."

She threw her shoulders back and lifted her chin. "So come on. Let me have it."

He stood and tossed the bone he held aside. "All right. I think ye don't appreciate yer father or yer friends." He spread his hands apart. "Satisfied?"

Sam tried to find words to fling at him. For some reason, they wouldn't come. "I'm going for a walk," she said.

Duncan looked taken aback. "What? Ye dinna want to duke it out?"

She lifted one shoulder. "What's the point? You've got it all figured out." She turned and headed away from him.

"Dinna go far," he cautioned. "Gwain's men could be anywhere. And soon 'twill be dark."

"I'm just going to the spring to get Blinky."

"Lass . . ."

Sam stopped and looked back. Duncan stood beside the fire, his brow furrowed. "I dinna mean to—"

"It's all right, Duncan." She cut him off. "I'm a big girl." She headed toward the spring.

Brogan had searched the forest all morning, but had come up empty-handed. The queen and her consort had hidden themselves well. Now he had retreated to his own hut to warm himself at the fireplace and think about what he should do next.

Others in the village had offered to help him search, but he'd refused, saying that he needed to be alone to "align himself with the deities" and "discern which way they would have him go."

In reality, he wanted to find them first and throw himself upon the queen's mercy, ingratiate himself to her and make her believe that Laird Gwain had forced him to go along with his attack upon the fairy queen and her consort. He would warn the queen of Gwain's plans and perhaps she would reward him. With fairy gold, perhaps!

He smiled to himself as he tried to picture what fairy gold would look like. White-gold, shimmering, worth more than anything on earth. His throat tightened and he coughed. He rose and poured himself a cup of spring water and drained the container.

Talamar's sickness had worsened, and four others

had fallen ill. Never before had he believed in magic. Never before had he believed in something bigger than himself. He had been as bad as Gwain in his arrogance, but now he, at least, had realized it. Friends of Talamar had come to him in the last day or two, giving him tribute, asking for his prayers. They still believed in such things as miracles. The only miracles he had ever believed in were the ones he created himself.

Perhaps he'd been wrong.

Brogan held his hands out to the fire blazing near the hearth. It must be growing colder outside, he realized, as a shiver slipped over his skin. From a peg on the wall he took down his good woolen cloak and placed it over his shoulders before turning back to the fire.

Once, back in his thieving days, one of his friends who stole for him, called Eidan, had suddenly given up his bad ways and become a priest. A priest of the one God, he had told Brogan. A God bigger than any of the others, he'd said, a God of love and kindness and joy.

Brogan thought at first the man was jesting, but when he realized his partner was serious, he'd been furious. As his friend spoke, though, and Brogan saw the look of utter peace in Eidan's eyes, Brogan had finally clapped him on the back and wished him well. He gazed into the fire. Last he had heard, his friend was in a monastery in the Northlands.

Brogan let his mind wander as he enjoyed the fire's warmth. Then he remembered another place he hadn't thought to look for the queen and her consort, a crag farther north of Nirdagh. Once he'd camped there himself, as it provided good protection from the wind and any bandits who might venture down the usual roadways.

Brogan stood and crossed to the door. He pulled

the brown cowhide back from the door and shivered again. The sunlight seemed uncommonly bright and he stood for a moment, regaining his balance. He took a deep breath and released it slowly, then headed out the door to find Fergus. The hunter had a small cart and mule. It would be a rough journey, but he would be wise to continue his search. Brogan pressed his lips together as he trudged across the village marketplace.

As soon as Samantha disappeared in the direction of the spring, Duncan cursed himself roundly and kicked a small piece of wood toward the fire.

All he had done was serve to reinforce—once again—that tough shield behind which Samantha Riley hid herself. All he had done was make everything worse.

Like telling her ye wanted to marry Talamar wasn't bad enough?

"I am an idiot," he said aloud.

If he had been in her position he would have turned the argument around. "And where is your concern for the human race, Duncan?" she could have asked. "Where was your concern for the villagers when we tricked them and forced them to wait upon us hand and foot while you played knight in shining armor for Talamar?"

And she'd have been right to accost him with her words, for they were words of truth. He'd put aside her safety and her needs to fulfill his own need to play God in Talamar's life.

He had finally been allowed to return to Talamar's time so that he could make things right—or so Duncan had thought. But had it been Providence or his own stubbornness that had brought him here? The end result of "making things right" might mean that Talamar was now doomed to spend the rest of her life with a man like Gwain.

Was Samantha right? Would Talamar prefer to die, rather than marry Gwain?

Of course. And he would not be the one to sentence her to such a miserable existence, nor would he sentence her to death by standing by and doing nothing. He'd come this far, he might as well go the distance. Talamar deserved a life with a man who loved her. Just as Samantha did.

Duncan ran one hand through his tangled hair, his head spinning. He was tired. He needed a bath and a good, hot meal of something other than squirrel. He needed to sleep on something other than the ground or the pitiful mattress in the hut he shared with Samantha. He missed his cabin back in Texas. He missed the computer he had come to appreciate in the twenty-first century. He missed the Crazy R Ranch and Griffin and Chelsea and Patrick Riley. He missed Samantha in his arms. Duncan stopped kicking bits of dirt and grew very still.

He smiled, feeling as if his face might split from the sheer, open expression of joy. An invisible burden rolled from his shoulders and he felt, for the first time in what seemed like a hundred years, as if he could finally stand up straight. He took a deep, cleansing breath and released the air from his lungs in one long, slow sigh of relief.

Samantha sat beside the spring, idly trailing her fingers in the water as the little dragon paddled around in the small pool.

Funny, she thought, *you'd think that a fire-breathing*

dragon wouldn't want to get into water. She frowned. *So that must mean whatever causes the flame isn't affected by water. Well, duh, of course not, or the poor little thing wouldn't be able to ever get a drink!*

She reached over and stroked the top of its blue-green head, and it closed its eyes in rapturous contentment. Blinky reminded her of one of the ranch cats who often wandered up to the front porch of the main house to be scratched or petted. She couldn't remember ever lounging on the porch, playing with the cats much—she was always too busy. One day, though, when she was about sixteen, she'd found a bedraggled and weak kitten on the front steps.

She'd taken care of it and nursed it back to health and it was then that she'd realized that her father's dream could also be hers. Just because he wanted her to go to medical school didn't mean that she couldn't want to go as well.

It had been a revolutionary thought. Up to that point she had fought him tooth and nail to keep from becoming a doctor, but when the cat appeared and she'd actually helped it get better, she'd realized that she'd been fighting him mostly for the sake of fighting.

"Well, that's what I do best, isn't it?" Sam murmured to the dragon. "I fight because as long as I'm fighting I don't have to really think about things, I guess. It's that old armed forces attitude—" She held her palm out sideways and squinted down the side of it as if sighting down a rifle's barrel "—set a goal and follow it through." She let her hand fall back to her lap. "Only in my case, the goal was simply to give my dad as much hell as possible." She shook her head and frowned. "I don't know why."

Her hand stilled on the little dragon's head and she

stared at the cool water flowing around the animal's spiny back as it bobbed up and down beside her.

"Why did I oppose him so much?" She laughed without humor. "Hell, why do I still oppose him so much? Because I'm spoiled rotten?" She took a deep breath, willing to face the truth, if only for a moment. "Well, maybe, partly, but that's not all there is to it." Sam scratched Blinky's head, and the dragon's tail bounced up and down in the water. "I remember being perfectly happy with my dad until I was about six years old and suddenly every time I looked at him I just felt angry inside."

For a moment Sam was silent, listening to the water as it rushed past her, even as memories rushed through her mind: living on different bases, in different states, following her father's career around, sometimes going to three new schools a year—she shifted uncomfortably. It was silly to be sitting here thinking about such things at the ripe old age of twenty-eight, but here she was, nevertheless.

Everything had been fine until her mother died. Up until then moving from town to town had been an adventure, because her mother had made it seem that way. And if her dad had to be away from home a lot, that was okay too, because her mother was there, and that meant everything was always all right.

Sam stood and with both hands lifted her hair from her neck, letting the breeze cool her warm cheeks. She stretched, grateful for the brown leggings Talamar had given her the day before. The leggings had allowed her to belt up short the long leine that usually served as a dress.

Talamar would be an awesome asset to any household, no doubt about it. *Wonder if she'd like to come home with me and be my valet,* Sam wondered, only half in amusement. *She'll make a great mom someday.*

That thought led her back to the conversation she'd had before with Duncan. Was he right? Would having a child go against the grain of who she was? He said she didn't appreciate her family or friends. Maybe she was too selfish to be a mother.

She closed her eyes and tried to imagine having a baby, holding it in her arms. A little boy who had Duncan's clear blue eyes. A little girl with his dark hair. How would it be to have that kind of responsibility? For a moment she felt tense and afraid, but then in her mental picture Duncan walked up beside her and smiled down at the baby she held.

Her eyes flew open, her heart pounding painfully.

She wanted that picture. She wanted that life. Duncan was wrong. She wanted to give the love inside of her to others. To her family, her friends. Her children. Her children with Duncan.

But she was too late.

She had lost Duncan, and he'd just made it abundantly clear what he thought of her. Again.

It was getting dark. Sam turned and started walking upstream, her arms wrapped tightly around her waist. Blinky jumped out of the water and trotted along beside her.

So what would she do when she returned to 2005 and Duncan told her good-bye again? How could she bear it?

I never even got to tell him that I loved him.

Sam sank to her knees. She'd never told Duncan she loved him. He didn't know. Would it make a difference? The memory of their night on the beach rushed back to her. He'd been so tender, so loving—he had to care about her. She knew he did, knew by the look in his eyes and the passion in his touch.

Maybe he was afraid to show her he cared. She certainly hadn't made it easy for him to tell her how he felt about her. What if—

Did she have the guts? Did she have the courage? What did it matter anyway if she told him? If he left her in 2005 and disappeared again at least she'd know that she said it. At least she would know that for once she'd taken a chance and opened her heart to another human being. He'd accused her before of being closed off, of being afraid. He was right. But suddenly she didn't want to live the rest of her life like that. Suddenly she wanted warmth and love and friends and family and she didn't want to hold back. She didn't want to protect herself from getting hurt, because it was better to risk it all than to hide behind a concrete wall.

The realization flooded over her like a tide, once and for all destroying that mighty fortress she had so painstakingly built around her heart.

Brogan squinted into the dying sunlight and pulled back on the mule's reins. He was lost. Moreover he was ill. Foolish, foolish, to ignore the warning signs of chill and dizziness. But he'd been so determined to find the queen and her consort.

A wave of vertigo made him grab the sides of the small cart in an effort to keep from falling off the crude wooden seat. Nausea clutched at his belly and Brogan moaned, closing his eyes and doubling over as he climbed out of the cart and sprawled on the ground. Bile rushed to his throat and he fought it back down as he tried to stand. He made it to his feet, then stumbled against the wheel of the cart and doubled over again, losing his hastily eaten lunch of bread and cheese. He felt better, but only momentarily, then another wave of nausea swept over him and left him shuddering.

With an instinct of one long used to determining his own survival, Brogan knew he must find water, and shelter, and if possible, help. He took a step forward and his legs gave way. He fell to his knees, and then flat upon his chest. He began to crawl as the fever burned within him.

"Samantha."

She looked up, startled.

Duncan stood staring down at her, his hair dancing in the soft wind, silvered by the moon. She stood silently and held out her hand. He took it and drew her to him.

"Samantha Jane Riley," he said, "I have been a fool. Forgive me."

She leaned her head upon his chest and closed her eyes.

Home. She was home at last.

"I love ye," he whispered against her hair. "Not Talamar. I have known since I returned here that I dinna love her."

Sam raised her head and looked into his eyes. They were midnight. They were forever.

"I am the fool," she said as she slid her arms up his chest to encircle his neck. "I've loved you for so long, but I was afraid. Afraid to love. Afraid to feel."

"I'm sorry if my words earlier hurt ye even more."

She shook her head. "Every word was true."

"And this," he said against her lips. "This is true, too."

Sam closed her eyes as Duncan possessed her mouth, branding her with his love, sealing the words he'd said with passion the last few bricks around her heart turned to powder.

Chapter Nineteen

"Have you ever looked into your own eyes, Duncan?" Sam asked, much, much later as they lay beside the stream in each other's arms.

He raised both brows. "I dinna ken what ye mean."

She leaned up on one elbow beside him. "Have you ever seen who you really are, inside?"

"Aye," he said.

"Ever since we arrived here, I've been having to look at myself." She shook her head. "It's not a pretty picture."

He turned toward her. The moonlight glinted across his body, sending shadows across his broad chest, his muscled thighs, and she wanted him all over again.

"Dinna be so hard on yerself," he said. "Whatever ye have seen, together we can face it."

"I think you're right," she said softly.

Duncan laughed at her words. "I'm right? Well, this *is* a day of miracles, isn't it, love?"

She let her gaze roam over his face. She traced the

planes and angles that time and experience had carved into his countenance, and the scar that always sent a thrill through her soul.

"How did you get that scar?" she asked.

He reached up and smoothed her cheekbone with his thumb. "Griffin gave it to me," he said at last, "when we were but children."

She blinked, and then laughed. "Why didn't you tell me when I asked before?"

"Because I was too proud," he said, leaning up until his breath was warm against her lips.

"Why did you tell me this time?"

"Because now I'm not too proud."

Sam ran her tongue across her lips.

"Before we go any further with this—"

Duncan raised one brow. "A little late for that, isn't it, lass."

"I need to tell you—I'm having an identity crisis. I'm not sure who I am anymore," she said.

He pulled her back down to him. "Then it's lucky for ye that I do." He touched his lips to hers, briefly, and she breathed his breath for a second, inhaled the warmth of Duncan and wanted more. "Ye are Samantha Riley," he said, "doctor, daughter, lover, friend, beautiful woman, and the self-proclaimed queen of the fairies."

"I'm not a doctor," she said. She slid down beside him again and leaned her head against his shoulder.

"Ye'll always be a doctor, lass. Ye have a diploma and everything." Sam smiled. "I've seen it. Whether or not ye choose to practice is another thing entirely, but ye are definitely a doctor."

"I'm a lousy friend."

He shrugged. "Jix and Chelsea think ye're a wonderful friend. Have ye ever thought how it would be if ye all were like Chelsea, shy and studious. Or if ye were all like Jix?"

"Heaven help the world," Sam said dryly.

Duncan laughed softly against her hair. "Aye. She's a wonder, but the point is, ye all bring different attributes to yer united friendship. Together ye balance out one another."

Sam looked up at him. "I never thought about it like that. And in spite of what you said before, I have learned to appreciate them."

"I'm glad to hear it,"

She sighed and smoothed her hand across his chest. "Next on the list?"

She looked up at him. "I'm a lousy daughter."

His eyes darkened with sympathy. "No, ye aren't. Ye're just human, lass. Your father pushes yer buttons. Ye push his. 'Tis the way of the world."

"I do love him," she said. "He just drives me crazy."

He nodded. "Aye, and ye drive him crazy, and me as well."

She glared at him and he kissed her for a full five minutes and then lifted his head and squinted one eye at her. "The evil eye is gone?"

"Very funny," she said, flushed from the embrace. "You know," she said, "I think we're talking way too much."

"I just want to say one more thing and then, I don't know about ye, but I'd like to return to our nice, warm fire."

"I thought we were building our own," she said and then leaned down and licked the center of his chest.

He closed his eyes at her touch, then opened them again. "Stop it, or I won't be able to finish my thought."

"All right, love," she said. "What is your thought."

"Yer father loves ye with all of his heart and ye love him just as much. We all make mistakes. We all do the best we can with what we've been given, and when we are given something more, we do better."

"Okay," she agreed, "but there's one last identity to reckon with. I'm not—"

"Now if ye say ye aren't a good lover, I'll have to kiss the words right out of yer mouth," he said, stopping just centimeters away from her lips.

"I'm not the queen of the fairies," she teased, then let her senses take over, allowing her brain to register every molecule of her skin being touched by his, relishing the curve and slope and pressure of their bodies pressed together.

"Aye," he murmured, "but ye are the queen of my heart."

"Duncan," she whispered.

He kissed the side of her neck, the sensitive spot under her ear and then found her mouth again. Sam lost herself in the fire and Duncan groaned as she arched against him—when all at once downstream the darkness lit up like a pagan bonfire.

"Duncan!" Sam cried. "The dragon!"

Duncan sat up just as a scream split the night and a small oak tree beside them burst into flames.

The little dragon sat contentedly beside what looked like a dead body lying face down on the ground.

"Great," Duncan said. "We needed more complications." Samantha dragged on her clothes in record speed and then raced to see who Blinky had just killed. Duncan pulled on his boots and leggings, then took his heavy plaid and soaked the material in the stream before crossing to the fire in the tree.

"It's Brogan!" she shouted. She knelt beside the man

and pressed two fingers against his neck. "He's still alive."

"Burned?" Duncan asked as he whipped the long, wet material against a tree limb. A shower of embers rained down from above and he ducked his head.

"No, I don't think so." Sam laid a practiced hand on the prostrate man's brow. "But he's feverish. Let's get him to the crag."

"I'm a little busy at the moment!" Duncan called over one shoulder as the embers on the ground ignited and he ran to stomp them out.

Sam was trying to turn Brogan over, with little success. "Don't burn anything important, will you?" she said. "His pulse rate is up, and he's really pale. Probably dehydrated."

"And ye said ye weren't a doctor!" Duncan grinned and wrapped the plaid around his waist and then started pushing against the trunk of the tree.

The few flames left in the treetop reflected in Sam's narrowed eyes. "And you're the one who reminded me that I *am* a doctor, remember? So stop playing lumberjack and help me carry him!"

"I'm no playing!" Duncan snorted. "I canna leave it to burn," he said, leaning his shoulder into the trunk. "'Twill catch the rest of the forest afire. If I push it over I can stomp it out."

"Oh, for pity's sake!" Sam hurried over to him and added her weight to his against the oak, undeterred by the dirt or the soot or danger of the flame. Duncan gazed down at her, once again amazed by the woman he loved.

"Ye're too lightweight for this job," he told her loudly over the crackle of the fire.

"Flatterer!" she shouted. "C'mon, now, push!"

After a few minutes of extreme leaning, the two

managed to send the remains of the tree crashing to the ground. Duncan's boots were still the ones he'd been wearing when they went spinning back in time, and the thick leather soles protected his feet as he tromped on the flames. Sam continued to use his water-soaked plaid to fight the last dying embers in the tree branches. When the fire was extinguished, Sam rubbed the back of her hand across her nose, leaving a sooty mark that made her look like a Siamese cat.

"What are you grinning at now?" she asked, frowning.

"Nothing, lass." He pointed at Brogan. "Let's get him to the crag." He turned to the dragon and pressed his brows together. "And as for ye—"

"Don't scold him," Sam interrupted. "Blinky was just trying to protect us."

Duncan stared at her in disbelief. "Trying to—that creature almost roasted us alive!"

"Blinky didn't mean to!" Sam patted the dragon's head as Duncan knelt beside Brogan and shoved him onto his back.

"Dinna mean to, but we would have been just as charbroiled either way!" Duncan told her as he pushed Brogan's limp body into a sitting position. "This man weighs a bloody ton!"

"Oh, stop grousing and help me pick him up," Sam said. "For someone who dispenses a lot of advice for the terminally whiny, you sure don't take many pages from your own book."

Duncan scowled as he lifted Brogan by the shoulders and Sam took the man's feet.

"I am not whiny!" he said. "Dinna ever use that word when describing me. I'm a warrior."

"Well, you're a whining warrior, then," she retorted. "And your end of this train is sagging."

Duncan locked his jaw. The woman was incorrigible. But as they headed for the crag, Samantha glanced over at him and smiled. The moonlight glinted against her hair, turning it silver, and her long-lashed eyes glittered with excitement.

"Ye love this," he said. "Dinna deny it."

She looked startled for a minute, and then laughed. "I love saving lives," she said. The pleasure in her face faded. "I don't like what it means to the person who's hurt. Even Brogan."

"And ye would take care of him, even though he's our enemy? Ye wouldna even think of leaving him here to die and end all our problems, as far as he is concerned?" Duncan watched her, enjoying the outrage in her eyes as they headed up the slope that led to the crag.

"Of course not! A doctor doesn't care what a person's politics are, or even if they're good or evil. I swore an oath to heal people, no matter what."

Duncan stopped walking and she looked up into his eyes again, defiant, daring him to say a word. "Aye," he said, " 'tis one of the many reasons I love ye." He started walking again, but Sam stayed rooted to the spot, bringing him up short. He frowned back at her, then smiled as he saw the look on her face. "Hey, Dr. Riley, yer end of this train is sagging sorely."

To his surprise she grinned at him. "Aye," she said, starting forward again, an exaggerated swing to her hips, "but baby, just look at my caboose."

"Ye need to get some sleep," Duncan told her at the end of her second day of caring for Brogan.

Sam looked up from trying to force water down the man's throat and nodded. The truth was she was too weary to argue. She brushed a strand of hair that had escaped from her improvised French braid—a little crooked from doing it herself without a mirror—and then rose and crossed to Duncan's side. She sat down beside him and let him put his arm around her as she leaned against his chest and closed her eyes. She must have slept for a few minutes, and when she opened her eyes and looked up, Duncan was gazing down at her.

"What?" she said groggily.

"Nothing. I was just watching ye sleep. Ye look like a little girl when ye sleep, innocent and sweet."

Sam drew in a deep breath and let it go. "Well, looks are deceiving, aren't they?" She let her head roll back against his shoulder and then voiced the question on her mind. "Are we ever going to get out of here, Duncan? Am I ever going to get back to my own time?"

"I canna say, lass," he said, curving his hand around the nape of her neck and pulling her back to him.

Brogan rolled over restlessly, flinging the cover back and Sam moved out of Duncan's arms to his side, where she helped him get more comfortable. That was the problem with Scotland, there was little in the way of strawlike substances to create padding over stone. They'd gathered humus from the forest to make a cushion and Sam had placed her cloak over the dry material, creating a rough mattress. She'd dried Duncan's plaid by the fire the first night and covered her patient with it, in spite of Duncan's protests that she needed it for her own comfort.

"I wonder where Brogan's staff is?" Duncan said. He linked his hands over his knees and gazed up at her, his eyes thoughtful. He'd been very quiet today. It made her nervous.

"Good question," Sam murmured. "If he makes it through the night, maybe we can ask him."

"Is he that bad?"

She hesitated, then nodded her head. "Yes, he's that bad. I may have to use the blue healing crystal."

"Ye have one?"

Sam nodded. "I took it from the cave." She patted the red velvet bag still tucked beneath her rhinestone belt. "If Talamar spoke the truth, it will cure him." Her eyes clouded over. "But then I won't have one for my father."

"Lass, ye canna—"

She interrupted him. "There's no reason we can't return to the crystal cave Talamar took me to and get more, is there?"

Duncan shrugged. "I wouldna think so, lass, but then, if they are anything like the green crystals, ye never know. They often seem to have a mind of their own."

Brogan shifted again and Sam patted his shoulder.

"I know," she said, softly, "I'm just trying not to think about that."

"Ye amaze me," Duncan said.

Sam stared at him, then laughed awkwardly. "You amaze me with such a statement. Why in the world do I amaze you?"

"This man would kill ye given half the chance, but ye are caring for him as if he were a member of yer own family."

She lifted one shoulder. "It's my duty. I took an oath to help anyone in need of health care."

Duncan frowned. "So ye dinna treat me—in Texas, when I was so ill—because of any affection for me. Ye treated me for the same reason that ye are treating him—out of duty."

Sam avoided his eyes. "Well, in the beginning, yes."

"And then ye crawled into bed with me."

A slow smile crossed her face. "Well, I'd have to say

that was above and beyond my usual devotion to duty." She looked back at him. "Don't you know how hard it was for me, every time I touched you, every time I *bathed* you, when you first came back with Griffin and Chelsea? I wanted to jump your bones every time I looked at you."

"You did?" he asked, sounding incredulous.

Sam got up and glared down at him, her hands on her hips. "Oh, I forgot, I'm the ice queen. I don't care about any of my friends or family."

She rose and stalked away from him. Duncan jumped up and ran after her. He grabbed her by the arm and jerked her to a stop.

"I know that isn't true," he said.

Sam arched one brow. "Oh, really?"

The breeze swept up around them and a strand of hair, loose from her braid, blew into her face. Duncan gently stroked it back behind her ear.

"Aye," he said. "And I'm sorry for ever saying it. Ye are a warm, giving woman and I believe ye love yer friends and family with all yer heart. In fact, I'm counting on it."

Sam caught her breath as Duncan bent his head and brushed his lips against hers.

Brogan moaned.

"Hold that thought," Sam said as she reluctantly moved away from the Scot and back to her patient. She knelt down beside him and opened the red velvet bag at her waist. With an oath, Duncan crossed to her side.

"Why in the world would ye do this?" he asked. "Ye must save the crystal for yer father, lass. There is no guarantee we'll be able to get back to the cave, or if we do, if the crystals will still be there."

"Lower your voice," she said, her own words

hushed. Brogan jerked his head to one side, his breathing labored. Sam tucked the plaid around him more tightly. "Now, you listen to me, Duncan Campbell, I do not want to use my blue crystal on this man, but I will if I have to!"

"But—"

"No buts!" Sam folded her arms over her chest and leveled her gaze at him. Duncan recognized that look from the time he'd spent recovering from his illness. He hated that look. It was a look, he was sure, that had sent terror through many a nurse's heart during her days in Houston. It was a look that said she wasn't going to take no for an answer. It was a look that said Samantha Riley was going to have her way—or else.

"All right," he finally said, shaking his head. "It's up to ye to decide."

She smiled without humor. "It always is. That's what being a doctor is all about." Sam laid her hand on Brogan's head again. "But there might be something else I could try first, before using the crystal."

"Ye have an idea?"

Sam nodded. "I'm going to attempt to burn the fever out of him," she said, and glanced up at the rising sun. "And no arguments!'

"Arguments?" Duncan pushed up the sleeves of his dark blue leine and smiled. "Just show me where ye want the fire built, lass, and tell me how long to make the spit so I can shove it up his bony ass and turn him over the flames like a rotisserie chicken."

Sam and Duncan built the fire on the flat rocks of the crag to insure that they wouldn't accidentally set the forest on fire. They dragged the already half-burnt tree Blinky had charred, and piled the wood in a half circle. Somehow Duncan coaxed the little animal to give a spurt of its inner fire, and the dry branches caught immediately.

"Okay, let's move Brogan in to the center of it," Sam ordered.

When all was ready, they carried their patient into the center of the circle. The blazing branches were far enough away that they posed no threat to Brogan or to them, as long as they stayed in the middle. She covered Brogan with the plaid and tucked it in around him. His sallow face already had a fine sheen of perspiration across his skin.

Good. Once again she had Jix to thank. Her friend had taken a course in Native American remedies and had actually taken part in a "sweat lodge." Intrigued, Sam had looked up more information on the cultural ceremony and discovered that in addition to being used for spiritual cleansing, something similar could also be used to break fevers in cases like Brogan's.

"I'm going to look for more wood, or perhaps peat," Duncan said. "I'm assuming ye want to keep the fire going as long as possible."

Sam nodded and he strode off without a backward look. Her heart seemed to constrict as she watched him walk away from her.

He'd said he loved her. There was no doubt in her mind or heart that she loved him. The thing she had tried to protect herself from all of her adult life had finally happened in spite of her best defense. She hadn't loved Mark. Mark had just been another way to stick it to her father, and now she knew why she had done it. She hadn't truly cared about any of the men she'd dated. She'd chosen most of them based on how much she gauged her father would hate them. The main reason she'd resisted Duncan for so long was because he'd been her father's choice.

How immature I've been, she thought, *shaking her head. I've guarded my heart against love and life because inside I've remained that hurt little girl who lost her mother.*

A new thought hit her. Maybe deep down she'd been afraid to love her father fully because she couldn't stand to lose another parent that she loved so much. Sam shook her head in amazement at her sudden insight.

Wouldn't Jix and Chelsea love to know that I've finally gotten in touch with my inner child?

Brogan moaned and Sam turned her attention back to him. His dark hair lay matted across his forehead and Sam brushed it back, gratified that his skin seemed a little bit moister, less like dry, hot paper than it had the night before. She was beginning to sweat herself.

Her braid had come undone during the work of building the fire. She leaned down and picked up a twig about five inches long, then twisted her hair up on top of her head, and secured it by sticking the twig through the way she used to do with her pencils while on her rounds at the hospital.

Those had been stressful days—days of decision and little sleep and pressure from higher-ups who didn't seem to like her very much.

She bent down to pick up the makeshift waterbag Duncan had fashioned from the leather jerkin he'd been wearing the day they escaped. She trickled a little water into Brogan's mouth, past his cracked, dry lips. He moved his mouth and the water went down. Dehydration was one of the deadliest enemies in this medical scenario, Sam knew, but she couldn't give him too much too fast. There were beads of sweat now rolling down his face and she took a piece of material she'd ripped from her leine and blotted the moisture from him.

"Come on, Brogan," she said aloud, "don't make me look bad. You've got to stay alive so you can prove I'm a fraud, remember?"

To her surprise the man's eyelids fluttered open and he gazed up at her, his eyes bright with fever. He opened and closed his mouth as if trying to speak, and finally managed to whisper a few words.

"Why—help—me?"

Sam met his glazed eyes with firm resolve. "Because I'm a healer," she said. "You were right, Brogan. I'm not the queen of the fairies, but I really am a healer and that's what healers do, they help sick people."

"But I am yer—yer—"

"My enemy?" Sam nodded and dabbed the sweat away from his forehead again. "Yeah, yeah. But I took a vow, to help the sick. Besides, doesn't God say to love your enemies?"

He shook his head almost imperceptibly. "Not—my—god."

"Well, I'll introduce you to mine later, now be quiet. I'm going to give you a little water and then I want you to rest. There will be plenty of time for questions when you feel better."

She dribbled a little more water between his lips and Brogan drank her offering greedily. He sighed and closed his eyes again. Sam laid practiced fingers on his pulse and then tightened her grip, alarmed. His pulse was slowing. She pressed her fingers against his throat to double-check. Definitely slowing.

In her last trip to Scotland's past she'd learned a great deal about using herbs as remedies, but even if she could find them in time, she had no way to cook them or prepare them out here in the wild. They would have to go back to the village.

Sam reached for the velvet bag at her waist and felt the edges of the blue crystal through the material. She'd waited long enough.

"Is he any better?"

She looked up into Duncan's concerned gaze. He deposited a pile of wood to one side and crossed to Brogan. He stood waiting for her answer and she ran her tongue across her lips and then swallowed hard.

"No," she said. "I don't think there's time to wait any longer."

"Are ye going to use the crystal?" he asked. She stared up at him. Duncan's dark hair seemed almost flame-like as the light breeze sweeping through the crag lifted the strands and sent them to dance in fiery points around his head, backlit by the circle of fire. His blue eyes glowed amber in the blaze, now beginning to die down around them, and Sam knew that whatever decision she made, Duncan would accept it. If Brogan lived or died, Duncan wouldn't blame her.

If he lived or died. Here it was again, this choice, this decision, only this time it truly was her choice. This time a man wouldn't die because she made a mistake or a miscalculation or a misdiagnosis. This time if the patient died it would be because she had refused to grant him life.

All right. She couldn't let him die. She'd taken a vow. First do no harm. Did that include doing good if you could? Of course it did. And there was a whole cavern full of blue crystals. Talamar would take Sam back to it again.

"Yes," she said at last to Duncan. She untied the velvet bag from the rhinestone belt always encircling her waist and pulled the drawstrings open. She took out the blue crystal and cradled it in her palm for a moment. It glowed with an inner light against her skin and her hand began to tingle.

"Wow," she whispered, and carefully placed the gleaming jewel on Brogan's chest as Duncan looked on, his face grim, but not disapproving.

Brogan's breathing slowed and deepened. His pale, sallow face flushed suddenly with color. The beads of perspiration disappeared. Sam and Duncan exchanged awestruck glances as the high priest opened his eyes.

"Where am I?" he asked. "What happened to me?" He pushed up on his elbows and looked around, his dark eyes dazed, but no longer feverish.

"You've been very ill," Samantha told him with a firm pat on the arm, "but you're going to be all right."

"She saved yer worthless life," Duncan said, a glint in his eyes. "So remember that in the days ahead."

"Saved my—" Brogan eased back to the ground. "I remember—ye talked to me—something—" he closed his eyes.

"That's right, go to sleep," Sam said. "Even with the healing powers of the crystal, I imagine that you'll need some recovery time." She glanced over at Duncan. "We need to get him back to the village. He needs broth, bread, warm clothes, a warm blanket, if we don't want him to have a relapse."

Duncan stared at her, his gaze unreadable.

"What?" she demanded.

He shook his head. "Again, sometimes ye truly amaze me," he said.

Sam shrugged and turned away, pretending to straighten the plaid over Brogan's feet. Duncan's words were like a balm to her soul, and she felt suddenly shy.

"But this is where I put my foot down," Duncan went on, his voice firm.

Her head came up and her eyes narrowed. "What do you mean?"

"We are not taking Brogan back to the village," he said, folding his arms over his broad chest. "And that's final."

Sam's temper flared. "The only thing that's final is what I say is final," she retorted. "I'm the doctor. I give the orders, at least where my patient is concerned."

"We aren't in Houston anymore, sunshine." Duncan's blue eyes were unwavering. "If we go back to the village, Gwain's men will kill us first and ask questions never. Have ye forgotten my swing over the cliff? I haven't."

"I know but—"

"No buts, as ye are so fond of saying," he said.

"I'm also fond of saying that you aren't the boss of me!" Sam heard the childish phrase coming out of her mouth and inwardly winced, but his male chauvinist, macho attitude was just too much to take. "I make my own decisions!"

"Not this time, lass," he said, shaking his head. His fiery hair was tousled and his jaw was locked, making him look even more irresistible than usual. His long, tapered fingers bit into huge biceps that were flexed and taut. Sam felt the pulse of desire quicken along her veins and took a step forward, then caught herself.

Focus, Samantha, she ordered, bringing her weaker side under control again. She'd just opened her mouth to continue the argument when there was a sudden rustling in the bushes near the edge of the crag.

"Is that Blinky?" she asked in a hushed voice, but Duncan pointed to the other side of the slowly dying circle of fire where the little dragon lay curled up, fast asleep. "Then—"

Duncan held up one finger to his lips and moved in front of her. The bushes shook again and then someone stumbled out and onto the flat stone surface of the crag. It was a dark-haired young woman. She stood for a moment, looking confused and unsure, then her eyes lit on the two of them. She stumbled forward a few steps and then sank to her knees.

"My queen," she said.

Sam frowned and stepped from behind Duncan. The girl looked familiar but she couldn't quite place her.

"It's Diersa," Duncan said. "Talamar's cousin."

Her cousin. Oh, yeah, the girl who had the hots for Duncan.

"Of course you'd remember who she is," Sam said, then ignored Duncan's puzzled look as she tried to find her old queenly persona. She stiffened her spine and lifted her chin. "Why are you here?" she asked.

"My queen," she said, her voice so low Sam could scarcely hear her. Her hair was a tangled mess and her clothing was torn and dirty. And she wasn't shooting Duncan any lascivious glances. Something must really be wrong. "I seek yer forgiveness for our village."

Sam raised both brows and glanced over at Duncan. He moved to her side.

"Who has sent ye?" he demanded. "Speak up, girl, and look at yer queen when ye speak to her."

Diersa looked up hesitantly. "The elders of the village have sent me, my queen. They hoped ye would have pity upon me because I am Talamar's cousin. They have asked for yer forgiveness for the actions of the high priest and Laird Gwain."

"Oh they do, do they?" Sam said and glanced at Duncan again. He shrugged. Maybe it wouldn't be good to give in too quickly. Why had the villagers gone to all of this trouble to send Diersa of all people out to find them? She placed her hands on her hips. "Well, give me one good reason why I should give it?"

The girl twisted her hands in front of her and Sam felt a sudden stab of sympathy. She looked truly distraught.

"Have mercy, my queen. Please have mercy. Yer plague that ye called down upon Gwain and his men has stricken the villagers as well, including my cousin Talamar! Finn would not leave her side and he added his plea to mine, to beg for yer pardon and mercy."

"Finn?" Sam and Duncan exchanged glances. "Has Gwain set him free?"

"Laird Gwain and his men are all terribly ill," Diersa said, her lower lip trembling. "Finn is one of the few unaffected by the malady, and he has been helping Aleric and myself, and a few others who were spared, to care for those who are sick."

"And he sent you to find me?"

"Aye, my queen." Diersa bowed her head again.

Sam beckoned for Duncan to follow her as she moved to one side, putting a few feet between them and the kneeling woman.

"What do you think?"

Duncan shrugged. "It could be a trap."

"But it could be the truth. Talamar could be really sick, even dying." Sam felt a pang at the thought. "We've got to go back."

"I will go back," Duncan said firmly. She opened her mouth to protest and he cut her off. "I will take Diersa back to the village and we will observe from a distance until I deem it is safe to enter. Then, if it isn't a trick,

I'll return for ye and Brogan." He frowned. "I dinna like to leave ye here alone with him."

"I have Blinky," she said. "I'll be all right."

"I'll leave ye my sword."

"I don't need your sword."

"Aye, lass, I'm leaving my sword."

Sam started to argue with him, but suddenly she was tired of fighting. Who said she had to always have her own way? Who said she was even always right? It was a novel idea and she decided to take a chance.

"All right," she said, noting the surprise that lit Duncan's eyes. "Just as long as you realize that this is typical male chauvinist behavior, through and through."

He smiled. "Aye," he said as he drew her against him for a good-bye kiss. "I do."

Chapter Twenty

Brogan opened his eyes and found that it hadn't been a dream. Queen Brigid sat in a filthy leine and trews, leaning against a small dragon, a sword at her side. Both were fast asleep. He lay on top of the queen's cloak with the consort's plaid tucked around him. A leather bag of water, or at least some clear liquid that seeped from its lashed sides, lay beside him. Although his clothing was soiled with sweat, he himself was clean, as though someone had bathed him while he slept.

He sat up, expecting to feel dizzy, surprised when it didn't happen. He decided to try to piece together what had happened to him.

He remembered taking the cart and mule—he had abandoned it once the fever set in and hoped the animal had found its way back to the village—and recalled stumbling toward the spring before losing his balance and falling to the ground. He didn't know how long he had been lying there unconscious before finally awakening. He looked away from the fairy queen and the dragon to discover a large black wolf not five feet away from him, his teeth bared, about to attack.

As Brogan looked down the throat of death, he felt a curious sense of peace. It would be over in a matter of seconds, all of his striving, all of his ambition and clever manipulations. It would all be over and as it turned out—what did it all matter after all? In a moment he would be just as dead as if he had lived as a king. In that instant, he wished he believed in God or gods or fairies, or anything that would take the fear from dying.

He kept his eyes on the wolf, determined to face death, determined not to die as a coward. But he longed to close his eyes and pray to whomever was out there. He had a sudden, fervent need to believe that there was someone after all.

"Whoever ye are," he whispered, "if ye exist at all, help me, please."

He didn't know really what he expected, but it wasn't a fiery miracle. Still, that was what he got. Moments after his prayer, he cried out as a flame burst across the open expanse where he lay, sending the wolf yelping into the forest nearby. The smell of singed hair hung in the air as the dragon—the one that had defended the fairy queen—toddled over to him and sniffed his feet. Brogan had barely had time to realize that the animal meant him no harm before passing out.

The next thing he remembered was hearing the voice of the fairy queen, telling him to live, telling him—he sat up straighter—that she wasn't the queen of the fairies, but a healer. Or had he dreamed that?

He was trying to clear the fog from his mind when he noticed the little dragon moving slowly out from under the woman who leaned against it. The dragon edged away from her little by little, until at last she lay flat on the ground, her head cradled on top of her arm.

Free from its burden, the creature bounded over to him and Brogan froze, his eyes wide with fear. Now that he was closer to the dragon he could see that it wasn't purely green, but variations of iridescent blues and greens that colored the tough scales across its back. The skin on its legs and neck and head was leathery, but also lustrous and speckled with silver. Its wings were edged in silver and its eyes were dark amber. The little horn on top of its head was a translucent blue. If ever there was a creature from the fairy kingdom, this was it.

The little dragon looked at him for a minute, sniffed his feet again, snorted, and then snuffled up the length of Brogan's leg until it reached his hands, clasped together so tightly in his lap he feared he might draw his own blood with his fingernails. The dragon lowered its head and bumped Brogan's hands, then his shoulder and arm in a similar manner. Brogan finally realized the creature wanted him to pet it.

Tentatively, he reached up and stroked one hand over the dragon's round head, unable to keep from smiling as it closed its eyes in obvious contentment. Brogan found a little soft spot behind the single protrusion at the top of its head, and scratched. The little dragon began making a low rumbling sound.

"Getting along, are we?"

He looked up, startled, into the strange lavender eyes of the fairy queen. He didn't know what to say. "Thank you" seemed hardly adequate. "I'm sorry for trying to kill ye" would be admitting too much. "Are ye the fairy queen or no" might be dangerous. Luckily, she spoke again.

"Are you feeling better?" she asked. He nodded and

accepted the leather bag of water as she picked it up and handed it to him. "You need to drink as much as possible. You're very dehydrated."

He didn't recognize the word, but discerned it had something to do with his water intake and so he drank, thankful for the cool liquid, even if it did taste of leather.

"You've been very ill," she told him as she sat cross-legged beside him. He realized suddenly that he was in a crag whose flat stones formed a kind of shelter, with a wall at their back and a floor of rock. No wonder his back ached.

"Why—" his voice was weak, scratchy, and the sound startled him. He cleared his throat and tried again. "Why did ye help me?"

She smiled at the question, but he could see there was no real humor in her gaze. "You do have a one-track mind, don't you?" He frowned at her response and she clarified. "You asked me the same thing before when you were extremely out of it."

She talked so strangely. Had she always spoken in such a way? He didn't remember her doing so in the village.

"Did ye answer me?" he ventured to ask.

The queen sighed and ran one hand through her long blond hair, dragging it back from her face. She looked tired and not like a fairy queen at all.

"Yes. I told you that I am a healer." She turned and met his eyes squarely. "Do you remember that? I am a healer and I was able, through the grace of God, to help you."

"A healer," he said, and took another sip of water as he thought her words over. He frowned. "Then why did ye help me? Why did ye not leave me to die?"

"Because I don't operate that way, buster," she muttered. He shook his head at her words and she sighed again. "Because where I come from healers are sworn to help anyone in need. Besides that, I have my own code of ethics that don't include leaving a helpless man to die."

Then the words came more easily. "Thank ye," he said. "What can I do to repay ye?"

"Nothing, I—" she stopped, a curious look in her eyes. "Well, actually, do you still have your staff?"

He frowned, trying to remember where it was. "It was in the cart, I remember that much. Yes, when I got out of the cart, when I realized I was ill, I leaned upon it. Perhaps it is near the stream? I remember the stream." He glanced up at her. "You want the staff? But why?"

She shrugged. "Um, I think it's pretty," she said, her eyes darting away from him. "But if you don't want to give it to me, I understand." Her voice trailed away and suddenly the high priest had a flash of this woman standing over him, telling him to live, giving him water, tucking the plaid around him, caring for him more completely than anyone ever had before.

"If I can find it," Brogan said, "it is yours."

The little dragon bumped his hand again and he patted its head absentmindedly.

"So you and Blinky have become buddies, eh?" she said. "I was afraid you might have been put off by the fireworks display the other night."

Brogan had heard that the Blessed Ones often tried to trick mortals into thinking them mortals too. Was this such a trick? But for what purpose? And why then would she have saved his life?

"Blinky?" he said.

She smiled and patted the animal's back. "I named it

that because it blinks a lot. He didn't mean to almost roast you. I'm sure Blinky was just defending us, not trying to hurt you."

Brogan shook his head. "No, he was defending me."

The woman's eyes widened. "You?"

"Aye." He cleared his throat, still feeling awkward sitting here with the fairy queen who'd said she wasn't really the fairy queen. "I had passed out—from my fever I suppose—and when I awakened, a wolf was about to attack. Yer friend here sent a lick of flame that chased the beast away."

"I think he's your friend as well," she said, "but right now"—to his astonishment she pushed him back down upon the stone and with a few efficient movements, tucked the plaid around him once again—"I want you to get some more sleep. You've been through a lot and you don't want to have a relapse."

Brogan was so stunned by her compassion that he closed his eyes and pretended to sleep, all the while planning what he would do next.

What Duncan saw from the shelter of the nearby forest shocked him. Where just a few days before had been a happy little village filled with men and women and children carrying on their daily lives, now Nirdagh looked like a battlefield, with bodies strewn across the marketplace and beyond. As they crouched behind some thick-leaved bushes, Diersa explained that Talamar and Gwain were among the most severely stricken by the illness, and not expected to live. They were both in the common building where there was the most warmth.

"Give me yer cloak," he told the girl. She untied the rough brown woolen garment and handed it to him. "Now, wait here for me. If I dinna return within an hour, go back to Sam—to the queen, and tell her that she must not return to the village under any condition. Do ye ken? That she must stay in the crag."

Diersa nodded, her pale face anxious. "Aye, I understand."

Duncan laid one hand on her shoulder in thanks and then tied the cloak around his broad shoulders and lifted the hood to hide his face. When he was sure no one was looking in his direction, he hurried out of the forest, running in a half-crouch until he reached a wide tree near the common building and flattened himself against it. After peering briefly around it to make sure no one was around, he strode out from his hiding place and headed for the common building.

Apparently he didn't need to fear that someone would see him. The building was empty except for the two patients, and Duncan was angered to realize that other sick villagers were lying outside because they were not deemed important enough to lie beside the Laird and his betrothed.

And yet no one seemed to be taking care of either one of them.

Talamar lay tossing and turning, just as Brogan had, while beside her on another pallet, Gwain moaned, moving his head back and forth. Duncan moved to the girl's side and laid his hand on her forehead as he'd seen Samantha do. She was burning up. Her skin was like heated paper. A flask of water sat nearby and he lifted it to her mouth, but she would not drink. She pushed his hand away.

"Talamar," he said softly. He slid his hand behind her head and lifted it, tilting the flask to her lips again. "Drink, darlin'. Just a little, please, for Duncan."

She opened her eyes blearily and stared up at him. "Duncan?" she whispered. He poured a little water against her lips. She didn't move for a second, then reached out and with a shaking hand turned the bottle up and gulped the water.

"Not too much, lass, 'twill make ye retch." He took the flask away and she lay back, already spent from her efforts.

"The queen—" she licked her cracked, swollen lips and Duncan's heart ached at the sight.

"She's fine. I'm going to bring her here, to help ye."

"No, ye mustn't," she said, grasping his arm with trembling fingers. "Most of Gwain's men—"

"Gwain's men are strewn across the ground, most of them. Samantha is a healer. She can help all of ye. Where is Finn?"

She looked around, her eyes a little wild. "I dinna know," she croaked. "I dinna think she would send her wrath upon us. I sent Diersa to beg her for mercy."

Duncan wished he could tell her that Sam was only guilty of trying to save his life by assuming the guise of the fairy queen, but that story would have to wait. "She dinna strike anyone down. I will explain later, but in the meantime, ye shall have yer mercy. Now rest until I return."

"Wait—" Her small fingers knotted on his sleeve with more strength than he thought she had left. "I knew in my heart she had not turned her back on us. But I do not wish to—to—ask too much from her. If the queen would but send the blue crystals," she whispered, "then she would not have to come herself."

Duncan clasped her hand in his. "Aye, 'tis a good idea. Tell me where they are."

"But the queen knows—"

"The queen is not with me. If I go to her, she will insist on coming back with me. You must tell me where to find the blue crystals."

Talamar licked her lips again and Duncan picked up the flask and gave her a little more water. "Aye, she is a merciful queen."

"Talamar, the crystals?"

Hoarsely, Talamar told him how to find the cave of crystals and closed her eyes. No matter how he tried, he couldn't rouse her again. He moved to Gwain's pallet, intending to give the man some water too, but the laird wouldn't respond. Duncan's heart pounded.

There was no way he could keep Samantha from returning to the village once she knew of their plight. If he brought the crystals back, there would be no need for Sam to risk herself, but if he didn't tell her, and Talamar died in the meantime, would Sam ever forgive him? Would he ever forgive himself?

He would go back to Diersa and send her to Samantha, bidding her come to the village. So many of Gwain's men were stricken they didn't pose much of a danger at the moment. Then he would find the crystal cave.

As Duncan hurried out of the building and through the people moaning on the ground, he saw Finn lying among them. He was pale, his eyes closed. Duncan stopped beside the man and knelt down to give him some water. Finn opened his eyes.

"I'm all right," he said. "Just exhausted from staying up all night with Talamar. I had to get out for a moment."

Duncan lifted the water flask to him and the man drank greedily. He had three days' growth of beard across his face and the sight jarred something in Duncan. Some nagging thought, some hidden realization that he just couldn't put his finger on. Then he saw it. Just a flash. Something in Finn's eyes, his chin. But it was enough.

"Better now?" Duncan asked. Finn opened his eyes and nodded. "Then we need to talk, and ye need to listen well, else ye are going to lose everything, including yer worthless life."

Samantha waited in the crag for Duncan to return, keeping the little dragon at her side. She wasn't afraid of Brogan exactly, but she did feel a little uneasy, now that he was well again. After he agreed to give her the staff he'd been curiously silent, speaking only when she spoke to him.

Diersa arrived back at the crag just after nightfall with Duncan's message. At first Sam was afraid he had been taken captive and the whole thing was a trick, but whether it was or not, she had to return to the village and see for herself. Diersa was too tired to lead her back to the village, and Sam wasn't so sure she wanted to make herself so vulnerable by venturing out in the darkness with the girl. They would wait until morning to leave. She slept off and on, waking often only to find Brogan sitting beside the fire, staring into the flames.

In the morning, the high priest was gone, and Sam's fears of walking into an ambush grew. But she had to go to Duncan. She had to make sure he was all right, and if Diersa's words were true, she had to help the villagers and Talamar.

She and Diersa headed for the village. After the strain of caring for Brogan for the last several days, Sam found she was exhausted by the time she reached the village, but the terrible sight that greeted her there sent a surge of adrenalin through her veins.

Sam wasted no time in organizing her "hospital," moving the more seriously ill into the common building, ordering the few able to walk and work to help her. She set the older women to cooking chicken broth for those able to eat, and the younger women to bathing the patients. At first the women protested that to bathe the sick would be the death of them. Samantha started to scream at them to obey her, but then she saw the fear in their eyes and remembered she was dealing with people in an ancient time that had no concept of germs or the difference cleanliness could make. She decided to make up a story worthy of Jix Ferguson.

"The goblins have done this, not me," she explained to the doubtful nurses. "And they have sent tiny little gremlins to make everyone sick. If we wash the ones who are ill, we might be able to wash the gremlins away too and they will not be able to harm you." After that, she didn't have any trouble with the bathing brigade. She prayed none of them contracted the illness.

She expected Gwain's men to arrest her as soon as they saw her, but instead, the men who weren't sick were eager to help her, eager to have someone take charge. After the first day, she had some kind of system worked out between herself and the ten or eleven "orderlies" and "nurses." The sickest patients had been bathed and given the warmest blankets, and those that would take it, a cup of chicken broth.

Finn bounced back after receiving some water and two cups of soup, and though he looked drawn and worn, he insisted on staying at her side to help. She put him in charge of the soldiers, and promised that she would take care of Talamar.

Talamar.

The girl was near death. Though Samantha recognized that the illness which had struck the village was nothing more than a virulent strain of influenza, in this time period it could easily be lethal, especially if those hit with it became dehydrated, or the sickness developed into a secondary infection.

That was what had happened to Talamar. Her lungs had become involved, and once Sam had things running fairly smoothly in the rest of the "hospital," she parked herself beside the girl, monitoring the lift and fall of her chest and the increasing labor of her breath.

Gwain was almost as sick as Talamar. He burned with fever and Sam put him and the girl closest to the huge fireplace that dwarfed the rest of the room, and hovered over the two of them around the clock.

By the end of the second day, she was beginning to panic a little. Where was Duncan? Had he found the cave? It shouldn't have taken him this long. Had Diersa mixed up his message?

She was just nodding off, sitting beside Talamar in Gwain's hard, thronelike chair, when the door to the common building burst open and she raised her eyes to the sight of Duncan.

He stood in the doorway shirtless, his broad shoulders and sculptured chest gleaming in the firelight. His discarded leine was draped across his arms, filled with something heavy—the crystals?

Sam jumped up and rushed to his side, her heart pounding with joy. Now everything would be all right. Talamar would be saved. The rest of the village would live.

But something was wrong. Duncan's face was a study in discouragement, not triumph.

"What is it?" she said, her hand on his arm.

"There were no blue ones," he said, and her heart

sank. "Only white and lavender. I brought those, just in case."

Sam had been running on little food and smaller amounts of sleep for three days now and when she heard Duncan's words, something inside of her snapped.

"Just in case?" she said, hearing the harshness of her voice whipping across the dimly lit room. "Just in case what? In case all of these people bump into a group of Chinese and need to understand their language before they die? In case we want to let them slip calmly into the next world? Duncan, I know the blue crystals were there, I saw them!"

She expected him to explode back at her, but instead he gazed down at her with compassion.

"Where do ye want these, lass?"

Sam looked around and saw a wooden tub near the fireplace. "Put them in that tub," she said wearily.

"Ye havena slept, have ye?" he asked as he crossed to the container and carefully dumped the crystals into it. He shook out his leine and pulled it over his head. "And probably haven't eaten."

"Don't change the subject! Where are the blue crystals?"

"Lass, I dinna know. They weren't there."

Sam felt her anger slip away as Duncan continued to look at her with gentleness in his eyes. She wanted to scream at him to fight with her, anything other than give her this promise of comfort and love. But instead, a sob broke free from her throat and Duncan made good on his promise, taking her in his arms.

She clung to him and let the tears come for a minute.

"Shhh, 'tis all right, lass. Ye are a fine doctor. Ye can help them yerself."

She gulped down her sobs and pulled herself together as she brushed the moisture from her face and backed out of his embrace, shaking her head.

"No," she said, dragging her hand over the long braid she'd fashioned sometime during the day to keep her hair out of her eyes. "Talamar is going to die. They're all going to die."

Her proclamation was met with silence. She looked up to find Duncan glaring at her. Sam lifted her chin defiantly.

"I canna believe ye just said that," he said.

"It's the truth, I'm just telling you the truth." Sam moved to the big fireplace and leaned against the waist-high hearth. She closed her eyes. This was why she'd given up medicine. No matter how hard a person tried, there was always this possibility of failure, of death.

"I never took ye for a coward."

Sam spun around, fists clenched at her side, suddenly longing for the compassion to reappear in Duncan's now stony gaze.

"How dare you! I am not a coward."

"Then ye are a quitter, and that's just as bad."

"I've done my best!" she shouted, and then clapped one hand over her mouth as Talamar and others in the room shifted in their sleep. She motioned for him to follow her outside. She walked quickly to the end of the building, and then turned to give him her best shot.

"I've done my best," she told him, "but it isn't enough! We need those crystals."

"Well, ye canna have them, so now what will ye do?" Duncan folded his arms over his chest and gazed down at her. "Give up?"

Sam turned away, shaking her head, hands on her hips. "There's nothing more I can do."

"So it's all up to ye, is it?"

She jerked her head up. "Who else?" She spread her hands. "Do you see any other doctors around here? Any EMTs? Any nurses? It's up to me, and I can't do it." She glared at him, feeling helpless and weak and a hundred times a failure. "Is that what you wanted to hear? I've failed, Duncan. Satisfied?"

"Not even a little bit," he said. "Why don't ye stop rolling around in that barrel of self-pity and face up to yer responsibilities?"

"Self-pity!? Why you—" Sam flung herself at him, fists flying, feet kicking, striking him again and again, impotent little taps no doubt against the hard muscled chest of a warrior. When she couldn't lift her hand again, Duncan slid one arm under her legs and the other behind her, and picked her up.

"What do you think you're doing?" she demanded. "Put me down!"

"Listen to me." His still, quiet voice shut her up like no amount of yelling would have. "Ye are a good doctor. Ye are the only hope these people have. If ye give up, most of them will probably die. If ye keep trying, some of them will live. Either way, yer choice will affect them for the rest of their lives—however long that may be."

Sam stopped kicking and lay back in his arms. His eyes were warm again, blue and deep like a hot ocean, one she wanted to bathe in. For a moment Sam felt protected. For a moment she felt that perhaps she could keep trying. The moment quickly passed.

"I'm so tired. Can I truly make a difference?" She asked weakly.

"Only you can decide that," he said, his breath warm against her cheek. "So what's it to be? Will ye try? Will ye help these people as much as is humanly possible?"

Sam closed her eyes. "You know I will," she said.

"That's my girl," he whispered. "Now, get some sleep. I'll watch them 'til morning."

"I hate you, Duncan Campbell," she muttered, the words muffled against his chest.

She felt the deep rumble of his laughter under her lips.

"Aye," he said. "No doubt."

Chapter Twenty-one

By the end of the week, Talamar was sitting up and drinking soup. Gwain had tried to get up and return to his men, but Sam had pushed him back down and threatened to sit on him, and the laird had finally relented. For the most part, everyone was well on the way to recovery, and there had been only one death, an elderly man.

Even though she had never met the man before—he had been already too frail with age to visit the fairy queen—Duncan saw Samantha take a few moments to weep for him, and then watched her wipe her eyes and visit the ones who had survived.

As her eyes lit up with the knowledge that she had helped save their lives, as she spoke encouraging words to each, Duncan knew that Samantha Riley would never be the same again. And neither would he.

Something had happened to him during this week of woe.

After he had taunted Samantha, she had risen to the

challenge, as he'd known she would. He'd expected her to find that great core of courage he'd recognized inside of her. He'd expected her to fight.

He hadn't expected a miracle.

But Samantha Riley had created her own miracle. She'd been everywhere that week, organizing, cleaning, cooking, bathing the sick. She'd hunted for hours in the forest for certain kinds of herbs and boiled them in the common room. As some of the villagers began recovering, she put them to work, helping her harvest the herbs, teaching them how to use them as poultices and tonics.

She had a water patrol that simply went from bed to bed, all day long, encouraging the sick ones to drink or eat, if they were able. Even Gwain received the best of care. She treated him the same as any other patient, even bathing him once to try to bring down the fever.

Every night she'd sprawled unconscious beside Duncan on the bed in their hut for a total of perhaps an hour before rising and tackling the next crisis.

And as he watched her fight the good fight, he gained something he'd never had for Samantha Riley before.

Respect.

Oh, he'd known for some time that he loved her, and had given her credit for graduating from medical school; but this was different, different from his love for her, and yet deeply intertwined.

Now he knew that Samantha was as much a warrior as he had ever been. He would never look at her quite the same way again.

One of his jobs for the day, as decreed by the queen herself, was to give each of the patients one of the lavender crystals. Talamar had suggested that perhaps the soothing influence of the crystals would keep the villagers from slipping into despair, and would speed their recovery.

As he handed out the multisided crystals, Duncan took a moment to look into the eyes of those Samantha had helped save, silently acknowledging her strength in the face of disaster. He would find a special time and a secluded place to tell her how much he admired what she had done.

One corner of his mouth lifted. A month ago he wouldn't have dared to compliment Samantha, knowing it would be something she would hold over his head in days to come. Now he had no such qualms.

He handed out the last crystal and headed back to the common building where Samantha was overseeing a new batch of herbal remedy. Perhaps he should make another trip to the crystal cave and procure more of the lavender crystals. Those he'd given them to already seemed calmer, more at ease. As soon as he pulled back the hide over the doorway, he realized he'd made a huge mistake. He should have started in this building.

The room was full of people, villagers and soldiers alike. Gwain sat in his carved wooden chair, his face pale, his cheeks sunken from his illness. In front of him stood Samantha, her face flushed, her arms held on either side by two of his burliest men. Talamar lay on her pallet, her eyes bright with unshed tears as she gazed up at Finn, also flanked by Gwain's men.

Duncan's hand went to the sword at his side, but two men grabbed him before he could draw it from the scabbard. His weapon was taken from him and he was shoved toward the laird.

"What's this about, Gwain?" he demanded. "Is this how ye repay Queen Brigid?"

Gwain's lips curled back in disdain. "She is no more Queen Brigid than I am," he said. " 'Tis as I suspected—she is a fraud."

"Ye are wrong," Duncan said, thinking quickly. "How else do ye think ye are alive this day?"

The man shook his head. "This plague came upon us as plagues often do. Who can say why?" His dark eyes narrowed. "However, just in case there is a real Queen Brigid, as these good people keep assuring me, I have decided to pay homage to her by sacrificing those who sought to imitate her power."

A cold chill danced down Duncan's spine as a sense of déjà vu swept over him. Duncan forced himself not to fight against the men holding him by each arm. "The real Queen Brigid stands right there in front of ye, responsible for saving yer worthless life."

Gwain chuckled. "Aye, so I've heard. But I am not a fool, consort. The true Queen of the Sidhe does not need herbs nor boiling water to heal those in her care. Just as this woman did not save ye from dangling over the cliff with her magic, neither did she save any of us with a spell or an amulet."

"I just finished giving out amulets of peace," Duncan said hastily.

Gwain's bearded face broke into a smile. "The villagers are gullible, easily swayed by such things. An amulet of peace is a simple way to convince simple people. It would be much harder—and prove more—to use such a crystal to invoke healing powers."

"I told you I needed those damn blue crystals," Sam said under her breath.

Duncan shot her a look that warned her to hold her tongue. She shot him back a look that told him where he could put his warning.

"That proves nothing," Duncan told Gwain. "The point is that the queen saved yer life. And this is how ye repay her?" He looked around at the soldiers and the villagers in the room. "Have ye no loyalty? Will ye let this happen?"

Gwain looked past Duncan and nodded. Duncan turned in time to see one of his soldiers nod in return and go out the doorway. They were up to something. Duncan glanced back at Samantha and saw she was staring down at Talamar.

The villagers began murmuring among themselves uneasily, while the soldiers stared stoically ahead. There was no way he could fight them all. Their only chance was if Talamar stood up for them.

"Talamar, say something," Duncan implored.

Talamar opened her eyes and turned them to the villagers and soldiers.

"Do not listen to Gwain," she said, her voice weak. "Our queen has spared us. Do not bring worse upon us."

"You'd better listen to her," Sam said. "This little game I've been playing with you is losing my interest."

Talamar closed her eyes again.

"What if ye're wrong?" Duncan asked the laird. "What if this is the real Queen of the Sidhe?"

Gwain laced his hands over his stomach, which had shrunken considerably over the last week, and smiled. "I have it on very good authority that she is not."

"Whose authority?" Sam said, her own tone queenly.

Gwain raised one hand toward the doorway. Someone outside pulled the hide back and a man ducked his head and entered.

Brogan.

"Just great," Duncan said under his breath. "Ye had to save the blaggart."

"I did more than that," said Sam, her face ashen. "Whoever said honesty was the best policy was an idiot."

Brogan approached them slowly, holding his staff. The pale green crystals sparkled above the wood.

The high priest stopped a good ten feet away from them, his eyes darting nervously from side to side.

"She is not the queen of the Tuatha De Danaan," the high priest said, his voice flat. "She told me so herself. We have been deceived." He looked down at the ground, oddly subdued.

"There ye have it," Gwain said to Duncan. He leaned forward slightly. "Talamar and I will be married this day, and ye and yer whore will be sacrificed to appease the beliefs of the village."

"And what does Finn have to say about this marriage?" Samantha said, her voice rigid.

Gwain glanced over at the silent, blond Finn, held firmly between two soldiers. "He will have nothing to say about it, else he will join ye in the fire."

Duncan's mouth flattened into a grim line. "Let us go," he said, "and I swear ye'll never see us again."

The laird's mouth twitched under his beard, whether in amusement or irritation, Duncan couldn't tell. The man's eyes remained steady. "And leave ourselves open to another plague from the Tuatha Da Danaan? We must atone for our sins, for ever accepting a false representation of the queen."

"Wouldn't a few Hail Marys work for you?" Sam said.

"Yer words have no meaning to me," Gwain said, "and soon yer lying tongue will be silenced forever."

He unlaced his hands and moved them to the arms of the chair where his fingers tightened around the wood in anticipation.

"Take them to the standing stones."

"Well, thanks for the good time," Sam said as she and Duncan were shoved forward along the forest path.

"Ye're welcome, lass. I always aim to please," Duncan answered, his voice light. She glanced over and their eyes met. He winked. Heartened, Sam lifted her chin and turned her attention back to the trail.

Talamar was being carried on a wooden pallet between Finn and another soldier and Sam was worried about her. The girl's eyes fluttered open. Her red-gold hair lay tangled beneath her and Sam spared a fleeting angry thought for the "nurse" who should have combed the girl's hair that morning. Her face was so pale.

Sam had to mentally restrain herself to keep from running over and taking Talamar's pulse. Out of the whole ordeal, she hated the most that in spite of everything, Talamar was still going to end up marrying Gwain. Well, that, and the fact that they were about to die.

They reached the standing stones, but there was some discussion about whether or not the prisoners would be sacrificed within the stones or outside. Apparently, the superstition surrounding the huge monoliths extended even to the mighty Gwain.

"Brogan," the laird said. "Ye are the high priest. Should we make our sacrifice within the circle of stones?"

"Aye," the priest said. "In the center."

A sob broke free from Talamar where she lay on the

ground. Samantha jerked away from her captors and threw herself down beside the girl, but the soldiers grabbed her and dragged her back.

"Trying for a hotter flame, lass?" Duncan asked lightly as she stumbled to a stop beside him. The soldiers took position on either side of the two, leaving them next to one another. Duncan's hand brushed against her thigh and Sam curled her fingers into his.

"A short life but a merry one," she said.

"Aye."

The gentleness of his voice made her glance up. His dark blue eyes seared into hers. " 'Twas merry," he whispered, "as long as ye were there. I'm sorry, lass, for ever dragging ye into this."

Sam leaned against him for a moment, head against his chest, caught by his heat, wishing hopelessly that she could lie in his arms just one more time. "I love you, Duncan. I don't think I can ever say that often enough, but I'm going to try."

His mouth eased into an amazing smile. "And I'm verra proud of ye. I'll be making a habit out of that phrase as well."

"Thanks," she whispered. "Boy, are you going to get lucky later. If there is a later."

"Quiet!" Gwain barked. A soldier jerked her away from Duncan and Sam fought the urge to deck the man. Her gaze fell on Talamar, who was now sitting up on her pallet. She stared at Sam, dismay in her eyes. Brogan stood at the edge of the crowd, his thin fingers clutched around the staff he held. He looked a little dazed.

"Place them in the center of the stones!" Gwain demanded.

Sam and Duncan were pushed into the middle of

the fairy ring, and a shiver swept over her as she stumbled to a stop. The last time she'd stood in this place the earth had tried to swallow her whole.

The soldiers positioned them and then ran out of the circle, obviously not immune to superstition or fear, leaving the two free at last to hold one another. Duncan's arms went around her and Sam felt a new surge of strength and courage.

Talamar had risen from her pallet and now took a step toward them. A soldier stopped her from entering the circle and she stood just outside the stones, watching, her hand to her throat.

A tingle swept over Sam and she looked up at Duncan, startled.

"Aye," he said, "I feel it too."

"Duncan, about that time I fainted here—"

"Aye, lass?"

"There was something I didn't tell you."

"Aye?"

"The earth tried to swallow me."

"Place the branches!" Gwain shouted.

"Thanks for the notice," Duncan said, and held her tighter.

Apparently this had not been a spur-of-the-moment decision on the laird's part since he'd started his recovery, Sam realized. At least forty or fifty saplings had been cut down, along with some dead growth that was now piled around them. The soldiers practically threw the wood into place in their haste to leave the fairy ring.

A tingling rush swept over her again.

"Hold on to me, lass," Duncan said. "Whatever happens, hold on to me."

"Talamar said the circle was how the fairy queen returned to her home," Sam whispered, her arms flung tightly around his waist. "You don't think—"

"I dinna know," he said, "just—"

"Stop!"

The command rang out across the standing stones and Sam and Duncan jerked their heads up. Brogan strode suddenly from the back of the crowd, his staff in hand, the people moving out of his path. He stopped just outside the circle, his dark eyes glittering with something that looked suspiciously like zeal.

"What are ye doing, Brogan?" Gwain demanded.

"Ye must not kill them," Brogan said. "She saved my life, and yers, Gwain." He moved his gaze to Talamar. "And that of yer betrothed. Ye have no right to take their lives."

"She lied," Gwain blustered, his fists clenched at his side. "She tricked us all, including ye!" His voice became mocking as he glanced around at the villagers. "She brought the plague of the Sidhe down on us, did she not? And she tried to stop my marriage from taking place! I have every right."

"Brogan is right," Talamar said. She swayed and Finn broke away from the soldiers at his side and ran to her. The soldiers took a step forward, but Gwain held up his hand.

"He is going nowhere."

"We must not kill them," Talamar said, Finn's arm around her. "To repay good with evil is wrong." She turned to the villagers and elders gathered. "Do not let them do this." The crowd looked uneasy at Talamar's words.

Finally one man stepped forward, Aleric, an elder. "We dare not anger Gwain," he said. "Else how will we defend ourselves against the Danes?"

"With my help," Finn said, pulling Talamar close as

he turned to glare at Gwain. "I've tried to be loyal, Father, but I willna let ye hurt Talamar, nor my friends."

"Father?" Sam said, her mouth falling open.

"Father?" Talamar whispered, looking up at Finn.

Duncan smiled. "Father." He glanced over at the tall young man and nodded. "Good lad."

Finn's face was flushed but he grinned at Duncan, and addressed the soldiers. "Men of arms," he said, his voice strong and decisive, "stop my father from this travesty of justice and I promise ye double yer pay, time each year to visit yer families, and," he paused dramatically, "I will personally give each of ye a parcel of land that will belong to ye for as long as ye serve me."

A cheer went up from the men as Gwain sputtered in fury. In a matter of moments the laird had been seized, his hands were tied behind his back, and he was sitting on the ground, cursing his son roundly.

"Who knew?" Sam said aloud.

Duncan raised one dark brow at Sam. "I knew."

"I dinna know," Talamar said.

"Och, love, I couldna tell ye," Finn said. "My father forbade it, and I was a weakling. A coward." He glanced over at Duncan and Sam. "These people have taught me what courage is. While you were ill, Duncan came to me and convinced me to take my father's power and use it for good."

Sam poked Duncan in the side with her elbow. "And you didn't share this little conversation because?"

He shrugged. "Just gave the lad a little friendly advice."

Talamar's eyes glittered with love as she gazed up at Finn. "I dinna know ye were the laird's son, but I knew ye were a good man."

"And I always knew ye were my own true love." He bent his head to hers and kissed her.

"And ye are mine," she said. Talamar smiled up at him and with a shout, Finn lifted one hand into the air.

"Remove that wood!" he cried. Ten soldiers rushed forward and carried the wood away as quickly as they had brought it inside the ring.

Talamar turned back to the circle of stones and walked into the ring. She stopped just on the other side of the stones and sank into a deep curtsy.

"Please, forgive the people of the village, my queen," she said, her eyes downcast. "They were just afraid and did not know what to do."

Sam wanted desperately to tell Talamar the truth, but she didn't dare. She'd already made that mistake with Brogan and look what had happened. If she didn't open her big mouth again they might just get out of this alive.

"Stand up, Talamar," she said. The girl hesitated, then stood, her head still bowed. "Look at me, please."

Talamar looked up, her green eyes luminous, and in that moment Sam felt a pain so piercing that it took her breath away. She would miss her friend forever, but she had to go home. Her father needed her.

"It's all right," Sam said softly, and held out her hand.

Talamar hesitated again, then moved forward and tentatively took her hand. "Ye forgive us?"

"There's nothing to forgive, and besides, not my job." She smiled and suddenly knew that she couldn't leave without telling Talamar the truth. She pulled the girl into her arms for a tight hug.

"My queen?" Talamar said, apparently too startled to hug back.

Sam held her close and whispered in her ear. "I'm not the fairy queen, but I am your most devoted friend and I need your help. I am a traveler from another time. I need the green crystals to return to my home. Will you help us?" She released her and Talamar took a step back, her mouth open in astonishment.

"My queen!" she said, and her hand flew to her lips.

"Samantha," Sam said. "Just Samantha."

Talamar blinked at her in wonder and then smiled. "My queen. Samantha. To say I am yer friend gives me more joy than I can e'er express. I welcome this new test." She sank into a curtsy again.

"No," Sam said, bending to pull her back to her feet again as Talamar continued to smile. "You don't understand. It's no test. I need the green crystals."

Talamar frowned. "But my queen," she said, "I dinna understand. Always before ye have returned to yer home through the standing stones."

"Yes, Talamar." Sam thought quickly. Obviously the girl wasn't going to accept her claims of not being the fairy queen. "There's a problem with the usual way I return to, er—" she stuttered to stop. *What was the name of that place again?*

"Tir Na Nog," Duncan said helpfully.

Sam picked up the conversation without missing a beat. "Yes, Tir Na Nog. And the green crystals can be used to gain me entrance again to, er, the land of the Sidhe." There, that was pretty good.

"Oh, I see, my queen—Samantha."

"Talamar," Duncan said, as Brogan continued to watch them, openly curious. The villagers were murmuring among themselves, casting the little group anxious looks. No doubt they were waiting for the next act in the show. He pulled the girl to one side and lowered his voice. Sam moved with him. "When I went to the cave to find the healing crystals," he said, "they weren't there. Why not?"

"I do not know, Sir Duncan," she said. "The crystals seem to come and go somehow, as is their wont." She glanced at Samantha. "Why would they hide from yer consort, my queen—Samantha?"

"Er, perhaps it's the doings of one of my enemies," Sam said.

"Aye," Duncan said, "one of the Unseelie Court, no doubt."

Talamar's eyes widened at his words and she lowered her voice. "Do ye have need of a healing crystal, my queen—Samantha?"

"Yes," Sam said. She reached out and took Talamar's hand as her heart began to pound a hopeful rhythm. "Yes, do you have one, Talamar?"

"Aye." The girl reached for the leather cord around her neck and pulled it over her head. A clear crystal, a lavender, and a blue were strung there. "Ye are most welcome to all three, my queen."

"Just the blue one," Sam said. "That's the only one I need." Talamar nodded and took the crystal from the cord and handed it to Sam.

"Ye healed me with a blue crystal, didn't ye, my queen?"

Sam turned, startled, as Brogan spoke from beside her elbow. "Yes, I did."

Talamar glanced at Samantha, her gaze knowing. "Ye were saving that crystal, were ye not? For someone special in yer life?"

Sam nodded. It surprised her that Talamar was so intuitive. "Someone in my family is near death. That's why I'm so anxious to return to er, Tir Na Nog, and I had intended to bring the blue crystal with me."

"Then why did ye use it to heal me?" Brogan asked, shaking his dark head. "I dinna understand."

"I told you before," Sam said. "You were there, you were dying. I had to save you." She shrugged. "Simple."

"To save the life of an enemy over that of yer own kin," he shook his head again. " 'Tis not so simple. Nor are my beliefs right now."

"But how—why didn't this heal you, when you were ill?" Sam asked, taking the precious gift in her hand.

"The crystal never heals the first person who touches it," she said, as if reciting a textbook. "Am I correct, my queen?"

"Er, yes, you are correct." Sam took the crystal. "Thank you, Talamar."

"My queen?" Brogan stood in front of her, the crystal-studded staff in his hands. Sam's heartbeat quickened. He was going to make good on his promise to give her the staff.

A wan smile touched his lips. "I thought I had a way to earn yer forgiveness for my treachery, but Finn stole my thunder. I had a wondrous escape planned for all of ye."

"Escape?" Sam said.

He pursed his lips together and whistled loudly. From the heart of the nearby forest there came a flash of blue and green across the sky, and then the sight of the little dragon hovering above them. The villagers and soldiers fell back, giving the animal a wide berth as he gently sank to the earth beside the high priest.

"He willna harm ye," Brogan said over his shoulder to the villagers. "Will ye, Donald?" He scratched the dragon's head and it turned its face up to the sky in rapture.

"Donald?" Sam blurted.

Brogan shook his head and moved into the circle of standing stones. "Blinky was no name for such a strong, brave lad," he said. He glanced at Sam and spoke apologetically. "I know that I said I would give ye this staff," he said, "but 'tis not mine to give." He held out the staff to Talamar. "This is yers," he said.

She started to protest, but he held up one hand.

"Nay, 'tis yers. I never deserved it, for I am the charlatan in this village." His gaze swept over Duncan and Sam. "Thank ye," he said softly, "for saving me."

He turned and walked away, the little dragon on his heels. "Come along then, Donald," he said.

The dragon started to follow, then stopped and looked back at Samantha. Again that tug on her heartstrings—what was wrong with her? Like she could take a baby dragon back with her! Too bad, though, that Jix and Chelsea couldn't see him. She walked over to the hesitant creature and knelt down beside him, draping one arm around his tough hide.

"Good-bye, Blinky," Sam whispered to him softly. "Have a good life." She glanced up at Brogan waiting impatiently. "You'd better take good care of him."

"I will, my queen," he said with a bow. "Indeed I will."

Sam gave Blinky another hug and stood. Brogan whistled again and the little dragon bounced happily to his side.

"Come along, lad," he said. "There's a monastery northeast of here and an old friend of mine there that I wish to see again. I have much to discuss with him. Mayhap we will stop on the way at the Loch of Ness and let ye take a wee swim, eh?" The two disappeared into the forest.

"Well, what do ye make of that?" Duncan said,

shaking his head as Sam crossed back to where he stood in the center of the stones.

Sam grinned up at him. "I make out the beginning of a beautiful friendship, and maybe the start of a very famous legend." She glanced down at the ground warily. "Do you think we could get out of this circle now?"

"Ye have need of this too, do ye not, my queen?" Talamar said, handing her the staff.

Relief swept over Sam. "Yes, thank you." She took the staff and handed it to Duncan. Their eyes met. It was time to go.

"Good-bye, Talamar. I wish you only happiness and joy in your life." She reached out and hugged the other woman tightly. "And remember, love is the greatest magic of all."

"Yes, my queen—Samantha," Talamar whispered.

Finn had entered the circle and now pulled Talamar back from them. "Thank ye," he said to Samantha, "for saving her."

"My pleasure," she said, giving Talamar a fond look.

"Rule yer father's lands wisely," Duncan said. "And love Talamar with all of yer heart."

"That is something I will never fail to do," Finn said. He put his arm around Talamar and guided her from the circle. They turned and stood outside the large standing stones and suddenly a hush fell on the murmuring crowd around them.

"Lass," Duncan said as he looked down at the staff, "these crystals aren't glowing, and they are not in water."

"Talamar said that the real fairy queen told her that the green crystals worked through elements of nature. They're lodged in wood, so maybe—"

"Just dinna get yer hopes up." Duncan turned the staff around in his hands and gripped the crystals.

"Hope is all we've got, laddie," Sam said. She reached out to touch the smooth sides of the magical stones, and then froze, her fingers inches away from the crystals as she looked up at the man she loved.

"What is it?" Duncan asked, his rugged, handsome face wreathed in concern as he gazed down at her.

"After we get back to my time, you don't have to stay with me." She ran her tongue across her lips. "I want you to," she added as uncertainty crossed his face, "but I want you to do what you need to do. I'll understand, whatever you choose."

And suddenly she knew it was true. She wanted what was best for Duncan, not herself. She loved him that much.

Duncan lowered his mouth to hers and she lifted hers to him. He burned his answer into her lips and her heart, and when he raised his head, she leaned against his chest and his sigh rippled all the way through her. She had her answer, at last.

"Let's go home, Duncan," she whispered, "to Texas."

"Aye, lass," he agreed.

"My queen!" Talamar called. "Are the two of ye getting shorter?"

Sam looked up, startled, toward the girl and Finn. Talamar had grown several inches taller.

"Duncan," Sam tightened her grip on him. "Look down."

They both looked. Their feet were gone. The ground had swallowed them up to their ankles. She and Duncan looked at one other.

"Lass," he whispered, "I canna move."

Samantha made a grab for the crystals and touched them just as a paralyzing sensation swept over her.

Sam filled her mind with thoughts of Texas, the

Crazy R Ranch, and the image of her father in front of his fireplace. Jix, Chelsea, Griffin, Jamie—she pictured all of them together in the colonel's den. She pictured herself, with Duncan by her side, back in 2005 Texas, where they belonged. Both of them.

The green crystals beneath their fingers began to glow, and just as Sam felt the earth disappear from under her feet, a swirling emerald vortex swallowed them whole and swept them away into the unknown.

Epilogue

"I can't believe I lost it," Samantha said as she paced across the waiting room and back again.

The new stroke wing at the Texas Medical Center in Austin was brightly lit, the waiting room filled with comfortable imitation leather chairs and stylish little tables flanking them. Sam was oblivious to the comforts. She was trying to work up the courage to face her father without the miracle cure she had worked so hard to bring him.

When the standing stone circle had begun its weird quicksand phenomenon, she had also felt what she hoped was the sensation of the crystals sending them through time. But most of all she'd felt Duncan's arm around her, holding her, keeping her safe. She was falling, dizzily, spinning around and around, when all at one she heard a big splash and then she was wet, and she opened her eyes to the wonderful sight of the two of them bobbing up and down in the middle of Jacob's Well.

The car she'd left nearby—how long ago?—was gone, probably stolen or impounded, since she'd left the key under the seat. They'd had to walk all the way to the highway before they caught a ride with a passing motorist.

At the ranch they'd wasted no time in explaining things to an excited Jix and Chelsea, who swore that only a few days had passed since their disappearance. Amazing, since they'd been in the past for over a month. They changed their clothes—Sam had been overjoyed to hand Jix back the rhinestone belt—then dragged the two women into her father's SUV and headed for the hospital. Duncan and Sam related a condensed version of their adventure along the way, promising more details later.

"A fairy queen? Really?" Jix and Chelsea had wanted the details right then, but Sam convinced them to call their husbands and tell them the news. The two women had pounced on their cell phones and were now headed downstairs to meet Jamie and Griffin and bring them up to speed.

Sam didn't realize she'd lost the blue crystal until she reached the hospital. She'd been pacing the waiting room, trying to work up her nerve to go into the ICU and see her father.

"Why didn't I put it in my pocket?"

"Ye dinna have a pocket, lass," Duncan reminded her from his prone position on the one long couch in the room.

"I had that stupid little velvet bag," she told him. "I could have put it in there." She paced some more. "I should have known I couldn't hold on to it!"

"Dinna kick yerself so hard, lass."

"It isn't fair, it just isn't fair," she said, shoving her hands into her jeans. "To go through so much and

345

make it back here, only to lose the one thing that could heal him—"

Duncan sat up and held his hand out to her. "Come here."

She crossed the room and sat down beside him. Duncan put his arm around her, but she was stiff and unyielding. He held her silently until she melted against him with a sob.

Tears burned down her cheeks. "In Nirdagh I could do something to at least try to keep those people alive. Here, I'm helpless."

He turned her face to his and kissed her tears. "Nay," he said, "Samantha Riley is never helpless."

"My father has the best doctors in Texas," she said. She pulled away and got up to pace again. "He's in a coma. What in the world could I do to make him wake up?"

"Talk to him," Duncan said. "Do what ye do best, Samantha. Save him."

Sam looked up into his warm blue eyes and slowly lifted her arms around his neck. She kissed him with all the love and fear inside of her, and when he lifted his mouth from hers, it was as if he had lifted a dark shadow from her heart as well.

"Ye can do it, lass," he said. "I believe in ye."

She nodded as she backed slowly away from him, then turned and ran toward the ICU, almost plowing down Jix and Chelsea in the hallway.

Duncan was right. She wasn't helpless. Her father was going to wake up or her name wasn't Dr. Samantha Riley. She pushed the door to the ICU open and went inside.

Colonel Riley lay tilted slightly upward in his hospital bed. He was attached to tubes and wires, the steady beep of a monitor near him declaring he was still alive as the oxygen from his mask hissed into his lungs. They hadn't put him on a respirator yet, but she knew it was just a matter of time, unless he woke up soon.

She crossed to his side and stood looking down at him. His face was almost the same, lined and solid, the laugh lines at the corners of his eyes slightly deeper than she remembered.

Suddenly images of her father laughing with her danced across her mind. She remembered as a little girl being bounced upon his knee, remembered him teaching her to ride, remembered him smiling down at her as he held her hand and walked her to school each and every morning after her mother died.

Then she was older, and they rode together across the ranch, and he told her jokes about Texas A&M, a Texas tradition, and teased her about naming her gelding Sugar, because she thought at first he was a mare. She remembered Christmases, just the two of them, how each and every item she'd put on her list was under the tree, wrapped by him, evidenced by the abundance of scotch tape and the bows that kept falling off.

She remembered graduating from high school, and how he had smiled down at her with tears in his eyes, then college, and then medical school. He'd almost busted his buttons off with pride over that accomplishment. And why shouldn't he? He'd helped her get there. It was his triumph too.

How could she have forgotten all of this, she wondered as she stood beside his bed. How had the fact that her father tended to be a little controlling, a little gruff, wipe out every other good thing he had ever done for her?

"Please, God," she whispered. "Don't let him die. Let me tell him I love him." She closed her eyes for a moment, took a deep breath, and then opened them again. "Daddy," she said softly. "I'm here. I had to take a long, roundabout way to get here, but I made it.

"Dad, you're the one who taught me to never say die, to never give up, remember? So I know you aren't going to give up without a fight. Besides, I won't let you." She picked up one of his long, lean hands from the bed and cradled it between hers.

"You see, you and I, we've got a lot to talk about, a lot to work out, and that's fine. I can deal with that." Her throat tightened and she stroked his hand. "What I can't deal with is being without you. Not yet. I'm not ready for that. So open your eyes, Dad, and stop being so stubborn. Open your eyes and tell me you're proud of me, because I know you are." She paused. "I love you, Dad."

Sam ran out of words and stood silent for a moment, half expecting her father to really answer her. But the only reply to her diatribe was the sound of the monitor beside his bed.

"If only I hadn't lost the crystal," she said aloud, beginning to sink into frustration again. Duncan's words came back to her—*Save him.* What would make him open his eyes? What would bring Colonel Riley back to her? She smiled.

Only one thing.

Sam leaned down closer to him. "Daddy," she said, "I have something important to tell you, so listen. I'm going to marry Duncan Campbell. Do you hear me, Dad? So do you know what this means?" She raised her voice and enunciated each word carefully.

"YOU—WERE—RIGHT."

She leaned back. She waited, hardly daring to breathe.

Colonel Patrick Riley's eyelids fluttered, and blinked. He opened his eyes and ran his tongue over dry lips. "What—what did you say? Samantha?"

"Yes, Dad," she said, her heart pounding. Tears burned her eyes, but she managed to keep her voice steady. *Thank you, thank you, God.*

"Did you hear what I said?" she asked.

"I heard," he whispered, "but I thought I must have dreamed it."

Sam shook her head. "You didn't dream it. You were right, Dad. Duncan Campbell is the man for me. Now you've got to get well so you can give me away at the wedding."

Her father turned his steel-gray eyes to hers and she didn't miss the twinkle reflected there as he lifted his hand to gently touch her face. Then he cleared his throat and frowned, his face falling into familiar lines.

"Well," he said weakly, but with a spark of his old gruffness, "what are we waiting for? Where are my pants?"

"Why did I ever let ye talk me into this?" Duncan asked, tugging at the stiff tuxedo collar around his neck.

"Me? Why did I ever let you talk me into it?" Samantha demanded as she shoved a long, gossamer bridal veil back on her head for the fourth time. No matter how hard she tried, the damned thing wouldn't stay on straight!

"I didn't." He glared down at her and then his blue eyes shifted from frustration to amusement. "As a matter of fact, neither one of us had anything to do with this." He pulled her to the door of the bedroom where they were both dressing and pointed down the hall to the kitchen of the Riley ranch house, where they could see Jix and Chelsea talking. "It was those two!"

After her father's miraculous awakening, and six weeks of recovery in a rehabilitation hospital, Duncan had asked him for Sam's hand in marriage and Jix and

Chelsea had begun planning with a vengeance. Since her father was still weak, the wedding would be a small affair with just their closest friends and family, held in the ranch house.

"Hey, that's right." Sam moved to her fiancé's side and slid her hands up the front of his tailored shirt. "Wanna run away with me? We could elope to Vegas."

Duncan closed the door to the room and slid his arms around her waist. She wore her wedding underwear, corset, lacy panties and a full floor-length slip. The corset was cinched tightly and made her curves above and below that much curvier.

"What are ye wearing?" he asked as he lowered his mouth to kiss her bare shoulder. "And how do I take it off?"

"There's a tie right here," she said, holding up the long end of a white ribbon.

He raised his head, interested, took the ribbon between his fingers and pulled, untying the bow at the top.

"Stop that," she said, slapping his hand away. "Hey, you didn't answer me." She put her hands on her hips and tried to give him "the look," but her heart just wasn't in it anymore.

Duncan gazed down at her and she slipped her arms around his waist, loving him, wanting him.

"I will follow ye anywhere, lass," he said, his voice soft. "Across time and space and Texas. Just give me the word."

"You know, you aren't half the male chauvinist p—" he raised both dark brows at her, "—er—that you used to be."

"Aye," he said, "and ye are not half the demanding b—" Sam narrowed her eyes at him, "—er—woman—ye used to be, either."

"Guess we've both learned a lot."

"Guess so."

"Guess that was the point."

"The—" Duncan's firm lips eased up into a smile as he nodded. "Aye, I believe it was."

"I'm going back to that residency program, you know," she said.

"I never doubted but that ye would."

"Oh." She leaned up and kissed him. "By the way, thanks for saving us back there."

Duncan shook his head. "Back where?"

Sam rolled her eyes. "Don't play innocent. You know you were responsible for Finn growing a backbone at the last minute and putting a leash on his bulldog of a father."

"Oh, that." He lifted one shoulder. "Well, 'twas no more saving us than the grand example of yer strength and honor in saving the whole village."

Sam ran her hands over his shirt again, feeling the incredible, totally yielded love she felt for Duncan Campbell wash over her. "You are getting so lucky later."

"Och, dinna tease me, lass."

She laughed and kissed him, then moved to open the door and peek out again. "Well," she said, pretending to sound long-suffering, "they've gone to all of this trouble. We might as well go through with the thing."

"Might as well. But first—" he turned her around and pressed her against the door, effectively shutting out the people milling around in the other rooms. He tugged on the white ribbon again.

"Duncan, I have to put on my dress."

"Later."

"But we're getting married in five minutes."

"Make it ten," he whispered against her ear.

"It's bad luck for you to see me in my dress."

"We make our own luck," he said as he kissed his way down the side of her neck. "Besides, I dinna want to see ye in yer dress. I want to see ye out of it."

Samantha slid down the door and Duncan followed her, unlacing her corset as she linked her hands around his neck.

"We're going to be late for our own wedding," she murmured.

"Och, lass, we've got all the time in the world."

"That's right," she said as she pushed him against the wall and crawled into his lap. "Plenty of time for sleepy mornings and sunsets on the beach and babies with your eyes and my intelligence—"

"Hey!" Duncan protested. "What about my intelligence?" Then his eyes lit up. "Babies?"

Sam leaned down and brushed her lips softly against his. "Babies," she whispered.

Thirty minutes later, after several frantic knocks on the door from Jix and Chelsea, Samantha Jane Riley and Duncan Fitzgerald Campbell were joined in holy matrimony in the living room of the Crazy R Ranch with their best friends beaming beside them. Still recovering, but well on his way back to health, Patrick Riley rose from his wheelchair long enough to give his daughter to the only man he'd ever deemed worthy of her.

Sam's diaphanous white gown drifted like a shimmering cloud to her feet. The matching sheer shawl draped beautifully across her shoulders, while the sparkling rhinestone belt at her waist matched her mother's earrings and necklace. Jix and Chelsea wore matching lavender dresses, and each of them wore a piece of the lavender crystal Sam had brought back in her velvet bag, smoothed and fashioned into a pendant and hanging from a silver chain. Jix had been remarkably calm for the entire day.

Duncan looked very *GQ* in his black tuxedo jacket and his tailored shirt tucked into the Campbell kilt. At Sam's request he had worn his leather boots. Jamie and Griffin wore their own clan kilts with velvet jackets. A local piper had played "Scotland the Brave" as Samantha walked down the aisle.

"I didn't know your middle name was Fitzgerald," Sam whispered to Duncan as the pastor began the wedding vows.

Their vows were simple, traditional. Griffin had the rings and handed them to Duncan at exactly the right time.

"Think I can handle it?" she asked as she took his hand and placed the white gold Celtic knot band upon his finger.

"I think," Duncan slipped the matching ring on hers, "that together we can handle anything." He brought her hand to his lips and his eyes met hers, blue and forever. "My queen."

"In the name of the Father, and the Son, and the Holy Ghost," the pastor said, "I now pronounce you husband and wife."

Samantha reached behind her waist and hit the switch. Dazzling, holographic white wings—reprogrammed for the wedding—shimmered up and out from her wedding gown; as her father looked up astonished, Jix and Chelsea squealed in delight, and Duncan laughed and kissed his Fairy Queen.

TO MY READERS:

The village of Nirdagh is fictional, as are all of the characters who lived in this fictional world, but my research shows that in the 9th century my made-up village isn't a bad representation of how things might have been in the past. The belief system of worshipping the Tuatha Da Danaan was a very real concept to the ancient people of Scotland and Ireland. The Sidhe (pronounced Shee) were considered both fairies and gods and were greatly feared and revered by the ancient Scots. The time crystals are my own invention, of course, but if they *were* real they would have to make their appearance in Scotland or Ireland where such magical creations are welcomed and understood! And in the magical waters of Jacob's Well near Wimberley, Texas.

Other interesting tidbits—when I came up with a warm spring for Samantha and Duncan to bathe in, I worried it was too far-fetched, but then I found an article on the Internet about an archeological dig that has confirmed there was once a hot spring in Scotland. It wasn't close to my hot spring, but hey, if there can be one, there can be others, right? And about my little buddy, Blinky? Sure, he's a fantasy animal, but folklore abounds with tales of such creatures and who are we to say they never existed?

Highland Magic was written to give you a smile and a chuckle. I hope you'll read it and enjoy Sam and Duncan's grand adventure, which wraps up my Highland time-travel saga! To find out what all the fuss is about, order your copy of the first two adventures in the series, *Highland Dream* and *Highland Fling* from your local bookstore or go to www.dorchesterpub.com.

TESS MALLORY
HIGHLAND DREAM

When Jix Ferguson's dream reveals that her best friend is making a terrible mistake and marrying the wrong guy, she tricks Samantha into flying to Scotland. There the two women met the man Jix is convinced her friend should marry—Jamie MacGregor. He is handsome, smart, perfect . . . the only problem is, Jix falls for him, too. Then a slight scuffle involving the Scot's ancestral sword sends all three back to the start of the seventeenth century—where MacGregors are outlaws and hunted. All Jix has to do is marry Griffin Campbell, steal Jamie's sword back from their captor, and find a way to return herself and her friends to their own time. Oh yeah, and she has to fall in love. It isn't going to be easy, but in this matter of the heart, Jix knows she'll laugh last.

___52444-9 $7.99 US/$9.99 CAN

☐ **YES!**

Sign me up for the Love Spell Book Club and send my
FREE BOOKS! If I choose to stay in the club, I will pay only
$8.50* each month, a savings of $6.48!

NAME: _____

ADDRESS: _____

TELEPHONE: _____

EMAIL: _____

☐ I want to pay by credit card.

☐ VISA   ☐ MasterCard.   ☐ DISCOVER

ACCOUNT #: _____

EXPIRATION DATE: _____

SIGNATURE: _____

Mail this page along with $2.00 shipping and handling to:
Love Spell Book Club
PO Box 6640
Wayne, PA 19087
Or fax (must include credit card information) to:
610-995-9274

You can also sign up online at **www.dorchesterpub.com**.
*Plus $2.00 for shipping. Offer open to residents of the U.S. and Canada only. Canadian
residents please call 1-800-481-9191 for pricing information.
If under 18, a parent or guardian must sign. Terms, prices and conditions subject to
change. Subscription subject to acceptance. Dorchester Publishing reserves the right to
reject any order or cancel any subscription.